Psaltery at White Oaks

By
Martha Benn Macdonald

"I will also praise thee with the psaltery."

PublishAmerica
Baltimore

© 2008 by Martha Benn Macdonald.
All rights reserved. No part of this book may be reproduced, stored in a retrieval system or transmitted in any form or by any means without the prior written permission of the publishers, except by a reviewer who may quote brief passages in a review to be printed in a newspaper, magazine or journal.

First printing

This is a work of fiction. Names, characters, places, and incidents either are the product of the author's imagination or are used fictitiously. Any resemblance to actual persons, living or dead, events, or locales is entirely coincidental.

PublishAmerica has allowed this work to remain exactly as the author intended, verbatim, without editorial input.

ISBN: 1-60474-186-4
PUBLISHED BY PUBLISHAMERICA, LLLP
www.publishamerica.com
Baltimore

Printed in the United States of America

*Dedicated to My Three Saint Bernard Dogs
for their unfailing loyalty and devotion*

Acknowledgements:

My special thanks to Kathy Sholl and Laura Dawley for reading and typing the manuscripts; to Jeanie Bristow, Laura Dawley, and Donna Henderson for reading and editing; to Elijah Hamilton, Diana Van den Heuvel, Bill Doar, Sara Boelt, Wynne Boelt, Heidi Hartwiger, George Edward Martin, Gail Ice, Sarah and Lee Kennerly, Phyllis Hefney, Janie Sigmon, Bob Dunbar, Cindy Mayfield, Linda Knight, Ruth and Wesley Starnes, Ruth Bell, Joan Carraway, Beverly Holbrook, the late Equator McCoy, Johnie Mae Coachman, and Edwin Harrison Stultz for listening, encouraging, and answering questions; to Kara Balarezo, Anna Wright, and Diane Roche for their artistic suggestions; and, finally, to the staff of PublishAmerica for their unwavering faith in my vision for this book.

Book One (1763)

The bells in the old stone church rang and rang as Katie Fears Lynch, still wearing her indigo-blue wedding dress, ran toward the harbor to meet her husband and sail away on MALCOLM'S CROWN for South Carolina.

Her stomach churning, bright green eyes fearful, Katie turned one last time to look at her beloved Ireland and wave good-bye to her mother, grandmother, and older brother.

"Oh, Hugh, I'm afraid," she said to her husband who caught her in his arms.

"Of what, my luve?"

"Starving, mutiny among sailors, maybe slave rebellion…you know all those stories we've heard about slaves being chained in the bottom of ships. What if the ship is blown off course from high winds or storms? What if you become sick? Or what if…?"

"Luve, don't let your name Fears rule you. I love you. We're together, and we'll find peace and religious freedom in the New World. We're going to Georgetown. My father says we may even be kin to Thomas Lynch, that wealthy gentleman who owns a plantation on the North Santee River. I'll find work."

"I know you will," she said, wiping her eyes, "I will, too. Mother always said I could do anything with a needle—from making an apron or fancy gown to a pair of shoes. And we're married now. Oh, Hugh, we've been sweethearts since childhood."

He nodded as they made their way onto the ship. A stone mason who had worked on churches most of his life and believed in symbols and signs, Hugh was thankful to be sailing, confident of fulfilling his dreams in another country with Katie at his side. "Ah, there's nothing like the smell of the salty sea and the caw of gulls overhead, is there?"

A few weeks later, Katie felt sick. She found her husband looking out at the ocean and went to him. "Hold me, Hugh. I have something to tell you."

He smiled and took her in his arms.

She caressed his red hair, then whispered, "Darling, I'm with child....I."

Hugh was thrilled. "Ah, my luve, what shall we name our bairn, our child who will be born in the New World?"

"We'll know when the baby is born. Meantime, we shall dream of our home and our little one."

Hugh was only able to dream for a few days because, like several other passengers, he fell ill from a fever and died. Following prayers, their bodies were dumped overboard. Katie groped about, wondering what to do. She was completely alone. Returning to Ireland would be impossible, especially when a sudden storm came up and blew the ship off course, lashing and ripping the sails.

MALCOLM'S CROWN drifted for months just as Katie feared. "A bad omen," she murmured to one of the women. "I'm afraid, and I know my child is coming soon."

Sure enough, a baby girl was born several weeks early, and Katie struggled simply to keep herself and her child alive.

Her fears were confirmed again when one still day in August, pirates jumped aboard the vessel and began firing pistols, laughing, and seizing goods. The passengers huddled together, frightened, staring at the leader, a big man with flaming red curls which shook as he marched up and down the deck and turned his head from one side to the other, his blood-shot eyes glaring at one passenger, then another. He wore a gold hoop in one ear, a plaid tam-o'shanter, a clerical collar, and a tattered kilt.

Lighting a match to one front curl, the buccaneer cleared his throat, then examined each passenger, one by one. "You'll be my mate, old laddie, won't you?" he asked a thin, humped man clutching a fiddle. "And you'll gloriously play whatever air I call for, won't you? Now, don't be daez't."

The musician with stringy gray hair and bangs nodded, "I will, Sir. My name's Roderick Maclaren. I was with Bonnie Prince Charlie at Cullodeen Moor."

"Ah, that's my mate," the pirate replied. "In case you've not heard of me, why I am the one and only Curly Motte Macaulay O'Toole, and my men and I intend to make merry on your vessel today. I believe the Romans celebrate this day as the Assumption of their Queen Mary, but we Presbyterians see it as our Lammas-tide if you will, our harvest celebration. And that calls for a bottle of rum. Now if ye don't celebrate with us, why ye'll have your throats slashed," he laughed, taking a swig of rum and passing it to his mates.

Silence gripped the ship as passengers looked from one to another for direction, wondering what could happen next. Only an occasional caw of a lone seagull broke the stillness until Katie's baby cried.

The pirate turned, listened, and commanded the young mother, not to hide, but to come forth. The baby sucking at her breast, her dark hair disheveled, Katie pushed her way through the crowd and curtsied before Curly Motte Macaulay O'Toole.

He looked at the baby with curly gold hair and blue eyes and knelt at her mother's feet, his eyes tearful. He took the baby in his arms and prayed. Katie trembled as she saw the flag with bones and skeleton face waving high above the other ship. Many passengers frowned, and even other pirates shook their heads.

"Oh, don't be a'feared, my lass. If you will simply call your wee bairn Cecilia in honor of my beloved wife, now deceased, who was murdered by elders in the church when she was playing upon her psaltery, why....why I will spare you and everyone on board, including the slaves."

Hearing groaning and rattling chains, Katie looked around, certain most slaves would rather be dead than live on a ship where they were often force-fed, waiting to be sold in Georgetown, Charleston, or elsewhere. Curly Motte Macaulay O'Toole walked up and down the deck, carrying the baby, Katie following at his heels. When he turned, she curtsied again.

"Be it so, my lord. Cecilia Fears Lynch her name shall me...Cecilia for your dear wife, Fears for my maiden name, and Lynch for my precious husband who died only weeks ago. I loved him dearly. We were childhood sweethearts, simply searching for a happier time in Georgetown. Now, I cannot do more for you, nor will I, even if you and your mates choose to murder me."

"It is right, Mrs. Lynch," he answered. "And I feel certain that this child must surely be akin to the Thomas Lynch who is known for his wealth, knowledge, and generosity. Why I've sold slaves to him. I have been to his plantation known as Hopsewee. A member of the Winyah Indigo Society and an influential man, he will help you, guide you. Trust him."

Katie listened and nodded, not ever revealing her husband's own hope for a connection with Thomas Lynch.

"And now I'm certain you're wondering about me," the pirate continued, his voice gentler. "I, too, was with the Scots at Cullodeen Moor, when our beloved Bonnie Prince Charlie was so brutally defeated by the English. Ah, we loved Bonnie Prince Charlie. We all wanted him to reclaim the English throne. We all fought hard."

Though she was weary, Katie listened to the strange pirate, wondering about his clerical collar. He seemed to need to talk.

"Yes," he continued, still holding the baby, "I saw how unkind some of the church fathers, our very own, could be. 'Tis a long story of misunderstandings. My wife played the psaltery, the harp, and the organ. Of course, she was named for St. Cecilia, as you may have figured. She could sing all the old melodies and airs as well. She was carrying our bairn when the priesties murdered her. That's why I forsook the church, turned buccaneer, and began roaming the seas. We go up and down the coast, block ships from entering ports, seize booty, burn, loot, and celebrate, all in the name of Master Scratch himself, and my ship there, EDWARD'S REVENGE…why she's the best ship I ever sailed."

Katie nodded as he paused to take another swig of rum.

"Now, I want you to have my wife's little clock. She called it her fairy clock, and I want you to keep my piece of emerald silk that came all the way from China. Prize it, and promise to turn this cloth into a fine gown for your lassie when she marries. I also want you to have this bag of gold. Now it comes with a warning. It came from a church, but I'll not tell you why or where. But you must use it only for something good for yourself, little Cecilia, or her heirs. Do you understand?"

Katie nodded again.

"Oh, now I've lain with every whore since my wife died, but I am a believer. Eccentric as I am, I still trust in the Lord God Almighty, Maker of heaven and earth. I say prayers every night. Finally, I want you to take the psaltery which my dear Cecilia cherished most of all. I always teased her and said playing it made her 'tapsalteerie.' Ah, we were devoted. She knew the psalms so well and often sang, 'I will also praise Thee with the psaltery.' I knew she was talking to God, but I imagined she was speaking to me as well." His eyes filled with tears again.

"Will you baptize little Cecilia, Mr. O'Toole?" Katie asked, surprising herself, knowing she was shocking many of the passengers, perhaps his mates as well.

Curly Motte Macaulay O'Toole nodded and called for a bucket of sea water, then dipped his hand into the water, and touched the baby's head. Looking up into the blue sky, he prayed, "And I baptize you, Cecilia Fears

Lynch, in the name of God the Father, God the Son, and God the Holy Spirit." He made the sign of St. Andrew's cross and walked about the deck, proudly showing off the baby.

Little Cecilia cooed as an old woman with one tooth and long white hair murmured, "That man is crazy...so is that young mother."

"But she saved your life, you tyke" a passenger responded. "I'm grateful."

"And may God look graciously upon you, Mrs. Lynch. Try not to fear, but be wary, for you are young and very beautiful. Go carefully among the crowds and streets, and trust your Father in Heaven. Know your child, and love her. Be kind to her, and share the meaning of my psaltery with her." He put the baby in Katie's arms and gave her a basket laden with the fairy clock, bag of gold, green silk, and the psaltery. "One last warning, Mrs. Lynch: never, ever, tell the good folk of Georgetown that Curly Motte Macaulay O'Toole baptized your child."

"But why, Sir? I'm thankful...you were once ordained, weren't you?"

"To be certain, in the Kirk of Scotland. But my father, so I always heard, was a very distant cousin of John Abraham Motte though, of course, I don't know for sure. That Johnie must have had a shrewd head on his shoulders, for he sold the same land in Georgetown along the Sampit River to different families, first to the Perrie family, then a few years later, to the Reverend William Screven. Everything turned out well, but nobody needs to know my connection with you. It might hurt you and the bairn, my leddy. Do you understand?"

"I do, Sir. Thank you. I will never forget you as long as I live."

He kissed Katie on the forehead and caressed the child's hair, then pulled out his spontoon, jumped to his own ship, and sailed away.

Because MALCOLM'S CROWN continued to drift about, many passengers blamed Katie. "The winds are still. That pirate put a curse on our ship. You're to blame because you talked to him...that psaltery is evil. It's a sign of the Deevil."

Roderick Maclaren glared at them and spoke, his voice cracking. "You're wrong...why, if it had not been for this brave woman, none of you would be alive now, and you know it...go back to your chores, and don't you even be thinking about snatching the treasures neither. I'll guard Miss Katie and spit foam upon you if you as much as come near her." He thrust his fiddle toward them.

Within a few days, the winds picked up, and the boat sailed again. Finally, in mid-November, the captain turned into Winyah Bay and sailed on up the Sampit River toward Georgetown. He anchored at the landing off St. James Street.

"I do believe 'tis St. Cecilia's Day, Miss Katie," the old fiddler said, "and I propose a round of music in honor of you, the baby Cecilia, our passengers, and the captain." He began playing "Hail, Bright Cecilia," and followed by singing "Baloo Lammy."

"One of my favorites," Katie mused, rocking Cecilia.

"Trust your little child. Little Cecilia will have gifts and wisdom. Encourage her. If there's ever a burden in your life, why turn it into something good, and trust in God. Come to see me in Charleston where I expect to put up my sign and give violin lessons."

Katie thanked him again, then joined the others on the gangplank. She watched gulls circling above the dock and enjoyed the river breeze, her reveries suddenly interrupted by a harsh voice. "Keep that young slave alive. His name is Numbers, and I'm hoping Mr. Thomas Lynch will buy him....he knows a heap about indigo, and he's strong."

It was the voice, so Katie learned, of Orange McTavish Steggerda, an Irish Dutchman who especially hated Gullah Negroes. And Numbers was Gullah. "We're headed for Charleston at dawn, then on to Nassau. Keep those slaves moving. I aim to sell Numbers today. I don't like his cinnamon-colored eyes. They don't fit a Gullah neither."

Katie cringed as she heard chains rattling and saw slaves being whipped. Alone with a baby girl in a new country, Katie wondered deep down if Curly Motte Macaulay O'Toole's gifts were a blessing or a curse, if she herself had made a big mistake. Only time would tell, and only God would show her.

"Thy word is a lamp unto my feet, and a light
unto my path" (Psalm 119:105).

Book Two (1763-1776)

Trudging along the sandy shore, Katie struggled to carry the pirate's basket, her own small trunk, and Cecilia. Nobody offered to assist. "Are they looking down at me? Are they jealous? Maybe they think I'm a witch because I asked a pirate to baptize my baby?" Katie asked herself these questions over and over again.

At last, she saw a woman gathering herbs in a kitchen garden on St. James Street. "Such a beautiful baby you have in your arms," the woman said, as she watched passengers walking toward Bay Street. "Indeed, you must be tired from such a long journey. Won't you sit on the stoop there?"

Katie introduced herself and little Cecilia. The woman said she was related to early settlers in Georgetown. "My name is Jane Frances Oliver; my husband and I have two girls, Elizabeth and Eliza."

Katie sat down and began talking of her husband's death at sea and her ability to do needlework, knowing she had to find lodging before sundown and earn a living. "Yes, my mother back in Ireland said I did the fanciest stitches of anyone she'd ever known, including my grandmother who was a fine dressmaker herself. I also crochet, knit, embroider, make hats, shoes, breeches, waist coats, and dresses. I sing and play several different instruments as well."

"Why, you're a mother, milliner, musician, and more," Jane Oliver exclaimed.

"My, you are talented. Suppose you wait while I speak to my husband, will you? He's in the stable."

Katie waited, grateful to rest under the oak trees and enjoy the gentle wind.

Jane returned. "In exchange for sewing for our family and teaching the girls to sing and embroider, you may have lodging and meals. You are free to sew for others, and whatever money you earn is, of course, yours to keep. I would naturally ask that you conduct yourself properly."

"Of course," Katie curtsied.

She felt comfortable with the Olivers and enjoyed teaching Elizabeth who was five and Eliza who was nearly three years old. Cecilia grew and learned her numbers from the fairy clock. Before long, she caught up with the Oliver girls and especially enjoyed playing on the psaltery and singing.

"Why, Mrs. Lynch, your daughter has the voice of an angel," the Anglican priest proclaimed one day following the service at Prince George Church, "and your beauty as well."

"I call Cecilia my flower nymph because she's forever gathering flowers and weaving them into garlands for me or for the Oliver girls. I've taught her and Eliza and Elizabeth how to sew and dance. My child is happy, but she longs to ride a horse. Do you know anyone who might teach her?"

The priest thought, and almost immediately, the name of Thomas Lynch came to his mind. Following the pirate's advice, Katie listened and said nothing.

A few days later, the priest introduced Katie and Cecilia to Mr. Lynch who immediately liked the child and offered to enroll her in the Winyah Indigo Society's school. Eliza and Elizabeth, in the meantime, had begun attending Mrs. Cuvier's School on King Street where they learned French, geometry, astronomy, and painting.

Cecilia enjoyed her studies and came to call Mr. Lynch 'Master Thomas.' She looked on him as a father. He was proud of her equestrian skills and often invited Cecilia and the girls to gatherings at Hopsewee where they listened to old Maum Lucy's story of the stick horse and dolls in the attic.

Katie continued to sew for the family and for others. She prided herself on being thrifty and nimble with her needle. She was happy, except for having to go to the wharf to meet the ships and pay for goods she'd ordered. She disliked having sailors stare at her, sometimes suspicious that they wanted to take her to Bolem's Tavern for ale or to one of the houses on Church Street. She followed the priest's advice and carried a pistol when she walked through the streets to the docks.

In time, Katie saved enough money to build a small Queen-Anne frame house farther down Bay Street and purchase a Gullah girl who was about Cecilia's age. Katie learned the girl was called Monica. Cecilia and Monica quickly became best friends.

When Monica wasn't doing chores, the two roamed the marshes, woods, and fields for flowers, roots, and herbs which Cecilia described in her journal, following Monica's advice. Monica had learned from her own mother exactly what to mix for a cold or fever, upset stomach, and more.

Cecilia tried to teach Monica how to read, write, and speak proper English, and the two began a lucrative business with their mixtures. Before long, several ladies in Georgetown were buying the girls' potions. Hibiscus tea for cramps was a favorite. Of course, some of the doctors resented the slave girl and her white friend.

"Why they're nothing but witches who should be burned," Dr. Edward Pringle bellowed forth one night at a meeting of the Winyah Indigo Society. Indeed, Nahum, the minor prophet, would call that slave girl a 'mistress of witchcrafts.'"

"You're just jealous because your practice is suffering," one member retorted, "Why if I had to pay your fees, I might resort to herbs myself."

And, of course, making clothing and shoes for various members of Georgetown society, Katie heard the latest news, gossip, and advice, most of it unsolicited. To her surprise, Jane Oliver said that allowing Monica and Cecilia to keep the coins they collected from selling herbs and flowers was not wise. "You're allowing your own slave to make money, Katie. Why I've never heard of such a thing! People are talking, my dear. I vow they are. If you were still living in my home, I wouldn't allow it. I simply would not. And you know, some people think it's improper for Cecilia to play the psaltery at church."

But Katie would simply thread her needle and shake her head. "It's the girls' knowledge of herbs and flowers, not mine. Monica has taught my Cecilia so much, and my child has taught the slave girl to read. You know, Monica rarely lapses into Gullah anymore. I think their devotion is wonderful. It's exactly what Jesus asked us to do…love and serve, and when Cecilia plays and sings in church, she is praising the Lord. That's Christianity, Jane."

"I hope you're right," Jane Oliver sighed, fanning herself, "It's no wonder you don't have any friends, but me."

"But I have customers, and they provide me with the money I need. I stay busy, and my Cecilia is happy. There's only one thing which troubles me."

Jane listened as Katie described her daughter's swollen breast. "Yes, it's swollen with an inverted nipple, and Cecilia's other breast looks like a shriveled apple. Sometimes I think I should take her to a doctor. What do you think?"

"You should, Katie…Cecilia is such a beautiful girl at eleven now…maybe a doctor could help her. Dr. Pringle has a good reputation, according to my husband. Since my husband is an apothecary, he would know."

Katie agreed and later watched Cecilia one afternoon during her bath. "My child, I'm concerned about that swollen breast. Do your breasts ever hurt?"

"No, Mother, they don't hurt. If I want to ride, Monica simply binds the bigger breast and I am just fine."

Her mother continued. "My darling, you are beautiful, despite those freckles...I guess you don't follow Monica's remedies."

"No, I don't, Ma...I'd rather ride in the wind or play in the woods than coat myself with creams. I'm a little different from other girls. You know that."

"Cecilia, your breasts worry me. I think we'll go to see Dr. Pringle."

Cecilia protested, but her mother remained firm. "Monica will accompany us. Now, the priest respects the doctor. So does Mrs. Oliver. Let's visit him, and I shall expect you to do as Dr. Pringle says. Do you understand me?"

Cecilia reluctantly agreed and stamped her foot. "This visit will come to ill will, and I know it. You do, too. So does Monica."

"Cecilia, why, I've never seen you so angry...is it that time of the month?"

Monica shook her head and patted Cecilia's hand. "I be with you, honey."

When they arrived at his house the next day, Dr. Pringle ordered Cecilia to remove her shift, and he began examining her body, kneading her breasts and stomach.

At first, Katie looked on, then turned, and began to pace the wide pine boards. "Oh, I simply can't bear to look at my child's deformity. Doctor, what do you think has caused her to be this way? Is it something I did...or the work of Satan? What?"

Deep down, Katie wrestled, for she wondered if the pirate's baptism with ocean water had brought on an evil spell, and yet she knew that such a thought was absolutely irrational.

The doctor didn't answer, only continued to pinch, press, and fold the larger breast.

"Dr. Pringle, I am not Sally Lunn dough," Cecilia screamed, sitting up on the table, pushing away his gnarled fingers. "You're hurting me."

But the doctor pushed her back down and tied her hands with a rope.

"Mother, please do something."

But Katie ignored her daughter.

"Tis true, young woman," Dr. Pringle said, his jet black eyes glaring, "that you are not bread dough. Your body is Cecilia Lynch dough, and I'll feel it as much as I am required in order to make a proper diagnosis. Do you understand?"

"No, Sir, I don't," Cecilia answered, squirming, kicking, and twisting.

"The longer you misbehave, why, the longer this examination will take." He leaned over close to her, his round spectacles resting on the purple, tangled veins of his bulbous nose, his breath the odor of rum. He squeezed the inverted nipple again and again, then the scrubby breast. "Do you have any feeling in any other part of your body, young lady?"

"No, I do not. Why should I? Besides, I wouldn't tell you, Dr. Pringle, even if I did."

Fingering her vagina with one hand, then squeezing one nipple, then the other, he asked, "Now, do you feel something pleasurable?"

Monica shook her head. Cecilia refused to answer and kicked her legs so high that doctor's glasses toppled off.

"No milk will ever be here for a baby, no matter how much tea you and that slave gal brew. Only surgery will rectify this abnormality!"

"Surgery!" Katie gasped. "Is this deformity inherited?"

"Well, I don't know. Tell me, Mrs. Lynch, are your breasts normal? Would you like for me to make a comparison?"

"I would not, thank you," Katie said, wrapping her shawl closer about her shoulders.

Monica frowned and held Cecilia's hand.

"I have studied this extreme abnormality," Dr. Pringle continued, "in young women at the University of Edinburgh, and without surgery, such women are useless to their husband and babies. They might as well join a nunnery and become sequestered from the world. I would recommend surgery. If you do not believe me, I beg you to go to Charleston and consult with Dr. Fayssoux or Dr. Ramsey. Really, I repeat, Mrs. Lynch, without surgery, your child will never be normal. She'd do better as a freak in one of the fairs."

"Dr. Pringle," Monica gasped. "That was not kind."

Dr. Pringle slapped the enslaved girl. "The very audacity, Mrs. Lynch, this girl knows nothing. Shackle her, and send her back to Africa, so that I may get on with my work."

"Monica," Katie said, "suppose you wait outside."

Monica brushed back Cecilia's sweaty hair and untied the rope.

"What is your fee, Dr. Pringle?"

Before he answered, Cecilia stood up and pushed him away. "I do not mean to be disrespectful, but you have taken advantage of me today, Dr. Pringle. You have threatened and humiliated me before my best friend and mother."

"Are you a lesbian, young lady?"

Cecilia burst into tears and quickly dressed as the doctor continued. "Well, the priest and I will both observe you, but in different ways. I'll ask him to pray for your soul and body as you struggle to feed a baby, and I'll pray that some man may find you amusing, at least interesting. You'll be as dry as a withered hag carrying peat moss for her cottage fire in the Outer Hebrides."

"Cecilia, you must apologize to Dr. Pringle. You've not been brought up to be disrespectful."

"And he wasn't taught to embarrass and hurt his patients, either," Cecilia answered. "I am hurting, and I am bleeding."

As she turned to leave, the doctor said, "Well, I'm considered one of the finest doctors in the South, but, go young woman. Go ride your horses, and keep your pleasures to yourself. There is no charge, Mrs. Lynch. You have enough penance to do with a belligerent child and a hostile slave. I would watch that relationship."

Before Katie could finish gathering her belongings, Cecilia and Monica were out the door and off to the woods. Cecilia despised the doctor, especially when she saw his menacing eyes glaring at her during communion at church, knowing he'd touched the most sacred parts of her body and probably those of other innocent girls as well. She resented his attitude that a woman's function was simply to bear babies and satisfy men.

"How much does that priest know?" she later said to Monica, "What exactly has my mother said to him? Is that why he touched my breasts last week when I was practicing the psaltery at the church and why he suddenly said to me, 'Cecilia, have you ever heard of the Reverend Thomas Bosomworth from Savannah? Why he might enjoy meeting you.' Monica, what do you think? I was so startled when the priest said that to me I hit him with my psaltery and left. I just regret chipping off a little piece of wood. I told him I'd never meet the Reverend Bosomworth."

Monica smiled at her. "Don't worry. You won't have to."

"And as I was leaving, the priest called, 'You are the Miss Bosomworth, young lady.' Monica, it was horrible. I hate him, and I hate that doctor."

Monica tried to comfort her friend as they sat in the woods and wove chains from vines. "Everything gwine be alright."

Between fittings and cuttings, Katie sometimes asked Monica to brew a pot of tea and asked Cecilia if she'd changed her mind. "My child, we could go to Charleston or Philadelphia for the surgery. I've saved money, and there's the pirate's gold."

Cecilia knew who the pirate was, for her mother had described everything about Curly Motte Macaulay O'Toole and the baptism aboard MALCOLM'S REVENGE.

"No, I don't want to go, Ma. I do not feel abnormal at all…I'd rather drown in the bottom of the Waccamaw River than have another doctor touch my body again. Mother, you have no idea how much Dr. Pringle hurt me."

Monica added, "Sho' did, Missus Katie."

Finally, Katie apologized and asked the girls for assistance. "Please thread your needles, and help me finish this frock for Mrs. LeConte's daughter. She's getting married next month. Then, there are shoes Mrs. Smith ordered. She wants the latest style with fancy buckles. And I almost forgot about the hats for Eliza and Elizabeth."

Cecilia and Monica helped and later went down to the river to swim.

"Monica, what do you want to be when you grow up?"

"Be your best friend, always, and get married and have a baby or two….I hope your mammy gwine free me. But I saved a heap of money myself. I might buy my freedom."

"I'll help you…I will. I only want to wear breeches and ride through the swamps, disguising myself as a young lad, and fight with the patriots if we ever go to war against the British. And I want to explore and discover. I don't mind having babies, but I want to do more. Monica, riding in the woods, hunting, scouting, sleeping under trees is what really excites me."

Monica nodded and cautioned her. "Rememba yu purty, and I want yu to get married one day. If yu ever has chillins and you can't nurse, why, I'll help yu out."

Cecilia hugged her best friend, then swam ashore, and dressed. "Mother will expect us to finish chores before dark," Cecilia said, her yellowish-green eyes twinkling, "I love you."

That night in bed, Cecilia dreamed that Mr. Lynch gave her a horse. She saw herself riding him along the banks of the river and hiding with someone in tangled grapevines.

"What does that dream mean?"

"Maybe one day, you gwine be a soldier, honey," Monica interpreted.

Indeed, the following day, Mr. Lynch invited Cecilia to ride in the races in Georgetown and Charleston. "I'm going to give you that chocolate brown horse with the muscular shoulders and sleek coat, the one we call Dark Moon."

Cecilia's eyes widened. "You mean it, Master Lynch? A horse of my very own? What will my mother say?"

"I'll tell her," he offered, "but you will have to talk to her about riding in the races. You figure that one out. I call this a gift from one Lynch family to another Lynch family. How do you like that?"

"Oh, I do, Sir…I do!" Cecilia swelled with excitement.

"You'll have to tuck those golden curls way up under this tri-corn hat I'm giving you or whatever chapeau you choose to wear. I'll find you a suit of clothes. My son always enjoyed dressing for the races."

"Oh, you're like a father, Master Lynch, and…and I'll disguise myself with a mask sometimes and wear breeches… I am so excited."

"You're welcome at our home anytime, and Curly, my old hound, is yours, too. I will speak to your mother…I vaguely remember an old cabin down on the river near her place. That could be turned into a stable."

Off Cecilia went to the stable to brush Dark Moon and ride him. She tossed a biscuit to Curly who followed at her heels. Before long that afternoon, Cecilia was trotting across the field, jumping fences and hedges, feeling so exhilarated she sang with the river wind. "And we'll scout in the army, old boy, if we ever go to war against the British, won't we?"

She nuzzled her head against his, certain Dark Moon understood and answered.

In time, even Katie came to love her daughter's horse and enjoyed offering him carrots from their soup or a hand of oats. "But I won't ride him."

"You don't have to ride him, Mother," Cecilia teased. "Thank you for understanding."

"You'll always play the psaltery, won't you?"

"Ma, I never go a day without it…that instrument means far more to me than you will ever know, I promise."

So Cecilia practiced and rode in the races, nobody ever knowing she was a girl. She won a lovely silver bowl at New Market in the fall of 1774. She could not believe that, at eleven, she was racing at one of the finest courses in the country and that people thought she was Lochland MacLeod.

"Oh, Monica, thank you for binding that breast. Disguising myself as a boy is so much more fun than going to those balls and having to talk to all those snobbish ladies. I enjoy parties, but I detest pomp."

"You sees a heap of dat. What wah de word you use one day? Hipocrosee?"

Cecilia laughed, knowing what Monica meant, and they had another reading lesson and told stories way into the night, long after Katie had embroidered her last stitch on the Oliver girls' hats.

Cecilia never regretted playing hosenrollen and introducing herself as Lochland until the afternoon of the oyster roast at Bayberry Woods Plantation in November of 1775, when she met Dr. Colin Macaulay Bain who owned nearby Sherwood Grove Plantation.

Dressed in a kilt, Dr. Bain seemed carefree, almost indifferent, the way Cecilia herself longed to be. Biting her nails, she would listen to his stories of the Highlanders in the Carolinas. His blue eyes blazed as he recounted tale after tale of Bonnie Prince Charlie and old Scotland. For some reason, Cecilia suddenly began to feel self-conscious about her breast and her clothing.

She was sweating when a voice from behind whispered, "Why that man's old enough to be your grandfather."

Whomever the voice belonged to pressed one hand against her vagina and, with the other, cupped her swollen breast. "I can make you happier by far. Meet me in the cemetery this evening under the cypress trees."

"Who are you?" Cecilia gasped, struggling to free herself. She turned and faced someone clothed in an exotic gown, face masked.

She'd forgotten the dance that evening was to be a masked ball, and she hated herself. "Cecilia, you're the greatest guise of all."

"Oh, but Miss Bosomworth, surely you know," the voice continued, and Cecilia knew. It was the menacingly mincing voice of the priest.

"Why are you taunting me?"

"Because you absolutely fascinate me."

"Please leave me alone." She walked closer to Dr. Bain who looked so big, burly, and lovable that she longed to have him hold her. She listened as he talked about roses, medicine, Robert Bruce, rice, indigo, and exchanging seeds with Dr. Garden in Charleston.

Cecilia bit her nails deeper until they bled. "Who is Dr. Garden?" she asked herself. "Did that horrible Dr. Pringle mention him? Am I a wizard or something? What caused my swollen breast and the other shriveled one, the inverted nipple?" Thoughts raced through her mind, as Dr. Bain came forward to introduce himself.

"I am Lochland MacLeod, late of Rosemont, Sir," she answered, trying to fake a Scottish trill.

"Well, I am Dr. Colin Macaulay Bain. I was trained in Edinburgh. I live over at Sherwood Grove Plantation, and I maintain a plantation in Blisland County in the upcountry of South Carolina as well. Indeed, I've built my home there with a tower exactly like the turret above my castle in old Scotland. I lived near the Black Isle in the Highlands. My home here on the river is rather plain. My slaves cultivate indigo and rice. However, my holdings throughout the Carolinas are extensive. Now, do you play the bagpipe, lad?"

"I am trying to learn."

PSALTERY AT WHITE OAKS

"Are you?" Dr. Bain caught Lochland/Cecilia's arm to walk toward one of the tables spread with sizzling oysters, sweet potatoes, and cornbread.

Cecilia felt something tugging at her head. She didn't know if it was the branch of a live oak or the hand of that horrible priest again. Whatever it was removed Cecilia's tri-corn hat, and her golden curls spilled around her blushing cheeks.

"My, we do have sizzling oyster curls right here, and they are golden," Dr. Bain laughed. "I do hope that you will tell me all about them over a glass of punch." He bowed, roared heartily, and tipped his tam o'shanter.

"Not if my life depended on it," she whispered to herself, as she turned and ducked under the long tables, then ran across the lawn to the stable where she found a horse and rode to Hopsewee. She explained her predicament to Jacob, an enslaved man who was brushing a horse. After securing permission, he drove Cecilia home to Bay Street.

"Oh, I fumbled today," she later confessed to Monica, "when I lost a boot and my curls tumbled down. I wondered about his middle name Macaulay, but that didn't matter. I was absolutely fascinated with his stories and his knowledge of so many subjects."

Cecilia and Monica giggled a week later when they heard Dr. Bain explaining to Katie Lynch that he'd found a boot which "surely must belong to your daughter." Katie thanked him and offered tea and scones.

When Cecilia realized conflicts were deepening between the colonists and King George, she was glad not to have confided in anyone the day of the oyster roast. "Monica, I will wear breeches and serve as a scout. I want to be like Mr. Lynch and do something for the colonies. Did I tell you that he or his son....I don't remember which...is to sign that document known as THE DECLARATION OF INDEPENDENCE drafted by Thomas Jefferson of Virginia. Maybe I should change my name to Thomas."

"No, you're not," Monica teased. "That name of Lochland is harder for folks to guess."

"Monica, we've given each other such valuable lessons, haven't we?"

She nodded...."Best friend, I'm going to buy my freedom. I've already told your mammy, and she agreed. I'll stay on, and she will pay me wages....I always want to be with you."

"It's a promise, Monica...even if I marry or if you marry, we'll be together. You will always be my best friend. Let's sign a pledge," she teased.

And they did.

In late June of 1776, shots were fired from the old fort on Sullivan's island, and soon thereafter, THE DECLARATION OF INDEPENDENCE was signed. "That means I will need a uniform," Cecilia said. "We'll pay mother to make one, and I'll tell her it is for some boy who cannot come to town for a fitting…will she believe me?"

"All you can do is try, and so long as she get her money, I don't think she's gwine aks questions."

"Oh, Monica, I'll be fighting for our freedom against the King of England."

"And I will walk at liberty: for I seek thy precepts. I will speak of thy testimonies also before kings, and will not be ashamed" (Psalm 119:45-46).

Book Three (Later, 1776)

But Cecilia could not begin that walk toward liberty as soon as she wished because her mother needed assistance. Stitching was required for Charles Greene's shoes, and Mrs. Dowling wanted christening dresses for her twins. "Besides the sewing, Cecilia, we must deliver Dr. Frothington's waistcoat. And you must be more sociable. You've received several invitations to balls. You're quite pretty, and you dance beautifully. Oh, your father would be so proud of you. You've grown up now. You're nearly thirteen years old, and you and Monica simply cannot always be running off to the woods, you know. Times are different now, my darling."

Cecilia stuck out her lower lip and looked at her mother whose hair was graying. "Ma, you're still pretty yourself. Have you ever thought of marrying again?"

Katie shook her head. "I loved your father so much I could never imagine marrying another man. Besides, as long as I can thread a needle and remain nimble, I am happy and at peace. Now, please do the hems in the little dresses, and take the waistcoat. Have you forgotten that the ball tonight is in the beautiful Man home with the ballroom upstairs? Oh, I can only imagine looking out at the Sampit River and the ships sailing into town. Isn't that exciting? Oh, Jane Oliver says the view is magnificent. I want you to tell me all about what you see on the river. Of course, it may be too dark. I don't know."

Cecilia ducked her head. "I hoped you'd forgotten about the party."

"Why, Cecilia, I've finished your gown. I even cut a few inches from the pirate's emerald silk and fashioned little flowerets to adorn your dress. We'll pretend they're green-gage plums."

"Thank you, Ma."

"Perhaps Dr. Bain will be there and dance with you. Maybe he'll even teach you the Highland Fling one day," Katie said, her green eyes twinkling.

"You know him, then, and you know all about the oyster roast?"

"Yes, I do."

"But, the priest? Ma, do know how he tormented me about a Mr. Bosomworth?"

"No...I've no idea what you mean."

Cecilia confided in her mother who put down her needle and said, "Well, we shall not be going to take communion with him again. I've heard that some of the parishioners want him to leave. I had trusted him, but no more...Cecilia, life is short, and if you can find someone to make you happy, enjoy him. God loves you, and so do I. I've been a little stern, I suppose, and fearful, perhaps too cautious. Your father always said that the name Fears suited me perfectly. Try not to let it characterize you, for fear only brings about unhappiness and suspicion."

"Do you really mean that, Ma?"

Her mother nodded.

"I'll try not to bite my nails tonight."

"My darling daughter, I used to do worse than that," her mother smiled. "I used to blink my eyes, and sometimes I got a crampy stomach, but that was long ago, and your precious father helped me. We loved deeply, and....I want you to find someone and be loved as well."

Cecilia appreciated the talk with her mother and later shared it with Monica who said, "Yo' mammy love you, honey. She just may not always understand your feelings."

A few hours later, Cecilia and the Oliver girls were escorted by Jane Oliver and her husband to the party where ladies and gentlemen in the latest fashions, many made by Katie Lynch, danced away the night in the ballroom overlooking the Sampit River.

Between dances, guests dined on delicate crab cakes, ham biscuits, ginger cookies, and an assortment of fine fruits and candies, along with rounds of champagne punch. When Cecilia saw Dr. Colin Macaulay Bain dressed in his kilt, her stomach knotted, especially when she realized he was dancing with Dr. Pringle's daughter, Charlotte Jane.

"Does his daughter know about me, Mrs. Oliver?" Cecilia whispered. "I mean, she's pointing at me, and I don't think I even know her."

"My dear, child, please do not fret over Charlotte Jane Pringle. She's not even pretty. Her eyes are too close together. Some people say Dr. Bain is in love with her, but I don't think so at all. I think he's sweet on you. Where's your mother?"

"Sewing," Cecilia laughed, then curtsied when she realized Dr. Bain wanted to put her name on his card for the next dance, 'La Belle Marie.' Dancing with him thrilled Cecilia. She was drawn to this older Scotsman in a way she herself did not understand. Her heart pounded as he admired her gown and shoes.

"Such bejeweled red slippers Master Lochland is wearing this evening! Why they are as enchanting as the boots, breeches, and dazzling golden curls." His blue eyes danced merrily as he gazed down at her. Why you're even more beautiful than you were that afternoon in November nine months ago. And you do fascinate me with your spirit and pendles. You're my jo for an evening, Miss Cecilia."

She smiled as they made a second figure 8, not having any idea of the meaning of pendles or jo, but too afraid to ask.

He asked her to join him for 'Mary's Wedding.'

Between dances, Dr. Bain drew Cecilia so close her larger bosom ached. He held her. "Oh, you remind me so much of my bride of long ago in old Scotland. Her name was Nancy Macdonald. She was a gorgeous lassie…died of a fever when she was carrying our bairn. Ah, she could sing. Do you sing, Mademoiselle Lochland?"

"Yes, and I play the psaltery as well."

"There's something about you young lassies I cannot resist…help it, I cannot; and help it not, I can, but do not and will not," he laughed.

"Dr. Bain, you're hurting me," she cried, "and your eyes are gazing so far away they seem haunted. You frighten me. What are you thinking about? You're glunching, as my mother calls it, when I frown. Have you seen a ghost? Are you mad? Please tell me."

"Tis nothing, my dear, really nothing, I assure you. I just yearn to marry you and hold you and, but…well the fiddlers are playing again. It's 'Flora and Zephyr.' Won't you join me again? The rhythm's a little slower. Between clapping our hands in the dance, perhaps I can clasp you once again. Ah, Mademoiselle Cecilia, C.C.C., it is clap and clasp Cecilia."

"Dr. Bain, you're being silly," she finally allowed herself to relax and say.

He bowed to the lady of his dreams. Gazing at her lovely, gently freckled face, and yellowish-green eyes, Colin knew that he could never marry Cecilia. He had no right to even imagine such a possibility. Back home in Blisland County at White Oaks Plantation, his second wife, Anna Catherine, was expecting their first child, and he'd left her. Except for her brown eyes and very frail nature, Anna Catherine reminded him of Cecilia.

"Ah, what is it about lassies that absolutely fascinates me?" he mused to himself. "There was Nancy. Then, there's Anna Catherine, and, now, here's Cecilia. She's different from anyone I have ever known."

"What is it, Dr. Bain? You are traveling far away from me, even though the music from the minuet is beginning. What are you thinking? I don't mean to be rude, but I'm a little afraid."

But he didn't answer. He only led Cecilia to the dance floor, picturing Anna Catherine's large, sad brown eyes as they were the night he left her weeping in their bedroom. And he was not at her side when she needed him the most, the poor girl whom he'd rescued from her arrogant, overbearing, cruel brother, Dr. Gavin Knox Dunn, the long-bearded preacher who pounded the fear of God into the hearts and minds of his congregation every Sabbath at Brick Tower Church, then threatened them with his cane if they didn't make an offering.

After the death of their parents, Gavin had taken his youngest sister, Anna Catherine, home and charged her take care of his six children. November of 1773 was the time Colin first met the poor girl.... "A year before I saw you, Cecilia," he talked to himself, as he continued to dance and replay the meeting in his head. "I'd taken a volume of Issac Watts' psalms to Gavin, the minister of Brick Tower and schoolmaster of Dunn's Academy.

'Read these psalms, Dr. Dunn,' I had said, thrusting the little book into the minister's hands, 'and I dare you not to judge anyone anymore. Oh yes, you can boast about your degree from Princeton and your royal lineage which I personally find dubious in light of all we know about your wife and the way you treat your baby sister here.'

As Dunn had walked about the schoolroom, plucking his long red beard, I saw a pretty, golden-haired girl with large brown eyes scouring the floor smile at the last student leaving the academy. Clad in a shredded shift, the girl looked like a waif that morning.

'You treat your sister like a slave, and I am laith to talk to you, but I will.'

Before I could finish, the red-haired Dunn fired back, 'I'll have you know, my dear Dr. Bain, that my wife and I have taken over my sister's life, not you nor anyone else, and we will continue to rule her with God's help and with a whip, if needed, until such time in her life when she can no longer serve me. Do you quite understand?'

'But your sister has a right to happiness. She has a right to the joys of marriage and giving birth to her own children. I've heard that you got your baby sister with child just so she would have milk and could nurse your youngest child. If that's not incest, I've never understood the meaning of the word, and I hear that your wife is expecting your seventh child. So will you impregnate your sister a second time, so that she can nurse the newborn at his birth? Does your French wife have an insufficiency?'

'My wife's milk is none of your business. Indeed, I will force myself upon my sister, if necessary, so that, once again, she may give birth to a baby about the same time my wife does and provide enough milk to sustain my wife's child. At least, I'm offering Anna Catherine the joy of carrying a child and being sucked. I understand that's rather sexual experience for most women.'

'And I hear you sold Anna Catherine's baby to gypsies at the fair in Millsborough. Is that true?'

'It is, but that's none of your business, Dr. Bain.'

I shook my head and continued, 'Your sister must be freezing in that shift which barely covers her body. Don't you care that she's cold?'

'No, it makes her stronger.'

'I knew that Anna Catherine was required not only to clean the church, school, and house but also to tend the children while Dr. Dunn's wife slept. Behind Gavin's back, most members of the church referred to his wife as 'Dr. D's Acadian Strumpet.'

'I've known her kind,' one old member had grumbled when Yvette stumbled into church forty minutes late one Sabbath, her dress unbuttoned, hair tousled, rouge heavy."

"Dr. Bain," Cecilia interrupted, "you're far away. Are you telling a story?"

Colin nodded as he continued to dance and remember his time with Anna Catherine, knowing deep down that he should feel guilt and shame for abandoning her, for hurting her.

Aside from this conflict over Anna Catherine and Yvette, Dr. Dunn had always resented Colin Bain. There had been a land dispute over the property originally known as Mulberry Bluffs, now called Burnt Bluffs, which Colin claimed belonged to him. Gavin Dunn had insisted that the land belonged to the Dunn family.

The dispute had been settled in court in Colin's favor. Gavin had also opposed Colin's offer to add a brick tower to the original frame Presbyterian Church called Kell Presbyterian Church because a Mr. Kell had put up the only money for the first building. The session, however, impressed with Dr. Bain's knowledge, not only of medicine but also of architecture and church history, had voted in Colin's favor.

"After all, old Stephen Kell has been dead for over ten years. I don't think he would mind a brick tower," one member had said. And the tower which Dr. Gavin Dunn declared Papish was added, and the church soon became known as Brick Tower Church.

"It's nothing but arrogance, Colin Bain, and you know it, and a papish abomination in the eyes of God Almighty," Dr. Dunn had shouted and rapped his cane so hard against the door that a window in the academy had broken and fallen to the floor. Anna Catherine, still nursing her little nephew, Barnie, had cleaned it up.

Then, there was an argument between the two over land immediately adjacent to the church. One of Dr. Bain's cows had wandered into what Dunn claimed belonged to the church. According to the surveyor's report, the land proved to be a part of Dr. Bain's land grant. Indeed, Gavin hated Colin, and the conflict only deepened whenever the two doctors met.

That morning was no exception. Colin had watched Anna Catherine wash the slate board.

"You're asking for the hickory stick, little sister, and I won't hesitate to use it on you," Gavin Dunn railed out. "Why that's the laziest way to clean a slate board I've ever seen!" He chased her under one of the desks.

"Bubba, I've learned all of my letters, and I recited my psalms to Miss Yvette. I am trying…I'm just a little tired. Your baby boy, and mine—our son; you sold him. And then your child Barnie with Yvette. Your baby just wanted to suck me all night long, and…"

"And you had no right, Anna Catherine, to smile at that pupil who was leaving the academy. Why that's a sin. You know what Saint Paul said."

Hugging her knees under the desk, her arms and legs bleeding, Anna Catherine said, "I was only smiling. And there's a verse from Hebrews about being kind to strangers, lest we entertain an angel unawares. Mamma used to say that to me before she died, and I never forgot it. Haven't you read that in Hebrews?"

"Well, I don't believe that particular young man will ever be an angel, and I have certainly had enough of your mouth this morning. Do you understand?"

Colin had felt nothing but contempt for a man who would rape his own baby sister, beat her, and then pound the pulpit, criticizing others in an effort to frighten them into believing in Christ. "Only the everlasting fires of hell await you if you don't turn to Jesus," Dunn often screamed, sometimes holding a shovel in hand, along with his cane.

"You're nothing but a hypocritical bastard walking the earth. I wouldn't blame anyone for not attending your services. This girl is your very own flesh and blood, and yet you sired a baby by her simply so she could feed your own child who is really her nephew because of your wife's inadequate supply of milk. Oh, you're evil, and so are the ellers in your kirk."

Of course, Colin Bain did not fail, ever, to think of his own needs. He wanted an heir, a white heir, and he was getting older. "Tell you what, Gavin Dunn," Colin said, as he looked from Gavin to his baby sister and back, "I will marry your sister this very day and claim her as my bride. That will take her off your hands and prevent you from being incestuous a second time. How about that, old boy?"

Colin grabbed Dunn's cane and slapped him across his legs and face.

Wiping blood, Gavin looked from Colin to his sister, then back, studying the difference in ages, wondering who would feed his babies. "Well," he snarled, "there's certainly no pleasure in penetrating my baby sister. With her gone, there would be fewer mouths to feed, especially if you take Squaw Daphne, a half-breed Indian, as well."

"As if you ever gave your sister anything but crumbs from your table! Look how emaciated she is and how rosy and plump that baby boy of yours is. I've seen him. Further, your wife is the very embodiment of health, and you don't look as if you've ever fasted on fish for Jesus, either."

Dr. Dunn wagged his head as his wife entered. "Miss Yvette needs me. What is it, Mrs. Dunn?"

"Oh, Dr. Dunn," the woman with tangled black hair, streaked rouge, and a low-cut shift wailed, her gold earrings dangling, said, as she bustled into the room.

"A harlot of your own choosing," Colin commented.

"Don't you dare belittle my petit Yvette. She's the joy of my life," the preacher retorted, tightening his white clerical bow.

"You mean joy of your bed," Colin replied.

Before her husband commented, Yvette complained that the children were fussy and fretful. "Where is that stupid sister of yours? Why the fire needs wood, and my back wants rubbing. Gabbe, you left me early this morning. I couldn't find my pearls. I wondered if Daphne stole them...or that dumb daughter of hers, Phoebe. Oh, if I weren't with child, I'd whip them both. I hate Blisland County. I'm not from here. Je suis francais. And where will I find milk to nurse this bairn....will you take Anna Catherine to bed again?"

"Enough, Yvette. Remember wives are to be submissive to their husbands. Now, Dr. Bain here says he wants to marry my sister and take her off our hands. I like that idea. Will you please see that her belongings are packed in your oldest tote and get Squaw Daphne ready to go? At least, Anna Catherine's marriage will mean two fewer mouths to feed."

As he snapped his fingers, Yvette sulked. "Your sums are not accurate. Deux gone and one born….what does that equal?"

"Yvette."

"I won't have enough milk to feed Barnie. Even after he's dried up your sister's breasts, he'll still be hungry, and…I can't provide."

"Drink more thistle tea. Now I have chores to do, and surely you must as well."

Colin roared with laughter. "Old boy, let your wife drink some spirits. Nothing produces milk in a mother's breast quite as rapidly as the ale and more. Don't forget that Jesus' first miracle was changing water into wine at the marriage of Can of Galilee. So stop your damned harshness. You're just silly. Now, Anna Catherine, please change your clothes and prepare to ride home with me to White Oaks Plantation where you will never, ever, be whipped."

"Do you really promise never to beat me, Sir?" she asked, her eyes swollen and red.

"Never, and you will have lovely frocks which I shall order from London and Paris, a harpsichord, and anything your heart desires, and we shall have a handsome baby boy. Unto us a child will be born."

"But, Dr. Colin," Anna Catherine said.

Within an hour, Dr. Dunn pronounced his sister and Dr. Bain man and wife. "Whom God hath joined together, let no man put asunder."

Continuing to hold Cecilia and dance another reel, Colin remembered Anna Catherine rubbing her nose as he had lifted her on his bay thoroughbred. Daphne had shuffled along behind toting her own bag and Anna Catherine's little trunk, tears rolling down her wrinkled paper-brown face, as she waved to her daughter, Phoebe. "I luvs yu, honee lamb. So do Jesus. Jes memba to do wat dem foks say, and Gawd's angels will bring us togeda soon."

Hearing Phoebe's sobs, Colin stopped his horse and rode back to the church where Gavin was beating the girl. "Damn it, Dunn, stop beating her, or I'll take this slave as well. I'll even pay for her, and then we'll see who nurses that young bairn Barnie of yours. My worst fear should be that you might rape Phoebe, have a yellow baby, and sell her as a slave. The very idea of raping your baby sister just so she could have a baby in order to have milk to feed your son. Incest! And to think you have the utter audacity to send your elders about the countryside to decide if your church members are worthy of taking the Lord's Supper, a free gift from Jesus for all believers, is beyond my comprehension. You have committed the unpardonable sin. No wonder membership at Brick Tower Church is declining! You should be defrocked!"

"Bain, you're not exactly innocent of not using enslaved women for your own purposes and pleasures, then working the offspring in the fields or selling them down the river. You know that yourself," Gavin said, as he began beating his stick on the brown grass. "Phoebe, go assist Miss Yvette before I become angry again."

"Dunn, the grass surrounding your church withered long ago. Even the pines are dying." Colin took off, Daphne struggling to keep up through swirls of red dust.

That night in bed, Anna Catherine's behavior had frustrated Colin. He knew she wasn't a virgin, but she shrieked each time he penetrated her. "Oh, it hurts, Dr. Bain. It's worse than a beating."

But unable to resist, Colin had pushed, twisted, and thoroughly satisfied himself. His new wife cried herself to sleep. Indeed, if it had not been for the old Indian woman's eyes pleading the next morning in the outdoor kitchen where she sat peeling potatoes, Colin would have taken Anna Catherine back to Brick Tower Church.

"Oh, Docta, yu ain't got no idea how day dun beet us. Iz a Catawba woman. I don eben memba weah de docta got me. He call Missus Anna Catherine and me wiches cauffin we node a heep about flowas. Yo wif jes plum tired. She dun nursed dat baby Massa Barnie til she ain't got strenth lef. Phoebe and me, we tends to de chillins and de cows and dat wun mule de docta gots."

Colin listened as Daphne described Dr. Dunn's rape of his sister, the birthing, and the immediate sale of the baby to gypsies at the fair in Millsborough. "Yessuh, soon as dat baby wah borned, why dat gal had to begin nursing Barnie. I had to give huh baby sugah tits. And dat ain't all."

Colin didn't think so.

"Be gentle wid huh, Docta Bain."

Colin learned that Daphne's husband, also part Catawba, had been sold to a plantation owner in Maryland, a man whom Dr. Dunn had known at Princeton.

That Anna Catherine ever conceived again was a miracle. Selfish as Colin was, he had delivered too many not to be aware of his young wife's brutally torn body. He found himself wondering just how big Dunn's penis was and the delivery. Had the girl really been cut as Daphne described?

Colin trusted Daphne's wisdom and instincts, found her easy to know on the pallet in the kitchen when she wasn't roasting a chicken or rolling biscuits. Before long, though, Daphne and Prince, the slave who served as blacksmith/medicine man/gardener at White Oaks, were married. Part Cherokee, Prince understood Daphne and loved her deeply.

Realizing how valuable they both were to him at the plantation and in his medical practice, Colin left Daphne alone and concentrated on spoiling his young wife. He ordered gowns for Anna Catherine, but after a time, grew weary of her whining, wiping her nose, and refusing, ever, to try something new. He encouraged her to play the harpsichord and learn to sketch, but she gave up and cried. One afternoon, he forced her to join him for a boat ride on the Patuxee River behind the plantation. She wept and rubbed her nose the whole time.

"She jes ain't be feelin gud, docta," Daphne always said. Daphne always defended the young bride.

Finally, Cecilia looked at him. "I am tired of reeling, Doctor Bain. I don't know what you're thinking about. It's as if you're having a vision. Are you telling yourself a story? You're dancing with me mechanically now, and I don't want to be a marionette."

Cecilia stomped one red slipper on the floor.

Colin ignored her, knowing he should be, right then, at Anna Catherine's side. It was time for their baby to be delivered, but he wouldn't ride through the swamps and woods and cross the rivers to be at her side in Blisland County. He was much too delighted over his new prize, Miss Cecilia Fears Lynch. Much as he despised himself for his behavior, he would not change. "I'm too old," he said to himself, "and maybe Anna Catherine will die."

"Dr. Bain," Cecilia persisted. "I am not going to dance again. Let's walk to the window and look out at the river. I promised my mother I'd count the boats."

"Silly, it's dark."

"Well, what are you thinking about? Please, tell me."

"About how absolutely ravishing you are and about riding one day with you at my side."

She cut her eyes at him and listened as he began telling more tales of his ancestral home in Scotland, of the hills and lochs, of the different houses and churches he had designed, and of Flora MacDonald and Bonnie Prince Charlie. Dr. Colin Bain knew that he could capture anyone if he talked and told stories. Even his mother, Miss Tibbie Bain, long ago had accused him of deceiving people with his stories.

"Do you miss Scotland?" Cecilia asked.

"Of course, but I won't be going back. I have too much to manage in this country as it is: my plantation here and White Oaks, to say nothing of working with other doctors, seeing my patients, exchanging seeds with botanists, hunting, trading, and fighting again for my country. I'll fight with the patriots even though, as a Highlander, I had to take an oath of allegiance to the British Crown. That oath I will not honor. I'm a stone mason, and maybe my ring will keep me from losing my head."

Cecilia listened. "I'll fight, too."

"Truly, Mademoiselle Lochland, you fascinate me. Shall we have more champagne?" He squeezed her so tight her breasts ached again.

After the last dance when he left her for more punch, Cecilia stole away and ran down the stairs and left the Man home. She walked along the river. "God, I am afraid," she whispered, looking at the moon rising over the water, "but I don't know what to do. Help me."

Hours later, she couldn't explain her fears to Monica. "And I lost one of my shoes, again."

"Honey, what's troubling you? Maybe you in love! Maybe dat bothering you."

Cecilia took her best friend's hand. "I don't know."

Toward the end of August, Colin departed for Blisland County where Daphne told him what had happened. "Oh, yo wif struggled. Huh cried and cried. It wah a long, hard birthin. Huh tried to nurse dat baby. Why he wah a purty little boy....look jes like yu, Docta Bain. But he had his Mammy's cuhls. I rubbed huh wid lavenda, giv huh brandee, and tuk de boy down to the Kwatahs to a wet nuhse. He didn't liv long, and Miss Anna Catherine beg Prince and me to aks yu to forgive huh for not being a gude wif to you."

Colin buried Anna Catherine and their child whom she had named Colin Macaulay Bain, Jr. over at White Oaks Chapel under the white oaks. Roland William Lemmon, the minister at Swann Creek Associate Reformed Presbyterian Church a few miles up the road, came to perform the service. Colin simply would not ask Gavin Dunn.

Daphne tried to comfort her master, for she knew that life for Anna Catherine was more comfortable than her existence with her brother and his family. "She was a meek lamb."

"But the meek shall inherit the earth, and shall delight themselves
in the abundance of peace" (Psalm 37:11)

PSALTERY AT WHITE OAKS

Book Four (Late 1776-1781)

One day in early October, Katie finally told her daughter about receiving the lost red slipper from Dr. Bain. "He brought it back one morning a few days after the ball, then said he was leaving for his plantation in Blisland County. He seemed troubled, but, of course, I didn't pry. Have you seen him?"

"No, Mother, I haven't. He was very strange the night of the ball. He held me tight, and his eyes got a faraway stare, as though he was recalling something painful. I don't know what it was. I asked him, but he said nothing. Finally, I left because I was afraid."

"Darling, remember not to let fear govern you. When fear grips us, we only lose. Fear is nothing but the old Devil trying to tempt us. And, of course, when I'm afraid, I always think of what your daddy used to say and what I've said to you, "Let's not use your name to express the predicate, 'Katie Fears.'"

"I'll try not to let Cecilia Fears feel fear, Mamma."

Yet it was not her mother to whom Cecilia turned. Deep down because her mother had taken her to Dr. Pringle, Cecilia felt an ambivalence, an uncertainty. She was devoted to her mother, but did not fully trust her. It was to Monica she turned.

"Monica, let's go for a swim in the river. The air's still warm, and we can talk after we swim and rest on the banks of the river. Nobody will see us, will they?"

Monica shook her head, and off they went to the river where they stripped and swam. "I feel like a mermaid, don't you?"

"Sho do...I jes hope nobody ever sees us....I don't know what you'd say...I'd have fears, sho nuff, then," Monica answered, rolling her dark eyes, then smiling, "Sho would."

"Well, I'll make up something. God knows I must learn to do that if I'm going to be a scout for the patriots."

Monica nodded. "Tell me how you're feeling about that doctor. Have you missed him much? You know, time tells us an awful lot."

Cecilia talked about Dr. Bain's knowledge of architecture, medicine, trading, gardening, and warfare. "Oh, Monica, he is so handsome, and he knows so much. He fought against the English king at Cullodeen Moor in Scotland. That was the time in history when Bonnie Prince Charlie who claimed he should be the king of England lost. A lady named Flora MacDonald helped the prince to escape. Oh, the Scottish people loved Bonnie Prince Charlie. Apparently, he had a sense of humor. Wasn't Flora MacDonald brave? She's my sort of heroine. Dr. Bain has the most sparkling blue eyes, Monica. Except for one dance with Charlotte Jane Pringle, he spent the evening with me. But then I left. Do you think he went back to Charlotte Jane? I don't like her. Do you think her father told her about my breasts?"

"Honey, I don't know…that don't matta. Tell me about what yo heart say. Tell me about yo feelins for Doctor Bain."

"I don't know. He brought my red slipper back to Mamma. She finally told me. He must care something for me. Oh, my stomach knots into butterflies when I'm with him, and, then, I calm myself down and think about his busy life. He exchanges seeds with some woman named Lady Skipwith in Virginia, whoever she is, and some Monsieur Michaux, whoever he is. Did I tell you that Dr. Bain owns two plantations? Isn't that exciting?"

They swam ashore and talked on the river bank and nibbled leftover tea cakes Monica had made.

"Cecilia, I don't care about what he owns or does or says. Things don't matter. If your heart ain't in sumpin, den whatever it be gwine dry up. Does the doctor ever aks you about yourself or what you like?"

Cecilia thought for a long time. "No. He just said I reminded him of his first bride who died in Scotland. Her name was Nancy Macdonald, and she came from the Outer Hebrides. Do you remember when Dr. Pringle said my breast would be dry like something from the Outer Hebrides? What did that mean?"

Monica shrugged her shoulders. "Sound like a name to me. Could be a gal's name or a boy's. I'm gwine name a chile Hebrides."

"Monica, you're funny. Divide it into syllables. He brides…maybe that means he will bride me….Dr. Bain will marry me. Oh, Monica, I want to marry him. Well, anyway, that Nancy died before their baby was born. Nancy must have had long golden hair and eyes that were a little like mine. Dr. Bain must have loved her, and to say I reminded her of him must mean he really loves me. Of course, he's old enough to be my grandfather. I'm surprised Ma didn't say that herself. Instead, she seems to encourage me to enjoy him. She keeps telling me not to fear. She doesn't want my name to be a grammatical construction. Oh, she's such a teacher. 'Let's not hear Cecilia Fears.' Tell me what to do, best friend. I can talk to you, not my mother. Surely you know that, don't you? Monica, I love you."

"Listen too yo heart. Dats the best advice I can ever give anybody. That's what my mammy always tole me…you're my best friend. You've taught me to read and write and speak. I know I make mistakes, but you've done give me yoself. The leestes I ken giv you is mine…and that's what my mammy taught me. Trust yo feelings. Trust yo heart."

"There's something about his shaggy brows and hair and……I want to curl up like a little girl on his big legs. He always wears a kilt. Do you think he wears pants under that plaid skirt, Monica?"

Monica shrugged her shoulders.

They began weaving a chain from the little vines running from the woods to the river bank. "He loves me. He loves me not. Dr. Bain loves me. Oh Monica, he does love me. If Tories have to leave Georgetown——and they will——that means Dr. Pringle and Charlotte Jane cannot remain in town. If she's not here, that means I won't have any competition. Oh, Monica, I should be ashamed. It's just that when I see Charlotte Jane I remember that horrible afternoon all over again when Dr. Pringle kneaded me and humiliated me before you and Mamma. Oh, it was awful, and then that priest…Mamma says he's no longer at Prince George Church. I think Mrs. Oliver told her that. What do you think Dr. Bain is doing? Will he really be my prince?"

"I don't know. Maybe we betta be getting home….Dat ole sun's beginning to set over the river. This is the purties time of day….when some boats be cumin in, an….well Gawd dun giv us so much to enjoy….honey, jes trus yo heart."

All through the fall, winter of 1776 and spring of 1777, Cecilia was restless. She rode Dark Moon, walked along the river or over the cobblestones on Bay Street, then up Broad Street where she stopped at the cemeteries, both Anglican and Jewish, to sit on tombstones and pray, or she paced up and down the hallway as her mother stitched away on someone's dress or waistcoat. "Mamma, tell me what to do."

"Darling, I don't know. I can't tell you if you love Dr. Bain. All I can do is encourage you not to fear," her mother smiled, never once putting down her needle.

"Mamma, remember that old rhyme, 'Jack be nimble. Jack be quick.' Well, you remind me of nimble old Jack who must have been quick as you thread and sew with that needle. Why we could make a sentence, couldn't we? And a rhyme perhaps? What do you think?"

"You're witty like your father."

"Tell me about him. What would he be doing?"

"Well, like you, he loved both the woods and the water, the church, and life. Whenever he cut stone for the cathedrals, why he'd talk to the bishop or priest about symbols and mysteries within the walls of the church. I couldn't understand that knowledge. Your father saw and understood light, and there were these various rules he had, rules I could never fathom. And yet he said I had rules. Maybe we both did. I think I'd hoped the priest at the church could explain things to me, but he didn't. Oh, he wasn't interested. He had no feelings, as you sadly had to learn. Your father helped me in so many ways. I only wish I could pass something of his deep understanding of symbols to you….and yet I think you already have it if you'll just trust yourself. His rule would be not to fear. That's what I wish mine were or could be, and yet, it's not, and I am sorry. I am just who I am. That's God's truth."

"Did you and Daddy really know each other as children?"

"We were born in cottages in the lowlands of Scotland…then we went to County Antrim, Ireland with our families, and….what else can I say?"

"I wish I could have married Thomas Lynch. He was the kind if man I would want."

Katie smiled as she listened to her daughter. "Darling, remember he was older, had a wife and son….you and I have no idea of his life before you met him. He was kind and good, and he did so much for Georgetown, but we don't ever really know people until we live with them. Do you understand? Sometimes, that's just a chance we must take, though. In the past, there were arranged marriages. There still are. It's just that I don't know anyone in Georgetown with whom to arrange a marriage for you. I must work for a living. I'm different from those who made investments and belonged to business companies when they came over."

While they were talking, Jane Oliver rapped on the door and hastened in. "I've just heard news that the General Marquis de Lafayette from France will be coming to nearby North Island to join the colonists in their fight against the British."

Those words were all Cecilia needed. Love or no love, she would fight for the patriots. Her father would be proud of that, her mother, too. "After all," she reasoned, "nobody could say Cecilia Fears because I will have no fear as I fight, and, after all, that's what Mamma preaches, and that's why Daddy came to the colonies. He wanted freedom. To have freedom must mean to have no fear. Mamma's given me a gift without realizing it. She's taught me to have no fear."

Cecilia kissed her mother, then snitched the breeches her mother was making, along with a shirt, tri-corn hat, and boots, and stole away on Dark Moon. "I'll meet that General Lafayette." Indeed, Cecilia spoke her best French on North Island and soon began scouting with General Francis Marion who came to be known as the Swamp Fox because of his maneuvers up and down the coast against the British, his fast pace, weaponry, and far more, all of which fascinated Cecilia, particularly his use of wooden shovels.

"Monica," she asked one afternoon upon returning home, "you do cover for me with Mamma, don't you? I mean, she encourages me not to fear, and I know she knew I posed as a boy, and yet I don't think she'd want me fighting. Posing and becoming are two different things."

"You don't even need to aks."

That was all Cecilia needed to return to the swamps. Like Marion, she knew the rivers, woods, and hideouts where British soldiers might lurk and plan an ambush, and she knew how to use a pistol, shovel, knife, or sword. Master Lynch had taught her riding and so much more. Whatever was necessary to defeat, challenge, or conquer the British, Cecilia would do it, even if that meant changing roles from patriot to Britisher or from Britisher back to patriot. "I'm Lochland MacLeod to Francis Marion and someone else, if needed, to a Britisher, and nobody will ever, ever know I'm just a thirteen year old girl whose mother is a dressmaker/shoemaker/milliner combined."

When Katie missed her daughter, Monica simply made up a comforting story which, even if Katie didn't really believe it, was sustaining. So long as her needle and money were in hand, Katie questioned little. Besides, there was Curly Motte Macaulay O'Toole's gold which she kept at her side, along with the psaltery, emerald silk, and fairy clock.

The months passed, one year melting into another, until Charleston and Georgetown fell to the British in 1780.

Houses and churches were burned and looted, Prince George Winyah included. It became a stable for the British as well.

One day when Monica was mending a soldier's breeches, she found a ring which she later showed to her best friend. "Dis here ring wid de blue stone looks special."

Cecilia examined the ring and agreed. "It looks like that Masonic ring Mamma has, doesn't it? I think Dr. Bain wore a Masonic ring."

"What you be getting at?"

Tucking her curls once again under a soldier's hat, this time a Britisher's she'd stolen, Cecilia smiled. "Now I'm a Red Coat, and I'll tell you soon. I have a mission now. Just don't tell my mother."

"Honey, I hate to tell you, but, truly, long as yo ma got that pirate's gold, she ain't worrying about nuthin, you included."

"Good."

So Cecilia did as she pleased. She hastened up Bay Street to Broad and stopped at the corner of High Market and Broad, the site of her beloved Prince George Winyah Church. She walked into the church where she saw British officers near the Baptismal Font. She paused and listened, then wandered down the long aisle, remembering all of her psalms and prayers, her psaltery. She saw horses in the very box pews where she and her mother and so many others had worshipped. A horse whimpered. She followed the sound to the box pew marked Smith. A beautiful bay thoroughbred was foundering, its back leg bleeding as well. Looking closely, Cecilia saw "Dr. CB" branded into the horse's shoulders.

This had to be the horse Dr. Bain called Emperor Augustus. All of Colin's stories and interests, his blue eyes, bushy brows and burly ways, rolling r's, the oyster roast, dances, even his teasing and hurting her breasts taunted, haunted Cecilia. She ached for him. Her stomach muscles knotted, and she didn't understand why. She had to see Dr. Colin Bain. Patting the horse, she made up her mind to ask the British officer a question.

"Oh, that horse," the officer answered. "Why that horse belongs to the Highlander who fought against the British long ago at Culloden Moor. He vowed to fight for the British, but he broke that law. He was caught for fighting against the Crown. Any Highlander who was at Culloden Moor was required to pledge his loyalty to the Crown. If we discover such a person fighting against the king, why, he's guilty of high treason. He's a traitor, and he'll be hanged. The officer who shot Dr. Colin Bain was Malcolm Keith. He's an old man now. He fought for Bonnie Prince Charlie. So did I. But we obeyed the law. Bain did not. Private Keith's dying at some house farther up on Broad Street."

When the Britisher turned, Lochland/Cecilia tiptoed from the church and made her way up Broad. Hearing screams, she knew this was the house turned hospital and walked inside, then up and down rows of soldiers on the first floor. Men screamed, writhing in pain, blood spattering and spattered on the floor, mosquitoes swarming over open sores and wounds. Cecilia vomited into the cuff of her coat and struggling to hold back more, remembered she'd eaten nothing since dawn, except for a cold biscuit. The stench was terrible — a blend of blood, vomit, urine, grunt.

She watched one soldier, in particular, turn from one side to the other, moan, and fling his arm up and down across his bare chest, the blue stones of his ring reddening in the afternoon sun. Cecilia walked closer and took the man's badly bandaged hand. "Can I...can I get you something? Some water perhaps?"

"Just forgiveness....I betrayed him, my childhood friend...if you ever see Colin Macaulay Bain, tell him I'm sorry. We fought at Cullodeen Moor. I followed the law. He didn't. Not seeing his Masonic ring a few weeks ago, I fired on him. I thought he was the enemy. He was, but deep down, he wasn't, never could be my enemy. Colin Bain was a true patriot because he followed his heart. I didn't. I just followed the law. That's Old Testament. The heart's Jesus. But it's all confusing. To follow your heart if it's war is not Jesus either. I don't know anymore....but Colin will be hanged at Brookgreen Plantation where the Allstons live. I'm dying. I just ask his forgiveness...and yours, if you knew him, and God's."

Cecilia clasped the man's hand, then gently slipped the ring off his finger onto her own bony one. "I have forgiven you; so has Colin Bain. But more, God has already forgiven you. Right now, he is saying to you, 'Today thou shalt be with me in paradise.' Hold to that, Mr... Your last name one more time, Sir?"

"Keith, Private Malcolm Keith," the man gasped and died, his hand in hers. She pulled a cover over his face and examined the ring. Sure enough, it was a Masonic ring, and she knew Brookgreen Plantation. She'd danced there with Benjamin Allston before his wedding. Those days seemed like yesterday. She left, then ran home to saddle Dark Moon, and gallop up the dark roads and through the swampy woods and cross the rivers to Brookgreen Plantation.

Oh, the thrill of riding under a full moon was something only a few would imagine. The smell of the salty sea, caw of the gulls, her breast bound as tight as Monica dared tie it down created a physical ecstasy itself. Not believing even Monica could imagine the pleasure, Cecilia bore down harder on the horse, the wind blowing strong across the river. "I don't care how many freckles I have, I am who I am, created in God's image, and so are you, Dark Moon." And they rode faster.

When she finally arrived at Brookgreen, Cecilia headed to the tree where she learned that Dr. Colin Macaulay Bain, traitor to the King, would be hanged. A Britisher, tightening the rope around Colin's neck, asked if he had anything to say.

Lochland/Cecilia dismounted and strode toward the tree. "Release this man. I am an officer in the regiment of your Captain Southwell. Here are my papers. The man whom you are about to hang is a fellow Mason. Malcolm Keith fired, not realizing Dr. Bain is a Mason. Here is Private Keith's ring. Here is mine as well. He asked me to bring it here as proof. This man there on the tree saved me months ago when patriots had a reaping hook about my neck. I was a Tory who had not departed from Georgetown. Now I do this man a favor. Release him at once."

The officer took the rings and examined them and the papers by the moon and his flickering candle. "This man is correct. The doctor is a Mason. Please untie the knot at once, and let him be released."

Colin Bain fell to the ground, his hands still bound. Lochland/Cecilia unraveled the last knots, then left. Colin struggled to his feet and limped into the woods, following his rescuer who waited on Dark Moon. Colin climbed onto the horse behind Cecilia, and they galloped through the swamps and woods to a grapevine arbor far, far away from Brookgreen.

"Oh, Cecilia, it is my lynx, my love," Colin said, when they finally stopped, when he looked into her eyes. "I love you. Oh, I have missed you."

He took Cecilia in his arms. She barely recognized him, for Colin's hair was totally gray now, his faced wrinkled, and burly brows completely white. He was gaunt. "I never dreamed I would ever see you again after I took the red slipper to your mother. Oh, marry me, my love, and we'll go home to White Oaks Plantation. We'll never, ever, meet another Tory. I promise."

"Colin, my sweet, you don't know that." She returned his kisses. "Besides, you're wounded." She looked at the blood on his legs and arms and tried to wipe his wounds with the sleeve of her jacket.

"'Tis nothing."

"Colin, Charleston and Georgetown have fallen to the British. Yes, I will marry you, but not until this war is over and the British have left and not until there's a priest at the church, a priest whom I trust. I'm older now, and I won't be hurt again."

They fell asleep, water lapping on the distant shore. Wakening between dreams, Cecilia and Colin loved again and again, until dawn. "Cecilia, we could sail away to the Highlands," he whispered, then fell back, exhausted.

"Shh...nobody will find us."

"Cecilia, did you really dance with Benjamin Allston? I didn't care for him. Maybe it was because I was attracted to his jo. I don't know. It doesn't matter now, does it?"

"No," she quieted, her finger over his lips. "But I need to tell you something about me you've probably already noticed...the swollen breast and the shriveled one. There's nothing I can do about them. I don't worry about them anymore. Besides, the sun is rising. That's hope. That sun is God's lamp for us all. I need to return home to my mother, and I suppose Sherwood Grove calls you. So I will kiss you good-bye for now."

"But, Cecilia, when...when will we marry?"

"When this war is over...that's what I said. Our marriage will be God's will. If it's to be, it will be, and I believe it will."

"Your talk is confusing. You speak in riddles."

"Not really, Dr. Bain...I know how you are suffering. We'll both be fortunate to get to our destinations without being caught. I have obligations."

"I suppose so," he sighed, "but I won't forget you, Cecilia Fears Lynch. I will marry you."

Cecilia continued to fight throughout the war. Not until the battle at Brattonsville in July of 1780, in York County, South Carolina, when Christian Hyuck, who particularly despised patriotic Presbyterians, was killed, was there any real hope of conquering the British. Skirmishes and battles followed, and there was a major triumph at King's Mountain in October of 1780, then another at Cowpens in January of 1781, followed, ultimately at Yorktown, Virginia, in October of 1781, when Cornwallis surrendered to the patriots.

The long struggle with the British was over, and Dr. Bain returned to Blisland County where he wrote Cecilia one letter after another, pressing for her hand in marriage. "I'll come to see you, and we will be married in Georgetown, then move to the hills of the Upcountry. Please do not disappoint me, Mademoiselle Lochland."

"The mountains shall bring peace to the people, and the little
hills, by righteousness. He shall judge the poor of the people, he
save the children of the needy and shall break in pieces the
oppressor" (Psalm 72:3-4).

Book Five (1781-1787)

"Monica, I just don't know," Cecilia said over and over again during the years following the war. "Dr. Bain keeps writing and pressing me for an answer. God knows I'm tired of making clothes, shoes, and hats with mother and doing all of those fancy embroidery stitches. You're the only one who knows my deepest feelings."

"Honey, I don't really," Monica answered, as they sat on the river bank and talked following a swim.

"Dr. Bain writes about his travels and the churches he's designed, but."

"Sista, I told you time and time that it ain't what he does. It's what you feels. Admiring a building's not the same as feeling in love or as giving love. Only you can know the difference. That's something I can't tell you. I know something gnawing way at you, and it's worse than a clawing crab, too."

"Oh yes. It is fear and humiliation. I just can't forget the night Colin squeezed me so hard. Yes, Cecilia Fears Lynch fears Dr. Colin. Isn't that a statement, Monica?" Cecilia laughed, then cried. "I'm mocking myself. Oh, much as I love to ride, sometimes I'm tired of pretending. I play a game so much of the time I don't really know myself anymore. I want someone to love me deeply and take care of me. Colin says he will, but I don't know. Mamma says not to let fear rule me and grip me. She says fear destroys life. But maybe fear is in my heart. I don't know. Sometimes, I think Dr. Bain's too worldly, and yet I'm drawn to him, pulled to him. He's irresistible. I would be pretty in an emerald silk gown, wouldn't I? If I get married, Mamma and the old pirate would be so happy, wouldn't they?"

Monica nodded. "Sho would. But what about you? Would you be happy?"

"I tried on Ma's old blue wedding gown. Of course, it's tattered. Monica, if I ever have a daughter, I wouldn't want her to feel my shame. Mamma has shamed and humiliated me. I'd want my daughter to ride in the wind with me and play the psaltery, be the psaltery, as I sometimes feel myself becoming. Monica, tell me what to do."

"Honey, I can't. I'm jes your best friend, your sister. I don't know your deepest feelings. You must trust yourself. Trust your heart. Ain't nobody else's heart but yours. God giv it to you long ago."

Cecilia understood intellectually, but remained confused, between fearing and yearning. Walking up Queen to High Market, she'd stop at the church, then go down Broad to Prince, and up and down every street in town day after day, season after season, until she finally said to herself, "Marry him, you goose. You cannot waste anymore time. If he loves you, he'll take care of you. If not, well, you will do something else. If you don't marry, why you're going to remain an old maid. An old maid in Georgetown? It's 1787. You're almost 24 years old." She wrote to Dr. Bain at once and told her mother and Monica.

Katie Fears celebrated her daughter's news with a little gathering, and Monica promised to accompany her best friend, "that is, if you want me."

"Wherever I go, you go, Monica. I need you." Cecilia settled on All Saints' Day of 1787 for the wedding.

Indeed, she was prettier than ever that day in the emerald green silk, her freckles covered with Monica's special buttermilk/marigold lotion, and her lips tinged with mulberry juice. Cecilia wore the tiny emerald earrings, a special gift from Colin. Her heart warm, she felt herself dancing when the priest pronounced the bride and groom man and wife. "Whom God hath joined together, let no man put asunder."

Following the ceremony, Katie invited friends for scones and Madeira. A little later, Cecilia and Colin departed, taking the hound dog, Curly Two, a gift from the Olivers, and Dark Moon. Monica rode with Cecilia in the handsome coach built in Charleston for the wedding.

The spokes of the wheels were painted to match the emerald green wedding dress, and the rims were etched in yellow. Above each door, the Lynch coat of arms with the lynx and the Bain coat of arms with the lion were painted, intertwined one over the other.

"How our children will interpret their family genealogy in the years to come is only a guess, my love," Colin teased, handsome in his tweed jacket, tam o'shanter adorned with a tiny St. Andrew's flag, and kilt. He kissed his bride.

Monica turned to him, "I jes pray we all has hearts, Dr. Bain." She rolled her eyes. He stared at her. He knew all about babies and their black mammies and about the relationships between enslaved women and their white owners, but this friendship which Cecilia and Monica shared puzzled him. It was different from Anna Catherine and Daphne's. "One day I'll find out, and I'll separate them," he said to himself.

Monica held the prized fairy clock and Cecilia the psaltery and bag of gold. When the coach and wagon behind, pulled by Dark Moon, passed the market, Colin saw a man chained to a post and ordered the driver to stop. "That man's a Gullah and just as smart as you, Monica. I intend to buy him today and have you marry him."

But Monica shook her head. "No, I won't be his wife."

"Of course, she won't," Cecilia called out. "Colin, you can't make Monica marry that slave."

"And why not?" He glared. The idea of his wife's contradicting him in front of everyone!

"Because Monica is free. She bought her freedom from my mother years ago, and there's absolutely nothing you or anyone can do to change that. Monica is my best friend. Wherever I go, she goes. Wherever she goes, I go, and…"

"The wench in the coach would be good for this slave, whose name is Numbers," the auctioneer interrupted, bawdily adding, "Just think of Numbers in the Bible, and pronounce it, 'Numb hers,' and you have the solution to taming that Gullah mammy. You know what I mean, Doc."

Something about the auctioneer and his curly black moustache irritated Cecilia, and something about the slave's cinnamon-colored eyes troubled her, and his breasts were puffy. "His eyes shimmer, Colin, and…No, don't buy him. I feel a bad omen." Cecilia jumped from the coach and walked toward the slave. "Mamma told me once about a man named Numbers who was sold when our ship docked in Georgetown long ago. Ma didn't like the slave trader then. I don't like him now…please, Colin. This slave is the same man who was mistreated then. He's just older. I don't like the way he's looking at me. Besides, why is he wearing a patch over one eye? Why is that auctioneer whipping him?"

"Because the slave's staring at you, silly goose." Colin lifted his wife in the air, then flung her on the seat beside Monica. "Now, don't move."

Monica shrugged her shoulders and patted Cecilia's hands. "Don't cry, honey."

"Numbers is from Peach Swamp down near Charleston. Yes, I did sell him years ago. He is older. That's true, but he's smart, just belligerent. That's why he wears a patch. You've got to work him hard and keep him away from the women. That's all."

Colin paid Orange McTavish Steggerda for Numbers, then led the slave to the wagon. As Colin was tying him to the wagon, Cecilia's fairy clock bonged twelve even though it was early afternoon. Numbers screamed and jumped so much Colin slapped him hard across the face and whipped his legs. Blood spattered on the cobblestones.

Only Monica understood the slave's words. "He's jes afraid of clocks. He's telling you that when he was a little boy long time ago a clock dun bong twelve times. That's when he got burned. Ain't nothing to do with being bought and sold. He jes has a fear that haunts him. That ain't hard to understand if you got a heart."

Cecilia understood and tried to tell her husband who only answered, "Hush. You've already angered me enough for one day." He chained Numbers under the seat of the wagon, then joined the coach driver, and the horses galloped over sandy roads toward the red hills of Blisland County.

Cecilia wept, her head on Monica's shoulder as the coach jostled along. "Honey, you chose him, and we jes got to make the best of it. Maybe he's jes tired or sumpin. Maybe he'll cool off riding outside with the men folk."

"Oh, Monica, I already miss Georgetown and Hopsewee and Mamma and....what have I done?"

Monica tried to console her.

Tired from riding for hours over the bumpy roads, Cecilia was grateful when Colin finally told the driver to stop at Talley's Tavern near Mill Springs. Following supper, Colin took Cecilia to bed and penetrated her again and again, then droned on and on about his duties until she finally fell asleep. At dawn he played a tune on the bagpipe, jumped under the quilt, and came to her, laughing, then splashed water from the pitcher on her face. "My sweet, it is morning, and it's time for my pretty bride to be up and about."

Relieved that her husband seemed in a good mood, she blinked her eyes and stretched. "Oh, Colin, let's sleep awhile, can't we? I'm so tired. Surely you are, too. Couldn't we just cuddle?"

"No, 'tis time for you to eat your oats and prepare to ride to White Oaks. It won't be long now, and may your big breast dangle like the earbobs I gave you. That's right, my love, I've gotten you, and you can't fool me anymore." He fingered the inverted nipple and squeezed the tiny breast. "You're mine, and I won't have you binding that big tiddie anymore. Do you understand?"

Stunned, she struggled to fight back tears, and finally boarded the coach where Monica waited. Cecilia closed her eyes against the morning sun.

"Harden not your heart, as in the day of provocation, and as in the day of temptation in the wilderness: When your fathers tempted me, proved me, and saw my work" (Psalm 95:8-9).

Book Six (1787-1788)

The wedding party arrived at White Oaks Plantation before noon. Gazing at the house which Colin had described, Cecilia tried to forget the painful trip. "Maybe all brides hurt a little bit after the wedding," she talked herself into believing.

She stared at the house, a Georgetown-style frame structure with a wide porch across the front and chimneys on each side. Connected to the house on the right side behind the chimney was a granite tower with tiny windows. Three climbing roses intertwined up the wall, and high above on the turret waved a dark blue flag with a white X-shaped cross.

"My cross of St. Andrew, my love," Colin said.

A large woman walked on the turret. Cecilia stared at the house and the woman.

"Do not be afraid. That's only Dido. She's my own Amazon who guards the tower. Didn't I ever tell you about her?"

"Is she….is she always there?" Cecilia asked, dreading a meeting with the woman.

"She comes and goes. Now, Cecilia, I want you to remember that the house and the land are all yours, except for one place. That's Chinaberry Grove. You must never, ever, go to the southwest side of the plantation. I beg you. That would not make Dido at all happy. Do you understand me?" He kissed her.

"Colin, you're not serious. You're teasing me, aren't you?" Cecilia smiled.

"No. I am quite serious."

Cecilia continued to smile as she looked at the magnificent boxwood, white oaks, and pines. "Oh, it's all so beautiful, Colin."

Monica nodded her approval.

Slaves came out to carry in the trunks and boxes, and Prince came forward to lead Numbers down to the Quarters. Colin introduced his wife and friend to Prince. For awhile, Cecilia was too tired to go inside, and she suggested that

Monica join her and rest on the porch. "We'll just enjoy the breeze from the Patuxee River. Oh, I almost feel as if we're in Georgetown again. I love the wind, don't you? We'll just pretend the Patuxee's the Sampit or the Waccamaw."

Monica agreed.

Colin found Daphne whipping up eggs for a custard. "Yo favrit desuht, docta."

Colin gave her a pair of gold earbobs and some salve. "All the way from Scotland," he boasted.

"Iz tickeled to deth. Cos I don't believes yu netha. You know, Docta Dunn neba gib me nuthin. He ripped off my earbobs wunz wen he tore me up. I bore him a baby wunz, but dat chile died, and I thanked Gawd."

Colin grimaced as he pictured old Dunn whipping a helpless Indian woman, then admitted he'd been almost as bad. He'd lain with Daphne and whipped her once. "Tell me, Daphne, is there any need to tell my new bride about Anna Catherine? You know, despite our differences, I treasure your advice more than anyone's."

He kicked off his boots, put his legs up on the kitchen table, and smoked his pipe.

"No, suh, ain't no need tu stir up dem coles. Dah's nuff brewin in de kettle already, an yu noz eczatly what I meens." She wrinkled her forehead and stared at him.

Colin nodded. He understood her meaning. He wanted Daphne to accept Monica and Cecilia. He knew that Monica resented him just as he resented her. But there was something about exotic women which intrigued him as much as young lasses, and he wasn't sure what. There was something broodingly sexual about Daphne.

Oh, but he adored his new bride. He teased Cecilia, tormented her, but he loved her deeply. "In one way or another, I'll draw milk from her nipples," he said to Daphne who simply listened.

While Monica and Cecilia inspected every corner of the house and ambled all through the gardens, sniffing flowers and herbs, figuring out where they would plant their own herbs, Colin disappeared from Daphne's kitchen. He was gone for hours.

When he returned late in the evening following supper, Cecilia, dressed in a pale blue silk trimmed with tiny roses, her breast bound, was playing the psaltery. Monica was listening and doing embroidery. Colin said that it was time for bed.

He took his bride to the tower and made love to her. "Oh, you're so beautiful, my darling St. Cecilia, even with those strange nipples, and I can pinch one, then the other."

She shrieked. "Colin, that hurts. Please don't."

"Monica might hear you and come over. Sh...thank God she doesn't sleep in the tower."

Cecilia finally fell asleep.

Daphne continued to preside over the kitchen, and Monica found herself settling into the role of gardener. Cecilia liked Daphne and Prince, and she walked to the stables each day, Curly Two nipping at her heels, to ride Dark Moon. She missed Master Lynch.

In time, Daphne and Monica began to trust each other, and Prince began to feel comfortable around her as well. They all shared their knowledge of medicines and herbs, each one complementing Dr. Bain's medical practice. Sometimes, Prince would set a patient's broken arm, or Monica would prescribe powdered herbs.

Despite Colin's encouragement and Daphne and Monica's support, Cecilia resisted becoming mistress of White Oaks. "I'm afraid, Monica. I don't exactly know why. Is it because Colin has teased me so much that I feel ashamed, or is it that I don't want to accept responsibility? I don't know. Help me understand myself, best friend."

Monica gave her a little passionflower tea. "This will settle your nerves. And I have some news. Elijah, what work in the brickyard, and me....well, we done fell in love, and we gwine be married. I'll be moving down to The Quarters."

"Why...why don't you buy his freedom, and you two could live here with us, Monica?"

"No, not now...I think maybe if I'm not in the house, Dr. Colin may be kinder to you. He resents us. Honey, you know that...I can feel his jealousy. Surely you can, too."

Cecilia cried, wondering what she'd do without Monica's presence. It wasn't jealousy, for she liked Elijah. He'd always been kind to Monica and thoughtful. He'd be good to Monica.

"Well," she said, wiping her tears, "I'll...'ll just have to pretend to be happy with my husband. Maybe if I try to believe I'm happier, I will be, and...and maybe he won't humiliate me so much."

"I know he loves you, honey, and why we'll be as close as always. Nothing's neba gwine change that, and you know it, don't you?"

"Yes," Cecilia answered, as she leaned her head on Monica's shoulders and muffled her tears. "I need you more than you need me. I always will. I love you."

"And I love you."

"Monica, you do know I'm happy for you."

Monica nodded, as Daphne shuffled in. "Yu noz my body be cripple up wid de rumatizm. Prince dun gib me some wiled yams, and Docta Bain brung me salve from Scotland....Missus Cecilia, I needs foh yu to take ova de runnin of White Oaks. I can't do it no moh....yuz de mistress."

Cecilia took Daphne's old, gnarled hands into her own. "I will, Daphne, if you will be my teacher."

"And lamb, don't be fraid of de docta. He luvs you so much."

They began making preparations for Christmas, gathering holly and cedar, magnolia and laurel for arrangements throughout the house and cooking all sorts of cakes, puddings, and pies out in the kitchen. Cecilia laughed and confessed that she would rather be out riding in the wind or tending to the garden than fretting over a plum pudding.

Daphne smiled. She understood. Monica had told her about their love and friendship. "We're like sisters, Daphne, and I don't think the doctor understands it. Lige does, and he's not jealous."

"I understand, Monica. I know."

Cecilia asked if there would be fish feasts or dances at White Oaks, and Daphne shook her head. "Ain't neba had uh party here."

Cecilia's stomach cramped. Something seemed wrong. Not to celebrate with friends at Christmas. Even though her mother needled her life away to make a coin, she never failed to celebrate special times with friends. She always invited friends in for a cup of wassail at Christmastide and adorned the tables with sprigs of bay. There was mistletoe as well. Above all, they sang carols from Scotland and Ireland, as Cecilia played them on the psaltery.

Daphne shook her head.

"Is there some evil spirit lurking here at White Oaks, or is life in the upcountry just more somber?"

Daphne shook her head again, then told a haunting story about her only child with Prince being burned one day down in The Quarters. "We call him Corinth, and one day somebody throwed a burning candle through our window, and the chile caugt fiah...I roll hem in a quilt, but I cudn't save hem...Prince buried hem up neah dat White Oak tree on the hill."

Cecilia trembled, thinking about the little boy, wondering if the Amazon woman had hurled a torch toward the cabins. "Who is that Dido, Daphne?"

"I neba noed dat, honey chile."

"Well, I'll just play my psaltery and the harpsichord, and sing. At least, you and Monica, Prince, and Elijah will join me, won't you?"

Daphne patted her hand, then explained that Dr. Colin stayed busy with his medicine or selling hides and spirits to traders coming in to the port cities or to merchants in Charleston and Georgetown. She also said that he exchanged seeds with other gardeners.

Later when Cecilia asked Colin about his travels, he explained that he liked to hunt as well. "You know, my sweet, I'm just not that social anymore. Besides, I'm older."

"But all the balls at the plantations near Georgetown, the oyster roasts and fish feasts? Didn't you enjoy those? Why you always dressed in your kilt, and we danced. You laughed and told stories. Were you simply disguising yourself?"

"Now, you're the disguise. Remember the young Master Lochland MacLeod and the golden curls. Come, my love, let me hold you."

Colin held her tightly and squeezed her breasts.

"Don't. Oh, that hurts, sweetheart. It does."

"But," Colin answered, his eyes twinkling, "you're my wife to enjoy. Remember that wives are to be submissive to their husbands. You're the one who is churched. I am not." He laughed again and smothered her with kisses on her neck and breasts, then sucked her nipples. "Ah, did you cover them with custard? They're sweet."

"Colin, you do shame me," she answered, then stood up and pulled up her bodice.

"Calm down. Why don't you sing something or play on the pirate's psaltery? Here, have a sip of brandy. The night is warm yet. Maybe, it's just our child stirring within you that has you a little upset. Cecilia, I do adore you."

To tease him, Cecilia did play a Renaissance hunting jig on the harpsichord and told Colin to gallop around the room. "Pretend you're a horse," she laughed, and Colin obeyed her, then collapsed, and called for another brandy. "My young wife, you weary me."

Cecilia laughed, then kissed him good-night, and went to bed, for she wanted to go to church the next day.

She hoped Colin would join her, but he declined. "No, you go. I prefer to light my own candles and have my own bread and wine. Daphne makes biscuits for these occasions, and my finest Madeira becomes Christ's blood given as a sacrifice for me. Far more meaningful than anything Dr. Dunn could ever bless and preserve. You'll come to share my feelings." He kissed her good-bye.

During the sermon at Brick Tower Church, Dr. Dunn railed out against Cecilia. Clutching his hickory stick, he walked down from the pulpit. "Woman, I know who thou art, and thou hast no tokens. I command you, therefore, in the name of God the Father Almighty, to remove thyself from this house of worship or be consumed in the everlasting fires of hell. Do I make myself quite plain unto thee?"

Without answering, Cecilia immediately left the church and rode home where she learned all about tokens.

"How utterly judgmental!" she cried. "I was denied the body and blood of my Lord and Savior, Jesus Christ, simply because I did not have a coin?"

"Oh, my little Saint Cecilia," Colin laughed, over his pipe and brandy, "don't take all of this so seriously. I simply forgot to give you a token. I have a number of tokens, and one day, mark my words, they will become collectors' items. They're like little buttons. One day, we shall bore holes in the tokens and sew them on my outer coat or your cape. We'll ride over to the church in the coach and four, and I'll laugh at old Dunn's expression when we interrupt his hideous services. The bastard's not worthy of your fretting. I'm just sorry he distressed you. I could challenge him to a duel. Ah, wouldn't that be spectacular? On the grounds of Brick Tower Church or right here at White Oaks Plantation, Dr. Colin Macaulay Bain challenges Dr. Gavin Dunn to a duel!"

"No, Colin, please don't," she smiled. "I'm weary."

"I know. So are your breasts, especially big dumpling? I'd think she's a wee bit worried about whether the baby can suck her. Perhaps, though, you'd like communion with me. I don't mind taking it again at all. Daphne's biscuits are delightful. They make a good broken body. The choice is yours. Have some, instead of biting your nails. That habit does not become you."

"Colin, stop scoffing my religious beliefs."

"Cecilia, I'm really not. I don't intend to sound that way. It's just that I know far more about old Dr. Dunn and his past than you do. He's a vicious preacher, a thorough hypocrite. Further, I have contributed heavily to that church, and Dunn knows it. I designed the brick tower and gave the money for it as well. That's why the church is called Brick Tower."

Cecilia left the room and took comfort in her old prayer book.

Colin busied himself with activities in Millsborough where he served as a trustee at Mount Hebron College. While he was away, Cecilia learned from Daphne that Colin had been a volunteer during the war and was known for his wealth and independence.

"But that doesn't entitle him to travel and leave me at Christmastide when I'm carrying our first child, does it?" she confided to Monica.

"Yu gwine make yourself sick, honey," Monica said.

"Monica, you are happy with Elijah, aren't you?"

"Oh, yes….he loves me, and I love him. He's good to me. His child is stirrin in me….maybe we'll have our babies bout the same time."

Cecilia said she liked Elijah. "He knows the signs, too. Whenever I ask him something about Dark Moon, he answers. There's only one slave who bothers me…he's that young man who helps Prince at the stable. I think they call him Caleb."

"Prince says he's not happy."

"Maybe we can free him one day…Monica, I would like to free all of the slaves at White Oaks, but right now, just tell me something…of course you've given Elijah your heart, but do you still have a little left for me?"

"Of course, I do, and you know it. Dat's jes de Devil tempting you. You put your best foot forward, and don't let Dr. Bain get you down neither. Sometimes I think he's jes a great big old chile. Now, don't let him be botherin you none about yo brestes. You're beautiful, and you're going to keep your chin up. Remember honey lamb, one of us got to name our chile Hebrides."

Cecilia laughed, remembering that afternoon when they'd talked about names. That seemed so long ago. Cecilia forced herself to smile and remain cheerful for Christmas. On Christmas Eve when she heard dancing down in The Quarters, she opened the windows, so she could hear the drums and merry shouting. She yearned to feel the slaves' joy over Christmas, but she felt nauseated. Monica gave her more ginger tea.

On Christmas Day, determined to prove herself mistress of White Oaks, Cecilia stood on the porch and passed out clothing and shoes to the slaves.

"This is our custom," Colin said, joining her. "You're doing well. I'm glad Daphne took the measurements weeks ago and the clothes and shoes were made. Your mother even gave me some old shoes, some mismatched, before our wedding day. In that way, I didn't have to give up more hides for the slaves. Next year I will expect you to supervise the task of measuring and cutting. It's something every plantation mistress does, and I am confident you will do a beautiful job."

"I understand," Cecilia answered, as she watched a cinnamon-colored woman approaching the porch, a basket on her head, belly swollen. The woman swayed back and forth in a low-cut shift, one breast exposed, her head covered with a blue turban adorned with tiny diamonds. She cut her eyes at Colin, then at Cecilia. "I don believes I noz you, Misses Ceceelya." The woman curtsied, and Cecilia extended her hand.

"Merci," the woman answered.

Later at the table, Cecilia asked if the woman was kin to Numbers. "Her eyes shimmer as his good one does."

Colin evaded the question. "Darling, I'll be leaving for Annapolis before New Year's, and I want you to be especially careful if you ride in January. Sometimes the winter days are quite cold and windy, and the horses spook. I don't want you to fall."

"Oh, Colin, take me with you."

But he shook his head. "Honey, you'd tire so easily. Besides, your tummy's swelling to meet the 'Big dumpling.' My sweet, I'll be stopping in Wilmington, New Bern, and Williamsburg along the way. I've been working on drawings for a church near New Bern."

"I wish you'd let me decide for myself, instead of telling me how I would feel." She stomped her foot under the table. "I am utterly bored and depressed."

"I know. I can tell sometimes, but you mask it very well. You really do."

"You're not fair to me. This isn't the kind of life you promised me, and you know it. Remember all of those letters you wrote to me describing life at White Oaks?"

"Love, eat plenty of Hoppin' John for me on New Year's Day, and play with the dolls your mother sent for the baby. Play the psaltery."

"I won't eat a thing."

Only Monica could comfort her. "Chile, you gave the docta yo heart. You jes got to make the most of it now. We agreed on that. Just don't fret over what he says. Sometimes I don't think he means a thing he says." Cecilia buried her head on Monica's shoulder and wept. "Why? Why did I ever marry him and leave Georgetown? Oh, he deceived me. He's played with my heart, and sometimes I hate him. I do."

Cecilia threw her glass of wine on the floor.

"Honey, you tricked your own heart, and you know it. Remember all the times you asked me, and we talked. You never answered my questions. You jes talked about the docta's flowers, his stories, his houses, and all."

"I know." Cecilia looked up, her face streaked with tears, hair falling about her face.

"Honey, you jes got to make the most of it. Lige and me...well we're here for you." Monica brushed back Cecilia's curls and wiped her face. "You jes go rest, and you'll be feeling better. Then, do something you really want to do."

"Ride now....ride across the fields and through the woods, not just around the plantation."

"Ain't nuthin stopping you but yourself....Remember sometimes you jes got to make believe. That's something my mammy learned me long time ago."

"I know you asked me about my heart, and I never answered you. I never answered myself. I've deceived myself. Maybe I didn't have a heart. Monica, I'm an odd one—a near orphan with irregular breasts baptized by a pirate. I want to go home to Mamma."

"But you can't. Tell you what. I need some more lessons cauf sometimes I be talking like those down in The Quarters....I find myself speaking the way they do."

"Maybe I could give everyone lessons. Why, Monica, if I want to free all the slaves, well I need to teach them, so that they can read and write, don't you think?"

"I sho do. Now, let's have a short lesson now."

So Cecilia gave her best friend a review of verbs and pronouns. "Thank you for assuring me, Monica. I could never live without you."

"And I'll cut yo breeches bigger, and we'll make a shorter cape. I need to make my own dresses bigger, too, so I can carry that Baby Hebrides," she laughed, as she left the room.

All through the spring, Cecilia gave lessons in the three R's to many slaves and rode Dark Moon. One night in April, she thought she heard gun fire and noises in the tower. She wandered down the stairs and crossed over into the rooms opposite the tower. The sounds grew fainter. "Maybe it was all a dream."

Scared, Cecilia crept across the lawn down to Monica's cabin and spent the night. After that night, Elijah and Monica stayed with her in the big house. "Dido dun disappeah," Lige said. "Ain't nobody seed huh netha."

Colin returned to White Oaks in the summer just in time to enjoy squash, beans, and other vegetables from the garden and fruits from the orchard. Peach Charlotte, one of Daphne's specialties, was his favorite.

Monica and Daphne were delighted with the aprons he brought them, and Cecilia was happy to receive some sheet music. Colin disappeared for a few hours, then returned, grateful to discover his wife seemed less anxious.

Cecilia never told him about all of the calming teas Monica and Daphne offered her. If chamomile didn't work, Monica gave her hops or pigeon grass. "We gwine mak yu seem happy," Daphne had said one day. "Sho is, honey lamb."

And Cecilia agreed. "Colin, the baby is fine. In fact, sometimes, I think I may be carrying two babies. Feel me. We'll name them George Washington and Martha Custis and call them Wash and Mollie for short. You know, when I used to ride at Brookgreen, Rachael Allston told me about naming her baby boy Washington for the commander. Did you know the Allstons? Her first husband died. He raced horses, and her second husband was a doctor."

Colin shook his head. "No....I never worried about meeting people. I was a volunteer known as a wealthy, up-country gentleman. I enjoyed that role."

"Colin, you will stay with me while the baby—-or babies—-are born, won't you? I have missed you so."

"Of course I will. But tell me how big dumpling and little dumpling are."

"Stop your silliness."

"Seriously, sweetheart, when I was in Annapolis, I consulted a physician who assured me that your abnormalities could easily be corrected with surgery. Why, I could operate tomorrow."

"Colin, you are absolutely crazy. No doctor, not even you, in his right mind would perform surgery on a pregnant woman, and you know that. You're absolutely not going to touch my breasts tonight," she screamed and walked to the window. "Why can't you ever simply put your arms around me and feel the breeze from the white oaks and listen to the tree frogs? Don't you ever grow tired of tantalizing me."

"Did I ever tell you that the darkies would call your little breast a chigger bump?"

"No, and I don't care. My God, Colin, didn't you even miss me?"

"Yes, I did. I consulted several doctors, exchanged seeds, and sold a number of our plantation products....I had important tasks which I don't think you always understand....Cecilia, you're such a child sometimes."

As she was about to reply, Daphne came in and announced supper and reported that Monica was going to be having her baby soon. "I gwine down to de Kwatahs, and Docta Bain, I hope yu be stayin wid yo wif dis time. You noz, Misses Ceceelya be habin yo babee soon."

PSALTERY AT WHITE OAKS

"Hush, Daphne. Of course, I plan to stay with my wife. Go on down to The Quarters, and mind your own business."

A few days later, Monica gave birth to twins whom she called Nessie and Memnon for characters in the Greek myths Cecilia had told her about. Cecilia struggled to waddle down to the cabin and visit the babies. She took them little dolls she'd made. "For Clytemnestra and Agamemnon. Oh, Monica, they are beautiful. Just look at Nessie's curly hair and Memnon's big brown eyes. Maybe you'll name your second child Hebrides. I'll write my mother a note. She will be so happy."

"Miss Celya, you gwine hab twins to," Elijah prophesied. "I dun seed it in de stahs."

"And I believe you, Lige. You're our prophet."

In late August, she went into labor. The pain seemed unbearable. Monica fanned her, Daphne brought cool tea, and Colin wiped her forehead between his sips of brandy. "You're almost there, my darling. Push one more time." Finally, on the morning of September the first, Cecilia gave birth to twins.

"Wash and Mollie," she sighed, "and I am exhausted."

"I know, and you did beautifully. I'm so proud of you. I do love you, Cecilia, and I'll record their names in the Bible, as you requested several weeks ago."

"Thank you. Please stay with me. I need you."

As soon as he patted the babies, Colin fingered his daughter's tiny nipples. There was no swelling. They seemed normal.

"Oh, aren't they precious?" Cecilia gazed drowsily at the twins whom Colin placed at her breasts. But she couldn't nurse them, and she knew it. 'Colin knows that, too,' she said to herself, 'why does he torment me so?'

He turned to Daphne. "You know where to take the boy child. He needs more nourishment than the baby girl. Monica, you take her, and see what you can do. Don't either of you drop them. I warn you, I could never forgive you for hurting these lambs."

"You ain't gwine have to, and you know it," Monica said, then turned to Cecilia. "Rest, honey lamb. You tired, and I know it. I'm so happy out chillins will be friends."

"Please bring the babies to their mother later after they're cleaned and fed, though she will never be able to nurse them. Maybe she doesn't want to. I don't know. Monica, I'll never understand why you bound my wife's breast. Did you enjoy it? Was it pleasurable?"

"Docta Bain, hush yo mouth! Yo wife jes brought you two beautiful chillins, and you be talkin about her brestes. Ain't you shamed?"

"No, I'm fascinated with your devotion."

Cecilia clasped Monica's hands as her best friend picked up Mollie, then turned over, and cried herself to sleep, clutching one of the dolls her mother had made.

Colin left the room. When she awakened later in the afternoon, Cecilia was alone, but she was too weary to care. Daphne brought chamomile tea. "I really don't want anything to eat," Cecilia sighed.

"Honey, yuz gotta eat to keep up yo strength."

"No, it doesn't matter. Not now, Daphne, maybe never."

"Honey, yu jes weeire...Prince will carry up sumpin fo' yu to eat. Don yu be cryin' no moh...dat ain't gud fo yu an' de chaps."

Colin forced himself to linger at White Oaks for a few weeks. The twins grew, and after a few days of Prince's remedies, Cecilia began to feel stronger. She rocked the babies and played with them, fascinated with their development and discoveries. "Mollie sucks her tiny thumb, and Wash looks at his tiny fists. Oh, they are beautiful children, Colin. God has blessed us."

Colin rode in several fox hunts and enjoyed walking over his land while Cecilia walked in the garden. One day before Christmas, he announced his plans to go abroad in the New Year.

"Oh, take us with you, Colin," Cecilia begged.

"Are you serious? Yes, you probably are. I could see us taking two babies and their mammies aboard a ship and sailing across the Atlantic. You'd probably insist on taking Dark Moon as well and maybe that mangy hound. My love, sometimes I think you have more feelings for that horse than you do for me."

"Please, Colin, let's not begin the litany again. It's always either the breasts or your many duties or your criticisms of something else."

"Well, you forget that I am a doctor, plantation owner, gardener, architect, and correspondent. What do you expect? I provide you with a beautiful home, servants, fine clothing, silver, more...you didn't have a pot to piss in when you married me, and you know it. I become tired of that Gullah woman, of her abiding presence. Neither one of you can move without the other. Sometimes I wonder about you two."

"Colin, stop. Please. You've insulted me enough. Would you like for me to leave?"

"Oh, sweetheart, no. Let's make love," he continued, lying down beside her. "And I have ordered a new horse for you for Christmas. So I'm not such a bad Scotsman, am I? And I ordered the rattles you requested for Mollie and Wash. You're my toy, Cecilia, and you delight me, even those breasts."

Cecilia gave herself to him, then prayed she would not become with child. "Not again, God, not so soon."

On Christmas morning, the ginger woman who balanced the basket came with a child at her breast. She curtsied, "Christmas gif, Madame. Any cloth for mon enfant? I needs to make hem sum suga tits."

Cecilia smiled and gave her extra material and another pair of shoes. "Daphne, who is that woman?"

Daphne shrugged her shoulders and went into the house.

Colin joined Cecilia later in the afternoon for Maderia while she was rocking the twins, and, true to his word, left on New Year's Day of 1789. Cecilia didn't go down to wish him a safe journey. She stayed in bed, claiming a fever. "What difference does it make?" she asked Monica who came for a visit. "Drink this willowbark tea, honey. It will calm you."

By spring, the twins were crawling and babbling. Cecilia laughed and sang to them, took them for long strolls near the river, and, as always tried to nurse her babies, but to no avail. "I'm determined to remain cheerful," she often said to her best friend, "but it's hard...oh, it's so hard."

"You want to talk about it?"

"Maybe...it's just the same thing over and over again, and I know it. Maybe the devil's just tempting me. My husband married me because I amuse him, and I married him because I was infatuated. How foolish! If it weren't for you and your family, I would go mad. What will become of me? Will I end up as a freakish old woman in some carnival?"

"No," Monica answered, rocking her and singing, "Steal away, steal away to Jesus." When I'm afraid, I jes sing dat old song, and I feels better. You will. Now, I want you to ride and play the psaltery. To feel blue after a birthin' is natural as the sun rising and setting."

"Monica, maybe I really should continue with my hope of teaching the slaves to read...maybe have a school."

"Ain't nothing to stop you, 'cept maybe youself or fear. And fear ain't nothing but ole Scratch, and you know it. Ain't nothing to stop you honey. Follow your dreams."

"I don't think so," Colin marched in, in early June, surprising them. "To follow your dreams is to follow me, nothing more...what's this I heard about reading?"

"Reading to the twins," Cecilia lied, working hard to remain cheerfully aloof. "You've played with my heart long enough," she analyzed in her head. "But don't hate him," a voice whispered back. "Oh, but sometimes I do," she argued with herself.

"Oh, my love, I have missed you. I went to Edinburgh and visited with the doctors at the University. Oh, I will have you." He tore off his clothes and lay on top of her. "Tell me you love me."

"I do."

"I hope I've gotten you with another child. We shall call him Colin Macaulay Bain, Jr., and he will be a Renaissance man just like me."

"Well, don't I count for being his mother?"

"Not unless he's grumpy. Then I can blame it all on you, my sweet," he teased. Cecilia was relieved that her husband was not tormenting her. "He seems happy. Just leave him be," she told herself.

During the summer, Colin played with the twins, then left abruptly one morning, only to reappear a month to the day he'd departed, then rode off again in September. But Cecilia didn't ask where he has been or where he was going. She only told him that she was carrying his child. She didn't even tell him that there'd been unrest among some of the slaves. Elijah said he'd fought off Numbers one day in the brick yard. "The man be tryin' to staht sumpin'… he set fiah to dem bales o' hay down neah Buhnt Bluffs."

Cecilia begged Elijah not to tell her husband about the slave's animosity. "He'd blame me because I've been teaching Numbers to read."

Elijah understood, but advised Cecilia not to come down to the Quarters. She wanted to know what started the unrest, and Elijah said that Colin had sold Numbers' wife and baby to a plantation owner down the river.

Cecilia shook her head and asked herself why her husband had to be so cruel, indifferent to people's needs. "Why would he do that?"

Elijah shook his head and assured her that things would settle down.

A few weeks later, Cecilia received a letter from Jane Oliver in Georgetown, saying that Katie Lynch had died.

> "They had to sell the house to pay your mother's debts. Your ma worked so hard. She just took sick and died one day. Apparently, she didn't have much money, but a lot of debts. The priest conducted a service, and your ma was buried near the river. Nobody realized what a pauper she'd become. For the last few years, her business had languished. I'm so sorry. Your ma was a proud lady. We took her food,

but she'd never invite us in. She took in stray cats. She told me never to write to you that she was sick. She appreciated all of your notes and stories about the babies. I promised your mother I'd send you her wedding ring and your daddy's spontoon. She began carrying it all the time as protection. May God be with you."

Cecilia read the letter to Monica, then broke down and wept. "I should have gone to see Mamma…she should not have died alone. I invited her to White Oaks, but she always said Georgetown was her home now."

"I know…you tried…you did the best you could, and you gwine show yo own chillins all the love you ken, so I don't want you to start feelin' fear and shame. You heat your best friend, Cecilia?"

She nodded. "You are so wise. Do you remember your mother, Monica?"

"Her being sold at the auctioneer's block in Charleston when I was seven years old, not long before yo ma bought me. My mammy was separated, for some reason, from her chillins. Oh, she was beautiful. Some plantation owner way down in Beaufort bought her. My mammy loved me. Why, she sang to me and we made baskets together. She was so tall, like a queen."

"The way you are, best friend."

"Huney, why don't you go riding," Monica said, changing the subject, "you ain't showing that much. I'll fix up the old breeches you wore when you was carrying the twins. They'd be so proud to see their mama ride. So will Nessie and Memnon."

"Yes," Cecilia said, her green-gold eyes suddenly flashing, "There's a jousting tournament over at the Lindsay Plantation in a couple of weeks. I don't remember who told me. Maybe it was Mrs. Wherry when she came calling. I could pose as a black knight. That way, I'm in mourning, of course, but nobody will ever know me."

"Where's that plantation?"

"It's called Leeds Landing. It's not far from Swann Creek Associated Reformed Presbyterian Church. Oh, Monica, this is just the pleasure I need. You don't think I'll scare the twins, do you?"

"Jes let them see you ride, but not in costume. 'Case that daddy of theirs comes in, you don't want them telling him about the tournament. You know all chillins love to tell what seems exciting."

Cecilia agreed. "And I'm going to teach Wash and Mollie to ride. I'm going to encourage them and absolutely spoil them."

In late October, Cecilia dressed herself and introduced herself as "The Black Knight" from Burnt Bluffs, and she won the prize for tilting the ring. It was her duty to crown young Leonora Elizabeth Lindsay queen of the tournament.

Leonora smiled, then invited the winning knight to dance as fiddlers tuned up and played and guests feasted on pheasant, sweet potatoes, fruit tarts and puddings. Beneath the mask, Cecilia blushed and felt nauseated and hot. She had to leave and managed to turn Leonora toward some lad dressed in yellow. "He will dance the reel with you."

She vomited and then galloped back home on the black horse Colin had given her for Christmas and had named Natas. To her astonishment, Colin was sitting in the library, the main room on the first floor of the tower. He was reading. "Wonder why he came back," she murmured to herself. "Surely not to celebrate our third anniversary or prepare for Christmas."

"Greetings, my dear," he said. "Odd that we're both in breeches as we near the occasion of our anniversary, particularly since you appear to be with child. Were you bored? Have you prayed? Have you missed me? Oh, I do love watching you pace and bite your nails. Then I know I've made you uncomfortable." He puffed his pipe and sipped his brandy.

"I'm cold, Colin. That's all. The wind picked up before I left the tournament."

"Tournament? Cecilia, you're more of a child than I thought! What poor judgment. You could have lost our child!"

"Oh, Colin, if you're embarrassed, nobody knew who I was. I posed as "The Black Knight" from Burnt Bluffs. Since I tilted the ring, why, it was my pleasure to crown the pretty young lady, Leonora Elizabeth Lindsay, queen."

"You mean you didn't pose as my favorite, Sir Lochland MacLeod? And did you know that Miss Leonora is a triplet?"

Cecilia shook her head. "Does it matter?"

"Mrs. Lionel Lindsay gave birth to three baby girls, each with a deformity, and I was privileged to do surgery on each one. Leonora had a hare lip. Didn't you notice her contorted smile? Then, there was the middle daughter, Louisa Lois. She had a club foot. I put a contraption on it, and, faithfully, that gal drags it around, even dances, I'm told. The father was disappointed not to have a son in the litter, so he called the last baby Latrobe. Oh, she's ugly. Her ears stick out like a donkey's. I tried something, but my surgery failed. Alas, what could I do?"

"You really are heartless, Colin. Tell me, were there sons?"

"Finally. Lionel. He's as arrogant as the old father. I think he prefers the company of young men, just as you and Monica seem to enjoy each other."

Cecilia slapped him on the leg, and he stood up, took her in his arms, and forced her to the hard floor by the blazing fire. "Oh, my love." They climaxed together, and she hated herself for yielding.

He withdrew and lay beside her on the floor. "You are beautiful half naked in black. Should I have a whip?"

"Stop it, Colin. Do not say anything else, please. Mama died while you were away. Not knowing where you were, I couldn't write. Colin, your penis, I fear, has visited too many homes."

"Now, please tell me who is being ugly. How did Miss Katie die? I truly liked your mother. She had spirit. Meantime, my love, how do you feel? You're still so small. You've not done anything foolish, have you?" He propped himself up, gazed down at her body, and stroked her.

"No, I've not taken any herbs or asked someone to do anything to take the child."

"Please don't ever do anything like that. It would be very painful. Besides, my love, I need you." He leaned down and kissed her breasts, his long white hair cascading around her. "You're still wearing your boots," he teased.

She put her arms around him. "I love you, but sometimes I think we should separate."

"And what would you do, my love? Make a living racing at New Market?"

She shook her head and pushed him away. "No, I could have a little school at the edge of the plantation. You could come and go, as you always do, but we would no longer be man and wife, just friends. You have betrayed me."

"Cecilia, it is you who deceived me. I never knew that your love for Monica was so deep. Even the slaves talk about it. I had no idea you weren't ready for motherhood."

"You've said too much." She stood up, her clothes on the floor. "Monica is the one who nurtured me and understood me. We have a bond, nothing physical, only spiritual. I taught her to read and write, and she gave me so many lessons. Maybe you have the unnatural fantasies. I will never know. You don't take me with you. I adore the twins. They walk, and we play and read. You have no idea how many teeth Wash has or how much Mollie coos and sleeps sucking her tiny thumb. You don't even care. True, you give them toys now and then. True, I've not been able to feed them, but I love them dearly. I am grateful to God for them." She began pacing.

"I'll follow you," he teased, "You can go all over the house naked if you'd like, but it is chilly tonight. And you'll be even colder, for I'm burning your black knight's costume." He threw it into the fire. "No more black knights, my love, no pun intended, for it's nearly our anniversary, and we must celebrate."

She ran upstairs, and he followed. They slept through the night, each exhausted, each dreaming of another beginning. At dawn, Cecilia reached for him. "Let's try again. I do love you."

"I adore you, my love."

And for a few weeks, Colin tried. His wife was right. She was a devoted mother who knew her children intimately. He didn't. Colin became fascinated with the twins' games and talk. "Why, they have their own brogue, don't they? I have no idea what 'gunda knee' or 'ole dollie baba' mean, but they do. If Wash fusses, Mollie wails. Sometimes she even sucks his thumb! Have you noticed?"

"Yes, they're very close, and Mollie does not have any abnormalities, except for a little rash on her face that comes and goes."

"Good."

Following breakfast, Colin disappeared.

"Daphne, where did my husband go? I was hoping he'd walk down by the river with us."

Daphne shook her head. "I dunno. Maybe down in the Kwatahs. Dat gal Lottie's 'bout to hav' a baby."

"I never knew my husband to deliver a slave's baby, did you, Daphne?"

The woman just shook her head.

"The heavens declare the glory of God; and the firmament showeth his handiwork. Day unto day uttereth speech, and night unto night showeth knowledge" (Psalm 19:1-2).

Book Seven (Christmas 1789-Christmas 1790)

During the weeks before Christmas, Cecilia sang old carols, supervised the cooking and clothing for the slaves, strewed the house with fresh greenery, and laughed as Mollie and Wash tossed the pigs' bladders and nibbled fried pigs' tails at hog-killin.

Even Colin appeared to enjoy being at home. Following Cecilia's advice, Monica stayed away from the Big House. "I know you love the doctor. Elijah and me, we both understand. Give him another chance, and when he leaves, we'll be together. Please don't fret over your best friend." Monica embraced her.

On Christmas morning there were fireworks up and down the Patuxee River. Cecilia distributed clothing and shoes to the servants and watched a light-bronzed woman walking toward the porch, a little boy holding her hand. "An Christmas gift to vous and le docteur," she said, and curtsied. "Now, ain't I gots a fine-looking garcon, Madame?"

Cecilia nodded and gave the woman clothing and extra shoes for the little boy. "The jewels on your turban are glistening this Christmas morning. They are beautiful, and may God be with you and the little boy. Let me clasp your hand and hold the little boy."

"Merci," the woman answered, smiling, then turned and tore her dress to reveal a scar on her left breast. "Dun got clawed il y a deux annees."

"Cecilia," Colin interrupted, motioning the woman to leave, "she is only a bondswoman.

Following dinner, Cecilia rested, then feeling stronger, the air warmer, yearned to go for a walk. "Let's see," she counted with Colin, "I'm seven or eight months along, or more. You're the doctor, Colin. Tell me."

He shrugged his shoulders. "Cecilia, I do not know." He poured himself another brandy.

"Maybe we'll have eggnog later, darling." She kissed him good-bye.

"Bye, Daddy," Wash said.

"Come wif us, Daddy," Mollie begged, tugging at his breeches.

"Go away, silly goose."

Mollie cried, and Cecilia comforted her. "Come on, sweetheart. Hold Mommy's hand."

They walked through the woods and down by the back creek, and on the way home, Cecilia and Mollie stumbled over fallen branches. Something was swarming, and Cecilia realized they were near a bee's nest. Before she could pick Mollie up, the bees were swarming and stung her eyes and Mollie's cheeks. Wash couldn't understand what his mother was saying, and ran ahead, for help. Cecilia picked up her little girl, but stumbled a second time, then a third, unable to balance herself. Daphne asked Monica to come up to the Big House, and together they made tea and salves, hoping to bring down the swelling.

On New Year's Eve, only Wash enjoyed the fireworks on the river with his father, and on New Year's Day, Colin insisted that he'd spent enough time at White Oaks. "I need to return to my duties and my business. I've spent two months with you, my dear."

When Cecilia begged him not to leave, Colin became ugly, accusing. "I think you deliberately stumbled. I don't think you ever really wanted our summer baby, Cecilia."

"Colin, that's not true," she wept. "You've no idea how happy I've been these last weeks. Our time has been just what I imagined it would be when we married. We've enjoyed the twins and each other, and….please stay. The children need you. I need you. Colin. Don't go."

Struggling to catch his hand, she fell to the floor.

"Cecilia, Wash needs me, and I'll be in and out to train him, but Mollie doesn't matter. You and Monica are her teachers. Just don't encourage her to travel to Lesbos."

Cecilia slapped her husband across the legs, then caught his foot. Colin fell down beside her. "Cecilia, stop it right now. I'm grateful that Mollie didn't inherit your deformity, but I regret she doesn't possess your zest for life. She's a dull child, my dear. She's not pretty the way you are."

"You've done nothing for your little daughter, Colin, and you know it. You're always pushing her away, and she feels it. She knows you don't love her."

"I admit that. Wash is the one who is important to me. I want him to follow in my footsteps and become a fine doctor. I want him to go abroad and study. You can teach Mollie in your so-called school, and we'll marry her off to someone."

Cecilia struggled to get up and collapsed on the sofa. "Oh, I am weary. Please give me a sip of brandy."

"Darling, you know, I will always be sorry I didn't do surgery. If I die, I don't suppose anyone would have you, despite your zest. Who would want an aging woman with breasts which are withered and decayed? I'll always be sorry I didn't perform surgery on you. I don't know if surgery would have enabled you to nurse or if it would have simply made you more pleasing to the eye. Still I wonder if this deformity is in your genes. I'll never know. I'm getting old, you know. I am nearly as old as George Washington. I wonder about my regrets, and yet I've enjoyed every minute of tormenting you and playing with the swollen breast and inverted nipple and tickling the little dried-up apple of the other one....if you'd been born natural, I may not have had nearly so many pleasures. Perhaps our very early summer baby will be a little girl with deformities. Perhaps she'll meet a man to whom she can bring pleasure simply on account of them. But she must not be dull. Ah, my love, I have enjoyed your spirit and your body."

"I know only too well," she answered. "Colin, carry me to bed."

"I will." He took her upstairs and gently put her down, then kissed her good-bye.

"Colin, come back soon. I do enjoy all of your stories. They are always spellbinding."

"Ah, they are, aren't they, dearie?"

He left.

On Candlemas, Cecilia gave birth to a baby boy. "Let's call him Little Colin Macaulay Bain, Jr." she said, as Monica shook the child, wrapped him, and gave him to her best friend.

"I can't nurse him, Monica. Please help me."

"You know I will, honey, and I gwine hab a baby soon, too. Iffn he bez a boy, I gwine call hem Hebrides."

Cecilia laughed, "Are you really? Monica, do you want a lesson?"

"I needs one," she answered, and took the baby. "It's time you started dat school. Remember you ain't gwine let de docta rule you no moh. He dun had his last chance, and he dun gone."

Cecilia agreed. "As soon as I gain my strength...I want to see Wash and Mollie. I want to tell them about the baby and read them a story."

"They be cumin."

"And best friend, if for some reason, Colin won't let me have a school...although Elijah could build one with leftover bricks, couldn't he?"

"Sho could...And would, honey. Lige has the best respects foh you. He don't admire the docta at all....he dun tole me some bad tales you don't wanna hear."

"What I wanted to say was that I want to teach every slave to read this spring."

"You can, and we noz it. God noz it, and He want you to do that. That's the talent he dun gib you."

The more excited Cecilia became, the weaker, so it seemed, the baby became. He turned yellow and couldn't nurse. Cecilia tried to nurse him, knowing she couldn't, and Monica tried after her baby boy, whom she did name Hebrides, was born, but nothing helped. The child died a few weeks later, and Cecilia became depressed, withdrawn. She blamed herself for the child's death. "If I hadn't gone walking on Christmas, I wouldn't have fallen. I might have been stronger. Our baby might have lived."

"Stop that, honey," Monica said, when Cecilia struggled to walk down to the cabin and see the baby. "Spring cumin soon, an you gwine feel betta. You gwine make yoself feel betta."

Cecilia believed her best friend, and before long the cold, dreary days passed, and she heard the bull frogs croaking in the creek, Cecilia knew spring was in the air. She went to The Quarters each day and took the children with her. She taught the slaves to read and count. She prayed with the older ones. She spent more time with Aunt Ella who claimed to be the oldest slave at White Oaks. "Yessum, Iz bout 101, but I ain't fo sho. Baut in Chalsun by way of Pote Royal, den sol to de Docta. He been gud to me. Cose I been gud to hem. U noz what I meenz. We had us a chile togeda, Lit'l King, but he dun been solt off long ago. Den I had a bad tim. A bull dun kick my foot...nobody did nuthin foh me....I meen Prince try...yo husbun finlee dun cut it off...I limps around, but Iz tired now...ready to go home to Gawd."

Cecilia took the woman in her arms as Monica sang, "Angel, Move Ova, Cauf Iz Cumin Home."

Spring passed into summer, and Cecilia worked every day down in The Quarters. Elijah even managed to build a little cabin which they came to be known as "The School." Cecilia made hornbooks for everyone. After lessons, she enjoyed walking with the children around the river and working in the garden, Nessie and Memnon, Mollie and Wash at her side. Monica visited with little Hebrides. They often laughed as they divided the name into syllables and sounds. 'He brides' or 'heb ree deez' or he bree deez."

"Siwee, Mommy," Wash said.

One afternoon in early July, while Colin was still away, Cecilia having long since given up asking, even troubling, over his whereabouts, Monica suggested a picnic down at Patuxee's Wharf. "I'll stay at home. You take the children, best friend," Cecilia answered, "for I promised to help Numbers."

She blew the children a kiss. Because Cecilia was a little late meeting Numbers at the schoolhouse, he became restless and walked up to the big house, knocked on the door, and came in before Daphne opened the door.

He brushed Daphne aside as Cecilia stepped forward and invited him into the library. Cecilia did not mind, for something about Numbers appealed to her, as it always had. Perhaps it was that shimmering cinnamon eye or curiosity over the bandage covering the other or in a peculiar way, his puffy breasts.

She reviewed letters on the hornbook with him, then read stories from the Bible, and asked him to identify words. If he didn't know a word, she would point to objects around the room. That afternoon, she pointed to the child in the portrait above the fireplace to teach the slave the word apple.

The fairy clock struck four, and the Gullah man screamed and jumped, as he had in Georgetown on her wedding day. Cecilia was frightened and pushed him away. Numbers panicked and ripped her bodice, clawed her breasts, pulled up her dress, and penetrated her, pushing, rocking, shoving back and forth, until he was satisfied.

She screamed, but nobody heard her. Numbers pulled off his patch and told Cecilia to feel his empty socket and look inside. "A hole...ain't nuthin dah but dahk...memba de clock...memba?"

She nodded under his massive weight as he talked on, bearing down again, telling her about the fire when he was a child, about his mammy trying to save his sight with evergreen tea. "Dat massa of de plandashun jes cuts it wid a nif....an my mammy cobud it wid a patch." He told Cecilia about being in a slave pen for months because nobody wanted a slave with one eye. He said that the cruel slave trader whom Dr. Bain finally hired had brought him to Georgetown. "I wah sold dah wunz, den again on yo weddin day. Oh, but yu sho is purty." And he came to her again.

Cecilia screamed, but Numbers was overwhelming. His rape reminded her of her own husband's days before their third anniversary. Hours later, Monica found her chilled and delirious. Monica bathed her best friend, put her to bed, and rubbed her with witch hazel. "Monica, why? What have I done?" Cecilia cried. "I try, and then something always happens. Does God hate me?"

"No...it ain't nuthin but de debil...Numbas is an ebil man...memba dat rebellion?"

Within a few weeks, Cecilia knew she was carrying Numbers' baby. She begged Monica to take the child. "I'll pay you. I have the gold to do it. Monica, I can't have a mixed child...I."

"But I ken hab a wite chile...what's the diffrenz, bes friend?"

And for the first time in all of their years of love and friendship, there was hurt, and Cecilia realized what she'd said. "Oh, I am sorry, Monica. I am....who am I? I know only too well. Please don't answer. A spoiled white girl who has never grown up. And yet..."

"Stop it...stop it, Cecilia."

Cecilia realized that was probably the first time her very best friend had ever called her by her Christian name.

"Monica," Cecilia said. "I don't know whether you realize it. We both have saints' names, and I don't know why."

"Cauf Gawd wanted it...I sho needs another grammar lesson."

"You're being kind and forgiving, and I don't deserve it, Monica. You know that. I hurt you and every enslaved person on the plantation when I made that remark, and I am sorry...Colin will blame me for being pregnant."

"Cecilia, that's nuthin new. He blame you for anything that don't go his way. He ain't worth fretting ova no moh."

"What will I do?"

"Have the chile, sam' as we do."

"But....but a black child born to a plantation mistress is a little different from a white child born in The Quarters, isn't it, Monica?"

"No...ain't no difference, and yu noz it. Jes yo pride. We ain't neba had a chance to hab pride..."

"Oh, I feel more shame now than I have ever felt, more guilt," Cecilia said. "But I'll bear it. I'll have to do that. You won't help me, and nobody else will. Why? Just to punish me?"

"Cecilia," Monica repeated, "if yo husband thought we tuk dat baby, why he'd whip Daphne and me, moh den he dun in de pas. Iz tired of hem. I node

Daphne iz. We dun hid it frum yu cauf we, like all dem servants, free or enslaved, luvs yu. Yuz been kind, gentle. Yuz taut em...but we ain't gwine trample wid Doc Colin...no moh. He beez an ebil man. Daz why I told you to try to love him because you married him. He played with your heart. He deceived you. But yu married hem foh de wrong reezuns, and yu noz it...oh, my English is bad frum libin in de Quarters. You giv me a lesson Friday cumin."

"I will," Cecilia answered, "and, again, I am sorry. I thought I was elected by God, but, of course, I'm not...I'm not at all. Oh, I am ashamed, Monica."

"If I dun offend, I'm sorry, too. At least, you was honest."

"You have never offended me, Monica. Never," Cecilia assured.

They forgave each other and made their way through the hot summer. As much as she tried, experimenting with various teas and brews, Cecilia could not lose Numbers' child. Despite deliberate falls, she still did not lose the baby.

When Colin finally returned in October, he kissed Cecilia, then ordered her to undress. "Oh, I have missed you, and I want to love you. The moon is full, and the air is warm, as it has been so many time in the past for us. See the candles flickering in the gentle wind through the window. Where's our summer baby, Cecilia?"

"He died, Colin. He lived for a month, and Monica nursed him."

"Well, then, pray tell me why your belly is swollen?" he demanded, as he undressed her.

"It's too painful for me to tell you, Colin," she answered, turning toward the wall.

"You'd better tell me the truth, Cecilia. You know that, don't you, or?"

"Is that a threat?"

"Absolutely...I'll whip you if you don't...I knew that I should not have been gone so long. I knew that you couldn't run the plantation without me."

"You never asked me to run White Oaks, and you know it. It's that cruel slave master who runs it. But I've not heard much of him lately. Maybe he leaves when you do. Maybe the plantation runs better with us just doing our parts. The crops grow, and we know what to do. We've kept you going. You've not kept us."

Colin slapped her hard, and she wept harder. "Now tell me who sired this child in your belly."

She told him all about Numbers' rape in July, hoping he would sympathize.

But he didn't. "That rape was your fault. You brought it on. You've done nothing but encourage that slave since our wedding day. You were fascinated with his one shimmering eye and the patch, and you know it. You began giving him reading lessons. That was your subtle way of hurting me, and it's backfired on you. Well, damn you, Cecilia! You're to blame."

"Colin, please, let me explain."

But he thrashed her again and vowed to whip Numbers and sell him to the highest bidder in Millsborough.

"Colin, please don't. Give us another chance. It was my fault. I was teaching him near the fairy clock, and…I should never have done that. If I'd been on time to the lesson down in The Quarters, nothing would have happened."

But the more his wife defended the slave, the angrier Colin became. "That's rubbish. It's all rubbish. The audacity of your believing that absurd story about a bonging clock and a fire, then a burn. Have his baby, Cecilia. Have his child, and we'll decide. Maybe I can impregnate you and fuck you once more before I die. It's your fault our summer child died."

"No, Colin…no. I admit his shimmering cinnamon eye fascinated me. Maybe on some level I identified with him because Mamma pitied him when she saw him on the ship years ago….long before you ever bought him. That Irish Dutchman mistreated him then. The slave has never received anything but cruelty, Colin."

"Well, he's a slave, Cecilia. What do you expect?"

"Slavery is wrong, and when this child is born, I intend to bring him or her or them up with the twins. I will buy this child's freedom with the pirate's gold, and there's nothing you can do to stop me, short of killing me."

"Oh, Cecilia," Colin cried, and fell down beside her. "I have missed you."

She said nothing, and he left a few minutes later to find Orange McTavish Steggerda.

Steggerda burned R A P I S T into Numbers' cheeks, hands, neck, and feet. Cecilia was sure she heard the slave screaming. Monica related that he'd been tied to a yoke, his wounds fresh from the branding, then whipped, manacled, and dragged about the plantation, and finally sold to the highest bidder in Millsborough. "The docta took the twins wid hem to the fair."

Cecilia wept. "Vengeance is mine, and I will repay, thus sayeth the Lord," she said to Colin after little Mollie had nightmares. "The sins of the third and fourth generation,…"

"You're a fine one to prophesy. It's your breast deformities which will show up in the third and fourth generations, love, not my whippings of a slave."

Cecilia was unrelenting. "This world will suffer from your whippings, and there will be other shames and humiliations to bear...you will never imagine them. You're incapable, Colin, and I am sorry."

"Why don't you ask Mollie about grinning for the plum pudding and chasing the greased pig or about the puppets. Ask her about the fortune teller."

"Mommy, I'm going to mawee a preecha."

"Oh, darling, I pray you'll always be happy," Cecilia answered, taking the little girl in her arms.

"Why not ask Wash about watching the boys drill on the grounds of Mount Hebron? Why not ask me about my meeting as a trustee there or about what the fortune teller told me?"

"Pray, Colin, exactly what did she tell you?"

"That I will see General George Washington in Georgetown next April; that our son may not wish to become a doctor."

"Colin, I have known that. Our little boy enjoys other activities. What Wash does with his life is his choice, not yours, not mine."

"Cecilia, would you like to accompany me and curtsey before General Washington? Why we could explain that you advocate freedom for slaves."

"Stop it, Colin. I do believe slaves should be freed. If I outlive you, I will free them. Meantime, I will teach them to read."

"No...no, you won't. I've already told Steggerda to beat any slave who comes to you for a lesson. Now, you can read stories, but no teaching. Steggerda will ride about, and he will report to me if you disobey me. No...your dreams of being a teacher are over, and I've already had the little house Elijah built torn down. If people know too much, they rebel, and, then, you have anarchy on your hands. I won't have that. Do you understand?"

Cecilia nodded, and Colin left. Later she talked to Monica. "I hate him. I hate the overseer. I hate slavery."

"I'm afraid of that man. He hates Gullahs. Eben though Iz free, I don't know. Freedom foh darkies really ain't no freedom at all."

Cecilia nodded. She agreed, then asked if Monica thought the twins had hearts.

"Sho do."

But Cecilia was restless. She could not be consoled and began to analyze again, as she used to, before beginning the reading lessons. "I'm to blame for so much of this, Monica, and you know it. You've told me. I dressed like a man and rode in the wind. I saw Colin as my father. Because he was a stone mason, I thought he was like my own father, a stone cutter deeply interested in the church and saints and angels. I listened to Colin's stories, spellbound, like a child. I was fascinated with all the roles he played. I thought I loved him....but it was just infatuation. I didn't even have a heart then. He didn't tamper with my heart. I didn't even have one, Monica."

"Stop it right now, Cecilia. You may not have had a heart. You may not have made the right choice when you married him, but yu sho dun tried, and we noz it. Docta Bain's jes a mean man....I don know what ails him. Nobody do...but whatever it is, he take it out on you and yo poor body."

"Maybe if I'd let Dr. Pringle do surgery long ago. Maybe if I'd gone to a carnival, why I could be a freak now, a pregnant freak. Maybe....maybe, Monica."

"You hush up your mouth right now....we can all say what if. But de pas is gwine. Yu can neba brings it back, and don't your forget dat. You gotta pick up and go from here, from there. And look how much you done love Wash and Mollie and me and all of us...."

"Did Colin marry me for my gold?"

Monica shrugged her shoulders. "I dunno. He de only one can answer dat question."

"Bury it for me, Monica. Bury my gold up on the hill under the white oak, and if I need it, I'll tell you, best friend. Will you?"

"Sho will."

"And when this baby grows up, I will send her north. She will never have a life here at White Oaks."

"No moh den dem white babies has down in The Quarters."

Cecilia wept from shame. She knew the dark Negroes sometimes looked with scorn upon the lighter ones. "Monica, all I can say is thank you for being my Holy Comforter here on earth. I know that when you talk, God is speaking to me. Even if it hurts, what you say is the truth. It is said for my good, for my learning, and understanding. Thank you."

"Sista...best friend, take up that psaltery again, and memba you can read. Sometimes reading really is a lesson. Long as you got that Bible open, Steggerda can't do nuthin to you. Do you understand?"

Cecilia hugged her.

Later, Cecilia was awakened by the twins' laughter and Colin marching up the tower steps. "Why are you lingering at White Oaks, Husband? Isn't it time for you to ride away?"

"I thought I would stay at the plantation. You've always begged me to spend more time with you." He tickled her breasts. "Ah, they're actually swelling this time. Maybe you can milk the little black child, Cecilia. Actually, I'm supervising slaves who are making barrels from the white oaks for rum. I discovered some slaves down in the woods making rum and using my white oak for barrels, for their own profit. Someone was helping them. So I broke up their trade and turned it to my advantage. Steggerda lashed the culprits."

"Nothing you ever do surprises me anymore, Colin. Why should it?"

"And now, my dear wife, this will soon be the whatever month, as the story goes, 'with the one who was called barren' Am I not waxing Biblical? Shall we call you Elizabeth? My mother's name was Tibbie. That's Scottish for Elizabeth. I used to believe all of those Biblical myths. But I don't anymore. We won't call you barren, only milkless."

"No more of your cynicism, Colin….no more. I will bear this child and move along with my life. Even though I have never understood what my purpose is, I may have one yet, even though it may be in death. I really long to die. If it were not for Mollie and Wash, I would probably drown myself in the river."

"And Monica could swim in and be your rescuing mermaid, my dear. Cecilia, I came to tell you that I will be spending Christmas in Charleston. I'll bring you a surprise."

"No. Please do not trouble yourself, Colin."

"My soul hath long dwelt with him that hateth peace (Psalm 120:6).

Book Eight (Late 1790-1807)

Without Colin's boots and hooves galloping from the bedroom to the bottoms and back to taunt everyone whom he met, Christmas was peaceful. Cecilia decorated and sang to the children, passed out clothing, and played the psaltery. She asked Elijah to set off fireworks in her husband's absence. "And, please, Elijah, allow my little twin girl to enjoy them with her brother."

"Sho weel, Misses Ceceelya, and yo babee gwine be bohnd soon."

The air was warm in January and February. When she heard the bull frogs croaking, she knew spring was coming and decided to walk about the plantation gathering herbs and greens, grateful for the sun bright sun piercing through the white oaks. Picking wild berries and nuts with no thought of where she was going, Cecilia suddenly realized she was surrounded by chinaberry trees. "The entire plantation is yours, my dear, except for Chinaberry Grove. Never, ever go there, lest a greater evil befall you."

"Where are you, Colin? I hear your warning." Realizing she was simply remembering his words from long ago, Cecilia shrugged her shoulders, and murmured, "What can be ill about a grove of chinaberries? Why some enslaved women have made the prettiest jewelry from the berries for years! That was just Colin trying to control me!"

Daring herself to go closer, she heard chains rattling and someone speaking. "Dat vous? I dun been waitin foh you, Mademoiselle Ceceelya. Venez-ici par les arbres. Comprenez-vous ce que je dis?"

"Un peu," Cecilia stammered. "Who are you?"

"Oh, you noz me. Sho duz. Lemme get a good peek at yu all to myself, sans le docteur, de lady what been baptiz by a pirate/priest, what hab dem strange brestes. I noz all bout em."

Cecilia chewed her finger nails and paced back and forth behind the chinaberries, listening, as she watched the woman sway one way, then dance another, as she rattled chains or paused to beat the drum which stood on the crumbling porch, her cinnamon eyes shimmering. Her eyes were bright like Numbers' good eye.

"I noz all bout yo ways….vous n'avez rien to hide from me. "Yu carryin Numba's baby, ain't you?"

Cecilia nodded, daring herself to push back a branch and walk into the grove. "Where have I seen you? I know….oui, oui. Je sais. Each Christmas, except for this one, you've come to the house."

"Das cauf yo husbun dun sold off de boy chile we dun had. About same time yo twins wah bohned, I gab birth to enfant aussi….my boy is half-brother to yo Wash and Mollie. You kept yo chaps, but Docta Colin, he dun solde mine off when he wah a little chap. Il s'était appelé Uriel…j'ai aimé cet enfant. You met him last Christmas. Yo husbun didn't like the little boy's lef hand. It wah small, so he solde hem. I didn't cum dis yeah cauf I dun been greevin."

Cecilia walked closer. "I'm sorry. I really am. Are you Numbers' sister? What is your name?"

"I ne suis pas sa soeur. Now Numbas and me, we dun had a boy together. We name him Caleb. He work wid Masta Prince in d'étables now. He ain't no baby Jesus, neither. I be called Caramel cauf my skin iz ginga. It be spice. Eba smelt spice on Docta Colin? Dats me…he gwine to bed wid many a lady, mais j'ai quelque chose nobody else ken gib hem…an he need it…well, what you gwine say foh yoselfin aujourd'hui?"

"Please tell me your story, Caramel. I remember seeing you, even shaking your hand, my husband criticizing me for holding yours. But I welcome strangers. Colin always belittles me."

"Cauf vous is toujours a chile. Il desire une femme complexe. I am complex, but culud. Iz frum Nassau. Mon père was French, and my mammy was a slave. Pa raped her, then sold us both later on. Your husband wants, needs, white chillins. De culud won't do. I noz it, but I ain't got no choice. He gon fuk me anyway, and my chillins gon be culud. Ain't nothin I ken do bout dat, but you, you gots a choice. You aint got to lay wit hem. He ain't chainin you."

"Did Colin buy you, Caramel?"

"Bien entendu. I tell you the details iffn you can stand em."

Cecilia sat on the rickety steps of the porch and listened as Caramel walked about, cackled, and stopped to do her chores—from plucking a chicken to picking collard greens or tossing crumbs to the crows and bones to a mangy hound.

"Long time ago when your husband was in Nassau, he saw Mammy and me for sale. I was young, but developed. Mammy always said I had the purtiest brestes. Somebody dun baught Mammy. Den de docta come ova to me. I wasn't wearing rien but a cloth round my lower parts and a straw hat pull down oba my eyes. Well, suh, he dun feel my chocolit nipples and my vagina. He tickles em and laugh. He paid gold foh me. Frum dat journee on, we made luv.

We soon had a boy. He était notre premier fils. He de wun what wuk at d'étables wid Masta Prince until he wah sold. Mon garcon s'appellait Chronicle. All my boys, they ken to yo chillins, whetha Docta Colin or Numbas be de pa. Ain't nothing gon change dat. Our chaps bonds you and me togeda."

"I suppose you are right."

"Iz tired, Mademoiselle. I dun been chained all dem yeahs. You ain't. You can't imagine being chained and slapt. You can't imagine being hungry or a baby taken from you. Well, you got time de parler with me?"

Cecilia nodded. "I do, and I'll be grateful."

"So we cum up to de White Oaks to dis heah cabin weah I libs....It wah his first home...I helped him wid his medicines cauf I node a heep, sam as Monica and Daphne duz now...we loved and time went by. But Docta Colin...why he wanted a white baby. And he tuk me to Gahttown and kep me ova in dem maisons on Church Street while he went about town. Whateva muney I made went to the Madame Princess of the brothel, and the res went to yo mari. Can't memba the yeah. He may hab seed yu den....I ain't too sho.

He node une jeune fille, Mademoiselle Mary Sophia Ravenel. She wah frum wun of dem plandashuns. He mislead her, used her, then refused to marry her. She beg and beg him to kill her, and he did. He dun gib her jimson weed. Den we went back to White Oaks, and he brung Mademoiselle Anna Catherine home...ceptin fo yo yeux verts, yu looks a heap lik her. Das a long story. She was a sad young gal, but I wah jealous cauffin he dun beelt de big house wid de tour foh her. De nite dey wah married, I cum ova cauffin J'ai desire poison her. I made a special brew. I heard hem getting on huh, and she wep and wep....he was mad and cum to de doh...he smelled my potion and snitched it, den hit me so hahd in la tete wid dat old thing he carry around——dat spontoon—he struck off my right ear...and clawed my breast..." Caramel removed her turban and lowered her torn dress, "sometime he mak me go bout jes lik dis, and he laugh, but den, I gets hem every time...I got sumpin nobody else got sexuallee. Comprenez-vou?"

Cecilia nodded. "Your scars, do they hurt?"

"Not anymore. Dey bled for long, long time…see mes souliers? They bez les souliers rouges that you lost. He dun gib me lots of yo old dresses and chapeaux. I sumtime dress up and walk around. He mak fun of you. But il vous aimé. Il vous adore. And you wanna know moh. Dat husbun….he ain't got no plandashun in Gahgtown. Dat all une histoire to impress foks….All he owns is White Oaks…he wah a pirate long time ago…he beez un cousin to dat homme what baptize you…"

"What? Your tales are hard to believe. I don't understand."

"I ain't sho pourquoi le docteur left Curly Motte Macaulay O'Toole, but he node all bout yo golde….so duz I. Where yu dun hid it, chile? Dat gold?"

Cecilia wouldn't answer…only asked the ginger woman how she was able to come each Christmas morning without the chains.

"Quelquefois I dun trik hem…den I broke loose wuntz and wandered oba to Mulberry Bluffs…Strange place wid dat French preacher. We didn't get along nun too well. Dat wah wun time wen Docta Colin left me here an went to Gahgtown."

"I can't even imagine how you've fared all these years, Caramel. I am sorry for you, but I don't want to have this baby. I can't. Won't you give me something to take the child early? I don't want it. Don't you understand?"

The woman cackled again, then held up three dolls. "Je sticks mes epinelles into chaque poupée. Dat beez my ritual. I sho feel sorry for vous, Mademoiselle Cecilia. Dat fust doll's de gal what died in Ghagtown. De second's Miss Cat, and you beez la troisième. But vous avez besoin d'avoir un enfant what be mix. Den you ken feel all de pains we had all along all these years, Monica, Daphne, and me. Wez all dun suffered par les annees by being raped by white men, specily yo docta. He dun tried us all, but Iz his favorite cauf I got sumpin nobody got."

"Stop it, you evil woman."

"Now when vous die, well…den de docta gwine mawee me…lessn he go bak to dat Lindsay femme. Mais I don't think he really love her. She got dat lip he dun surgery on. He always lik dem deformities. He played wid huh few years ago. Nobody much lik hem around heah netha."

Cecilia laughed, mocking Caramel. "Please don't tell me something I don't already know. Please. Maybe you've told my husband how cruelly to treat me. I don't know. Just give me something to cause the baby not to live."

"Je comprends, Mademoiselle. Dites-moi ce que vous desirez."

"I don't know what you use, but I know you must have ended unwanted babies many times. Please give me something so the baby dies, and if Monica and Daphne need to know, tell them. Just don't tell Colin."

"Non, je ne vous donne rien, and I noz all bout yo ridin in de wind on dem hohses….bet yu bear down hard on de saddle, don't yu and feel good, something….sexuelle, missy?"

Shocked at the woman's brazen words and losing patience, Cecilia finally screamed "At least, then tell me what to do for a quick delivery, lady."

"Go ride and wiggle wid pleashah on yo hohse. Ride unda a full moon, an yu hab dat babee right quick now, mind yu."

Cecilia thanked the woman, hopeful her suggestion might work.

"But dat jeune fille of yours, la petite Mollie, elle gwine hab trouble in de years to cum. Hep her."

Cecilia slowly stood up, confused as the woman babbled on. It was dark, and the wind was picking up, the moon a big yellow face welcoming her above the white oaks. She'd stayed in Chinaberry Grove far too long.

Cecilia made her way to the stable, saddled Dark Moon, and rode hard through the woods for hours. Just as Caramel had predicted, Cecilia began to cramp. By the time she reached the house, she was going into labor and called for Daphne and Monica.

They gave her ginger tea, and shortly before midnight, Daphne delivered a baby girl. Black kinks frosted her head. "You gwine try to nurse her, honey lamb?" Monica asked, giving the child to her mother.

Cecilia gazed at the baby and forced herself to realize she'd given birth to a mixed child, just as Monica, Daphne, and so many others had all these years. "I'm going to call the baby Abbie for John Adams' wife, Abigail, and I will grant her freedom. Why did you never tell me about Caramel?"

"Yu dun meet huh, Misses Ceceelya?" Daphne asked. "I thought so. You has dat spicy smell."

Cecilia nodded. "I did, and she told me everything. Why didn't you all?"

"Fear, honey lamb. Das bez all."

"I understand….I really do. I want to try to nurse my baby this time. Maybe without Colin mocking me, I can." To her surprise, the milk let down, and a little flowed as the baby sucked. "This is so comforting, Monica, Daphne. I can do it…I'm exhilarated. After all these years. I feel such contentment. I feel like a mother. Thank you."

"We knowed you cud, honey," Monica answered and seeing the twins hesitating at the door, called for them to come in. "Yo mammy dun had a fine baby sister. Come on in, and see her."

"Ma, can we hold her? Oh, she's pretty. Did we look like that when we were babies?" Mollie asked.

Cecilia smiled as she patted the twins' hair and invited them to climb into bed.

"Can I suck you?" Wash asked.

"Of course, honey." Cecilia drew her son toward her, as the baby fell asleep. "Me, too, Ma," Mollie added.

"You, too, sweetheart."

Monica and Daphne smiled and tiptoed from the room, grateful, at last, to see their beloved Cecilia happy and unafraid, unashamed.

All through the spring, Cecilia laughed, nursed, and played with her three children. Bowing the psaltery, she often sang to them. Sometimes they walked by the river, had picnics on the lawn, where Wash and Mollie made little chains from the yellow jasmine bejeweling the woods, or sat under the ancient white oak which seemed to beckon them on the hill above the kitchen.

"…weeping may endure for a night, but joy cometh in the morning" (Psalm 30:5)

Book Nine (Spring 1791-Fall 1807)

April passed into May, and Cecilia and the twins, little Abbie in her arms, celebrated with a Maypole party on the back lawn. Happier than she had ever felt, Cecilia invited Monica and Nessie and Memnon, Daphne, and a few others to come. They had a tea party and played games, then danced about the Maypole, a fence post which Monica had decorated.

When Abbie whimpered, Cecilia walked up to the old white oak and began nursing the baby. All at once, she heard a horse galloping up the lane. Her muscles tensed when she heard Daphne cry, "Dat beez Docta Colin."

Colin tethered his horse and came toward her. "What? A butterscotch-colored gal at your breast, is it? Now how ironical it is that our twins could not nurse, but yet you have Numbers' baby sucking away. How dare you, Cecilia?"

Monica defended her best friend, "She relaxed, Docta Bain. Dat's all. You ain't got nothing to fret about."

Colin slapped Monica so hard across the face she fell. Nessie and Memnon cried, and Elijah came forward, carrying a brick, not realizing at first that it was his master. "Doc, don't do dat."

Colin pulled out his pistol and fired it. "Leave…go back down to The Quarters. That means you, too, Daphne, and don't come back."

"Colin," Cecilia pleaded.

"Daddy," Wash and Mollie called. "Don't hurt Mammy and the baby. We…."

Colin pushed Mollie away. She began to cry and nestled her head against her mother under the tree. "It's alright, honey. Don't be afraid."

Wash joined his sister.

"Oh, Thomas Gainsborough could paint the perfect portrait and entitle it 'Mrs. Bain and Her Children under the Mulberry.' How idyllic! Only you're not worth his paint and brush, Cecilia, even his palette. How dare you! You mock me!"

"Colin, when the baby was born, she just put her little mouth to my nipple, and the milk flowed. I can't tell you the joy I felt, and our children have sucked, too. I've more than made up for my weakness in the past, for my inability to nurse them. They've been so thrilled. We've all enjoyed simply playing and being together. That's a mother's most natural feeling. Do not humiliate me. Do not shame me. Please do not be unkind. Why can't you be happy for me?"

Colin turned and marched up and down in front of her. "Aren't you curious to know where I've been?"

"No more....Colin, it doesn't matter. I stumbled upon Chinaberry Grove one day and met the ginger woman with chocolate nipples. She told me everything. Now I know who the young lady wearing the pink sash in the portrait is, the one that's slashed in the garret. I know all about Caramel, the lady in Georgetown, the Lindsay girl, and more. I know you are kin to Curly Motte Macaulay O'Toole. At least he told my mother the truth, as I told you that night at Brookgreen when I rescued you. I begged you to tell me all about yourself, but you wouldn't. You only regaled with fascinating tales. You don't own a plantation near Georgetown, and you may not even be a Mason or a member of the St. Andrew's Society. You may not even belong to the South Carolina Medical Society. I don't know. I don't care anymore. Oh, Colin, your penis has visited too many mansions. At least when I played Lochland, I told you the truth."

"I never knew you felt passion for Monica."

"Stop before you say too much. Monica has been my sister, my best friend, all these years, so don't go make up stories that have no resemblance to God's truth. Don't. You have hurt me enough."

Colin stared at her, began pacing again, then turned. "Cecilia, maybe we could start over again, just you and me, just the two of us. We could go to Edinburgh. Maybe we could take Mollie and Wash. They're nearly three. One of the wenches could go and nurse the baby. Your milk will be drying up."

"It already is, I know. I feel it. I'm afraid again, as I used to be. You torment me, humiliate me, and I don't seem to be able to control over my feelings. I...I despise myself for allowing you to make me fear. Mamma always said not to fear, and God knows I have tried, but... oh, I wish you'd never come back home to White Oaks, Colin."

"Me, too, Daddy," Mollie chimed in.

Colin slapped his little daughter.

"Don't you ever do that again," Cecilia said, standing up, the baby whimpering. "Wash, call Monica, please. Tell her to come take your little sister. Tell her Mammy's milk's not sweet right now. She'll understand, sweetheart."

Aware of his father's fury, Wash took little Abbie from their mother and carried her toward Monica's cabin, Mollie following.

"Cecilia, I met General George Washington in Georgetown when he was making his tour in our Southland. I didn't explain to him that you were birthing a mixed child....no, I didn't."

"I imagine he would have understood. God knows you've sired enough and left them to rot in The Quarters. I plan to take care of little Abbie and give her freedom, but...I'm weary now, and I'll go to bed. Besides, I've come to know now that you leave in the early winter and return in the spring. There's sort of a pattern I've finally figured out. It took me a long time, but…. There's no point in asking, for you never answer. It doesn't matter. No more, Colin."

She struggled past him and went up the stairs of the tower, flung herself on the bed, and wept.

When Monica was sure Colin had left, she came to Cecilia.

"Oh, Monica, I could feel the milk stop flowing and my breasts stiffen. Oh, they hurt. I don't know which is worse, labor and childbirth or this…Can't you give me something?"

"I dun already. "I've made a lotion from the leaves of the partridge-berry, and I'm gwine rub your brestes wid it."

Cecilia was sweating. "Monica, cut my curls. I don't want to worry over my hair anymore. I want to feel completely shorn….I don't like myself for being afraid, but no more….I will not ever let Colin Bain rip apart my body, and I'm struggling so he doesn't tear my soul. Please, best friend. You understand, I know."

"You sho?"

Cecilia nodded, and Monica snipped her curls.

"Oh, I want to die…promise you'll take care of the children. Please…please poison me."

But Monica shook her head. "You'll feel that joy in the morning again."

"I don't know…I've sunk pretty low. I pray God 'to bring my soul out of prison, that I may praise His name again.'"

"He will, honey…and Daphne's going to give you something to ease your fears. The last two hours have just been a shock to your system. You done gone from happiness to despair all because he cum home and humiliate you. Oh, I needs another grammar lesson. I listen to Lige and Daphne too much," Monica laughed.

"They are so kind. Don't ever be ashamed of your speech. It's pure. It's from the heart. Oh, Monica, how I have botched my life."

"Honey, you gwine get back to living, to the chillins, and to dat psaltery. You iz, and you'll begin teaching again, too, if you want. Do you?"

"Yes," she wept, her breasts bare, aching.

Colin surprised them both. "Now, really, what am I to think? One woman rubbing another's breasts. Cecilia, your hair. What have you done?"

"Cut my locks....I don't care anymore, Colin. I long to die."

Monica looked at him, her dark eyes warning, threatening, as she dared herself to say, "Enough's nuff, Docta Bain. Yo wife is sick. She ain't gwine get no betta unless you hep her. You may hate me, but don't blame her. We just been lik sistas all our live cauf her mammy bought me when we was both little. We growed up together."

Colin came to the bed. "Cecilia, I need you. Please take me back. I can't live without you."

"Colin...you have taken away any passion I ever felt. I have loved you deeply. I still do, but I cannot give anymore. I am weary. If I had jimson weed or foxglove, I'd take it and die now."

Colin finally made himself realize that his young wife, after pregnancies, rapes, and losses, was worse. He apologized. "I'm sorry, Cecilia....I've really tampered with your heart."

"I didn't have one," she wept..." I married you, not only because I loved you, but perhaps more than anything, because your stories fascinated me. I've sinned, too, but a lesbian I have never been."

"Not even a hosenrollen when you traveled with Francis Marion?" he said.

"Maybe," she smiled faintly, "but not for the reasons you believe. Colin, if you won't give me jimson weed, as you did the Ravenel lady in Georgetown, at least give me some comfrey tea. Nobody will know. I won't even tell Monica."

"Oh, Cecilia," he said, trying to gently massage her breasts. "I am sorry."

"Stop," she screamed. "That hurts too much. Don't. Give me something to sleep."

"I will...I'll give you a little Mary Jane. It will calm you and help you feel better. Oh, my love, I need you, even if you do look like a boy."

A few days later, Elijah and Daphne died, nobody ever knowing the exact cause. Monica wondered if Colin had poisoned them, but, of course, she had no proof. She didn't tell anyone what she suspected. "After all," she said to Prince, "it would be the doctor's word against mine, and, Prince, if you'd like, I'm going to buy your freedom. I got the money."

And she gave it to the faithful old slave.

A spirit of mourning darkened White Oaks, relieved only by the laughter of Wash, Mollie, and the baby, and Memnon and Nessie. They all hovered together.

Colin stayed at his wife's side. When he realized she was worse, he decided that the family should leave for the new pools at Hot Springs in the mountains.

"We'll take Delilah from The Quarters. Monica says she's a good woman who can tend the children and nurse Abbie, and I'll hire a mountain woman to take care of you. I promise not to ever torment you again, my dear."

"You can't," she feebly answered. "Go tell Caramel good-bye if you'd like."

"Oh, Cecilia, you don't believe me, do you?" he answered, lying down beside her.

She shook her head. "But I'll make the trip for the family."

They went by coach a few weeks later to Traveler's Rest where Colin hired someone with a wagon and team of horses to pull them up the mountains. Wash and Mollie babbled incessantly, excited over going to the mountains, and Cecilia enjoyed the fresh air, the flowers, and, finally, the mountains.

She found the daily baths so soothing and comforting that Colin decided to build a cabin and stay indefinitely, at least until his wife felt stronger. The children loved the mountain streams. Delilah nursed little Abbie who was a beautiful little girl with curly black hair, big brown eyes, and smooth caramel skin. She loved the twins, just as they loved her. Colin hired a young woman named Jeanie to take care of his wife. She played with the children and taught Cecilia to play mountain ballads on the psaltery.

Knowing Cecilia was grieving and in pain, Jeanie offered her brandy mixed with star grass. "This is our remedy for sore breasts, Missy."

Cecilia thanked her and frequently drank the beverage. She read, bathed in the hot tubs, occasionally painted, wrote letters to Monica, and kept a diary. She said little to Colin. There was nothing to say although she suspected him of sleeping with Jeanie, but kept her suspicions to herself. But that no longer mattered. Cecilia simply smiled forlornly at whatever happened, grateful for the children's happiness.

"They're growing before my eyes, best friend," she wrote to Monica one night, and the doctor is down at the tavern, "Jeanie keeps my hair short, and she has taught me some ballads and taught me more about the psaltery. She tells the children Jack stories. I miss you and long, now, to come home. I think Colin is ashamed. I still love him. I always will. In a way, I pity him in a strange way, but I can do no more. I know he is finding a woman's warmth from Jeanie. I am tired. My breasts ache, and I have a fever, and oh, Monica, I miss you and White Oaks."

Cecilia fell asleep, the quill pen in her hand. When he came in later, Colin read her letter and knew it was time to go home.

"Would you like to go back to White Oaks?"

His wife nodded. "I don't know what year it is, but the children are growing up. I fear Mollie's rash from childhood has returned...or maybe it's pimples or something else. I don't know, but please do something for her, Colin. She's in her teens now. I was in my teens when Dr. Pringle told me I should be in a fair because of my abnormal breasts. Colin, don't torment our daughter. She's a gentle girl. She's afraid and impressionable. Don't hurt her, as you have me, please."

He didn't answer, for he'd already humiliated Mollie. He knew that deep down only too well, and he was ashamed.

They closed the cabin and said good-bye to Jeanie, Colin promising to come back.

Everyone boarded the wagon for the jostling ride down the mountains. Cecilia lay in the back on quilts, the children around her.

They made several overnight stops because she tired easily. At one rustic inn, when his wife went to bed unusually early, Colin played cards and drank ale with the men. Before dawn, Cecilia left the inn and wandered along the banks of the stream. Colin found her staring into the red sun, holding mountain laurel.

"One of the women at the inn told me this was toxic, so I ate some," Cecilia said, weakly holding up the branch, offering it to her husband, "I want to die."

Afraid of losing her, Colin mustered forth all of the herbal lore Daphne and Prince and Monica had ever taught him and handed Cecilia some daffodils he saw growing along the creek.

"Eat these," he said, as he crushed them into a fine powder. "You'll vomit. Oh, I can't let you die, my love. I need you far more than you realize. I've tormented you, and I am sorry."

She heaved and heaved, as Colin held her, until she fell down, exhausted. "Please let me die. Leave me here to roll down into the creek."

He lifted her up and put her in the wagon and gave her the psaltery to hold. The children climbed in again for another bumpy ride to Traveler's Rest, where they boarded the old coach and headed home. At last they reached White Oaks. When Cecilia opened her eyes and saw the trees, she longed to jump out with the children and run up the lane. But she couldn't. She simply did not have the strength.

"Colin, I am sorry," she said, as he carried her into the house. "I don't think I will ever be well again. Thank you for taking me to the mountains, to the baths. I liked our time there, but I'm glad to be home."

He sat down on the wide veranda and looked into her eyes, tears in his own, "I understand. Please forgive me, my darling little Lochland. It is my fault. You are not to blame, no, not at all."

His wife said nothing. Cecilia later gave Monica the diaries and listened to her best friend's stories of the plantation. Even though Wash and Mollie, Memnon and Nessie had been separated, they played together as if they'd been apart for only a day, Abbie joining in. Abbie enchanted her mother. The color of the child's eyes engaged everyone, as their shade changed from copper to green to blue, depending on the dress she was wearing.

"When you become all grown up....and I don't remember how old you are now, honey," Cecilia said, "I want you to go north to school...and have a position. You'll be happier there, and one day, you will understand."

"But, Mamma, I would miss you."

Cecilia stroked her hair, as she did the twins' curls, listening to their dreams.

"Mamma, I want to be pretty like you," Mollie said, scratching her face, the pimples bleeding.

"You are already, honey...Mammy's tired, but you will take her place...try not to scratch, and Wash. What would you like to do?"

"Just run the plantation. I don't want to be a doctor."

"You don't have to be a doctor. Just be what you want to do, my son, but be kind to your sister. Promise me you'll always be gentle with your twin. She needs you."

"I do, Wash. I don't think Pa likes me...he seems to laugh at me. Mamma, once when you weren't looking, he made me strip and walk in the sun. He said the heat would help my acne. It was humiliating, especially when he tied me to a tree, as a man tethers his horse. Why is Abbie's face so clear?"

"Oh, darling, I am so sorry." Cecilia embraced her daughter. "I'll speak to your father again. You go play graces with Nessie on the front lawn, and wash your face. Sweetheart, try not to scratch. Monica will give you something."

Monica made a paste of oats and comfrey and rubbed on Mollie's face. "It'll get better. It will. Now, you try not to rub it, and I'm gwine to be wid your mammy."

"Monica, I can't walk anymore," Cecilia said. "At least I don't think I can. My legs hurt now, and…"

Monica rubbed her with arnica, and the two talked, remembering the past, then dreamed of better times ahead. Monica confessed she'd slept with Prince because they were lonely and became pregant. The baby boy had been born dead.

"Oh, best friend, I am sorry I wasn't there for you." Cecilia said, holding Monica's hands in her own. Thank you for always being here for me, listening, explaining. Please watch out for Mollie. I'm afraid her father sometimes humiliates her, and that grieves me, but…but I won't be here to watch."

"He has. I seen him…he forces her to strip, then ties her to the tree, and makes her walk up and down in the sun, telling her walking will make her thin and the sun will clear her skin. Sometimes while she's walking, he whips her. She cries. Ain't nuthin I can do, except bathe her when he through and comfort her. He the same mean man all over again. Thank God he ain't raped Miss Mollie."

"He wouldn't, Monica. At least, I don't think so. Oh, I really want to try to walk again, at least one more time. Do you have a cane?"

Monica brought one Prince had carved from a white oak. But Cecilia couldn't use it, so Prince designed a wheelchair. Sometimes when the days were mild, Wash, Mollie, and Abbie would roll their mother to the garden where she painted or simply enjoyed listening to the birds and sniffing the flowers, her hair graying now, her body wasting away.

Colin insisted on enrolling their son at Mount Hebron and sent Mollie to learn French, geometry, music and spelling at Mrs. Miller's Seminary a few miles from Essex. But Mollie was miserable. "Ma, why do the girls call me plump and ugly?"

"Because you eat too many biscuits," her father answered, listening to the conversation. "You must discipline yourself."

"As if you do," Monica dared to blurt out. "How many brandies do you drink each night?"

Colin ignored Monica's remark, told her to leave, then handed his daughter a handful of mulberries. "Eat these. They're laxative, and you'll shed some fat."

"Daddy, they're sour," Mollie answered.

"Eat them anyway."

Cecilia tapped the white oak cane on the ground and played her psaltery. "Enough. The utter audacity of such a proposal. Why that's reprehensible, and you know it, Dr. Colin Macaulay Bain. I don't care if you were a pirate. You've shamed me, but to humiliate your own daughter. That's more than I can or will bear. Stop right now. Do you hear me?"

"Ma, this is not new," Wash said. "Pa has already required Mollie to strip, walk naked in the sun, and eat mulberries. I've seen her obeying his orders. Mollie's afraid of pa. What Monica said is the truth."

"Come here, Mollie," Cecilia coaxed. "Tell Monica to try a little witch hazel or lavender oil...your skin will clear, and you don't have to go back to Mrs. Miller's school anymore. I'll try to teach you here. Maybe teaching you and Abbie here will help me, too. I yearn to teach the slaves to read...I...and I want you to play the psaltery. I've neglected to share the pirate's psaltery with you, and I'm sorry, sweetheart. You can learn."

"Ma," Mollie wailed, "nobody will ever marry me. I'm not pretty like you and Nessie and Abbie. My face is ugly, and I'm plump. I know it. You're just being kind to me."

"Sh," Cecilia answered. 'Pretty is as pretty does' is an old expression. Wash will look out for you. I've asked him to, and he will. You both must be true to yourselves, to what you want to do...don't let anyone get in your way, honey. I can't anymore."

"Ma, there's a twinkle in your green eyes," Wash said, as he watched her talking to his twin. "What is it. Do you feel better?"

"Wash, I want to ride one of the horses...I don't know about Dark Moon anymore. He's old. What about that horse your father gave me? Natas?"

"No, Mamma. That's Satan backwards," Abbie warned..."Don't."

"Before I ride," she answered, her eyes staring far away, "I want one of the dresses the ladies are wearing in Paris. I'm so old-fashioned in my petticoats and breeches. Mollie tells me the girls at the seminary look different. I'm afraid I dressed her in antiquated frocks, and I'm sorry. Wash, go to Charleston, and bring Mollie and Abbie and me some new clothes. Will you?"

Wash was delighted. "Charleston? By myself? Ma, Father never has given me permission to grow up? It's 1807, and Mollie and I are almost 19 years old. I'd like to ride to Charleston. I'll take Memnon with me, and Monica's baby boy. She named him Hebrides. I want to show him off. Mamma, did you really tell her to call him that?"

Cecilia laughed wearily. "Monica will tell you that story one day."

"Wash will finish Mount Hebron while I'm a trustee there, Cecilia. He'll have to for my sake, don't you think? Don't you understand?"

"No." She shook her head. "Let them do as they wish, so long as they are happy. I am leaving my children the pirate's gold. All I ask is that you be kind to them and stop tormenting Mollie. Nobody deserves that."

Colin agreed, thankful for his wife's command, grateful in a way which he himself did not understand. "You'll be beautiful, my love, in a new gown with puffy sleeves, the kind made of that gauze-like material. It's the latest fashion from Paris, so I hear. Even with your shorn hair, you'll enrapture me."

She said nothing, only smiled faintly at him.

Wash brought her a beautiful white gown with an empire waist and tiny puffed sleeves, along with one of the bands fashionable ladies were sometimes wearing in their hair. She donned the dress and asked her son to push her to the stable. "I want to give Natas an apple."

"Nothing more, Ma?" Mollie asked, listening. "Natas is spooky."

Cecilia smiled. Wash pushed his mother to the stable where she gave the horse the apple, then begged her son to put her on Natas' back. "Please, Wash, once more, and remember me in this white gown on the black horse."

"I will. Oh, Mamma, you so are beautiful. I hope one day to marry someone exactly like you, someone who sings and…well, you know, Mamma."

Cecilia patted his blonde hair and looked into his blue eyes. Before she could lean down and kiss her son, Natas took off, as she knew he would, and jumped one fence after the other, riding his mistress in the cold October wind, the moon rising. Cecilia heard the sound of bells coming from somewhere far off, and Natas spooked, throwing her to the ground. Hours later, Hebrides found her. She was delirious. He picked Cecilia up and carried her toward the house, listening as she feebly called, "Colin…Colin, I'll find you in the woods at Brookgreen. You won't hang. I promise I'll save you from the Tories."

Sure he heard her muffled cry, Colin came out and took his wife from Hebrides, then carried her upstairs to their room in the tower, and undressed her, sponged her body, and clothed her in a fresh gown. He kissed her.

"Colin…is our rose, yours and mine, does it still bloom at the window. It's almost…"

"I know, my love. Our anniversary, and our rose is blooming. I love you. I always have. I've been unkind, and I am ashamed."

"Please call the children and Monica. Be gentle with Mollie. She struggles so, and let Wash be himself, Mollie, too. Let Abbie go North. Promise?"

"I do, my darling." He kissed her again. "I will."

Soon the children and Monica gathered around her. Her voice quite weak, Cecilia continued to talk. "Mollie, your father promises to be kind. Wash, cultivate and enjoy your interests. You, too, Mollie. Remember you can sketch, and be someone's psaltress, my darling child. All of you read the psaltery. Abbie, trust your decisions. Monica, my very best friend for all these years, thank you for teaching me. The gold is to be divided among you. Please give your father a little if he's a pauper. The gold is to be used only for something good, never, ever, anything evil. Play the pirate's psaltery, and treasure the fairy clock. Mollie, my emerald green silk wedding gown is yours when you become a bride. Keep it in the family. Colin, let Caramel go. Free her, and, above all, love the children. I'm sorry for disappointing you…I have always loved you, and…and…I wish we could begin again, but….and the rose…nurture it…it's our love. Colin, God be with you, and… and we'll meet…in heaven…."

She looked up into her husband's eyes one last time as he kissed her. "Cecilia, I love you. I am sorry." He squeezed her hand as she took her last breath. Colin clung to her, even as her body stiffened. He could not release Cecilia. Finally, Monica led him away and prepared her best friend's body for the funeral.

"I'll call you Aunt Monica," Wash said, following, "for now you're the oldest woman on the plantation. Ma wants to be buried in her white dress. She said as much when I took her to the stable. After I put her on Natas, she looked down at me…and asked me to remember her in the white dress. Let's honor her wishes."

"Course we will, honey." And Monica told Wash all about his mother.

Colin didn't dare ask Dr. Gavin Dunn to bury his wife. Instead, he called on the services of John Livingston, the new minister at Swann Creek Associated Reformed Presbyterian Church. "Yes, young man, if you will simply conduct the service and use the psalms which my wife especially cherished….those which I have marked, well I will do something great for you. Why I will build you a far more beautiful church than the meeting house you have now. You will like the church I design. I saw it on my travels."

John Livingston, a shaggy-haired young man with a mole on his right cheek and one missing front tooth, nodded.

"Yes, to your meeting house I will add a portico and steeple. Then there will be five windows with shutters across the second story and double doors flanked by windows on the first floor. You will attract many new members to your church on the hill above Swann Creek. Perhaps you'll even take some members from Old Dunn's congregation. You do know I design churches. I was the one who added the brick tower over at Dunn's church."

Livingston batted his eyes and nodded.

"Pa," Mollie interrupted, "ma used to like a psalm....in fact, she sometimes sang it as she played the psaltery....it was 'Come, dearest Lord, descend and dwell By faith and love in every breast.' Ma wanted God to dwell in her breast."

"Enough, Mollie," Colin said, putting up his hand, his face reddening. "That's really not necessary to say. I have given the minister your mother's favorite psalms."

The minister blushed and turned from father to daughter. From the mountains of Tennessee, he'd struggled to finish Princeton and never imagined anyone would be interested in him or his church, except for Almighty God and perhaps his mentor who now conducted an academy in Georgia, an older man named Dr. Cuthbert Thaddeus Wemyss.

"You know, Dr. Bain, most ministers do not like me because I don't believe in slavery and because I talk about new lights."

"Goodness, don't tell me you're an Abolitionist. Surely you're not mocking me because I have slaves. We will discuss theology and philosophy after the funeral. After all, as I have read in the Bible, there's something in Colossians about not changing one's beliefs because of vain philosophers. Are you one of those vain preaching philosophers?" Well, you'll not change me, for slavery is an institution ordained by God. To hell with your Abolitionist beliefs! You won't last long around here."

The Reverend John Livingston conducted a quiet service, just as Cecilia would have wanted it, on November 2, 1807. Cecilia Fears Lynch was laid to rest beneath the trees at White Oaks Chapel a few feet from Colin's second wife, Anna Catherine Dunn Bain.

Beyond Anna Catherine's grave was the marker of a child: "Little Colin Macaulay Bain, infant son of A.C. Dunn Bain and C.M. Bain, M.D., born 1774, died 1774," a lamb carved at the top of the marker; then on the other side in the opposite direction was Cecilia's tombstone and another child's marker bearing the inscription, "Little Colin Macaulay Bain, infant son of C.F. Lynch Bain and C.M. Bain, born 1790, died 1790," the cross of St. Andrew through a palmetto carved at the top.

"Pa," Wash said, after the preacher said, 'Dust to dust,' Mollie, Abbie, and Monica dressed in black, weeping, "Why did you have two sons who died, each bearing your name? I thought I was your only son. I never knew Ma had any children but Mollie and Abbie and me. Who were the babies named Little Colin? Who is A. C. Dunn Bain? Were you married before?"

"Tell us, pa, so we can record the names in the Bible," Mollie said.

Colin's face rosacead, his eyes meeting the red afternoon sun.

Continuing, Mollie asked, "Pa, was A.C. Dunn Bain the lady whose portrait Wash and I saw in the tower one afternoon when we were playing? She looked a lot like Mamma. Only her eyes were brown. She was wearing a dress with a pink sash and red shoes. I asked Mamma about her once. She didn't answer, but her eyes filled with tears."

Colin stared at Mollie, his face turning a deeper shade of scarlet, "Shut up, you ugly lassie. Don't talk about what you don't know!"

All eyes were on Colin, who stood with hands balled into fists.

Monica broke the silence. "I'll tell you what Daphne told me. Your pa's second wife was Anna Catherine Dunn. Your father left her here at White Oaks when she was about to bear his son. The baby lived a short while and died. So did his mother. Your father courted your ma while Anna Catherine was still alive. Your mother was the very best friend I ever had. I even sang on the choir sometimes with her in Georgetown, that was, until the priest humiliated her. She fought for the patriots in the American Revolution, scouting up and down the marshes and swamps. She saved your father from hanging. I bought my freedom from Miss Katie, your grandmother, but your father always resented me. Your pa forced himself on your mother one summer day when you were little. He called that baby their early summer child. The little fellow lived for a month. Your pa accused me of taking the child, your ma of doing things she never did. That child was born weak. And if you don't know anything else, you needs to realize yo pa rode off every winter. He never knowed what was going on at de plandashun, but he always blamed Miss Cecilia. No matta what happened, it was always the mammy's fault. That's why there are two Little Colin boys buried here."

Colin knelt at his wife's marker and wept.

Monica continued, despite his tears. "You ain't never understood anything but your own importance, Dr. Bain. You tricked your wife. You played with her heart, and she adored you. You laughed at her psaltery."

"Monica, I adored her. Stop right now." He slapped the black woman across her face, her blood spattering on the earth. Mollie wiped Monica's face and dared to push her father. "Stop, Pa, please."

"Pock-marked, gal. Shut up, and leave me alone." Colin flung his daughter against a nearby tombstone where she fell. Clutching the marker, Mollie sobbed so hard she split a seam in her dress.

"I pray that God will heal this family in your hour of grief," the minister said. "As the good book sayeth:

'And it came to pass, when I heard these words, that I sat down and wept, and mourned certain days, and fasted, and prayed before the God of heaven, And said, I beseech thee, O Lord God of heaven, the great and terrible God, that keepeth covenant and mercy for them that love him and observe his commandments: Let thine ear now be attentive, and thine eyes open, that thou mayest hear the prayer of thy servant, which I pray before thee now, day and night…O Lord, I beseech thee, let now thine ear be attentive to the prayer of thy servant, and to the prayer of thy servants, who desire to fear thy name: and prosper, I pray thee, thy servant this day, and grant him mercy in the sight of this man. For I was the king's cupbearer.'

I am quoting to you, Dr. Bain, from Nehemiah, Chapter 1. Perhaps you should read the whole chapter to comfort you in your mourning."

Colin looked at the minister, "Is this the scripture you use to console the members of your church?"

The minister looked at him grimly. "Yes."

"Your words do not seem especially comforting to me today. If I am wrong, I beg your humble pardon. I wish that you had offered a personal prayer for my family. Of course, since you did not know my wife, that may have been difficult for you. Unlike me, my beloved wife was deeply religious."

"Stop it, Father," Wash said. "You insulted my mother, and now Aunt Monica, and my twin sister, and Mr. Livingston as well. You don't even know this minister who graciously agreed to do the burial service for Mamma. I should challenge you to a duel right here at the chapel, and I would not be ashamed to draw a sword against my own father. We have witnesses, including this new minister, and Abbie is here. So are the white oaks, Mamma's favorite trees. There is absolutely nothing you can ever say or do to take away what Mamma left to all of us, so don't you even try, you old bastard."

"No, Wash," Mollie pleaded. "Don't be so hard on Pa."

Before Colin defended himself, the shaggy-haired Abolitionist minister departed.

"Precious in the sight of the Lord is the death of his saints"
(Psalm 116:15).

Book Ten (Late 1807 on)

A silent gloominess hovered over the plantation. The psaltery rested on the harpsichord gathering dust, and the white oaks seemed too still, almost harboring the winter winds. Colin moped about, sometimes hoping Monica would console him.

But Monica refused. She was taking care of Nessie who was about to deliver London's baby. "I ain't got nothing else to give my gal, Docta Bain. Her baby gwine die, and you don't care." So he spent time with Caramel who wearied him with her request for freedom.

"I can't release you. I won't, Caramel. I need you. You understand me more than anyone else, and you know it. We'll grow old together."

Caramel served him brandy with ginger and cinnamon, then busied herself with fashioning an effigy of Colin and sticking pins in it.

Angry, Colin left and turned to the girls for comfort and amusement. He began giving them lessons in French, spelling, geography, fencing, and riding.

Abbie learned quickly, but not Mollie. Rather than help her, Colin actually enjoyed teasing her as she made mistake after mistake in pronunciation, worse even, in mounting her horse.

"Go," he called, as Mollie sat astride Natas a few days before Christmas. "Go." He slapped the horse's rump, clapping. "This is your chance to prove you're a better rider than your mother." Natas jumped over a fence, and Mollie tumbled off, injuring her head and leg.

Abbie stopped and went to her sister's side.

But not Colin. "Get up, Mollie, and remount. Go with the wind, as your ma did." Mollie couldn't. She struggled to get up and ended up limping home.

"You'll never ride well until you lose weight!" her father rebuked, then mounted Natas, and rode with Abbie through the fields.

PSALTERY AT WHITE OAKS

Monica met Mollie and gave her salves, then asked Prince to set her ankle. "Yu dun broke yo ankle, Misses Mollie," Prince said. "Sho hab."

Mollie thanked him and later said to Monica who was making pies in the kitchen. "I never liked riding. I never have wanted to compete with Ma. I'd like to be pretty like her, but I just enjoy my embroidery and sewing."

"Ain't nothing wrong with that, honey. Nothing at all. God made each one of us different. Each one of us has a gift. Enjoy yours, and don't compare. It only leads to misery."

While they were talking, Nessie came in crying, telling them that the overseer had whipped her for being late to the fields. "I dun tole Wash, and he gwine fire dat mean man."

"Good. It's time he was fired, and I'm going to buy your freedom and London's, Nessie, but I want you to marry dat boy. He new here at White Oaks, ain't he?"

Nessie nodded. "Yessum, Ma. He cum from Leeds Landing. That Mista Steggud dun brung hem to take Pa's place in the brick yahd."

"Steggerda did bring London here," Wash said, as he joined his sisters and the black women in the kitchen, "but I just fired him, too. Nobody ever needs to be whipped for simply being late, and surely not you, Nessie. That's absurd."

"What" Colin blurted out, the purple veins in his nose swelling. "What have you done, son?"

"I fired the Irish Dutchman. I fired your overseer. He has carried your cruel rules too far, and so have you with your own family, especially my twinny. Oh, I've done my share of teasing her, and I probably always will. But Sis is not afraid of me. She's scared of you. So was Mamma. You taunted her, and she finally died of a broken heart. We all know that."

Colin glared at his son, then said, "Do as you please. But I will hire another overseer, and I will endeavor not to trouble you with my presence. I can stay either in the tower or in my coach. Which do you prefer?"

Abbie started laughing.

"You'll make him angrier, Sis," Mollie whispered.

"I don't care."

"Stay in the tower, Pa," Wash finally answered.

Christmas was difficult. With Monica and Nessie's assistance, Mollie passed out the clothing and shoes. After Christmas, Colin hired Jeremy Wherry as overseer. Unlike Steggerda, Wherry was not harsh. He tried to get along with the enslaved and with everyone at White Oaks.

Nessie and London were finally married, and Monica bought their freedom. Wash said he would pay them wages to stay. "I'm going to buy Memnon's freedom, too, and pay him to help me. I don't care what my father thinks. I have the money, and this is for a good cause. There's nothing evil in buying good slaves their freedom."

Monica decided to practice midwifery. Tired of being paid nothing by Dr. Bain, she made her services known throughout Blisland County and was successful. Mollie and Abbie began giving the slaves reading lessons. Colin came and went, ignoring his family, leaving the running of the plantation to his son.

Colin knew that Wash's beliefs differed somewhat from his own, but they both believed in the institution of slavery. "I intend to expand the grist mill and invite friends over for fish feasts and dances. I will have the kind of merriment at White Oaks Ma always wanted," Wash announced to his father in the spring.

Colin shrugged his shoulders and went down to Chinaberry Grove.

The months passed, one year blending into another, and in July of 1810, Colin, the twins, and Abbie attended a patriotic celebration at the old Hamilton place known as Cork Hill because of some legend about lone cork tree growing a mile or so from the house. Many of Colin's friends from the war were there, some in uniform. They exchanged stories and reminisced about the long struggle for freedom.

While Abbie, Wash, and Mollie were talking, Abbie startled the twins. "You know, I've never thought much about it, I'm different. I'm light-skinned, and my hair's kinky, isn't it? Oh, you won't hurt my feelings if you agree, Mollie. I know I don't look like ya'll. My eyes are different, too. Sometimes....sometimes I've wondered if I'm really Caleb's sister, you know that older slave that works in the stable. Maybe....maybe Ma just felt sorry for me when I was born down in The Quarters and took me in."

"I don't think so, Sis, not that we know of," Wash said.

"And I was unkind to Caleb the other day. Oh, I was, and I'm so ashamed. I asked him to saddle one of the horses for me, and he wouldn't. He stared at me and said, 'You ain't a white gal. Youz really a slave, jes lik me. I knoz all about yu. You ain't de docta's chile, and wun day yu'll find out.' I slapped Caleb hard and ordered Prince to give him thirteen lashes. Prince stripped that man and beat him hard. I watched and laughed as his back bled. Caleb vowed revenge. Oh, I'm ashamed. You know, the plantation system is ugly. It's evil, Wash, and I want to go North. I don't want to be a part of it."

"You don't have to stay here. I promise. But, meantime, let's enjoy some refreshments and meet some friends. This is, after all, a social occasion. Hey, Sis, there's that preacher, the one who buried Ma," he continued and thumped her behind. "Go get him. Maybe you can persuade him to get a tooth and marry you. Go on, Sissy."

"I don't know what to say, Bubba."

"Just tell him you're glad to see him," Abbie encouraged, "and we'll join you in a little while. You can do it, Sis."

Mollie obeyed, and Abbie turned to her brother again. "Wash, I want to go to Boston to school and become a teacher. I know our father will not make the arrangements. Can I really trust you?"

"I will not let you down," he answered, as he caught a glimpse of Mollie sitting with John Livingston and another young lady. She had dark hair and gray eyes. She wore a white gown which resembled the one his mother was buried in. "Abbie, look at her, at the young lady wearing a white dress and straw bonnet. Except for her eyes and hair, why she looks like Ma. Wonder who she is?"

"I don't know. Let's go meet her."

So they joined Mollie and her friends. John introduced Wash and Abbie to his sister. "This is Agnes."

Agnes smiled and chattered easily. "Mollie tells me you're a teacher, too," she said to Abbie, "and a graceful rider, too, and that you're a skilled hunter known for your wit and humor, Mr. Bain."

Wash felt himself almost stammering, something he never did, even with his father. He was delighted when the fiddlers tuned up. "Will you join me, Miss Livingston?"

"No, she won't. My sister and I do not dance," the minister interrupted, tipping his hat. "Even though I'm broad-minded, that's one diversion of which I do not approve, Mr. Bain. You will excuse us."

"Well, one day, mon frère," Agnes said, "I will reel and waltz, sing and recite my poetry. I shall not live with you forever, and there's nothing you nor anyone else can do to stop me anymore than you with your Abolitionist leanings can do to prevent people from owning slaves." She curtsied to Mollie, Wash, and Abbie, and followed her brother. "Au revoir," she turned and called."

"A vous," Abbie answered.

"Oh, she's charming," Wash said. "Why she has such a flair for fashion, doesn't she?"

Mollie agreed as she watched the sun setting over the river beyond the pines. Slaves served a light supper of fried fish, cornbread, and cole slaw from long tables. Wash invited his sisters to dance, then offered them a cup of punch. They all watched their father as he invited old spinsters fanning themselves on the porch to dance.

"Isn't he an old fool, still wearing that ancient Macaulay kilt and chattering away? He continues to roll that Scottish r. Angry as he makes me, there's something admirable about the old boy."

Mollie shook her head. "I'm afraid of him. Let's go home now. Can we, Bubba? I'm tired."

"Of course, we can. There's no reason to linger. I'm sure the old boy will linger for several hours with the ladies. We all know that. He'll ride a horse home later. I'll just whisper in his ear that we're departing."

They left in the coach, and Colin tipsied into White Oaks after midnight.

The next morning he slept late, then spent the rest of the day riding over the plantation and talking to Jeremy Wherry. Mollie, Wash, Abbie, and Monica were playing charades in the parlor when they heard footsteps on the piazza. Mollie tiptoed to the window. "Bubba, there's the biggest, old darkie I've ever seen. He's wearing a patch over one eye. He's at the front door. The word RAPIST is carved on his forehead."

By the time Wash stood up, the man had pushed open the heavy door and was walking through the hall, throwing candlesticks and vases on the floor, slashing portraits. He came into the parlor and stared at Abbie.

"Yo sho iz purty, gal, and I dun cum fo you. Youze my gal. You knowed it, don't you?"

"What? Who are you? Wash, who is this man?"

Mollie clinging to him, Wash stammered, "I....I've never seen him."

"I have," Monica said. "You get away from here, ole man. You understand?" She hit him with her cane.

"Iz free as yu iz now. I dun payd off my massa in Chalstun weah I was sold afta de brandin and wuppin by dat ovaseeah. I dun cum foh Caleb. He outside. We dun tied up Prince. I cum foh dis heah gal. She Caleb's haf sista. Iz huh pa. Dat docta, he ain't yo pa, gal. Sho as I standin heah, he ain't yo pappy. I iz, and Monica knowed it, too. Sho do."

Wash drew his pistol and fired as Numbers broke a window and jumped to the ground. Wash called the hounds, and the dogs chased the man and his son down to the river. Monica and Mollie covered their ears to block the screaming.

"Numbers will not be coming back, Aunt Monica, but it's time you told us all the truth."

They sat down as the old woman related the episode in July of 1790, when she had taken the twins for a walk along the river and their mother had insisted on giving the slave a reading lesson. "When we cum home, she was naked on the floor. Yo pa was away. He came and went and left us home alone so much of the time. Yo mammy begged us all to take the baby, but we was afraid. I hate to tell you, but we been wupped too many times ourselves, Daphne what was living then, and me, and…well a few months later, this beautiful gal was born, and yo ma named her Abbie. Your ma loved her as she did you and Miss Mollie, and she promised Abbie her freedom. Das what happen."

Colin came in later for a brandy, and Wash confronted him. "Tell us more about the slave named Numbers. He was just here."

"Do tell. Is that why I heard the shots?"

"But who is he?" Mollie asked.

"Simply a slave whom your mother pitied for one reason or another. They made love one afternoon, and Abbie was conceived. Your mother was always attracted to the man, something about her mother Katie seeing him shackled on their boat at the landing in Georgetown years and years ago and something about his shimmering cinnamon-colored eyes." Colin shrugged his shoulders. "That's all I know."

"She didn't encourage dat man, and you knoz it, Docta Bain," Monica interrupted.

"Hush….I wasn't there, and neither were you."

"Pa, where were you?" Mollie persisted. "We all know Mamma had compassion and enjoyed teaching the slaves to read, but I don't think she would have freely given her body to anyone."

"Oh, Mollie, stop scratching those ugly pimples. You only make them bleed. Anger doesn't become you. Monica, perhaps you should try a new paste for her skin. Of course, my old remedy is Dr. Sun. Strip, and walk in the sun, Mollie, and munch those mulberries. I've even thought of making wine from them."

Wash stared at his father. "That was very cruel, Father, and you know it."

"I suppose so…Mollie's not pretty like her mother."

"And you're not kind like your wife," Monica said.

Abbie put her arms around Mollie who began crying. "It'll be better, Sis."

"Tell you what, Wash. Why don't you marry and bring us some children? Mollie and Abbie could be their governesses, and we could all stay right here at White Oaks!"

"You're tipsy, Father. Tell me one more time. Did Numbers really rape our mother?"

"I didn't. I'm not black. And this beautiful butterscotch child was sucking at her mother's breast when I returned from visiting General Washington in May of 1791. Your mother was milkless when you twins were born."

"Hush, Docta Bain," Monica said. "Enough's enough."

"Maybe your mother encouraged the black monster. I don't know. We'll never know. Nobody was there but your mother and Numbers. At least Mollie doesn't have a swollen breast with an inverted nipple and a shriveled breast. At least, I don't think so."

Before anyone said anything, Colin stood up and ripped the girls' bodices. "No, you're not deformed, neither of you, and Abbie, you have delicious little chocolate nipples. Daughter, yours are so pink."

Wash slapped Colin, as Monica covered the girls with her apron. "The devil got into you today, Docta Bain."

"Oh, Monica, you weary me. We've argued for so long, haven't we?"

"Yes, we have. You've always made fun of people with afflictions. You have tormented them. You accused these chillin's ma of being a lesbian with me. We never was nothing but best friends all these years, and you knew it. Your wife died of a broken haht. You know that, too. I apologized. We forgave each other, but I will never forgive myself."

"There was nothing for Miss Cecilia to be forgiven for."

"Since I am surrounded by enemies, I think I'll lock myself in the tower for good. Mollie, why don't you marry that preacher, John Livingston. You know he owns Burnt Bluffs now. It was originally called Mulberry Bluffs until the fire. I had leased the land years ago to that French Huguenot minister, Dr. Boucher. It's a long story which I'll relate one day when you're all less antagonistic. I gave the land to the preacher when I changed his plain meeting house into the beautiful church it is today. But remember that I still own White Oaks. You all don't. Not while I still breathe."

"Free the slaves, Father. That's what Ma wanted."

"Never!"

"Free my people," Abbie begged. "Mammy wanted you to."

"Never, ginger girl. You're free. Go on North. I don't know why you're waiting."

"Wash is making the arrangements, and I will certainly not linger here, Doctor Bain, now that I know the truth."

Several weeks later, when Mollie, Wash, and Abbie were enjoying supper in the dining room, Mollie pressed her brother's hand. "Wash, John Livingston has asked me to marry him."

"Does he love you, Sissy? Will he take care of you?"

"Of course, he'll take care of her, Wash. He loves Mollie," Abbie said. "You marry him when I go north to school. We'll write letters. Oh, my life here could have been so different if Mamma had not loved me as she did and if you two had not been kind to me. Why I could have grown up in The Quarters and be scratching in some garden with chickens or sleeping on a cold pallet....or on the floor and eating nothing but fat back and greens, corn bread, and sweet potatoes."

"Please, Abbie. Here at White Oaks, an enslaved person's life is not that bad, is it?" Wash asked.

"I think so, and my mission is to teach my people and to free them. Why don't you begin here, Wash? Ma would be so proud."

He shook his head. "In time, but not yet."

"What are you waiting for?"

"Well, I'm glad John Livingston is an Abolitionist and does not believe in slavery," Mollie said.

"Fine, but will he take care of you? I mean, you know what a lavish lifestyle we have here. We eat and drink as we please, play and sing and dance when we wish, order clothes, travel, hunt, go boating. We lead a life of leisure."

"Because of slavery, you do," Abbie interrupted.

"Mollie, you've never scrubbed floors or slopped hogs, gathered wood or made a fire. You've never even washed clothes, Sis," Wash said, "that's hard work, and you're not accustomed to it at all!"

"Maybe you're a little jealous, Bubba, that your twin sister would be marrying," she smiled. "John will learn me what I need to know to be his helpmate. He wants to rebuild the orphanage that Dr. Boucher started at Mulberry Bluffs before it was burned. We'll all work together. Maybe some of the girls in The Quarters would help me."

Wash poured himself a glass of bourbon and said, "Maybe you could take that gal named Da. She still lives with her mammy, Delilah, the mammy who went to the mountains when we little."

"Yes, I could buy her freedom and pay her wages with part of the gold Ma left me."

"Or I'll pay her, Sissy. I won't have you slopping hogs," Wash said.

Abbie said nothing.

"Only if John will allow me to have a paid servant, Wash. The decision is his," Mollie insisted.

"Damned Abolitionist preacher. Well, if he doesn't agree, you won't be marrying him. I will not have you laboring like a slave. You weren't bred for that, and you know it."

"Oh, Wash, you've said too much. Nobody was ever born to be a slave, and you know it," Abbie said, her voice angry. "Have you really made plans for me, or are you lying?"

"Yes...as a matter of fact, Sis, you can take the coach from Essex next week."

"Well, Pa thinks I'm bred to work," Mollie said. "He says I'll bear babies easily and nurse them."

"Please excuse me," Abbie said. "I think I'll go upstairs and pack. I'll be certain to scour the floor before I leave this house."

"Abbie, I'm sorry."

But Abbie left the table. "Excuse me, Mollie and Monica."

"Sis, doesn't John Livingston's missing front tooth bother you...and that shaggy hair? Why he looks like some sort of monarch from the seventeenth century! And his legs are so thin. At least, get him to cut his hair so he'll resemble a Cromwellian round head."

"Bubba, you're silly," Mollie laughed.

"Mollie, do you love him?"

"Oh, I do...well, I guess I'll join Abbie upstairs. John has asked me to read what St. Paul says about marriage. Would you like to read with me?"

"God knows I don't. When I marry, I will love my wife passionately and absolutely spoil her and know Ma's looking down from heaven, happy and proud. You mean Abbie's not going to come back down and play the psaltery for me tonight?"

"I don't think so. You hurt her feelings. Maybe you could play a few notes on the harpsichord with your last bourbon. Good-night, Bubba."

Wash staggered from the dining room into the parlor, played a tune, then fell asleep on the floor, awakened in the night by his hounds.

"Harden not your heart, as in the provocation, and as
in the days of temptation in the wilderness" (Psalm 95:8).

PSALTERY AT WHITE OAKS

Book Eleven (1810-1811)

A few days later after Abbie left for Boston, Wash made a call on the Reverend John Fennell Livingston, hoping to find out exactly what this minister believed, what he was like.

Wash galloped up the road toward Essex in the hot August sun, corn tasseling in the fields, and stopped at Swann Creek Church to water Natas and look at the church. He could not believe that his father had actually turned the plain meeting house into such a beautiful church. Indeed, the church had five windows across the second story, double doors with windows on each side on the first, and a portico, in addition to a steeple. "Why? What motivated our father? Was it simply because John Livingston conducted Mamma's burial service, or was this designed to make old Dr. Dunn jealous?" This church surely surpassed Brick Tower Church.

Wash shrugged his shoulders and led the horse to the creek behind the church, then rode on and turned up the lane leading to Burnt Bluffs. The landscape was ugly. Only stumps remained from the pines and mulberries which had burned so long ago. Some folks said there had been a brush fire. Prince told everyone a witch lived over at the bluffs. Whatever, it was gloomy and hauntingly dreary. Even the house where John Livingston lived was partially burned.

Picturing his twin living in this house covered with tangled vines troubled Wash. He tethered the horse to a stump and pushed his way through the vines, climbed the rickety steps, and rapped on the door.

Much to his surprise, Agnes answered the door. "Bonjour, Wash," she curtsied. "Welcome to my brother's paltry abode. Though he's a minister, I cannot even say psaltered home. He rarely reads psalms."

Wash laughed. He found John's sister to be enchantingly witty.

"I can offer you a milk stool or a broken settle to sit upon, even a bench made from granite slabs." Agnes led him into the barren parlor. "We mostly live in this room because it wasn't burned, and we sleep in the shell of a room back there which my brother managed to put together. He separated the room with some of my grandmother's quilts. Mamma and I slept in one side, and John stayed on the other. Our mother died shortly after I came to live here.

The kitchen outdoors is still standing, and there's one slave cabin and, of course, the burned chapel. The house where the orphans lived burned to the ground. Then, there's another building that's so covered over with vines and old boards I don't know what it ever was, maybe a stable. John added a lean-to to the side for the mule and wagon. A few books that belonged to Dr. Boucher and a woman named Jeanette de Calmes survived.

I can assure you, though, that we didn't live like this when our father was living. He preached in Virginia, and then we crossed Cumberland Gap and lived in the mountains where he built a cabin for us. John doesn't even bother to chink up the cracks."

Wash was spellbound. Not only was Agnes beautiful, but she was a fine storyteller, just like his mother.

"My brother left for Hampton-Sydney College, for Pa insisted on educating him. I learned music at home. When I was young, I married an old French soldier who had served under Rochambeau in the Revolution, and we sailed for France. My husband's name was Jean Duval. Soon after we arrived in Dieppe, he died. Sometimes I think I married Monsieur Duval to satisfy my mother's dream. A French Huguenot, she wanted me to go to France. Of course, I wanted adventure. My father died after I married, but Mamma stayed in at home until John finished at Princeton. He went there after finishing Hampton-Sydney. For some reason, he took this church here in Blisland County. I don't know why. That's when Mamma moved. When I came home later——and that's a long story I won't go into now——I joined them here. I cook for John, but he doesn't appreciate all of my herbs. He just wants plain food. I can't even vary the potatoes. C'est tout. But I do cultivate my own grapes. In fact, I have a small vineyard way down toward the river where Dr. Boucher apparently had his. I make my own wine. Would you like a glass?"

"Why, yes, thank you."

"Oh, it's not fine wine," Agnes teased, "but the taste is pleasant. Even John enjoys a glass on occasion."

Wash felt himself falling in love with Agnes. She was witty, playful, beautiful, and her voice musical. She was so much like his mother. He gazed at her as she walked across the splintered floor. "My sister says your brother wishes to marry her."

"Yes, he does, and Mollie would be his ideal helpmeet. I think they're both suited for one another. They're rather alike, don't you think?"

Wash nodded.

"You know, I don't know what changed John. When he was younger, he used to be animated, but he doesn't have that joie de vivre anymore. I've often wondered if it was that friend he met at Princeton, the one who has an academy in Georgia. I forget his name now. It's not important. I met the man one time, and that was enough. One of those dreadfully stern ministers, you know, always glaring with ferocious eyes, trying to make people feel guilty, sort of like that despicable Dr. Dunn."

Wash wanted Agnes, and she felt it. She yearned for him, too. They were kindred spirits. Wash knew that she would enjoy the fish suppers and fox hunts which his mother had enjoyed in the low-country. He envisioned Agnes in his mother's emerald green silk wedding gown. Mollie was far too plump to wear the dress.

"Why my brother thinks I'm Catholic simply because I lived in Paris and because I dislike the whole idea of tokens for 'The Lord's Supper.' Do you know that an elder refused to give me a token because he heard me singing one of Lully's arias, instead of a psalm? Sometimes I'm going to pack my valise and take the stage coach to Savannah or Charleston and give music lessons."

"Please don't leave now," Wash said.

"Sh....I hear footsteps on the porch. It's probably John. Sometimes I hide my wine glass behind the logs near the hearth, but I won't this morning."

John walked in, removed his torn hat, and shook hands with Wash. "Have you prepared tea for our guest, Agnes?"

"Oh, mon frère, we're enjoying a little wine. Would you like a sip?"

"No thank you, Agnes. Please go to the well and dip some water for me."

"As you please," she curtsied.

"And put the rage of the Bastille in it," Wash teased, as he watched Agnes dance through the door, singing, "Allons enfants,...."

John sat on the milk stool and explained that he would be conducting a burial service for Mrs. Jane de Graffenreid's baby. "The Lord gives, and the Lord takes away."

Wash nodded. "But I believe Jesus said something also about letting the dead bury the dead and getting on with life. Seriously, Brother John, I've come to talk to you about your proposal to my sister, and I also want to ask you for your sister's hand in marriage."

"Marry Agnes. She is useless to me, really only a frivolity who never assists with chores. She babbles in French half the time and enjoys her vineyard. You're welcome to have her hand in marriage, and I would like to take your sister's. I love Mollie."

"I will allow the marriage only if you agree to her bringing two former slaves. Mollie will pay their wages, or I will."

"That would not be right for my wife to pay wages. That is my duty, and I do not wish to employ any human being for such menial tasks. My wife will do the work. After all, that is a woman's duty. If the chores become too cumbersome, I will allow her to pay someone. I will make that decision. I hope you can get some work out of Agnes. After all, St. Paul says women are to be submissive to their husbands."

"John, apparently you don't understand me. I don't want my sister doing menial labor. You think about what I have said, and, now, if you will excuse me, I will bid you good day and share news with your sister at the well."

"By all means, Mr. Bain. I will marry you two at Swann Creek Church. The sooner the better, too. Then, I shall have more time to devote to my sermons. I think that would make Agnes happy and your father as well."

Wash found Agnes at the well and took her in his arms. He proposed, and she accepted immediately. "I pledge to be your loving and faithful wife, and I would be honored to wear your mother's gown and play her psaltery. But I won't obey you, Wash."

"You don't have to," he laughed, "and I promise to order the finest clothes for you and a new phaeton. Indeed, White Oaks will come to be what my precious mother always longed for, a lively plantation with gatherings, merriment, music, and laughter."

Wash rode home to share his tidings. Mollie bit her nails and scratched her face. "Bubba, you've not been fair to me," she wailed. "I won't come to your wedding and feel humiliated when it is I who should be marrying first. After all, John asked me to marry him."

"You will, but not until he comes around, Sissy, not until he agrees to a paid servant. He claimed you shouldn't pay the wages and that he did not want to. We know he will never agree to a slave. After all, John is an Abolitionist. Besides, you would never fit into mother's wedding gown, and you know it. What's more, I am worried that you'd become a Cinderslut if you married John Livingston. That house is a burned hovel. It's not fit for humans, really."

But Mollie refused to listen. "I hate you, Bubba." She stormed upstairs in tears and flung herself across the walnut bed. Monica found her later, the cat curled up beside her. "It's not fair, Monica. I won't go to that wedding and hear the man I want to marry pronounce his sister and my brother man and wife."

"No, honey, it is not fair." Monica washed the blood off Mollie's scratched face and brushed back her hair. "Why don't we go sit in the garden a spell? We'll figure something out. Wash was plumb wrong, and he knows that deep down."

Monica chastised him later that night, and Wash tried to cajole her into forgiving him. "I'll buy you a present in Charleston."

She shook her head. "You're acting just like yo pa when you're unkind to your twin Sissy, and you know it. You ought to be ashamed."

When the wedding day arrived in October, Agnes laughed as she dressed. "I have to rip a seam to fit into this emerald gown, and nobody knows why." She was already carrying Wash's baby.

Colin attended the ceremony, for Agnes had insisted that he be invited, and Monica persuaded Mollie to go as well. "Something good will come of it, honey lamb. You wait and see." Wearing her brown dress and bonnet, Mollie forced herself to be pleasant.

After the service at Swann Creek Church, John followed Mollie to the portico and took her hand in his. "I will come for you in a few weeks, and we will marry without your brother or father's consent. I know a minister in Essex. You may bring Nessie and her husband if you wish, so long as they are free. I will figure out a way to pay them."

Mollie's eyes filled with tears of joy. "You mean that, John."

"I do, Mollie....I will take care of you."

As Wash and Agnes were ready to leave for their wedding trip to Pawley's Island, Wash kissed Mollie. "Sissy, don't resent us. And remember, I'm counting on you to be the old maiden aunt for our children."

"No, Wash," Agnes answered, raising her voice above his laughter, "Your twin will be my sister very soon. Mollie, I promise to bring you a surprise and something for Monica, too."

Oak leaves whirling in the crisp breeze, Mollie stooped down and picked up a clump of red dirt and hurled it at Wash. He ducked. "Come on, Sissy. I was only teasing."

"No you weren't, Wash Bain. Nothing would please you more, and I know it."

Later to Monica, Mollie said that she was a little jealous of Agnes. "She's far prettier than I'll ever be, and she rides beautifully, like Abbie. But I would never be unkind to her."

Monica listened and nodded. "I understand. Miss Aggie would, too, if you tole her. It will all be alright, honey." The two women busied themselves making dresses for Mollie and finishing a quilt. "Yo mammy would be happy for you. Oh, she loved you and Wash. Always rememba that."

Mollie nodded. "When Agnes returns, I'm going to confide my wedding plans to her. I don't think she'll tell my brother, do you? I don't want him or pa to know."

In November, Agnes and Wash came home, and Mollie told Agnes. "I won't tell Wash, but please don't let my brother require too much of you. He's different from me, Mollie. He's become very strict, almost harsh. Don't let him take advantage of you."

Mollie chewed her nails, waiting for John to come. "It's been nearly six weeks, Monica."

"He comin tonight. I seed him in a vision. Now, you be ready when I aks London to lead Mr. John to your window."

Mollie finished packing, and, sure enough, around midnight, London banged the window. That was the sign. Mollie went down the ladder and rode away with John to Essex. There was no wedding trip, and the very next day, she settled into a pattern at Burnt Bluffs, one of duty and drudgery.

Wash, however, lived luxuriously. He began to raise peacocks and ordered a piano for his wife. He added an extension with a narrow porch on to the back of the house, making it in the shape of an L.

"You'll regret being such a spendthrift, Son," Colin said, when he occasionally came down from his self-imposed isolation in the tower. "You know what your ma said about wasting the gold, using it only for something good."

"Father, I think the old pirate himself would approve of spending gold on his wife. I believe, from all the stories I've heard, he spoiled his Cecilia. I'm sorry you didn't spoil my mammy."

"Did you know your sister was planning to elope?"

"No...all I know is that Nessie and London and their little baby Lafayette are over at the bluffs now. Monica bought their freedom."

Colin sat down and puffed his pipe. "Well, I'll pray for their happiness. But God knows now, this gout is paining me. I'm growing old, Son."

"Wash laughed. "I don't believe a word of that, Father.""

At hog-killin time, John and Mollie came to White Oaks, and Wash teased his sister unmercifully, but added, "I do rejoice with you, Sissy."

Mollie said nothing.

Agnes embraced Mollie. "I hope you and my brother will be as happy as your brother and I are. I'm carrying our child."

"You are radiant."

"Mollie, I want our children to be close. They'll be double-first cousins. That's most as close as twins, isn't it? And I want you to take your mother's psaltery."

"Oh no. I couldn't play that around John. You keep it, Aggie."

"Well," she said, her gray eyes searching Mollie's, and looking beyond at her brother reading a book as he paced up and down, anxious to leave, "You and John join us for Christmas. We'd like that."

"Yes," Colin added, as he hobbled in. "This is always your home, and come as often as you will. I am sorry for mistreating you all these years. Isolated in the tower, I've done a great deal of thinking, and I am remorseful. I beg your forgiveness. I've asked for God's. I'm growing old, Daughter, and I've even turned to Monica and Prince's remedies. It's cherry juice. Can you imagine? I have two colored doctors!"

"They may know more than you do, Dr. Bain," John said. "I hear you made Mollie eat mulberries and peaches regularly."

Colin's face reddened. Mollie only nodded. She could forgive her father, but she could never forget his ugly words all those years......the time he had ripped open her dress, the afternoons he had tied her naked to the trees near the garden.

Frowning, she agreed to come for Christmas. "But my husband is ready to leave now."

Agnes understood and kissed her good-bye. During the next few days, Agnes supervised the cooking and adorned the house with greenery and fruit. Mollie and John came for Christmas Day. There were fireworks, and merriment was the order of the day at the plantation from sampling tasty puddings and pies to singing and drinking rounds of Colin's favorite Arrack punch. Agnes and Mollie visited in The Quarters and distributed clothing and shoes to the slaves.

In the New Year, Colin confessed that he was absolutely bored. "Otherwise, I shall begin seeing patients again and give lectures at Mount Hebron. Otherwise I will become a miserable, old, crippled man."

Monica listened and encouraged him to work. "Maybe you understands now why yo Misses Cecilia wanted to keep busy."

"I do."

And, of course, Colin liked Agnes immensely and found her company pleasurable. She reminded him of Cecilia. He and Agnes shared stories, but he never revealed anything about sailing with the notorious Curly Motte Macaulay O'Toole or about imprisoning Caramel. He hoped Monica had not given away all of his secrets, but he would never know. "So, why worry?" he laughed to himself, pouring himself another brandy.

Wash never resented his father's time with Agnes until one night in June. Wash was at the stable with a lame horse when Colin was returning from his quarterly meeting of the Gwynneth Society, a club of men of Welsh descent who celebrated the patron saint of Wales. Since Colin's grandfather on his mother's side was from Wales, he felt a certain loyalty to St. David, almost as much as he did to St. Andrew.

A little intoxicated, Colin had fallen from his horse and limped into the tower and up the stairs, his chin cut, one eye swollen, and his right thigh bleeding. Hearing his screams, Agnes climbed the narrow steps to Colin's room, cleaned his wounds, and bandaged his cuts. "I fear this one on your chin may need stitches," she said, holding the candle and looking closely.

Colin pulled her down on him. "Oh, I love you, Agnes. If you weren't carrying my son's bairn, why I'd get you with my own child, sure as the moon riseth there above the white oaks. You're a pretty lass, and you remind me so much of my beloved Cecilia. Now I know why Wash adores you."

"You nasty, old drunk," she slapped him. "I won't ever take care of you again. You're just as evil as Mollie said." Agnes left the room, but never told anyone about the incident, not even Monica, not even her husband.

A few days later when he knew Wash was out in the fields supervising planting, Colin went to the parlor door and asked Agnes' forgiveness. "I am sorry. I've been taking laudanum for pain."

She invited him to join her. "Of course, I forgive you. That's what God asks us to do. Have you forgiven yourself and others?"

"I have tried," and he found himself telling Agnes all about taunting his wife. "Yes, I hurt her. I teased her unmercifully about that breast deformity. The truth be known, she had two deformities. Cecilia was really my third wife. I was hard on her, but absolutely adored her. She bore the twins and another baby boy whom she named for me. Thinking she aborted that child on purpose when she fell, I was angry and left her. I never realized the baby was actually born and lived until I returned home. I'll be buried between Cecilia and my second wife, Anna Catherine, who also bore a son she named for me. Frustrated with Anna Catherine, I left when she needed me the most. My first wife lies on the hillside of an old kirk in Scotland. Oh, Agnes, I have been a bad boy. I have been so cruel, and I don't really know why."

"Did you ask your wife's forgiveness?"

"I did, and she accepted it. She asked me to forgive her. I had nothing to forgive her for, and she was so beautiful. I was jealous of her relationship with Monica."

Agnes took his hand. "We've all done things we're ashamed of. We all have a past. You know, I never dreamed I would ever be blessed with Wash. When I was younger, I married a French soldier."

"So you're older than Wash?"

"Two years. I was young when I married the soldier. He was older. After he died, I discovered there was very little money. I used most of it to take music lessons in Paris. Well, I fell in love with my music teacher, the man who gave me lessons in voice. I gave birth to a little boy. Monsieur LeClair wouldn't marry me, though. He was angry. I trudged the streets of Paris in rags. I was cold and hungry. I sold my grandmother's ring. My baby starved to death, and I gave myself to others. I sold myself to others. Finally, one day a wise, old nun at a cathedral took me in. Her name was Sister Madelaine. I'll never forget her. If I ever have a little girl, I'd like to name her Madelaine for the nun and Elise for my mother. The nun secured funds for my passage back to America. Father had died by then, and mother was living with my brother. Dr. Bain, I have never told Wash that story."

"He doesn't need to know. I'll never tell. If you've told Monica, she will never reveal it either. I've been very unkind to her, and I have tried to ask her forgiveness."

"She will understand. Oh, I worry about Mollie. As you know, we didn't grow up in a gloomy household. Mother was cheerful, and Father was gentle. My brother changed when he was away in college. I am truly afraid that Mollie has become his Cinderslut, and I don't know who will save her. There's no fairy godmother. I could never have stayed indefinitely with John. If I had not fallen in love with Wash, why I would have left Burnt Bluffs and gone to Savannah to teach music. Burnt Bluffs is dreary. It is depressing."

"Are you up to traveling in the coach to visit my daughter tomorrow?"

She nodded, and the next day, Colin and Agnes found Mollie, great with child, down on her hands and knees, scrubbing the hearth. Her forehead was covered with beads of sweat, pimples bleeding, and hair tangled and matted. She could scarcely stand up.

When Colin saw her, he knew his daughter was John's Cinderslut.

Agnes and Colin learned that John Livingston had been tarred and feathered by members of Swann Creek Church.

"That's right, Pa. My husband no longer preaches at the church. One Sabbath, when he gave a sermon on the abomination of slavery in the sight of God, all the elders of the church were furious, so they stripped John of his robe and clothing, covered him with tar, and bound him in a cart, after which they drove him around the church and up to Essex, then back to the church. As if that wasn't punishment enough, why, they called him a 'stang.'"

"Why on earth did they say that?" Agnes asked, as she struggled to sit on the milk stool.

"Because I'm ugly and have bad skin, some of the women think he beats me."

"Does my brother beat you, Mollie?"

"No, but they thought so. So they strung John up on a pole which they carried home, as people watched. It was terrible. John now insists more than ever that it is even wrong for us to pay servants to do tasks which he says I should do. Before long, Nessie and London and little Lafayette will be returning to White Oaks. Will you and Wash pay them?"

"Of course, but where's Nessie now?"

"Probably in the garden. You will excuse me. I must gather wood. It's a little cold yet. I've enjoyed my flowers, though. Will you watch Lafayette for me, please? He's in the box there."

"I don't mind, but why is Nessie's baby in your parlor?" Colin asked. "Did John tear down the old slave cabin?"

"Oh, no. That's his library now. He spends most of his time there. He reads and meditates, and he's writing a book now on Dr. Boucher and the Huguenots. The rest of us divide the chores and wait for John to interpret the scriptures for us. He gives us our orders each day. After all, my duty is to serve my husband. He is my master."

Colin was shocked. "But, my dear child, you do not have to live in this hovel. Why don't you come home?" Colin hobbled toward her.

"Yes, come stay with us, at least until after the baby is born," Agnes interrupted. "We'll have our babies together in a warm house, and Monica will be there for us. This hovel is no place for a newborn, Mollie." Agnes picked up Lafayette and held him.

"Daughter, I beg you. This is not equality for anyone. This is cruelty. This is punishment. This is the sort of slavery your husband preached against. Can't you understand?"

Mollie only shook her head. "Father, I married him. At least, John never hits me or teases me. He never calls me plump or ugly, as you did. He doesn't make me walk naked in the garden, as you did. He simply tells me what I am to do, and I obey him."

"Oh, Mollie, I grieve for you. Your mother would, too, if she were alive."

"Father, I will bear John's babies and nurse them. Truly, I have come to cherish the beliefs of John Calvin and John Knox and Dr. Cuthbert Thaddeus Wemyss. He was one of John's friends at Princeton, in fact, his mentor. After serving as a tutor at some of the finest plantations in Virginia, he moved to North Carolina, then, more recently, to Georgia, where he has an academy near the Savannah River."

"I...I am about to be sick," Agnes murmured. "I am sorry. What is that odor? I feel nauseated."

"Probably the sow. She got away from me one day and got into my honey. I chased her for hours through the vineyard and into the next room where she is now. Actually, she's about to have piglets any day now. We may all be nursing together. Maybe Lafayette will be that little child leading us....I must ask John about that verse from Isaiah. But, then, he may disapprove. What do you think, Agnes?"

Then, suddenly, Mollie let out a piercing wail that made the sow respond and Lafayette cry. "Call Nessie....I....it's time...it's....early."

Agnes went for Nessie, and Colin stretched out his waistcoat on the dirt floor. "Here, my child, let me help you lie down. Take some deep breaths now, and push. It's coming. The baby's coming."

Mollie pushed and pushed, screaming, the pain unbearable, unable to hold back. "Father, it hurts..."

He squeezed her hand, and within a few minutes, delivered a baby boy. "Oh, he's a fine boy, my dearie...just look at him! Daughter, I am proud of you. Tis June 20, 1811, and you're a mother; he's decided to come early, this bairn." Colin slapped the baby and turned him upside down, then gave the child to his mother.

"I want to call the baby George Fennell Livingston. Do you like that name?"

"Why I do, indeed. The name is patriotic, it's French Huguenot, and it bears your husband's surname. That is a merry choice, to be certain." And he still rolled his r's.

"Father," she whispered, "I know I've disappointed you, but one day, I will be pretty, and one day, I'll have a beautiful baby girl and name her for

Mamma. I'll call our daughter Cecilia. Please don't worry about us. Before long, John will open a school, and you will realize how brilliant he is. He can't help being stern."

"Sh...rest now. Nessie's here, and she will take care of you." Colin kissed Mollie as the baby sucked away at her breasts.

"Give her all the love you can."

"Take Aggie home. She's about to give birth herself."

Agnes covered her sister-in-law with a torn quilt she'd found near the mother pig. It was a quilt which her grandmother had made so long ago.

As soon as they returned to White Oaks, Agnes went into labor and suffered for hours. She clinched her husband's arms. "Oh, this is so hard, Wash. I...I don't bear babies easily like Mollie." And she wailed through the night.

"Bear down, honey child," Monica said, giving her more thyme tea. "It's comin." She asked Delilah for more cloths and water. Colin finally had to force the baby out, its little feet coming first. "It's June 21, 1811, my darling," Wash said, as he looked at their baby, marveling, and he kissed Agnes. "Try to rest." She smiled through her tears.

"The Lord is my strength and my shield; my heart trusted
in him, and I am helped: therefore my heart greatly rejoiceth;
and with my song will I praise him" (Psalm 28:7).

Book Twelve (1811-1814)

"Did I really have the baby?" Agnes suddenly asked, "I think I'm dreaming...I was crying, and, then...I fell asleep...maybe I'm losing my mind. Oh, I am exhausted."

"You gave birth to a handsome baby boy, my dear Aggie," Colin said, as he gave the child to her. She nursed the baby easily.

"Oh, he's hungry. Isn't he a big boy? Where's Wash?"

"Right here, my love...right here. Monica called for me. And what shall we name him?"

"I want to name him Andrew Washington Bain...do you like that, Wash?"

He nodded and sat on the bed beside her.

"And, Dr. Bain, I want you to be a part of our children's lives. I'm sure Wash will agree. You've delivered two little boys, and you've been right at our sides. Thank you."

Colin held her hands. "Thank you...thank you. You've made me so proud I'm going to whistle."

"Yes, Pa. Do that. And if I had a sheep here on the plantation, why we would pipe in some haggis in honor of little Saint Andrew's birthing," Wash added.

A few weeks later, Mollie brought little George over to meet his double-first cousin and visited with Agnes and the family. "Aggie, we'll want to have our babies baptized."

"We will. Mollie, I want to have lots of babies. Do you?"

"Yes."

Within a few months, Agnes was expecting her second baby. "We'll have sons, my darling," she said to Wash.

"A baby girl would be fine, too, as long as she's as pretty as you are, my darling Aggie."

"And we'll spoil our children and pay Monica to take care of them if she's willing."

The old woman beamed. "I'd be proud to raise yo chillins. I tried to raise you and yo Sissy right. I'm jes sorry I helped her elope with that preacher. I know he's one of God's chillin, but the more I see him, the less I like him. He's just not a happy man. He's miserable, and he act like he want everybody else to be miserable, too. Prince and I rode over to Burnt Bluffs Tuesday past, and we seen him. He was screaming something from Exodus. Mollie's baby's growing same as little Masta Andrew."

When Andrew was nearly fifteen months old, his mother went into labor and, after a long struggle, gave birth to another little boy.

"Let's call him James Jefferson Bain," Wash suggested, as he carried the child about. Do you like that name, Aggie?"

She nodded, then fell asleep, spent, her face drenching with perspiration.

Colin took his son aside. "My boy, I must tell you that having a third child would be very dangerous for Aggie."

"Pa, you're just jealous. Look at you with your long, tangled beard and hair and that fancy cane," Wash laughed.

"No, we almost lost Aggie this time." Delivering the baby, Colin was surprised at how torn Agnes was. "Something brutal must have happened when she gave birth to that baby in France," he thought to himself, but he said nothing. He'd given Aggie his word. "Your beautiful wife nurses easily, but giving birth is difficult for her, very difficult."

Wash finally realized his father was serious. "Thank you. I love Aggie deeply, and I never want to lose her, Pa. I know you understand."

Colin turned away, his eyes swelling with tears. He missed Cecilia, and he had so many regrets. He knew Wash would never have such regrets, for he was kind to Aggie.

"You know, I finally understand what your mother meant when she used to quote the psalmist" he said, turning to his son, 'Keep me, O Lord, from the hands of the wicked; preserve me from the violent man.' I was the wicked, violent man. I used to torment her, and I am deeply sorry."

"She knew you were, Pa. She loved you. She forgave you. Forgive yourself."

Within a few months, everyone knew something was wrong with Jamie. He was yellow, and he didn't respond to treatments. When he was five months old, Jamie died. He was buried at White Oaks Chapel in early February of 1813, not far from Colin's baby boys.

Agnes grieved and became depressed. Colin tried to comfort her. "This is the second baby you have lost."

Agnes talked for a long time one afternoon while Druzie, as she called her little boy, played in the parlor. Colin listened, then began reading to her from Cecilia's prayer book. As he read, Druzie crawled up in his lap and played with his grandfather's beard.

"Oh, Druzie, would you like a Welsh pony and a sheep dog?"

The child clapped his chubby hands.

"You know, I offered to buy a collie for little George, but his father said, 'No.' Aggie, I have trouble believing he's your brother."

Agnes laughed quietly. "So do I. I will always pamper Druzie, Dr. Bain, even when he's grown and married, just as I'm sure Miss Cecilia would have Wash, had she lived. He was her only son. Druzie is mine."

And Wash pampered Aggie. He feared her becoming an invalid as his mother had. Monica kept telling him that the situation was different. "Your ma's was physical from milk fever and that's a long story, but, finally, it was emotional. She died of a broken heart after years and years of humiliation and shame."

Wash listened and gradually figured out his parents' conflicts. "Monica, Nessie and London are coming back to White Oaks because my brother-in-law will no longer pay them. I feel sorry for Sissy, but I tried to warn her."

"I know you did. Will you give Nessie and London wages?"

"Of course I will, Aunt Monica. Why we all grew up together, and Druzie will welcome Lafayette's company. I've never asked you, and I'm changing the subject, but…do you think I shot Numbers and Caleb that afternoon?"

"I don't know. No bodies ever washed up." Monica shook her head. "I want you to free my son, Hebrides, the one yo mammy and me named together."

Wash laughed. "I'll free him. He's never married, has he? And neither has Memnon."

"Memnon's crazy about that silly gal named Antigone, the one what they all calls 'Anteegwine.' She's not right in the head, and I hope he won't marry her, even though they have a son, Josh. Now, she's one whose freedom I wouldn't buy. Of course, she's got a little boy. I don't know whether he's my grandson or not."

Wash listened and remembered all of their discussions about slavery. "By the way, Abbie wrote a letter to me. I need to share it with Sis. Abbie's in Boston and says she has a position as a teacher in a girls' seminary. She sent her love. The tone was happy. Astronomy and drawing are her favorite subjects."

"Do tell. She sho was a pretty baby."

"Who?" Colin asked, walking into the parlor with Druzie. "Stay with Grandpappy a little while. Your mother's resting."

"Oh, Mollie and I had a letter from Abbie, and I've just told Monica that I'll pay Nessie and London to work here on the plantation if they choose. They're coming home from Burnt Bluffs because John refuses to pay them."

"I think I'll go over and help Mollie then. Someone needs to be there with her, don't you think? And maybe Hebrides would enjoy helping out. I'll pay him," Colin volunteered.

"Ma," Druzie called, his blue eyes lighting up. "Can Druzie give the puppy some ham?"

"Yes, sweetheart," Agnes answered, slowly walking into the room. "I couldn't sleep, and, Dr. Bain, you cannot go hobbling around that burned hovel at Burnt Bluffs, and you know it. Why not send Anteegwine over for awhile? She could take her little boy. I'll pay her wages. I don't think my brother can refuse if I say it's a gift, or something like that, do you?"

"I hope not," Wash answered, "and I'll drive Anteegwine over tomorrow and Hebrides if he agrees, and be back for a glass of Madeira with you, Aggie."

"Can Druzie go?" the little boy asked.

"Of course."

The next day at Burnt Bluffs, John was unfriendly, almost rude, to Wash. "I resent your interfering, Brother Wash. My Mollie is a strong woman. In fact, she's with child again. I want a number of children, and my wife can bear them. That's why I married her. I strongly agree with that quotation from the good book: 'Thy wife shall be as a fruitful vine by the sides of thine house: thy children like olive plants around thy table.' My wife is a fruitful vine, and my children are olive plants. Mollie's milk flows easily. She's like the sow in the next room; only Mollie doesn't root. Mollie follows my orders."

Mollie welcomed her brother, then sat quietly on the milk stool, as her brother watched Druzie and George play. "Your little boy's a handsome child, Sissy, but he doesn't smile much."

"No...I make him help me. He doesn't have time for frivolity. Excuse me, Bubba, but I must milk the cow. Would you like to help me?"

"Mollie, I wouldn't know how to do that, but I've brought Hebrides. He's Monica's youngest boy, and he might watch George and Josh. Why don't you tell Anteegwine to do the milking? She's come to help you. Anteegwine is Aggie's gift to you, Sis, and I am paying Hebrides. He's free. We all love you. We want your life to be easier here." He kissed his sister good-bye.

Mollie looked at her brother and smiled as he left.

John followed Wash outside.

"I must have naively, stupidly, anticipated some miraculous change, John. I guess I thought you would change after you married my sister. She deserves far better than this life you give her."

John shrugged his shoulders. "Well, to quote the good book again, 'If she's poor and I am the oppressor, God will break me into pieces, as the psalmist has written,' but I think not, for I am obeying the commandments. You are not! You have actually committed adultery, for my sister was once married."

"John, you are a madman. I do not care. I love Aggie dearly, as I had hoped you would my twin sister. Look in the mirror and see yourself face to face."

"You're mocking Paul, and the Lord will smite you down, Brother Wash," John prophesied.

"No, I am only telling the truth. Surely you know that when you share your life with someone else, you have to change and grow together in a new light, shedding your selfish ways. God knows that I have learned to do that. My sister has never, ever, been selfish. I pity her. She simply transferred my father's unkindnesses to her onto you. That's all she's ever known in a man. I must tell my sister that she can come back home."

Wash picked up Druzie, and they found Mollie milking the cow. "Sis, you can come back home to White Oaks."

"No, I will not forsake my husband and little child."

"But he little George looks like a sad grown-up. Mollie, your son is just a little older than two, and he's withered. He looks like an old man. Do you feed him?"

"Hush, Wash," John screamed, "and leave my home. I will pay the Negress and her boy child, Josh. Hebrides can stay, too. I will not accept my sister's gift, or yours."

"Please talk to Anteegwine. She's not the smartest darkie we ever had at White Oaks."

Mollie smiled at her brother. "No, you've not changed."

On January 6, 1814, Mollie gave birth to a baby girl with light brown hair and crystal blue eyes. "I will call her Cecilia Fears. I always promised to name my first daughter for my dear mother, and I will call the child Celie for short. And I want her and George to be baptized together," she whispered to her husband.

John patted her hand. "That is a beautiful name, my Mollie. That's fine with me. We'll have the children baptized at White Oaks Chapel. I imagine you would prefer that to Swann Creek." Mollie nodded.

"My boy, he ain't neba been baptiz," Anteegwine said, as she took the baby girl. "Huh beez a purty babee, Misses Mollie, but huh ain't rite netha. She dun got three brestes. Huh look like a witch. I beez 'feared."

"Hush," Mollie said, as she looked with a mixture of love and hate at the naked baby. "Anteegwine, you're going to help me take care of her and little George, and you are not going to tell anyone about my baby's breasts. God will heal her. Do you understand? A baby isn't going to hurt you."

"Yessum…yessum, I sho doz…I tend to de boys."

Mollie nursed her baby and went to sleep, praying John would not be harsh to their child because of her deformity.

"But it is good for me to draw near to God:
I have put my trust in the Lord God, that I
May declare all thy works" (Psalm 73:28).

Book Thirteen (1814-1822)

At few weeks later at White Oaks Chapel, Druzie, George, and Celie were baptized by a preacher from Essex. Colin felt his granddaughter's deformity when he held her, but he said nothing.

"I've said too much in the past," he murmured to himself. "I have hurt too many people. I can only pray now."

George noticed his sister's three nipples one summer afternoon when she was lying on the pallet. He squeezed them over and over again, laughing. "I can squeeze Cewee." Mollie ignored him and the baby's crying and continued sewing until she heard Celie screaming.

Reluctantly putting down a shirt she was mending, Mollie got up and slapped George. "Hush, George. You should be ashamed of yourself. Ask God's forgiveness, and pray to God to make your sister normal."

"What does mean normal, Ma?"

"Sh...sh...you might disturb your father."

The daily rituals at Burnt Bluffs continued, and after a visit there, Colin told his daughter-in-law, "Mollie is so accustomed to her life at Burnt Bluffs that she doesn't realize how dreary it really is. I am concerned about little Celie and George. George is malnourished and somber. I don't like the way he plays with his sister's breasts."

Colin had seen Mollie scrub floors, tend the garden, slop hogs, milk the cow, make soap, feed the chickens, and nurse Celie. "Anteegwine cooks and tells stories to the children. She takes them for long walks through the barren land while their father bellows forth about the Bible and worships in the ruined church originally called Mulberry Bluffs Chapel. My daughter was so excited over discovering the name of the first church. While she was showing me the little volume of session minutes she'd found under some bricks, John walked in and snatched the book from her and said that 'wives were to be submissive and not interested in worldly lore.' He didn't want her to become joyful, but it was fine for him to make a discovery."

"I'm so sorry to hear that," Agnes said, "so sorry he humiliates my sister-in-law."

"He does, for he said to me, 'I will tell you, Dr. Bain, that I found remnants of the old chair which Dr. Boucher used, and I have learned more about the beliefs of the French Huguenots and Covenanters.' Mollie smiled, but said nothing. She's learned not to ask John anything. She seems to keep the children quiet and rebukes them if they seemed naughty. Aggie, it's very somber there. It's a sad household."

Mollie's children soon grew bored with Anteegwine's stories, especially George. "If she's going to tell us about the devil and his demons, she could at least make them real, couldn't she, Sis."

Celie shuddered. "Anteegwine scares me."

George asked his sister, Josh, and Hebrides to play with him in the old vineyard. "If you won't pull my little titties," Celie answered. "That hurts."

When Mollie wasn't paying attention, the children wandered away from the hovel and built a fort from scraps near the old stable. "I don't like Pa," George said. "He never plays with us. When I ask him to play marbles with me, he just says that games are an abomination and tells me to recite 'Work for the Night Is Coming.' All we ever do is work."

"Come on. Let's play hide and seek," Celie called, running down the path. Then, sometimes Hebrides would take the children all into the woods and tell stories about the animals and fairy people that lived there. George especially liked these times because Hebrides had a way with words, and he would tell George just to smile at his father but then to do whatever he wanted. "That doesn't work, Hebrides. You'll see."

Except for such afternoons of play, the children's only excitement was an occasional wave from children who now came to their father for tutoring. If children did not do well at old Dr. Gavin Dunn's academy, now run primarily by his son, Dr. Wylie Dunn, they came to the Reverend John Livingston for help in the three R's.

Mollie made clothing from leftover clothes. Sometimes the children were half naked, for John never offered anything new for them to wear. Many winter nights, they nearly froze, for John never built a fire, and Antigone didn't know how. Mollie never asked Hebrides to do anything. There was something about the boy which made her uncomfortable, and she didn't know why.

Mollie finally said there was no fire because she'd forgotten to go across the fields to White Oaks for wood. "So you'll learn to make do. That's what poor people have to do, and I don't have any money to spare." Mollie taught the children to live off sweet potatoes, greens, apples, and cornmeal. Occasionally, they had a piece of meat from the hogs. John sold all the eggs and most of the hogs. There were never cakes or cookies.

If her father came calling, Mollie threw an old quilt over the children. "Daughter, you pretend too well. I am sorry. I know what is going on, and I have brought clothes for the children. They do not have to dress like paupers," Colin said one afternoon when he surprised them all with a visit.

"John will not like that, Pa."

"Well, I don't care. Just tell him that the clothing was an unexpected surprise. My little granddaughter deserves some frocks, and George should have something special, too." The children looked suspiciously at their grandfather, until he began laughing and throwing little plaid balls Aggie had sent. And, of course, Druzie, comfortable with anyone, began talking and picking up objects. "What is this, Cudn Celie?"

"Why don't you come play with me at White Oaks? Lafayette and I go hunting and fishing, and we've learned to play a game called rounders on the front lawn. And croquet."

"Who's Lafayette?" Celie asked.

"He's Nessie's child," Colin answered. "George, remember him? Surely, you do, Hebrides. After all, he would be your nephew."

"We dun most growed up together," Hebrides laughed. "Tell dat boy be good."

George nodded. "We'd like to come, but you'd have to ask Ma."

"We'll ask your father, George. Now run along outside, and don't bother me."

Colin looked at his granddaughter running about half naked with the boys. "Mollie, the children deserve better."

"Father, do you remember making me walk naked near the garden? This is no different."

"Oh, Mollie…please don't punish little Celie for what I did to you. I have apologized again and again. I am ashamed. The sun was something physicians were recommending for pimples in those days. Mollie, you had beautiful dresses. Clothe your little girl. I mean, please don't go along with all of that so-called naturalness Rousseau writes about in France. Celie shouldn't be running around half-naked with all these boys, you know."

"Father, clothes are simply riches which moths corrupt. You know that yourself. You, of all people, should not be telling me not to let my daughter go naked when you're the one who made me strip."

"Oh, it has come back to haunt me in my old age, Daughter, but if nothing else, the boys shouldn't be looking at Celie's little breasts. Oh, I grieve for you, my dearie. And if you don't start teaching the children, I will insist on sending them to school. Would you like for me to discuss this with your husband?"

"Please do. He makes all of the decisions. You know that, Father. My job is simply to obey him."

John agreed for Colin to send the children to school. "I don't have time to teach my children. I am too busy tutoring and doing my own studies. Mollie teaches them more than you realize, Dr. Bain."

From that afternoon on, Colin made plans for the boys' schooling. He took Druzie and George to Dr. Dunn's School and began teaching Celie himself. He told her stories, taught her to play the psaltery, and played games with all of them. Wash took the boys fishing and hunting, Lafayette and Joshua, too.

Agnes sang and showed Celie how to embroider. "Oh, your grandmother would be so proud of you and your great grandmother, too. I understand that she did fancy stitches and made shoes and hats as well."

Celie loved to spend time with her Aunt Agnes and Monica at White Oaks. It was such a happy house, and she longed to live there. She adored her grandfather and often climbed up into his lap. Playing with his long white beard, Celie would beg her grandfather to roll his r's and tell her another story or sing a song. Colin always did, and she would fall asleep in his arms. Sometimes he played croquet with her on the lawn.

Those happy times for the children ended in the fall of 1822, when their grandfather, riding the large bay horse with a star on his face, was jumping a fence at the Cameron's steeplechase. He missed and died instantly.

Never really wanting his children around him, John decided to send George to Dr. Wemyss' school in Georgia, and Druzie, wishing to be with his cousin, begged to go, too.

Wash and Agnes agreed. Mollie kept Celie at home and taught her to read and write. Celie dreaded the lessons, and she became afraid of her mother and Anteegwine.

When Anteegwine called Celie a little witch because of her three small breasts, Mollie would search the scriptures, insisting that her child was not a witch. Antigone called the middle breast a 'big chiggarbump' and asked Celie if it itched. Once Mollie tried to burn it off, but Celie cried so much her mother stopped. "Hush that screaming. Your father will hear you. I know what to do. I'll show it to him. After all, you're his child, too."

John insisted that his own daughter was an abomination in the sight of the Lord and vowed one day to cut the third breast off. "This generation is paying for the sins of the fathers," and Mollie thought of her own mother. If Celie ever cried, Mollie gave her a whipping, and Anteegwine laughed. Celie longed to run away. She missed Druzie and George, even though George himself was often a big tease. The only people Celie could talk to at all were Josh and Hebrides. They were kind and listened. Celie spent as much time with them as she could.

One afternoon, they heard wagon wheels churning up the lane. When she realized it was Monica, Celie jumped up and down. "Monica, take me with you to White Oaks, please."

"I am, honey. Memnon drove me over to invite you to come for a tea party—-just you and me, and if the boys want to visit for a little while, why that's alright with me, too." Mollie asked her husband who reluctantly gave permission.

Monica served beaten biscuits and lemonade and gave Celie a little quilt. "I made it for you, and I made you a baby dollie, too. Every little girl needs a doll, and I want you to remember that a piece of yo grand mammy's wedding gown is in the quilt." Celie didn't know what to say. She'd never had a doll to hold or love.

"Can I keep them, Monica?"

"Course you can. They foh you, honey." And Monica sang to her and told her stories about Georgetown and her grandmother. "I want you to be like her when you grow up."

"I wish you were my mother, Monica. Mamma is so mean to me. Half the time she doesn't give me anything to wear, and they laugh at my breasts. I can't help it." Celie began crying, and Monica rocked her, just as she had her grandmother so many years ago. "I want to come live at White Oaks, and I want Druzie and my brother to come home…Monica, Burnt Bluffs is so gloomy."

Monica sighed, for she could only imagine. "Play the psaltery for me before we go back, will you?"

And Celie played the songs Colin and Aunt Agnes had taught her.

"Where's Aunt Agnes?"

"I believe Massa Wash took her for a boat ride on the river. He'll take you one day, too, and you know, it won't be too long before Christmas. The boys will be coming home then. Let's look forward to that time, and remember I love you. We all do, and so does God. When you get tired or upset, say a little prayer to him. He's always there for you." Monica read her comforting passages from scripture which the little girl had never heard.

PSALTERY AT WHITE OAKS

When George and Druzie finally came for Christmas, Druzie insisted that his cousins come to White Oaks to spend Christmas Day. Celie and George could hardly believe their parents gave permission.

George had nothing but contempt for his father and absolutely no respect for his mother when he came home from Dr. Wemyss' Academy. He hated his parents and told Celie and his aunt and uncle exactly why.

"Father does nothing but write and shout down in that burned chapel, and all mother does is slop hogs, mend clothes, milk the cows, and criticize. Whatever that crazy father tells her to do, she does it. They've both threatened to cut off my sister's little breast. They're insane, and I detest that Dr. Wemyss. Druzie and I, like all the other boys there, had to build huts to live in. Dr. Wemyss is a squatty, red-haired man....he looks a little like old Dunn, but he's stockier. And he's always carrying a hickory. If you can't recite properly, why he whips you. The boys from Charleston and Beaufort make fun of our clothes and the way we talk. I mean, I can understand why they laugh at my homespun attire, but not at Druzie's. Druzie's clothes are fancy. Except for an occasional picnic on the Savannah River, we work all the time. It's drudgery. We work in the fields and eat potato porridge. If it weren't for the cakes and cookies Monica sends us, why I'd be thin as a cattail. And there are exercises, too, and there's always chapel or church. Oh, I hate that place. I'd rather be dead than have to go back."

"Is it that bad, son?" Wash asked.

"Yes, it is. I hate being there, and Dr. Wemyss is harder on George. I don't know why. Maybe Uncle John told him to be that way."

"I pray every night to come to White Oaks," Celie said.

"Just this morning, I described my school days to mother," George answered, "and she said, 'George, hush, and go ring that rooster's neck for dinner.' When I tried to talk to Father, he told me I was a sinner who did not deserve to live. One day, I am going to leave and never come back. And I'm going to take Hebrides with me. I'm teaching him how to write, and he tells some of the best stories."

"Our father was certainly never the way my brother is," Aunt Agnes explained. "True, he was stern, but he never raised his voice, and he always assured us of God's love. I fear my brother worships this Dr. Wemyss."

"Oh, I hate that man. And that scowl makes him look like Mephistopheles," George continued. They all laughed.

"Why don't you boys try to stick it out a little longer. Try to make good marks, and I'll plan to make other arrangements for your schooling after that and attempt to persuade your Uncle John. How about that?" Wash suggested.

"Let's enjoy Christmas Day," Aunt Agnes insisted. "Memnon and Josh will be shooting fireworks off tonight on the river, and we've persuaded your mother and father for you to stay with us for at least two days."

Celie spent her time with Monica and Aunt Agnes, and the boys played with Lafayette.

The night before his departure for Georgia for the spring term, George confided in his sister that he discovered the pleasure of yellow jasmine. "Actually, it numbs me. Try it sometime, and write to me, will you?"

"I promise."

As the boys were leaving, Celie clung to her brother so long that John separated them and threw her against one of the stumps. Celie began crying.

"That's incest, Daughter. Get up right now before I whip you, and go help your mother. Then, ask God's forgiveness. Certainly, you know you were conceived in sin."

George rode away in the coach with Druzie, wondering how anybody, especially a baby, was born in sin. Deep down, George believed God's spirit was in the flowers, trees, rivers, and streams, in people who imagined. Whatever flourished and bloomed with love was God. Whatever did not was not born of God. George was convinced that his parents were not God's children. "They do nothing to love or inspire others, Druzie," he said, as the coach rambled over the dusty roads toward Georgia. "My father is an agent of Satan. How could he ever think of my little sister as sinful?"

Druzie shrugged his shoulders. "I can't imagine. I love Cuz Celie. One day I am going to marry her."

"You sound prophetic," George teased. "Pa would say that's incest, wouldn't he?

"I don't care what Uncle John says," Druzie answered, lowering his voice and quoting a psalm. 'Behold, how good and pleasant it is for brethren to dwell together in unity.' That's what I believe anyway. Besides, Cuz, we're all three saints. Did you know that? I'm St. Andrew, you're St. George, and Celie is St. Cecilia."

"Druzie, I'm glad you're my double-first cousin and my best friend."

"God be merciful to us, and bless us; and cause his face to shine upon us" (Psalm 67:1).

Book Fourteen (1823-1825)

Troubled over the boys' stories about their treatment at Dr. Wemyss' school, Wash and Agnes decided to travel to Georgia. The day before their departure, Celie was visiting, and she was so excited to see Uncle Wash that she ran and jumped on his back. "Carry me piggy back," she squealed.

He did not mind obliging her, for he loved his niece as if she were his daughter. But when Uncle Wash stood up to carry her, his back snapped. He winced with pain.

"Oh, I'm sorry, Uncle Wash. Please don't tell Ma and Pa," Celie cried.

"Our secret. Even Aunt Aggie won't know, but we'll have to wait to make the trip to Georgia."

Rheumatism set in, and Wash struggled to get around the plantation. The next months were grueling for him. He often stayed in bed and drank sassafras tea to ease the pain, along with various poultices and ointments.

Not until time for graduation exercises months later was he able to make the trip to Georgia in the ancient coach with the family. Old as he was, Prince insisted on driving.

"You payin me, and I want to see dem boys. Sho do." Mollie and John accepted Wash's invitation and made plans to travel to Georgia.

"But we won't go to see the boys without Celie and Hebrides," Aunt Agnes insisted, when John had said that his daughter could not join them.

"She might get ideas of marriage when she sees all the young men," John protested.

"Rubbish, Bubba, and you know it," Agnes answered. "Shame on you, John, for being so negative all of the time and for denying your children the pleasures of life."

Deep down, though, Celie knew why her father didn't want her to go. He wanted her all to himself. More than once, John had fondled his daughter and lain with her behind the old cabin. Yet when Celie had tried to tell her mother,

Mollie always told her to hush. "You ought to be ashamed. No man's going to enjoy those, except somebody in a carnival."

After that, Celie kept these fears and thoughts to herself and tried to avoid her father. Occasionally, she told Hebrides. "I have to tell somebody," she wept one day, and he promised to stay with her whenever possible.

So they all crowded into the coach and journeyed to Georgia where they began to see what the boys had tried so desperately to tell them.

Known for his wit, highest marks in recitation, and geniality, Druzie was to deliver the address at the graduation ceremony, and George, often hailed "The Wemyss Thespian" because he entertained the boys with endless satires on his father and Dr. Wemyss, was to give a short presentation. However, both students, to their parents' disappointment, were too sick to perform or walk across the stage for their diplomas.

"Where are the boys?" Agnes asked.

"I don't know, my darling. I'll hobble around and find out."

But Celie knew where the boys were. She'd listened to her brother's descriptions of the hut where he lived with Druzie. She knew the location and would take the family there. Though her father bellowed against the idea of his daughter leading her own father, she led the way.

"How did you know?" John asked.

"I always listen to whatever my brother and Cudn Druzie tell me. As I listened to their stories, I pictured the school, the church, and the huts, the fields and woods around."

"Don't be thinking you're a prophetess," John said. "You're not that child leading the animals, as prophesied."

"Pa, don't...please don't hurt me for showing the way."

George and Druzie lay on pallets in the dark hut. George twisted in pain, and Druzie could barely see. He was almost blind, so an ophthalmologist later confirmed, from a fever.

Much as he hated his father, George had written several letters and addressed them to the Reverend John Livingston, Burnt Bluffs, South Carolina, begging his father to ask Uncle Wash to come for Druzie. John had looked at the letters, then burned them immediately. "Rubbish," he always muttered to himself, pounding the broken pulpit in the ruined chapel. "Nothing should interfere with my words to God, surely not requests from my own son who has disobeyed me."

"Celie," Druzie called. "Do I hear your voice?"

Agnes was shocked when she leaned down to kiss her son.

"Mamma, you didn't know?"

"Know what, sweetheart?"

"That I'm blind. George wrote letter after letter to Uncle John telling him to come for us."

"Pa, did you not receive my letters? Didn't you tell Uncle Wash and Aunt Aggie and my mother?

"Of course, I received the letters, George, but I burned them. I knew that whatever you asked for was foolish."

"You've never given me anything but a scorpion, ever."

When George tried to stand, his legs went numb. Celie sat beside him on the pallet, for Mollie wouldn't. She stood in the doorway, unable to look at her son or nephew.

Wash was furious that he'd not been notified.

"Pa," Druzie said, "I also asked Dr. Wemyss to write to you all for me and tell you I had a fever and couldn't see. That was after the boating accident. I don't guess he ever wrote you. George wrote to Uncle John. We both did the best we could to let you know we were sick. The only medicine I ever got was something from an old Indian woman. Dr. Wemyss did not believe I was sick. He accused me of just not wanting to recite my lessons...I believe it was Cicero or Virgil that day, so he thrashed me with that hickory he always carried, even when I had a fever and couldn't see...I was lying on this pallet, and he whipped me 'til I bled. The woman rubbed me with mulberry leaves to stop the bleeding and gave George something for pain, until Dr. Wemyss sent her away and told George the pain was all in his head. Uncle John, why didn't you at least show my father George's letters?"

"I told you that I've never believed anything my son ever said."

Agnes sat on Druzie's pallet. "Darling, tell me what happened." She held her son's hand.

"Let George tell you. I almost died, Mamma."

"Cuz and I went fishing on the river one afternoon in the early spring following an examination. I was a little tipsy, but Druzie wasn't. He never drank anything. Well, it began to get dark, and the boat tipped over. Druzie couldn't swim, and neither could I. The Charleston boys who made fun of our clothing had vowed we didn't know how to fish. That's one reason we went. Druzie got tired of their insults, and we were going to prove we could fish. After all, Grandfather taught us how. Well, we took Reuben, one of the slaves who keeps the school clean, and a classmate, Neilly Dulligan, from the mountains. When the boat tipped over, Neilly was able, finally, to get hold of

Druzie and pull him ashore. Reuben and Neilly took Druzie to school and begged Dr. Wemyss to come help me, but your old friend, Dr. Wemyss, never came. He beat Reuben and Neilly and threw Druzie on the pallet. I held onto the boat for a long time and finally made it ashore. I froze there in my wet clothes I can't remember why I waited on the shore for so long. I kept thinking somebody would help me get the boat out."

"Why does Dr. Wemyss dislike you so much, George?" Wash asked.

"Because he's a troublemaker," John answered, glaring from his son to his nephew.

"No, Father, you are wrong. I was sometimes in trouble, but, more than that, I was always the winner in those debates we had nearly every night by candlelight. I was logical, rational, and I could pick apart whatever was not a well-constructed argument. Wemyss was jealous. He always wanted the Charleston boys to win. All Wemyss said to me was 'Boy, your father will be so embarrassed when he finds out about your behavior. If your cousin has gone blind, it is your own fault, and God will punish both of you.' After that, I didn't care anymore. I limped around, trying to help Druzie."

Mollie finally sat down beside her son and shoved Celie to the floor, but he pushed away. "It's too late, Mother. I tried to tell you so many times, but you wouldn't hear me. All those times when I was a little boy and just asked you to love me and play with me, you wouldn't. Instead, you scrubbed the floor and did whatever that crazy man who calls himself a minister of Jesus told you to do. You made Sissy go around half naked. We were cold and hungry. And you call yourself a Christian woman. We weren't even allowed to have eggs, only scorpions. Pa sold all the eggs to make money for his books. The first time Sissy ever had cookies was the time Aunt Monica invited her for teacakes at White Oaks. I hate you and Father. Please don't touch me. I want Celie and Hebrides."

Wash had heard enough. He was disgusted. "I have nothing but contempt for you, John, and for this Dr. Wemyss and…and, most of all, for myself for believing in you. I should never have trusted your judgment. Druzie, I am sorry, and I can only ask your forgiveness, yours, too, George. Why? Why, Mollie, did I ever allow you to marry this worm who calls himself a child of God." Deep down, of course, he knew why Mollie had yearned to marry John, and he said no more.

Agnes tried to console her husband, but at the time, he simply couldn't accept it. He could not forgive himself as he saw his son lying sightless on the pallet. "I won't go to that graduation supper which Dr. and Mrs. Wemyss are giving in their home. The thought of breaking bread with such a man is disgusting, especially when Druzie was the honored graduate and our nephew was to perform in the historical drama on the lawn."

"Druzie, can you see anything?" Agnes asked.

"Only a little. Mamma, take me home. I don't want to be here anymore. I hate it here."

"So do I," George said. "Why do we have to wait? Surely not to honor the cowardly, august Dr. Wemyss or my father."

"We will leave at once, George," Wash said.

"Do you know that Druzie and I were even whipped again on Good Friday?" George continued. "I'm sure old Wemyss couldn't bring himself to admit that to you, Father. Rather symbolic whippings, don't you think?"

"No, he did not write me anything, Son."

Just before they left for White Oaks and Burnt Bluffs, Wash confronted Dr. Wemyss whose only explanation was that he simply never believed George. "And the thrashings were verily to teach the boys a lesson, to encourage them to tell the truth, and to be good examples to others in the eyes of Almighty God."

"Amen," John said, his eyes meeting his old mentor's. "Mollie, you and I will ride home in a wagon I've arranged to rent. Celie and Hebrides can walk behind."

"Celie's riding with us," Druzie shouted."And so is Cuz George and Hebrides. My cousin risked his own life to save mine."

Wash insisted Druzie would see the finest doctors in Charleston and in Philadelphia, but Druzie answered, "I just want to go to White Oaks. One day I will be able to see again. I'm sure of it, and I can always ride Nellie, Natas' colt. I'll always remember how to ride, even to the hunts, and I can run the grist mill."

Agnes clasped her son's hands. "Let's go home to White Oaks."

Druzie could forgive, but George could not, would not. The wounds were too deep. "Father, do forgive me, for I may not know what I do," he said, crossing himself.

John slapped George. "Shame. 'The Lord will not hold him guiltless who taketh His name in vain.'"

George hated his mother and father and turned more and more to laudanum which he managed to secure in one way or another from Barnie Dunn, old Dr.Gavin Dunn's youngest son. And, of course, Celie gathered yellow jasmine, which grew wild, even at Burnt Bluffs in the spring, and gave it to George.

"Let not the water flood overflow me, neither let the deep swallow
me up, and let not the pit shut her mouth upon me" (Psalm 69:15).

Book Fifteen (1826-1828)

At White Oaks, Druzie surprised his parents by remaining active, for Hebrides stayed with him and decided to go back and forth between the plantations. "Afta all, I'z free now, and I'z heah for dem boys. I ain't gwine marry, and I likes strumming the banjo Misses Cecilia giv me one Christmas before she died."

He taught Druzie to play the banjo, and they rode and practiced shooting in the woods. "Some things you don't ever forget, Mamma, and firing a pistol's one of them. Besides, One day I'll begin to see more. I still see a little bit now."

"Are you certain you don't want to see an ophthalmologist in Charleston, Druzie? There are some fine doctors there."

"I don't....I don't like to be confined or have people hovering around me, pitying me."

Agnes was glad Druzie couldn't see her tears. She adored her only son and grieved over his blindness, blaming herself for ever being persuaded to send the boys to the school in Georgia.

If he worried, Wash never showed it. "I can't," he would sometimes tell Agnes. "We must both always encourage Druzie to do as much as he will, to be as independent as possible. I'm glad he wants to run the grist mill." He can, you know. He will, my sweet. Try not to worry." And Wash took Agnes in his arms and held her as she quietly wept. "I understand, Aggie. I do."

Druzie sometimes sensed his mother's anxieties and comforted her himself. "Mamma, you could drink a little Madeira with Pa or some chamomile tea. I might even join you. Please don't worry. I'll be fine. White Oaks is my home. Besides, I have the psaltery and Father's portion of the pirate's gold given to my grandmother."

"You do, indeed," Wash said. "Only your not having the diploma bothers me. I would send you to Mount Hebron, but now that your grandfather's passed away, I think the experience would be different. Much as I dislike the Dunns, I was thinking of having you enroll in their academy. Of course, Prince would drive you in the coach. No boarding at all!"

"As if reading Latin and Greek will help me run the mill or understand Nellie," Druzie laughed, "but if that will please you, I yield. But only if Cudn George goes....and only if Hebrides takes us. I won't go alone."

So Wash prevailed upon his brother-in-law to allow George to finish his education with Druzie. "I will pay your son's tuition. Please understand, John, that I dislike the Dunns as much as you do. I simply want the boys to finish their schooling. Perhaps in another year or so, we might enroll them at the South Carolina College if they are interested."

When his father ordered his son to gather his books and prepare to attend the academy to finish his education, George laughed. "You old fool. You don't really think quoting Homer and St. Augustine will diminish my pain, do you? You're more of a fanatic than I believed. Whoever heard of learning anything from the Dunns. They're dung, Pa."

"George, hush. God will strike you for calling me a fool." John slapped his son's aching thighs.

At enrollment time, Wash asked Dr. Gavin Dunn "around ninety-five years old," according to members of Brick Tower Church, and his assistant, Dr. Wylie Dunn, to teach the boys. "No whippings at all. Do we understand one another?"

Gavin nodded.

"But you may certainly whip my son if he is insubordinate," John said.

"My youngest son, Barnie, now a medical doctor, knows all about whippings and physical exercise."

Wash asked where Barnie received his medical degrees.

"He read under Dr. Tucker in Millsborough. Barnie delivers babies, sees some patients, and prescribes medicine. He's a good doctor even if I say so myself. He invented a special remedy for his mother's rheumatism."

"Well, that's mighty fine," John said, "and if George gives you any trouble, whip him, and advise me, so that I might thrash him again."

"If you ever so much as raise a hand against my child, we will square off in a duel, and I will win. Do you understand? My father had nothing but contempt for you, Dunn. Even though I've never exactly known the cause, I am inclined to agree with him. Do we understand each other, Dr. Dunn?"

The old man nodded. "He will receive a good education, and I understand that the boys are not boarding."

"That is correct, and Hebrides will be driving them each day."

George and Druzie were delighted to be together again with their childhood friends: John Burns Hamilton and Llwellyn Jacobs. Of course, they detested Barnie who forced the students to call him "Dr. Barnabie" and who especially enjoyed taunting George. "That Livingston boy's my gopher" Druzie was sure he sometimes heard Barnie say.

Knowing George's body ached most of the time, Barnie would sometimes whisper, "Tell you what…I'll give you some laudanum if you'll answer my riddles for the class. A covenant or not?"

"Agreed," George said.

And George never minded making a fool of himself for a little laudanum to ease his neuralgia.

Back at Burnt Bluffs, Celie was miserable. Even though she was nearly fourteen and suffered terrible menstrual cramps, her mother made her daughter plow. When George came home in the late afternoon, he would find his sister crying. "Ma called me a witch, and Anteegwine laughed at me. Pa took my dress off in the chapel and fondled me. Bubba, let's run away. We could hide in the tower at White Oaks. We could find medicine in Grandpa's cabinets to ease your pain, I'm sure. Hebrides would help us."

"We will one day. I hate the Dunns and those stupid military drills we do. I'd rather write poetry about the full moon or the falling stars. Sis, I don't know how Druzie tolerates the school."

"Bubba, Druzie has always been loved and pampered. We've never received any affection, ever, except by Grandpa, Monica, Aunt Agnes and Uncle Wash, and Cudn Druzie himself, and Hebrides and Josh. Sometimes I lie awake at night thinking about us. Then, I pray. God answers my little prayers, and I fall asleep. George, do you ever count the stars?"

"All the time, Sis. I describe them to Hebrides, and we talk. I tell him about the demons in trees, and…he understands. I love Hebrides, Sis. Pa and Ma, they wouldn't understand. Do you?"

"Yes, Bubba, it's alright."

He hugged her, then limped to the stable and wrote until his mother called him to supper and told Celie to go slop the hogs."

"Ma, I'm so tired tonight. My breasts are aching, and my stomach is swollen. It's that time, you know, and I just don't feel good. Why did Father take off my clothes and make me lie with him in the chapel. Why, Mamma?"

Opening the family Bible, Mollie ignored her daughter's question.

"Ma, please answer my question."

"Because your father believes your breasts betoken evil in your body. He must believe that labor will work it out of you and take away that deformity. Now, do as I say, and please do not bother me again. I am reading what your father asked me to read about family life."

"But, Ma, lying with my father is not labor. It is incest, isn't it?"

"Hush, child. Don't say such things."

"I think Jesus loves me, don't you? I don't believe God wants my father to whip me. Ma, did somebody hurt you? Is that why you don't love me? Tell me why you've never loved me, so that I can understand and help you love me. Would it help for me to try to love you more?"

Celie looked at her mother, her hair now white, pulled back severely from her wrinkled, pock-marked face, her ears crusty.

"Your father would call your questions digging under," Mollie answered, pulling up her daughter's dress. "Don't you see how hideous you look? No man would want a body like that. You'll be lucky if you can be some family's maid. Now go see what's delaying your brother."

John heard his daughter whimpering when he came in and hit her again.

"If you persist in disobeying, I will lock you in the slave cabin. Do you understand, Daughter?"

She ran from the hovel and found George and Hebrides asleep on the rope bed near the stalls in the stable, George holding an empty bottle.

"Where'd you get that rum?"

"Down at the free Negroes' still way down in the woods. I buy it...Sis, you don't really think I could endure my pain without something, do you?"

"I don't know," she answered, sinking to the floor, her head against the bed post. "Help me, God. George, I'm going to White Oaks tonight."

"You can't. Please wait another day or so. If I can get some laudanum from that idiotic Barnie Dunn, maybe I'll feel strong enough to join you. We could stay with Uncle Wash and Aunt Agnes. Monica and Druzie would like for us to come, I am sure. Sis," his eyes brightening, "I'll bet there's leftover medicine for pain up in the tower from Grandfather Colin. Hebrides saw Pa whipping you."

Hebrides said he was afraid. "I wanna go to White Oaks to stay at my Sissy's, but can't leave your Bubba...we're too close, you know."

Celie nodded.

"Will Druzie understand?"

"Of course, he understands. He knows everything, and he doesn't care. Bubba, imitate the Dunns the way you sometimes do…so I will laugh. If Pa thinks I'm still crying, he'll beat me again. He really is crazy."

And she wiped her eyes when George stood and started mimicking old Dr. Gavin Dunn. "Even though that bastard must be 100 years old, he stands up there and pounds his gavel, then recites, 'Thou Shalt Not,' and he always looks right at me as if I'm some terrible sinner. Oh, I detest the Dunns, Sis. I'd love to fire a pistol at just one of them. Some of the boys say Barnie's father committed incest."

"What do you mean by that? You're talking out of your head, George. You're drunk."

"No…the boys say Barnie's pa raped his own baby sister, Anna Catherine, before she married Grandfather."

"So grandpa's first wife was raped before she married Grandfather? Is that what you are saying, Bubba? That seems like nonsense. Is that what you're saying?"

George shrugged his shoulders. "That's what I said, Sis. Try to get some sleep."

"Can I stay here in the stable? If I go to the house, Ma or Pa will hurt me. It's going to rain tonight. Maybe you won't have to go to school tomorrow."

"Sis, now you know that will not happen."

The next day after exercises, George asked Barnie for some laudanum. "Please, I'm in a lot of pain."

Barnie laughed. "You're always in a lot of pain. My head hurts today, but I'm not complaining. Besides, George Livingston, why should I keep giving you medicine? You never do anything in return." About fifty years old himself, Barnie looked like all the Dunns and like old Wemyss, red-hair graying, gray eyes reddening, glaring, bushy brows, bulky bodies, prancing with canes, each boasting, each struggling to make everyone else feel inferior.

"I've used all of the herbs and teas I can….and the alcohol. I just need something stronger."

"So what will you offer me in exchange? I don't ever do anything anymore for free. I'm not a disciple. I only attend church and pretend. Surely you, of all people, understand. That's what your father did."

"I do, but I've nothing to give you."

"We've all heard the rumor that your grandmother received a bag of gold from some pirate who was kin to her husband, your grandfather, the late Dr. Colin Macaulay Bain. So where is the gold?"

"It's not mine to give. My mother gave her share to my father, the most fanatical human who ever lived. You know that. Please, Barnie, help me out one last time. I've answered your silly riddles. I've never done anything to harm you."

"Your pain came from lingering in clothes that froze. And who made the decision to stay in wet clothes on the river? You…you…you! You brought about your own neuralgia. Jesus didn't. So don't ask for his mercy."

George shrugged his shoulders. "I couldn't…it was that overwhelming sense of responsibility I felt, believe it or not."

"You, responsible? You expect me to believe you have a conscience?"

"Yes, something of one! I really do."

Barnie roared. "If you did, you wouldn't be sleeping with that Negro boy."

George slapped Barnie, and the two got into a fight, and George succeeded with the help of Hebrides in throwing Barnie on the ground. All the boys clapped and cheered.

"Thirty laps around the fields, and that means you, too, Druzie Bain. Georgie Boy's lover can lead you."

"Oh, Dunn, if you knew the way we lived, you wouldn't mock us," George shouted, as he began limping, "Hear what my father saith, Dr. Dunn… 'Mollie, thou shalt not eat a second helping of cornbread, for you would be setting a bad example for George and Celie.' Yes, while the old bastard eats meat, we must enjoy the potatoes Anteegwine burns and the beans so boiled down with fat back you wouldn't know we were eating anything like green beans. Why, the hogs eat better than we do…and then Ma's pock marks only redden more when I remind her of how ridiculous it all is. We live in a crazy household."

"Well, so do I, but I am not bitter, George. Aren't you ashamed?"

"No…I'm not. I hate you, Barnie. You've become like your old man and mine… The only difference is that neither can do anything for me, except scream, and screaming does not ease my pain. Please don't make me run around the field."

"Why?"

"Bastard, I ache. Please give me something to ease the soreness. Don't you have some opium?"

Barnie lowered his voice. "Really, old boy, if I had more poppies, why I'd give you some, but, actually, I don't have any, and whatever I have, I must keep for myself. My situation is almost as bad as yours."

"Barnie, please!"

"Well, make it worth my while, then. I want something tangible, something I can hold in exchange."

"What about my grandfather's Masonic ring?"

"We already have one in the family. No, a ring will not do."

"What about my ability as a Thespian? I could entertain you and your friends at a gathering and make you laugh. You know I was good at that at Wemyss' School. Even the old fart admitted as much."

"Nonsense. But....but you do have a sister. I've seen her. In fact, I think I met her once at a fish supper. She was sitting with Catherine Rebecca Mobley and Sara Anna Nicholson. You were there, too. Yes, I remember her crystal blue eyes and light brown hair. A little homely, but pretty. In fact, except for her eyes, she looks a little like my Aunt Anna Catherine. She died when I was just a wee boy."

The comment about Anna Catherine confirmed what George had heard, but he said nothing. "Well, my sister has three breasts, and she's homely, but she's really pretty. Even our pa thinks so. I've not teased her in years. But...maybe I could use her so-called deformity to my advantage if you're able to help me. Hebrides might enable us to make a deal."

"Meaning you'd put your lover in a bad situation? I don't understand."

"Well, my sister's breasts... they're different, unique if you will." As he talked, George quieted his own guilty voice, murmuring within that his pain transcended any guilt.

Barnie tilted his head, "Now, that sounds interesting, indeed. A bargain, George. Now, how do you plan to arrange an exchange of breasts? That really sounds like something for a carnival."

"You're right, and I am betraying my sister. In truth, she could make money traveling up and down the coast with a carnival. Working for my fanatic parents will exhaust her. Oh, I am Judas, your laudanum, the silver. Now, my sister is a virgin, Barnie. I warn you. Be gentle if that is possible. Do you understand the exchange?"

"Indeed, now get on with them...the arrangements for the exchange, George. Tell me."

George asked for the laudanum as proof of Barnie's commitment. "I'll take my sister for a ride in the wagon this evening before supper. You be at Swann Creek Church. Our wagon will suddenly break down...a bad wheel, you know, and you come offer to help. You just happen to be returning home from delivering a baby. My sister will go with you because the air will be chilly. Hebrides won't be able to go because of some condition I'll invent. You'll understand? Use your noggin, man, the one your mother still coddles."

"Enough, George." They shook hands, and, later that October afternoon, when the sun was setting, Barnie was at the church waiting when George, Hebrides, and Celie rode up the lane toward Essex. "Whoa, Buddy," George called to the mule, steadying himself to get down.

"It's the wheel, Sis," he said to comfort Celie. "We'll have to mend it. Buddy's leg is badly cut. I don't know why. Probably something before we ever left home. Hebrides, will you hold the mule? And I'll need some water and cloth. Please give me your apron, Sissy."

She did, and her brother dabbed the animal's leg.

"Bubba, there's a spring behind the church. I remember hearing Pa talk about it. I think the darkies used to call it Mully Creek"

"Then go fetch some water, will you? But give me your dress to stop Buddy's bleeding."

"What if somebody sees me? I'm only wearing a dead slave's torn shift. You know how Ma makes over leftover clothes for us. You know that's why the boys made fun of you at Wemyss' School. She made you wear slave's garments. I sat there naked and helped her remake them for you. George, please don't let anybody hurt me. Couldn't Hebrides go?"

"He'd get scared…night coming on. Sis, nobody's going to see you on this lonely road on a cold evening. Come on."

And that moment, Barnie Dunn appeared in his buggy. "Need some help?"

"Oh, no thank you, Sir," Celie answered, folding her arms across her breasts. "My brother and I will manage. We are fine."

"Sis, this is Dr. Dunn. He'll know what to do to help us. You go with him to the spring and fetch the water. I'll stay here with Buddy and begin working on the wheel."

"But…"

Despite her protests, Barnie lifted her into the buggy and winked at George. "Here's a blanket if you're cold, young lady."

Barnie cracked the whip so hard his horse took off in a canter. The buggy ran into the creek, and Barnie and Celie tumbled out. Barnie got up immediately, but Celie could not. Her knee was sprained. "I'm hurt, Dr. Dunn."

"Ah, that's unfortunate," he said, his teeth glistening.

He tethered the horse, then ripped off the blanket he'd given her, and gazed at her body.

"Absolutely astonishing! Why, I have never seen such breasts. They are fascinating. Did you inherit these from your grandmother? Your brother was right. You would be a celebrity at any fair, especially a local one. Have you ever thought of going to Millsborough? Just imagine the advertisement: 'Fanatical Minister's Daughter in Fair. Come one and all!' Why you could make money and get away from your harsh parents. You could also give your brother an endless supply of laudanum and anything else to ease his pain."

Barnie pulled Celie to him and held her tight.

"Let me go," she screamed, loosening her hair and covering her breasts, trying to kick him with her uninjured knee.

"Oh no, you're not going to cover those circus tits," Barnie answered. He pushed her against one of the pines and began fondling her breasts, sucking each in turn, fingering her vagina. "Ah, I imagine your father does hail you as something diabolical. Has he ever talked about burning you at the stake? My father surely would have. Before the moon rises above the pines near this creek, I will have you. You're bewitchingly beautiful, Celie Fears, and you are mine."

He pulled her to a tree near the water, tied her, and raped her. "Oh, oh…this is ecstasy. Celie, you are…"

Tugging and twisting, she kicked Barnie hard more than once in the groin. He fell into the creek, and she untied herself and his horse, then galloped through the woods to Burnt Bluffs.

"Oh, you'll pay for this, you damned witch," Barnie railed out in the dark water. "No one ever, ever, scorns or rejects Dr. Barnabie Dunn. You remember that."

By the time Celie reached home, George was stumbling toward the hovel where his parents were praying. He still held the broken wagon wheel.

"Why, George, why?" Celie screamed.

"Sis, why are you naked?"

"Bubba, how can you ask that question? You know…why did you betray me? Why did you leave me? Why did you sacrifice me? I've never, ever, hurt you? Why did you sell your own soul to the devil?"

"For pain, Sis…I'm sorry. Please forgive me."

"Surely you knew Barnie Dunn was going to rape me. George, how could you have betrayed your baby sister?" She cried. "Oh, it hurt. He pushed me up against the trunk of a tree, making fun of my breasts, and raped me, saying I could make money to pay for your laudanum if I joined the fair in Millsborough. He insulted me, violated me, and you arranged it all. George,

I should hate you," she wailed, tugging at her brother's arm. "I'm bleeding. Bubba. Where's Hebrides? Help me before Mother and Father hear us and see me. Couldn't you have done something other than use your baby sister for laudanum?"

Hysterical, Celie pounded her brother with her arms, and he caught her and held her until John opened the front door, as Celie knew her father would. He held a lantern. "What are you doing, Daughter? Naked before thine own house and in thy brother's arms? This is incest! Wife, search thine own heart. What hast thou done?"

"John, Celie and George are our children. They love each other. She's been hurt, and."

"Our daughter takes after your own mother, not mine. It was your mother, Cecilia, for whom our daughter is named, who had the breast deformity. It's been passed on from one generation to the next. You are all sinners, and God will punish you." John's voice thundered above Celie's wails.

George stammered a few words of explanation which made no sense to either of his parents. John jerked Celie toward him. "Mollie, look at your daughter, a grown woman, naked and deformed before God. 'The Lord wilt not hold him guiltless…"

"John," she answered, shaking him. "You have seen our child. I asked you to look at her. Now, who is guiltless? I've seen the Livingston coat of arms with a warrior bearing his breasts. Even Antigone tried to tell me she'd seen you hold our daughter and draw her to you in the church when I sent her there. And our own daughter told me, but I never believed either of them. Have you, Husband? Have you raped my Celie?"

"Oh, Mamma," George said, "your pock marks are reddening under the lantern. Are you saying that our father, the minister who claims to be without sin, has violated his own daughter and you knew it, wondered about it, and…and yet did nothing? Mother…you and I, and Pa, we have all humiliated Sissy."

George wept as Celie held him against her breast. He covered her with his ragged coat. "Oh, Sis, I…I am so ashamed. I will make it up to you."

"I'm going to cut off that third breast," John interrupted, "and you won't have to make it up to her. Yes, God has commanded me to do it. I must perform my duty, as Abraham did his, and then this generation will be exorcised of all sin." With those words, John lifted Celie in the air, then flung her down on one of the gnarled mulberry stumps. "Bring me a knife, Mollie."

"I will not, John...no more, no more. I am ashamed. I can only ask God's forgiveness. I hurt my children because my father and brother humiliated me. I took my anger out on my babies. I allowed you to treat me as they had. I made a bad decision. I...God forgive me." She threw herself on one of the stumps and wept. "I thought you loved me, John. You didn't. You tormented me, and believing Paul's words, I tried to obey you. You and I are the sinners, John, not our children, not Hebrides. George turned to a colored boy because you and I didn't give our own son what he needed most of all."

Anteegwine began singing and moving around Celie..."De moon bez full...mo brestes growz if dey be cut on de risin. Betta wait, Preecha man."

"Hush, you crazy woman," George said, as his father turned Celie over and glared.

"The knife. I am waiting, and God's servants do not wait."

"I've sinned. That's for sure," George interrupted, firing a shot into the air, "but no more, and, old man, God's servants do wait. I learned that from the absurd Dr. Wemyss if I learned nothing else, and I've heard you shout a verse about waiting upon the Lord for strength as you pounded the broken table in that ruined church. I think it's from Isaiah. Oh, Celie, I... I am sorry. Father, it's time for you to die. Yes, Grandfather gave me his pistol, and I intend to use it. You have made all of us suffer long enough."

"George," John begged, but George fired again. And his father fell to the ground next to Mollie. "Wife, I am dying. Help me. Submit yourself to me one last time. It is right in the sight of God."

But Mollie said nothing, only clutched the stump and continued to weep. "Father, forgive me. Children, forgive me...I don't deserve to live."

"Help me, Daughter," John cried. "I'm bleeding."

"I can't, Father. I don't have the strength."

George threw the broken wheel on his dying father, then began tying his arms to the spokes, and kicked him squarely in the testicles.

"Old man, 'It were better that a millstone be dragged around his neck and he be drowned in the bottom of the sea than one of the little ones be frightened, or something like that from Scripture.' We were the little ones, Sis...Father hurt us. He half clothed us, often left us hungry, hurt us, whipped us, Mother, too, and I have no regrets whatsoever for drowning him in the Patuxee River. If there are dragons lurking...and Antigone said there are, why Pa will have plenty of company. I don't care. He never gave us anything but a scorpion."

The more his father screamed in pain, struggling to free himself, the more George laughed. Celie called her brother to stop, saying they should forgive their father, but George ignored her cries and dragged the old man down to the dark waters and threw him in, then began hurling one dead mulberry branch after another over his body. "Grab one, you old bastard, if you're still breathing, and float on down the river to die. I don't give a damn."

George staggered back to the hovel, where his sister crouched by the fire, turning her back to Mollie. Hebrides strummed a spiritual on the banjo, Antigone moaning. "Where dem witches?"

"Shut up," George said, hitting the black woman with the fire poker. "You're the second witch. My mother's the first. Leave, Anteegwine...get away from me, and go find the third witch. Go down to the woods. Go to the river and drown. I don't care. I'm sick of your superstitions. Go back to White Oaks. Mother, you are the witch... you know that, don't you? You have never done anything but humiliate Celie and me...I hate you. I don't care if you die."

"Son, please...I'm so ashamed. I want to die."

"Maybe you will. I hope so, and I will write a long narrative poem about this family living in the burned woods with witches and a maniac of God, my own father, the man you married. I will sell the poem and make money for Celie and me. Then...then we will restore the land. Oh yes, I am waxing Biblical tonight, filled with the scriptures. God knows I had to recite them often enough. 'I will plant in the wilderness the cedar, the shittah tree, and the myrtle, and the oil tree; I will set in the desert the fir tree, and the pine, and the box tree together:'"

"George, stop it...you don't even know what a shittah tree is."

"Shittah...shit," he laughed, adding, "Sis, I don't give a damn." His eyes were fierce, angry, penetrating her teary ones. "Sis, I'll have visions. Why I'll be like Ezekiel and see that wheel way up in the middle of the air."

Hebrides turned and stared, "I ain't gwine wid you."

"George, you are mad, and I am afraid. Please stop shouting," Celie cried.

"No...if we hadn't been sent to that hideous school, why I never would have gotten neuralgia, and Druzie wouldn't have gone blind. You may not have ever been humiliated and violated by your own father, Celie. My God, for someone who claimed to be an Abolitionist, that bastard was brutal. And, Mother, you knew exactly what he was doing and never once questioned him. I'm surprised he didn't suggest that you rape me."

Mollie hugged her knees and trembled. The fire was low. "Shoot me, George. I am so ashamed. I don't deserve to live."

"That would be too easy. No, I want you to suffer, Mother. I want you to writhe in emotional pain and feel the guilt and hurt and fear you passed on to us...Remember all the times I wanted a little slice of ham. 'No, George. You cannot have your father's meat. Celie, go gather the eggs for your father to sell. I should strip you and tie you up.'

I'm sorry for what you suffered when you were growing up, but Celie and I...we didn't have to be your victims. We're the offspring of two maniacs."

"George, where does forgiveness begin, except in our hearts? Just because she never forgave does not mean you and I can't. We need to try. She has asked us to forgive her. Maybe we can all begin to heal," Celie said, putting her arms around her mother.

"Sis, I can't begin jumping and leaping in the air for joy. I can't begin to forgive. I am crippled. Celie, I am crippled physically and spiritually. Don't you understand?"

"Bubba, don't become Pa...don't. We are the ones who must break the inheritance of abuse, this sin which has passed from one generation to the next. Bitterness only hurts the mind, body, and soul."

Mollie reached for Celie's hands. "I am sorry. I am so ashamed." Celie patted her mother's hand.

George put the pistol down on the milk stool and stumbled out into the cold, dark night. Hebrides followed.

"I'll go to White Oaks for Monica," Celie whispered. "She will know what to do."

"No, just let me die, Celie...please give me something, anything," she heaved. "I...I don't know what to say anymore. I wouldn't know how to live. Whip me...shoot me with my father's pistol."

"I can't, Mamma. I can't. Monica will tell us what to do."

"Hm...hm...I...I," her mother moaned, and Celie took the mule through the woods to White Oaks.

"O deliver not the soul of the turtledove unto the the multitude
of the wicked: forget not the congregation of the poor forever"
(Psalm 74:19).

Book Sixteen (1828-1830)

As Celie tied the mule to the hitching post at White Oaks, she heard the fairy clock strike twelve. The house was dark. "I had no idea it was midnight," she muttered to herself, "but I have to see Monica."

She rapped on the front door. "Misses Celie, wat de matta?" Lafayette asked, opening the door.

"I need to see Aunt Monica."

"Come on in. I gwine call Massa Andrew, too."

"Please don't wake everybody up. I need to see your mother."

Within a few minutes, Monica, Uncle Wash, Aunt Agnes, and Cudn Druzie gathered around Celie and heard the story.

"I'm going to Burnt Bluffs," Monica said, "and you gwine stay here, honey lamb. You been through enough for a life time. That was far more than your grandma ever had to face."

"Yes, darling," Aunt Agnes said. "I insist. Nessie will lay a fire in the bedroom next to Druzie's."

"Oh, Cuz, I'm so sorry," Druzie said. They sat on the sofa, and she wept, her head on his shoulder.

"Father," Druzie asked, "Did you and grandfather really humiliate Aunt Mollie when she was younger?"

"I used to tease her unmercifully, and I am ashamed. My father was downright cruel. Ma always rebuked him and took up for Mollie. As long as Mamma lived, he didn't get away with much that pertained to us. He was sorry. We both were. But I guess my twin's wounds were too deep. Monica and I will leave for Burnt Bluffs at once."

"And White Oaks is your home now," Aunt Agnes said. "We believe in God's love. That's what my mother and father taught us. I'm sorry my brother went astray."

"Thank you, but I don't think George will ever leave Burnt Bluffs. And Hebrides won't leave George. I don't know that I can leave the bluffs either, much as I love all of you. It's the only home I've ever known. I know it's a gloomy place, a haunted place, but I intend to change all of that. I will restore the land. It will become Mulberry Bluffs again, and I will build a school there, and I will name it in honor of my grandmother who so desperately wanted her own schoolhouse here at White Oaks."

"And I'll help you, Cuz," Druzie said, patting her hand. "We'll make your dream come true."

Aunt Agnes smiled. "You know, I had always believed my brother was going to turn Burnt Bluffs into the orphanage Dr. Boucher once had….before it burned, but he never did…I guess that's why I never wanted to go back. It was such a dreary place. Celie, let me get you some tea, perhaps even some brandy. You need something after all you've been through."

"No, I'm going with Aunt Monica and Uncle Wash now. I need to take care of my mother. She needs me."

Aunt Agnes listened, her eyes watering, remembering when she'd taken care of her own mother at Burnt Bluffs so many years ago. "I can only pray your brother George won't become the tortured soul my brother was."

Celie kissed Druzie and Aunt Agnes good-bye.

"Memnon, we'll need you….and maybe one of the boys to help us. Tell them to go in the wagon, and you take us in the buggy," Wash directed.

When they arrived at Burnt Bluffs, Anteegwine was tending the fire. "I cum back," she said.

Mollie was lying face down in a pool of blood by the milk stool, the pistol on the floor. She was naked, her long white hair wound tightly around her neck.

Celie stared at her mother's body. "Mamma must have taken off her clothes the way she'd stripped mine off so many times. She must have shot herself with the pistol. George left it on the milk stool when he stormed off. Anteegwine, was she dead when you found her?"

"Anteegwine, did you shoot her or wrap her hair around her throat?" Monica asked. "You must tell us."

Anteegwine's eyes widened in disbelief, and she looked from Monica to Celie, then to Wash and Memnon. "I ain't dun nuthin. She was dead when I cum in. I laid the fire cauf I thought huh might be cold."

Memnon dragged his childhood friend's body outside and asked Anteegwine to go to the well for water. "We gwine hav to wip up dat blood. Yu got any cloth, Missus Celie?"

She shook her head. She couldn't make them understand that there never had been many clothes or material, that she herself had gone half naked much of the time. They wouldn't believe her.

Monica said there were worn woolens in the wagon.

"I killed my mother," Celie wept…" If I'd stayed, she wouldn't have shot herself. She wouldn't have died."

"Sh, honey," Monica quieted. "Ain't nuthin you nor anybody else could of done. Yo mother was a desperate soul by then. She was weary."

A few days later, John Livingston's body washed up, and he and his wife were buried in a private service beside the burned chapel. George would not attend the service, and he and Hebrides continued to stay in the stable with the mule. George wrote poetry and took whatever he could find to ease his pain.

Celie tried to take care of him and began cleaning up the hovel. Memnon moved to the bluffs to help out, and he finally married Anteegwine. They stayed in the old slave cabin.

When she went through her father's ledger, Celie discovered that there was virtually no money, that John Livingston had spent most of her mother's gold on books for himself. In addition, he'd made donations to Dr. Wemyss' school and, on occasion, contributions to Brick Tower Church and to the Abolitionist Society. She found her father's will, and when she read that Burnt Bluffs had been left to George, her stomach knotted. She felt a kind of resentment, desperation. Whatever gold might have been left, Celie discovered George had exchanged for bills at the bank in Essex a few days before shooting his father. And she remembered all the times her brother would take the wagon to Essex, then return hours later, a little tipsy, sometimes less brooding and bitter.

In November of 1830, Celie reluctantly accepted Monica's advice to move to White Oaks "if for no other reason than to get well, honey. You plain tired, and you noz it."

Monica told Celie about the origin of the gold and the warning that had come with it. "Yo mammy knowed, and so does your Uncle Wash. Yo mammy disobeyed when she gave the gold to yo papa. He squandered it and so has Massa George."

Celie agreed. "I'll suffer for it, and we'll lose the bluffs."

"No…Aunt Agnes won't let that happen. Mista Druzie, he won't neither."

Leaving George behind bothered Celie, but at least Hebrides was with him. Anteegwine and Memnon would stay and begin cleaning up and rebuilding. "You don't think Memnon would get into trouble with the free Negroes down in the bottoms, do you?"

"No, honey. My son's good. He noz right from wrong, same as my daughter, Nessie. do. Memnon, he jes married someone who ain't got lot of sense. Did you believe Anteegwine when she said she didn't shoot your ma?"

"I did. She's superstitious and afraid, but I've always thought she was an honest woman. You know, I think about my brother. I just wish he'd forgiven Ma."

"Chile, you got to take care of yourself now…you ain't well right now. You need to rest, and you can't be frettin over that brother."

"But I believe I am 'my brother's keeper,' as the scriptures say."

Monica shook her head. "Not always, huney."

Celie packed her few belongings.

After breakfast the following morning, Celie found her brother to tell him her plans. "George, always remember that I love you and want you to write a beautiful poem for me. Hebrides, if you need anything, let us know."

He nodded, and George promised to write a long poem for his sister before he died. "Thank you for your forgiveness, Sissy, and be happy with Cudn Druzie. He loves you. He always has."

"I just wish he weren't my double-first cousin. Bubba, that's closer than twins," and they laughed.

"Celie, find me some of Grandpa's medicine at White Oaks, and bring it, will you?"

She nodded and put her arms around him one last time, uncertain of when she would return. "Bubba, Josh will drive us home, then come back to the bluffs to live with Memnon and Anteegwine. They're all here to help you. I'll send some medicine back by Josh."

"I'll be good," he winked.

Riding up the lane to White Oaks a little later, Celie heard shouting and told Josh to stop the buggy. She jumped out. "I'll be right back, Aunt Monica."

The old woman smiled, realizing how much Celie resembled Grandmother Cecilia. "She's going to make it, Josh."

He nodded. "Sho is, Grandma."

Celie recognized a prissy young lady named Rhoda Kathleen Henderson. Celie had met her once at a strawberry social at Swann Creek Church and didn't like her.

Rhoda Kathleen was mocking Druzie.

"How can you possibly tell me you'll ride your horse up to the drive at the fox hunt, Druzie Bain? You're crazy," she shouted, her gray eyes mottled brown, flashed. "You're blind. You're not fooling anyone but yourself."

"Don't mock me, Rhoda Kathleen. That's not necessary. All I did was invite you to a fox hunt and a dance. I see far more than you ever will, and one day you'll understand the meaning of my words. I run a successful grist mill and tutor children in arithmetic and reading. There's no need for you to be unkind."

Jeering even more, the girl picked up a chunk of moist red clay. "Here, Druzie, Take this. I'll pretend to be Jesus. Rub your eyes with this clay, and let's see if you can see. Of course not. You never will. Whatever made you think I'd consider having a blind man escort me. I simply came to bring some lavender to your mother, and you insulted me by inviting me to a social function. Do you think I want to embarrass myself in front of family and friends?"

"How dare you say such things to my cousin!" Celie said, as she spattered the girl's riding jacket and skirt with a handful of wet dirt. "And don't you ever come back to White Oaks!"

"Cuz," Druzie called, recognizing her voice. "I'm so glad you have come."

"Me, too, Druzie Bain."

He took her in his arms, and they walked inside where Aunt Agnes celebrated Celie's arrival with a glass of Madeira. Following supper, Celie played the psaltery and then tried the piano. She was excited. "I've never played the piano before." She surprised herself by being able to play Mozart so easily, so gracefully. "Aunt Agnes, you're a wonderful teacher. Remember when you taught me how to read music?"

By spring, Celie felt much stronger. She and Druzie spent hours together. Celie would read to him and accompany him around the plantation, telling him about the flowers and the clouds. "That one looks like a great swan, but now it's fading, and the pink is seeping through. Druzie, the sky is an ocean now."

He drew her close, and they made love under his grandmother's favorite white oak on the hill. "You're my eyes, Cuz," he whispered.

"And you're my soul."

When she heard a branch fall in the woods or a strange noise, she flinched in fear. "Celie, I didn't hear anything. Don't be afraid."

Celie found herself telling him all over again about the night Barnie Dunn had violated her. "It was terrible, worse than anything Pa ever did...I. Oh, Druzie, let's restore Burnt Bluffs. Isn't that a wonderful dream? We could make it come true. Do you know why it was burned?"

He shook his head. "Nobody does."

So they dreamed and anticipated together, Celie drawing sketches, then putting his fingers over hers, showing him the plans, explaining the original plat she'd found with her father's belongings in the burned chapel. "Once, there was a chapel, slave quarters, a stable, a lodge for the orphans, a kitchen, and that hovel we lived in. Wonder what it was like long time ago. Druzie, you could tutor and teach, along with me, and maybe George would do something. Anteegwine could cook, and…"

"Yes…we will."

"Sometimes, I become terribly anxious as I think about the future, though."

"Coz, I have had to learn just to trust the moment and latch on to whatever it offers. As long as I can put one foot in front of the other, I am living. I don't worry about tomorrow, and I don't want you to either."

"I will be your disciple," she teased, as she put a flower chain around his neck.

"Silly."

One afternoon when they were on the front lawn where Celie was gathering acorns for a game she'd devised, she saw someone riding up the lane. "Druzie, somebody's coming up on a mule. It's a young man, but I have no idea who he is. I'm a little afraid. I."

"No, sugar pie, don't be scared. Remember what we talked about. I'll do the talking, and I'll listen to his voice…then, I'll know who this person is unless he's a stranger."

The horse and rider galloped closer. "Welcome to White Oaks, to our home," Druzie said.

"Druzie, I had to come…I had to find you. After Ma and Pa died, life near Swannanoa Town was so lonely. My brother and I never got along too well. And I just took off one day. I had this need to see you and your cousin…George…that's right. I told you the night I left Wemyss' School that I'd never forget you. I was wonderin' if you might have some work for me. I…I don't have much money, and I'd be mighty obliged if you could help me."

"Neilly…it's Neilly Dulligan," Druzie said, bursting with laughter. "Oh, Neilly, I could never forget you either…you used to talk about rivers and cricks and frost on the mountain…and you sang these long poems…"

"Ballads is what we called them in the hills."

Druzie stood up and embraced his friend. "And, Neilly, this is my Coz Celie."

"You're welcome to stay here with us at White Oaks," Celie said. "I'm sure Aunt Agnes and Uncle Wash will be happy to know you, just as I am."

Druzie invited his friend in, and they all had a glass of brandy. "Oh, I feel a little light-headed, Cudn," Celie admitted, and Neilly smiled. Neilly was stocky, with gray-green eyes, and dark red hair that framed his face. He laughed heartily, nothing bothering him at all.

Aunt Agnes and Uncle Wash welcomed their son's friend from the mountains. "We raise cotton and some tobacco and other crops. We have a brickyard and grist mill. Druzie operates that. We have livestock. I could hire you as the overseer. Slaves are rebellious, and they need some discipline. I fired my father's overseer, a cruel Dutch Irishman, years ago. We hired someone, a Mr. Wherry, but he didn't stay long. Old Prince tries, and so does London, Monica's son-in-law."

"May I ask who Monica is?" Neilly asked.

"Oh, she has been with our family for years," Wash explained. "She's free and works as a midwife. Her story is such a long, complicated one that few people would ever believe us. But we're all fairly happy here, even the slaves for the most part. I treat them extremely well. Orange McTavish Steggerda did not. That's why I fired him. Many of the colored folks are free and work for wages."

Neilly hesitated. "Sir, I wouldn't know how to punish people or even manage slaves. Pa didn't believe in slavery. Neither did my ma. We worked hard. Sometimes I'll tell you....I appreciate the offer, but...but I can't accept it."

"Well," Celie interrupted, wanting to help this young mountaineer with his gentle ways, "Maybe my brother, George, would pay you to work over at Burnt Bluffs, I mean, if he has any money left. You see, he doesn't own slaves."

"That's the home where Celie was raised....and where I lived with her father before marrying Druzie's father," Aunt Agnes explained. Wash told Neilly the story of the burned plantation once known as Mulberry Bluffs. "We're still trying to discover why it burned."

Neilly was fascinated...."Well, could I buy the place and fix it up? I mean, I could farm the land and make something of it"

"Certainly," Aunt Agnes answered. "You could farm, restore the buildings, and open the orphanage again, as Dr. Boucher had it. I had hoped my brother would do that, but he didn't."

"Restoring the school is a dream Celie has and one which I share," Druzie said. "I want to be a teacher there. Celie has figured out all of the details."

Neilly nodded. "Well, I'll drive over to the place and see my old school buddy George. We were all so close once, weren't we, Dru?"

"Yes."

"My brother isn't as you remember him. You'll soon realize the changes, and he mostly stays with Hebrides. He's Monica's youngest boy."

"Do they live with each other?"

Celie explained.

As they talked, Neilly found himself telling Celie all of the experiences which he had shared with her brother and cousin at Dr. Wemyss' Academy. "Oh, it was a horrible place, especially for the three of us. Well, I mean, Dru dressed well, but George and I didn't. We wore homespun clothes."

"My brother went there because our father had known Dr. Wemyss at Princeton years earlier. My father persuaded Uncle Wash to send Druzie to the school with George."

"I went because an aunt of mine had known Mrs. Wemyss somewhere. My aunt had given my father money for my schoolin and my brother's. You see, Aunt Rena had married up. Her husband had money, and he took a likin' to all of us, and you can guess the rest. We all had to work hard at the school. We had to toil in the fields and got very little to eat. I hope never to return."

Druzie agreed and listened as Celie explained her vision to Neilly. "Yes, Druzie will teach geometry, astronomy, rhetoric, and grammar. I'll give the young ladies music lessons, and Aunt Monica has agreed to teach needlepoint. She's had a way with the needle ever since she was a child. She and our grandmother for whom I was named grew up together in Georgetown, South Carolina. Our great grandmother, Katie Fears Lynch, settled there. She was from Ireland."

Neilly found Druzie's cousin spellbinding. "We'll all work together, provided Georgie boy is willing."

"Just tell him I insist," Druzie said. "George and I will always be indebted to you, Neilly. You saved our lives."

"Oh, Coz, there will be trees again on the barren land and vineyards and gardens and orchards. The mulberries will grow and flourish again. Do you think Bubba will sell Burnt Bluffs?"

Druzie nodded. "I'm certain of it, Celie."

"He maketh me to lie down in green pastures: he restoreth my soul: he leadeth me in the paths of righteousness for his name's sake" (Psalm 23:3).

Book Seventeen (1830-1841)

The next day Druzie accompanied his school friend to Burnt Bluffs where they found George slumped over a table, bottle in hand. Hebrides had a terrible cough. Neilly sobered George up and made the proposal. George agreed to sell on one condition.

"And what's that, old friend?" Neilly teased.

"That Hebrides and I be able to remain tenants without paying rent. This has been my home since childhood. Humble though it is, Burnt Bluffs is all I've ever known, and I'd like to enjoy it awhile longer. With all of the pain I've suffered, I don't want to move, even to White Oaks. Can you understand?"

"Of course, I can," Neilly answered, studying George's face and hands. His fingers, wrapped in woolen scraps, trembled, and his facial muscles were taut. He was quite thin, his skin dry. When George shifted his legs, he winced.

"And I will build you a cabin, so you won't freeze anymore. How have you stood living in nothing but the lean-to of a stable in your condition?"

"Rum, Neilly Dulligan, and Hebrides' love. We understand each other. Have a swig," George offered, tipping the bottle. "Numbs the pain, you know," He offered the bottle to Druzie, too. "And you will watch out for my Sissy, won't you? I know Cudn Druzie always will. Celie's been hurt, and, well, you know how big brothers are toward their sisters."

"Of course, I will. Now before I can enter into a permanent agreement, I must return to the mountains and my portion of our family land."

"Burnt Bluffs will be waiting for you."

"And I promise to bring you some spirits from one of the stills near Swannanoa Town. You know, my brother might even be interested in buying land nearby. We don't get along too well. We're different, but he is family."

Druzie gave his cousin the basket of food from Aunt Agnes. "I'll see you soon, George, and remember you're always welcome at White Oaks. It's your home, Hebrides', too."

"Thank you both for coming," George answered, as he limped a short way up the path to where their horses waited.

A few days later, when Druzie and Celie were in their grandfather's room in the tower, looking for medicine, Celie asked her cousin about Neilly. "Did he laugh during his days at Dr. Wemyss' Academy as easily as he laughs now?"

"Yes, he was always the prankster. Now if somebody angered him, why he'd lash out, Irish style. He had a temper then. Tell me, is his hair still that auburn color?"

"Yes. It's combed down close to his cheeks. His eyes are olive green. I picture him as a character in a story. Do you?"

"Possibly. I've never thought about him in that way. Coz, I love you." Druzie drew her to him.

"And I adore you, too. We'll be together all the time from now on."

"Celie, are the three roses still climbing up the tower?"

"Yes. Why?"

"Mamma told me stories about the roses and Grandpa's tower. He must have been a powerful man and so knowledgeable; at least that's what Pa told Ma."

"Yes, and...and do you remember the times he would bring us up here and we'd all pretend to be knights in some remote castle?"

"Those were merry times for all of us, weren't they?"

Aunt Agnes' voice interrupted their reverie for supper. She reminisced about Burnt Bluffs and, of course, anticipated Neilly's return. "That boy's different, isn't he? But I like him. I want him to restore the bluffs.

Then, Druzie began to tell Celie and his mother and father more about the academy in Georgia and all of Wemyss' old tricks. "Sometimes I thought if poor George only had a fancier suit of clothes, something other than that slave's woolen shirt Aunt Mollie made him wear and those ancient boots, life there for him would not have been so miserable."

"Yes, we would gladly have provided for him, but my fanatical brother wouldn't hear of it. Your father and I should have insisted, but we didn't."

"No, Uncle Wash interrupted, his voice wistful, "My twin sister's head became as stubborn as her husband's. Well, we did the best we could, and there's no point in looking back. It doesn't do any good."

"That boy's sweet on Celie," Monica later whispered to Agnes. "Sho is. Can't you tell?"

Agnes nodded, knowing in her heart that her son loved Celie. Deep down, Agnes hoped Druzie and Celie would marry, but she only said, "I don't want there to be any more hurt around here. There's been enough. I pray that God will bless them all and direct each one."

As though he could hear the Bains all whispering about him, Neilly Dulligan returned from the mountains to White Oaks, cash in hand, and invited Druzie and Celie to ride with him to Burnt Bluffs to pay George. More sober that day, George was in particularly good spirits after Neilly paid him in cash.

"You'll put that money in the bank, won't you, George?" Druzie asked.

"I'll take the mule to Essex one day this afternoon. In the meantime, I'll tuck it under my pillow."

"That's not safe, Bubba, not with those free Negroes in the bottoms. It's just not, and you know it, and Hebrides doesn't look well. Is he sick?"

"Yes...Anteegwine says he's got consumption. She's been mixing up potions and teas for us. I've just tried to keep him as comfortable as I can. He coughs a lot, and he has a fever."

"All the more reason for me to drive you to Essex."

Once the land was in his possession, Neilly set about, with the assistance of Josh and Memnon, to restore the place. After building a cabin for George, Neilly completed the chapel and the lodge. Celie and Druzie's curriculum plans seemed to motivate him, just as his restoration inspired them.

One afternoon, Druzie asked Celie to walk with him to their favorite white oak tree. They sat on the grass. "Coz, this is serious."

"What is it, Druzie? You look worried. What's the matter?"

"It's hard for me to say it, but I think I'm a little jealous. Neilly wants to marry you, and..."

"Oh, darling, I love you. My heart says to marry Druzie Bain, but...we're...we're double..."

"I know what you're going to say. No need to repeat your fears again, Cecilia Fears Livingston. Please don't. Sometimes, I suppose I become tired of hearing that our kinship has to affect our deep feelings. Can you understand?"

"Yes, and I am sorry. Oh, Druzie, you're waxing philosophical this afternoon, and you know it. Is that your therapy for me?"

"Do you suppose my blindness has made me become philosophical?"

"I don't know."

"I do. I know I've had to learn to adapt and to grow up rather quickly. I just never want to lose my ability to laugh. I never want to become bitter the way George is."

"You won't," she assured. "Druzie, surely you know how much you have helped me overcome my terrible childhood at Burnt Bluffs and feel stronger. You've no idea how much your love and encouragement means to me."

"Coz, that goes both ways, you know. After all, you're the very light that pierces my darkness. Celie, Neilly wants to marry you. I feel that he will be a good husband to you and for you. Do you love him?"

"Well, yes, I do feel an affection toward Neilly. It's a feeling I can't quite understand, perhaps because I've never had feelings for anyone but you, Druzie. The feeling frightens me a little."

"Oh, my precious cousin, I yearn to hold you."

"Hold me again, as you've held me so many times. Druzie, will...will Neilly be bothered about my breasts? You've felt them. You know absolutely everything about me. How would another man feel?"

"I feel awkward, uncomfortable. I almost don't know what to say, and yet I have to be fair. You are my double—first cousin, and that's what keeps you from seeing us in an you abiding relationship. I must understand that. I must respect your feelings, so I must be truthful. To answer your question, Neilly will not be bothered. Oh, Celie, nothing bothers him. Besides, he already knows about your breasts. George told him a long time ago when we were in school together. Boys talk about girls, and girls talk about boys. You know that."

She laughed. "Then, I suppose it's all settled. You've all arranged my marriage behind my back, haven't you?"

"No. The decision is yours, but I want you to remember that I will always be here for you. I will wait for you until I die. If Neilly had not saved my life, why I wouldn't be here to say that, would I?

He smiled, feeling Celie's tears moisten his cheek. "I love Neilly as a brother, and that will never change."

"I suppose people make fun of us, but we have something, Saint Druzie Bain, that nobody will ever have. We have a deep intimacy and understanding. It's spiritual, physical, lyrical like the pirate's psaltery, isn't it?"

"Yes." And they sat for a long time under the tree, the breezing wrapping around them.

Druzie finally broke the silence. "Ask Neilly to tell you about the time we all had to defend ourselves in a debate one night against those boys from Charleston and Georgetown. They were such snobs at times. I'll never forget Jeremiah Pringle Smith from Georgetown. He claimed Grandfather used to court his mother, Charlotte Jane Pringle. I never knew whether to believe him or not. I hated Jeremiah, and I'll tell you why. Neilly and George and I were all really logical in these debates. And yet Smith who was something of an imbecile would always win. I later found out old Wemyss paid another boy from McClellanville to count the votes in Smith's favor. It was an odd situation. Then, old Wemyss whipped us hard just because we asked, and then we'd limp back to those cold huts and wonder if we had food to eat. Raccoons always slipped in and ate the apples and cakes Mamma had sent. Old Wemyss never said anything but 'learn by recitation, and recite from learning,' whatever that meant. Well, Coz, when we open our school, the children will enjoy our lessons. There won't be all of this recitation. We'll encourage our pupils to ask questions, won't we?"

"Yes, my philosopher, they will, and we will, too."

"And there will never be any dunce caps at Mulberry Bluffs School."

"Absolutely not, only dancing caps," she laughed.

"No shame or humiliation. Oh, Coz, we'll be pioneers in developing a curriculum where mirth and merriment reign, won't we?"

Within a few weeks, in early December of 1831, wearing her grandmother's emerald green silk dress, Celie was married to Neilly James Dulligan at Swann Creek Church. Uncle Wash gave her away. Druzie and George sat together, and Monica, just before the ceremony, whispered, "Trust yourself, honey, and stay gentle as you are. You're your grandmammy all over again. Don't be afraid. And you take the psaltery. It's a dream. It's a gift from God through that old pirate a long time ago, and don't ever forget his wife's name was Cecilia, just same as yours and your grandmother's."

Celie kissed Monica.

And Uncle Wash reminded his niece of the horse sired by Dark Moon's son. "He's Moonlight Bay, and he's yours, Celie. Ride him the way Ma rode Dark Moon. Memnon will bring the horse to you later."

Following the ceremony, Celie lingered to embrace Druzie, then rode to the bluffs to make a home with her husband.

As though he sensed her fears and uncertainty, when Neilly took her to bed, he said, "I promise I'll never, ever, hurt you. I will love you until death do us part and more, and if I ever feel angry, it wouldn't be toward you. I promise." Neilly had listened to Druzie's words. "Never hurt my cousin. Let her bloom and be. She cherishes music and children, and she will be kind to you. To hurt her, ever, would be to destroy her soul. That almost happened in the past."

"Neilly, I will make a good wife to you." She straddled him on the rope bed, then turned, as he eased into her body, and they became one flesh.

Their first child, Neil Dulligan, was born a year after they were married—1832, but he was a sickly child. Despite Monica's remedies, he died when he was nine months old. Two weeks later, Uncle Wash died from a stroke. Little Neil and Uncle Wash were buried at White Oaks Chapel. Celie attended both services, then forced herself to pour all of her energy into the restoration project.

Two years later, Hugh Fears was born. He was a thin, pale baby with blue eyes like Celie's. He seemed rigid, frightened. The fact that he never cooed troubled his mother, but Neilly assured her, "I'll play with him. Don't worry. When you have another baby boy, why, they'll grow up laughing." In 1836, Burr Fennell tumbled out, merrily laughing, so it seemed to his mother. He had red hair, just like his father's, and green eyes mottled gold. Neilly loved his sons and took them about the plantation. Within two more years, Martha Josephine was born. "We'll call her Josie," Celie said. A beautiful baby with large, dark brown eyes, she was spoiled by her brothers. They carried her everywhere, even managing to intrigue Uncle George who babbled most of the time, wrote poems, and stayed drunk from the rum he secured from the free Negroes down in the bottoms. "Rum numbs my thumbs," he'd occasionally rime, then laugh.

Celie and Monica continued to offer herbs for pain, and Neilly made frequent trips to the apothecaries in Essex for George and Hebrides. Addicted as he was to these various remedies, little worked anymore. Realizing how sick Hebrides was, George gave up his will to live.

Celie and Neilly were happy, and they enjoyed their children, always listening to their needs, encouraging their interests. If Burr got into trouble, as he often did, for mischief, Celie would hold him or sing to him. When she realized how much Hugh Fears enjoyed working with his hands, she encouraged him to follow his daddy. She taught Josie to embroider and play the psaltery.

She and Neilly took in a few orphan children from Essex, and Druzie came over to teach. He said that Barnie Dunn had finally married Rhoda Kathleen. "Somebody told Mamma that Barnie had waited for you, Celie, and that he resented your marrying Neilly. Isn't that the silliest thing you ever heard?"

She shuddered at the name of Barnie Dunn. "Maybe they'll be happy together in the misery they impart to others. In fact, I hear old Barnie Dunn still gives the students the same rigorous exercises he gave us. Celie, I hated him as much as I did Wemyss, but I must forgive him, but I can't, can you?"

"No. Not yet. He hurt me so much that night at Swann Creek."

"Tell me, are you happy, Coz?" Druzie continued.

"Oh, yes, and we want more babies. Druzie, is being a teacher here at the school everything you imagined and dreamed it would be?"

"It is, and I don't think the pupils realize I'm blind. I have the children describe the stars to me, and we talk about the moon. Even old George hobbled down yesterday to tell the girls about a poem he's writing. He finds the goddess of the moon his inspiration. Oh, Coz, this school is almost too good to be true."

"We never gave up, and I am so grateful that you're fulfilling our dream. I'll teach when our children are older. And you know, I want to begin calling this place Mulberry Bluffs again. Don't you agree? It's no longer barren and ghostly. The bluffs are alive with joy and the laughter of children playing in the garden."

He patted her hand. "I agree."

In the late spring of 1841, Celie announced that she was carrying their fifth child. "We'll call him little Neilly, won't we?"

"You shouldn't," Druzie warned. "That may be bad luck. Besides, Coz, the baby might not be a boy."

"Druzie's right," Neilly said. "Why the baby might be a big baby girl with bright blue eyes just like yours, Celie, and I don't think she would like being named for her father."

"Well, you both win," Celie smiled. "I'll have this baby in February and name it. Is that agreeable with you both?"

After hog-killing at White Oaks and Mulberry Bluffs, all of the children wanted to go hunting. It was still early morning. As though they had banded together from a spell cast by George who repeated stories of talking deer in the bluffs and fairies on the moon, Burr insisted on finding out. "Let's go for a hunt. Maybe we'll find a unicorn, too. Uncle George has been telling us the legend of the unicorn."

Always encouraging the children to express their hopes and dreams, Druzie listened and said that it was an interesting idea. "A little irrational, Celie," he confessed, but, after all, we agreed that as teachers, we'd encourage our pupils, didn't we?"

She nodded.

"And so do I," Neilly added. "Whatever is the opposite of what old Dr. Wemyss supported is what I recommend. He never believed in the power of the imagination. I do. I would never have come to find you, Druzie, and

George, if I had not followed my dreams. We cannot always be rational. I don't care how irrational hunting for fairies and unicorns may seem, it's what encourages children to think and learn, so let's go hunting."

But Celie shook her head. "I'm not sure, Neilly, and you're not either. I see doubt in those green eyes of yours."

Druzie laughed, "I won't get in the middle of this one. I think I'll ride on home on Nellie and anticipate hearing about the unicorn and fairies you find on the hunt." He kissed the children and Celie good-bye. "By the way, what did Hebrides say?"

"He told us not to go, but he and George were arguing about something," Burr said. "Hebrides may have just been angry. I do remember that he hasn't been feeling very well lately, though. He'll be glad for whatever we shoot, even if it's possum."

"I'll ask Nathan and Lafayette to come go with you. How about that?" Druzie said, as he left.

Neilly turned to Celie. "I promise I'll be back. After all, today is our tenth anniversary, and I have a surprise for you. I want to give it to you tonight at supper."

"I'm still afraid, Neilly. The children seem so young, but if you feel this is the right decision, you know I trust you, and I will follow your wishes. As Druzie has told me so many times, I cannot go through my life fearing, as my middle name conjugates."

"I don't want you to fear either. Honey, I'll be home later. By the time we're ready to leave, Lafayette and Nathan will be here. I would take Memnon, but he went to Essex earlier to the apothecary shop."

She kissed her husband, gave all of the hunters, young and old, her blessing, then returned to the hearth with Josie. "Mamma, don't be afraid. God is with us." Celie caressed her child's dark curls, knowing in her heart that for three years old, Josie was very wise.

As the day wore on, fear tugged away at Celie, the baby swelling in her body. She smiled at Josie and tried to relax.

A few hours later in the afternoon, she went to the door. She paced the floor and looked out a second, then a third time. Nathan was running through the woods struggling to catch up with Josh. "Missus Celie, yo huzbun…he was teaching Massa Hugh to hole dat gun, and it went off. Massa Neelee, he dun got killed. Josh dun took them chaps to the chapel. I cum to tell you. I sho iz sorry. Sho iz. Massa Hugh, he think he killed his pa. He's taking on. I'm going for my mother. She'll know what to do."

Celie's body chilled. "Yes, Monica will know what to do. Tell her to come, please. Who is with the children?"

"Little Miss Eliza, dat olda gal, one of dem chillins in the school."

"Please go at once. I...I can't prepare my husband's body for the burial by myself." She sank to the floor and wept. Neilly James Dulligan died on December 6, 1841, on their tenth anniversary. "Is this an omen from God? I...I don't know."

"Mamma, I'll help you," Josie said, her dark eyes assuring.

Celie patted her daughter's hand, wondering who would take care of the children, knowing her brother was helpless. "Oh, this baby's big, honey," she said.

"Mamma, don't cry. I'll help you. I'll play the psaltery for you."

Celie held her daughter and wept. Finally, she stood up and lead her child outside. The December wind was chilly. They saw the boys coming from the chapel.

"Ma, Bubba didn't kill Pa...he didn't. It was an accident."

"Darling, I know that." Yet deep down, she wondered how her husband's death really happened. "Where's your father's body?"

"In the chapel waiting for you, Ma."

Celie sat on an old stump and wept fresh tears. She hugged the children and felt Hugh Fears stiffen in the embrace. "No," she said to herself, "Neilly could never help the child relax, and I've not been able to either. He fulfills his name, 'Hugh Fears,' just as I do."

"Son, I want you all to go to White Oaks and stay there....Druzie will be there, and your Aunt Agnes, and the others. You know the way."

"Ma, I'm scared. Anteegwine says there are witches in the woods, and it's nearly dark. The sun's going down."

"Honey, Nathan and Josh will be with you. I need you all to go, Josie, too. Hold her hand, but please ask Anteegwine to tell Uncle George to come. I need him. We'll all be together again soon. I promise."

Josie insisted on staying at her mother's side and sponging her forehead. "Mamma, you're hot."

"I'll make a cup of tea, and Antigone will be here. You go with your brothers, darling. You will be alright."

So the children left. Several hours later, Nathan returned and told Celie that everyone at White Oaks had a fever. "All exceptin my mammy. She say she gots to take care of em. Massa Druzie can't. You and me gwine hav to dress your huzbun, Misses Celie. We can do it."

She put the kettle on for tea, then began to prepare her husband's body for burial. She found herself wondering how Druzie was, then said to herself. "No, what are you going to do? Christmas is nearly here. You are by yourself, and…you must rest. That's what Monica would say."

She sank in the chair. Anteegwine sauntered in later. "I ken take care of you. When the time cum for you to deliver, why we'll put a shoe unda the bed. Some folks say that'll bring on the baby. And Mr. George, he cumin. Don't worry, Misses Celie."

Celie thanked her and fell asleep. George limped in later, tipsy. "Well, Sis, did they find the fairies and the unicorn?"

"No, Bubba. My husband was killed. There was an accident while they were hunting," and she related the details. "George, where are the orphan children? And what about Hebrides?" And he said that they were in the lodge and that she need not worry. "Little Eliza, as I call her, is almost twelve, and she knows what to do, Sis. But Hebrides won't live long. I've spent the last few hours with him. I want you to promise to bury him with me if anything happens to me. Do you understand?"

She nodded wearily. "I am going to have to rest and stay off my feet. I know that.

Bubba, I may need you to find someone to help me these next few weeks, especially with Christmas and the baby coming. Are you able to?"

He said he was better and could assist. To her surprise, George managed to tell Antigone what to do and stayed in the house with his sister. "It's not changed much, this old hovel, has it, since we were little?"

She agreed. "I told Neilly to finish all of the other buildings first…having spent my childhood here, I knew I could manage."

"And Neilly's been awfully good to me…he loved you, Sissy. He surely did."

"I know…will you go with me to the burial, that is, if I am able? I want him to be buried at Swann Creek."

After another swig or two of rum, George began to ramble on about their childhood, life at Dr. Wemyss' School, and more. Filled with her own grief, Celie couldn't respond.

Memnon returned with medicine for Hebrides and George, then went back and forth from Mulberry Bluffs to White Oaks in the old wagon, bringing food and supplies, sharing the news. "The chaps miss you, but Missus Agnes, she say they be having Christmas there, for you not to worry. Massa Druzie, he real sick with the fever, and Ma she ain't no better. My

Sissy say she'll come when she can. Missus Agnes dun told me to drive Mr. George up to de church where you want your husband buried and make the arrangements wid the preacha."

Celie thanked him and asked her brother to make the decisions. After quickly making over a black dress which one of the servants had brought from Aunt Agnes, Celie clothed herself in black and began the mourning. A few days later, her husband was buried at the church, and in late December, she felt the baby stirring more within. "It won't be long, I don't think, Bubba."

But the labor was long, and Celie twisted and turned. The child would not move, despite Antigone's teas. "Give me thyme, please."

"Ain't got none in de gyaden, Missy, and Memnon he ain't brung nothing else from Essex for having babies."

> "Will the Lord cast off forever? And will he be favorable
> no more? Is his mercy clean gone forever? Doth his promise fail
> for evermore? Hath God forgotten to be gracious? Hath he in
> anger shut up his tender mercies?" (Psalm 77:7-9).

Book Eighteen (1841-1850)

Christmas passed, and raw winter winds whipped around Celie's childhood hovel, ripping apart the make-shift curtains as she struggled to bring the baby herself. She sat up, then sank back, tried to stand, then lay down, twisting, turning, screaming, at last saying,

"Please, Bubba, can't you send for a doctor? Won't you send for a doctor? Anteegwine can't help me. Would you go for me yourself?"

That question was all George needed. A doctor meant pain medicine for him, and George knew exactly whom he'd find and called on Josh to help him mount the old mule. A few hours later, George returned. "The doctor will be here presently, Sis. He'll deliver your baby."

Sure enough, within a short time, Dr. Barnie Dunn strolled into the hovel, laughing, "So this really is the hovel where you grew up, you little bitch? And this is my hour of revenge, and I intend to savor every minute of it. You can bring the baby yourself if you wish, for it's your brother who needs me, not you. He needs laudanum. That's why he summoned me. Oh, little Celie Fears Livingston, watching you writhe in fear far surpasses ale, Madeira, rum, or mulberry wine. No, you rebuffed me, and I vowed to avenge myself, and here we are."

Cold as it was, Celie sweated and begged. Antigone wiped her forehead. "Dr. Barnie, she dun aksed me for thyme, but I ain't got nun in the gyaden."

"Did you look?" he asked.

"No……I wah sceared of de ghosties in dat gyaden."

"Thyme would make her delivery easy, and I want her to suffer, so don't worry, silly woman. Let 'Misses Celie,' as you call her, twist and turn, as you must have one day done yourself…Say, Georgie boy, I thought you told me your sister was a virgin that day we met near the church. She wasn't."

George confessed that he didn't know his father had violated her.

"Bubba, don't let Barnie Dunn hurt me again, please!" Celie screamed. "How could you ask a doctor who raped me to deliver my child? How could you do that when my husband has just died? How anytime, George...why?"

George ignored her question, then finally said nobody had told him about Neilly's death.

"Bubba, don't say that. I know Hebrides told you."

"Well, at least, Mrs. Dulligan," Barnie said, adjusting his pince-nez, then spreading his beard over Celie's swollen belly and squeezing her breasts, "you have a bed now...what I should do is tie these ropes around you and turn you, so you drop the baby on the floor yourself. As it will turn out, I'll arrange for your baby to drop. 'Vengeance is mine, and I will repay, for I am the Lord,'" Barnie scoffed, "God... Now you and I both know, Mrs. Dulligan, that you humiliated me by rejecting me after I offered, penetrating you, but we also know you could be richer by far in a carnival or fair. There's the fair in Millsborough in the spring. Your baby will probably be four-titted, and you could take it, whatever. I could have made your life far better, but you rejected me that evening at Swann Creek Church and took another man, your double-first cousin's friend, so now I'm rebuffing your baby. We'll just spend a late winter afternoon together before the setting sun, you and I; I will wait and watch. I have plenty of time. Georgie has paid me, and I've given him his laudanum. Oh, I wish I had a cigar, Celie Fears Livingston."

Barnie drank more wine and sneered as Celie pushed and pushed, trying to deliver the baby herself. As she pushed, he would shove his hand against her vagina. Hours later, unable to tolerate her screams, George walked into the dark, cold room and confronted Barnie. "You've tortured her enough. Stop!"

"Ah, well, then, let the delivery be done. Bring whatever teas you have, Antigone, if you wish. I have relished every minute of this afternoon. Now I'll count to sixty, and if your sister can say, 'Go,' why then I'll deliver the baby."

He counted slowly until Celie finally murmured, "Go." Then, Barnie pulled out a baby girl and tossed her to George, laughing, "Georgie, Georgie, Puddn and pie, catch that gal and make her cry."

The baby dropped on the floor, and George stooped over to pick her up, as Barnie tickled Celie's breasts and vagina one final time. "Your baby will be retarded exactly as I intended. I retarded your delivery and retarded your baby to pay you back for rejecting me and marrying that mountain boy. You can always tell your friends that Dr. Dunn's revenge brought about your baby's retardation. And I hope this baby causes you to suffer! And, Georgie boy, thank you for giving me the opportunity not only to rape your sister once but also to achieve revenge. Here's more laudanum. Writhe in pain in peace with your boyfriend."

"He...Hebrides is dying, Barnie."

"Not in your arms?"

George slapped the doctor and knelt at Celie's bedside. "Once again, I must ask your forgiveness, Sis. I am so sorry. I am so ashamed."

Celie said nothing, only nursed the newborn baby, Antigone speechless beside her, in the room, lightened only by the moon sailing across the dark sky. The next morning Celie named her baby girl Mary Caroline.

Finally in early January, when Monica and Nessie had recovered from the fever, they came to Mulberry Bluffs and brought the children. They found Celie shivering,

"Honey chile," Monica whispered, "Nessie's gwine take care of the others, but lemme take the baby and make you a pallet by the fire until you get stronger. This baby gal is beautiful. She's got Massa Neilly's green eyes, but they tinged with your blue also, and his reddish hair. She's gwine have a temper, though. She's already kicking."

"Monica, she's not right," Celie said. "Something's wrong, and I know it." Celie described the long, complicated delivery, the pain, and the baby being dropped on her head. "I'd rather die than go through anything like that again. Monica, I don't want any more babies, precious as they are in God's sight."

"You ain't gwine through no more pain."

"Can we send Antigone away? Maybe Memnon will take her to White Oaks for a change. I think she tried, but, Monica, I can't have her around anymore....she didn't bring me the thyme I knew was in the garden and would relieve my pain and make a quick delivery. Tell me about Druzie."

"The fever finally broke. He wants you to come home to White Oaks. We all do. Celie Fears, you can't stay here in this hovel and raise your chillins. You noz dat, don't you?"

"I want to come to White Oaks, but I have an obligation to take care of the orphan children which Neilly and I brought here to teach. I cannot forsake them. Please make Druzie understand that. Monica, you understand, don't you?"

Monica smiled, knowing how Druzie felt about Celie. "I'll try, honey. We going to keep Anteegwine here, if it's the same with you."

For the next few years, Celie stayed at Mulberry Bluffs and taught her children and the orphans, Druzie, finally, agreeing to come and teach again. Sometimes he stayed at the lodge overnight.

Raising Mary Caroline proved difficult. The child did not have Celie's deformities. Her breasts were small, but normal, and she didn't have rosacea or acne. It was her behavior which troubled Celie. Mary Caroline would break into sudden fits of laughter, or she'd cry and stomp her foot. Sometimes, she'd slap the boys or Josie, and she despised Cousin Druzie. "His eyes are funny-looking, and I don't like that poke hat he wears. You have three titties, Ma, and I've seen them. You're odd and you look like a witch with that black veil." The child ripped it off and ran from the room.

When Druzie laughed at Mary Caroline a few days later for making fun of him, she became angry, slapped his arms, and hit him in the face with a broken hornbook. "Now, this child does have problems, Coz," Druzie said to Celie.

"Sometimes Antigone says Mary Caroline needs to go to the asylum, but then she can be very gentle and helpful. Just this morning, Mary Caroline picked blackberries and helped Nessie with the clothes. She even took Bubba some blackberry cobbler for supper. I think it's because Hebrides is dying, and she pitied her uncle. I honestly don't know what to do with her. I do agree with your analysis, Saint Bain."

"Well, then, do what you think is best. You're her mother. Oh, Celie, I have missed you.

"As I have you."

Druzie took her in his arms and comforted her.

"You really don't want me, I don't think, not anymore, surely not now. If Antigone told the children I was a witch and if Mary Caroline believes it, why what else can I do? What can I say? I'm ugly and drawn now, and I know it. Please feel my breasts again. Druzie, punish me. I've begun to drink Bubba's brew, whatever it is, to numb the pain. Sometimes, I have mulberry wine. Other times, I have rum. I don't care as long as it numbs my pain. I even took some of his laudanum. I stole it when he wasn't in the cabin. I've stooped quite low."

"I had no idea you were so depressed. I do think it's time for you to stop wearing black, don't you?"

"I suppose so."

"Let's go to the chapel and talk." He linked his arm through hers, and they walked to the chapel where they heard tree frogs thrumming in the woods through an open window and felt the heat of summer. Not a breeze stirred.

PSALTERY AT WHITE OAKS

Celie showed her cousin the altar. "This is the place where my father pounded and hurled messages and threats to anyone who would listen. This is where he violated me and raped me, Druzie."

"I'm sorry, but remember that he's not here anymore, honey. Your father is dead." Druzie gently drew her down to him and caressed her body. "Oh, Celie, I do adore you. You're my angel with light brown hair and crystal blue eyes. I remember your looks when we were little before I became blind. I don't think you've changed. You'll always be the light that pierces my dark world." He touched her face. "You have never, ever, hurt anyone, and I want to teach you, once again, to dream and allow yourself to be loved. Do you understand?"

"I do...Druzie. I want that. I don't like feeling as I do. I'm robbing myself of life. Did Neilly really love me? I have to be sure."

"With all of his heart, and I know you loved him."

"I did. We had a good marriage. I wasn't ever afraid of him. But....but my feelings for you are so different. We understand each other. Druzie, I have missed you, but I feel guilty for even saying that. You know Pa also said I was a creation of the devil."

"Stop it right now, Cecilia Fears Livingston Dulligan, I abjure you in the name of the Father, Son, and Holy Ghost, and I am crossing myself with the sign of St. Andrew. I am exorcising you of guilt this day. Do you understand? And when you start these doubts and fears, I want you to remember this afternoon and the words of an old hymn Mamma used to sing to me. The words were something like giving our fears to the winds. Those words have comforted me."

"You sound like a blind prophet."

"I am," he said, drawing her closer. "You're irresistible."

"You, too....do you think Neilly knew we loved each other?"

"Yes, but it didn't bother him. He understood and trusted himself and us. He knew that we understood each other. It never worried him."

"Oh, Druzie, we've been soul mates since childhood, haven't we?"

"Yes, we're double-first cousins. We understand each other. We're almost as close as twins."

"That bothers me, and you know it," she continued.

"It does not trouble me at all, and I want to spend the rest of my days on earth with you." They made love and lingered in the church until after sunset, Celie agreeing to move to White Oaks within a few months.

"I'll always protect you," he assured, "for I have money. Pa left me some, and I have his gold."

"I have very little," she answered. "I discovered that Neilly gave Bubba a lot of money for medicine and, apparently, gambling. I was never suspicious, but I've looked at my late husband's books. I've been surprised and…and hurt, I suppose. I guess that's what George was doing all those times he took the mule and left the bluffs. Maybe he was going to the tavern in Swannkell. I don't know, for sure. Maybe he went to Essex. I do have enough to pay taxes and keep us going here for a few more years, especially if the crops are successful. I don't know what will ever become of my brother. At least, he has Hebrides' company. Maybe he'll find someone to love after Hebrides passes."

"I'm glad. Hebrides never did quite fit in with the colored folks, did he? I'm glad George paid Ma for the man's freedom." Druzie sighed. "Such a wasted life, George has lived these last few years, but he's that way because he saved my life. I will never abandon him. And if he and Hebrides enjoyed each other, who is anybody to judge? It never worried me at all. I'll pay the taxes on Mulberry Bluffs until I die, and then, I'll leave my money to you. Ma will leave what Father left to me. We'll be comfortable."

"Thank you, my darling Druzie. Let's go to the hovel and have peaches and cold biscuits. Shall we? And I need to see what my little girl is doing."

"Shall we have a glass of wine, too?"

While they were talking over wine, Mary Caroline stormed in and kicked the milk stool. "I hate Harriett DeGraffenreid. She tagged me when we were playing hide and seek. So I bit her arm, and she told Josie. My big sister says I deserve a spanking."

"You probably do," Druzie said. "That was naughty of you. After all, aren't the rules of hide and seek to tag the one who's caught?"

Celie picked up Mary Caroline and rocked her, soothing her tangled hair. "Sh…now tell me all about it, honey, and lower your voice. There's no need to make a ruckus, sugar-pie."

"Mamma, why is the man with the funny eyes still here?"

"Because I invited him to stay for supper. I'm sure Cudn Druzie would tell you a story if you'd settle down for a little while."

"No. I don't like him." Within a second, the child jumped off her mother's lap and ran from the hovel.

"Oh, Druzie, I'm sorry," Celie said.

"MC doesn't hurt my feelings. I don't think she'll ever love me or like me. I just worry over what she will become."

"She's different from the others, as we said. But I will never punish her."

Druzie kissed his cousin. "It's late. I think I'll stay at the lodge tonight if you'll take me there."

Celie gave him one of Neilly's night shirts and led the way. When they arrived, Celie saw all the children gathered around Eliza who was reading them a story. "Miss Celie, can Mary Caroline and Josie stay with us tonight in the lodge?"

"Why I suppose so, so long as Anteegwine stays with you. I think the boys better come on to the house, though. By the way, Master Bain will be staying in the first room tonight, so please mind your manners. Have a happy time. If anything bothers you, tell Anteegwine, or call on Master Bain. Or just come on home. The boys and I will be there."

Josie told her mother that they had all enjoyed a picnic in the woods.

"And you didn't even know it, did you, Ma?" Burr asked, a twinkle in his eyes.

"No....sleep well. Eliza, will you tuck the little ones in bed?"

"Yes ma'am," the older girl answered.

During the night, Celie smelled smoke and immediately got up and ran down the lane, calling the boys to come help. The lodge was blazing. She heard screaming in the woods and recognized Josie's voice, then saw Mary Caroline dart behind a tree.

"Mary Caroline," Josie said, "did you start that fire with your candle? Where did you go after Eliza finished saying prayers last night? I went to brush my hair, and Eliza tucked the girls in bed, then worked on embroidery for a little while. Were you with the younger children?"

"No, I was playing by myself. That's what I do most of the time because you are mean to me. If you're ugly to me again, I'll spit out my tongue and run away. I don't like you, and I don't like that cousin with the funny eyes either."

"Shame on you, little sister. He's one of the nicest people I have ever met, and he's a kind teacher. He makes our lessons interesting, and you know it."

"Where are you, Josie, Mary Caroline?" Celie called, frantic, as the fire crackled away, spreading to the stable. "The mule and Moonlight Bay, and the old pony the boys sometimes rode...Druzie, the girls, Antigone, Nessie," she whispered to herself. "Where are they?"

"We're over here, Mamma." It was Josie.

"Where's your sister?"

"I don't know. She was here a second ago. Where are Hugh and Burr?"

"Gone to the well for water."

"And Nessie and Antigone?"

"To the river, Ma. All I remember about last night was finishing prayers and brushing my hair and Eliza working on her embroidery. The younger girls had gone to their room. Then, all of a sudden, we heard a crackling sound and smelled something burning. It was scary. I realized the lodge was on fire. I called everybody. I looked for Mary Caroline and went to the little girls' room. Their door was locked, and I couldn't push it in. I called Eliza, but she went back to her room for something. I ran down to Cudn Druzie's room. His door was locked, too, but I got in through a window and found him. His hands were burning. All I could do was put them out with his quilt. Then I took him to the church. Mary Caroline was there. She was laughing and lighting candles. I took the candles from her, and she ran outside. Ma, I think Eliza's dead and the little girls. If she jumped from the third floor and if the little girls were trapped."

The boys came with buckets of water and struggled to put out the flames which competed for brightness with the full moon. Seeing the woods blazing, London, Memnon, and the others came from White Oaks, but they could do nothing. By morning, the lodge and stable had burned to the ground. Only a dinted gold cross glistened in the rubble. "That was Eliza's, Mamma," Josie cried.

Celie's stomach knotted, and her breathing was heavy. She trudged to the church and found Druzie shaking, his night shirt charred, torn. She listened as he prayed.

"Your hands, darling," she said. "They're..."

"Oh, they hurt...Celie, I can't describe the pain. And my eyes."

She wiped her forehead and his. "I don't know what to do now. I don't even have any salve or wash, and I am so ashamed and sorry."

"Take me to White Oaks," he trembled. "Monica will have something. But the children?"

"The orphan children burned to death, Druzie...I..."

"Celie, don't start that damned guilt, please. I can't help you tonight. I can't."

"Do you...do you remember anything that happened?"

"I was sleeping, dreaming, I think. I felt the moon smiling down on me, and we were talking, the moon and I...and then all at once, I sensed someone's presence, someone standing over the bed, and the fragrance of mulberry. I stretched out my hands to feel who it was, and the person slapped my eyes, then gave a cruel, demonical kind of laugh, and shouted, "You'll burn and burn, and I'm going to put wax in your funny eyes." Within a second, the person poured a little wax in my eyes and put the lighted candle to my hands. I tried to beat the flames out with the quilt, and...I walked to the door. Something was against it, like a chest. I tried to shove it and unlock the door. The laughter continued. I screamed, and the next thing I remember was Josie coming in and leading me to the church."

"Do you know who that person was?"

"I can't say, Celie."

"Or you won't say?"

"Celie, please stop it. There's no point in saying anything. We both know that. I am exhausted and suffering. Please get me home to White Oaks, and come when you are able. I need you."

She led Druzie to the hovel and soothed some lard on his hands and put cold tea compresses on his eyes. Burr came in with his father's clothes. "I'll carry you to White Oaks, Cudn Druzie. The animals and the wagon all burned."

Celie and Nessie prepared the orphan children's bodies and buried them on the slope behind the chapel. She wept. The bluffs were barren again. The chapel and the slave cabin, the corncrib, and another cabin down near George's survived and, of course, the hovel. "It will always be here," Celie sighed. "And I still have my black dresses. How many years will I mourn?"

Mary Caroline heard her mother. "I'm not mourning. I'm glad they all died. Eliza was mean to me, and so was that Harriett DeGraffenreid."

"Mary Caroline, tell me. Do you know who started the fire?"

The child, now nearly nine years old, looked up into her mother's face and said, "You....you put a curse on the lodge. Or maybe God just wanted it to burn. Maybe your Cudn Druzie's eyes began blazing. I don't know."

"Oh, Mary Caroline, your attitude hurts me so. Surely you understand I want to know who set the fire. Surely you know most everyone thinks you did. I....I won't punish you. I just want to help you. I'm not a doctor, but...I am your mother, and... Were you playing with mulberry candles last night? Please tell me. I know burning mulberry is fragrant, isn't it?"

"Ma, you're stupid if you think I'd tell you anything. I wouldn't tell you if I could, and I couldn't tell you if I would, and I won't ever tell you what I know." She stuck out her tongue and ran from the room.

"You speak in riddles, Mary Caroline. Please don't torment me so," Celie called.

"Mother," Josie said, hearing the end of the conversation, "you have to do something with my sister. I'm know she started the fire, and so do you. Why...Why do you always protect her?"

"Because, Josie, I....I am afraid of my own child."

"Ma, let's leave for White Oaks. It's our home. We don't have to stay here anymore."

"For not being thirteen, you are so wise, my dear Josie. You are the mother I would wish for."

"And the psaltery's at White Oaks for you to play."

"And it definitely does not create tapsalteerie as my harsh father used to say. Oh, sometime I'll tell you that story."

"I could make words from that word. Let's go to bed. I can only imagine how tired you are. I love you, Mamma."

"My soul waiteth for the Lord more than they that watch for the morning: I say, more than they that watch for the morning"
(Psalm 130:6).

Book Nineteen (1850-1852)

By late September, Celie and her family had settled into the daily rituals at White Oaks. The boys helped Druzie at the grist mill, along with Lafayette and his son, Nathan. They also often hunted and fished. Mary Caroline and Josie busied themselves with embroidery and reading.

Celie spent her time with Monica and Aunt Agnes whom she looked on as the mother she'd never had. They usually worked in the kitchen garden, sewed, and sometimes simply talked. "Aunt Agnes, help me. I am afraid of my own Mary Caroline. I know it, and so does everybody else. I imagine they all laugh at me for calling myself her mother. Please tell me what to do."

"I'll try. I would do with Mary Caroline what I did with Druzie when he was a little boy, what my mother did with your father and me when we were young, long before he left home and changed into the raging fanatic you knew. We were always encouraged to stay busy with what we enjoyed. I wrote poetry and kept a journal of flowers and herbs in the garden. My brother used to enjoy looking for gems in the mines when we lived in the mountains. Because Druzie seemed to enjoy fencing and riding, I encouraged him to concentrate on those activities. Of course, his father made him learn to operate the grist mill. Druzie enjoyed that. The activities were practical and pleasurable. We simply need to find out what Mary Caroline really enjoys."

"I have no idea, except playing games and then hitting the children who follow the rules," Celie sighed.

"Well, we could teach her croquet, rounders, and graces and encourage her to knit. She won't know how unless she has a teacher, and that is Biblical....and, ultimately kind and practical, and really compassionate. But you must never, ever, allow her to ruin the joy of others. I know she doesn't like my son. She's jealous of your affection for Druzie. You do know that, don't you, Celie."

"I do." Celie's eyes filled with tears as she retold her aunt of the child's birthing. "That's why it's so hard for me to punish her. She didn't ask to be born like that. Can you understand, Aunt Aggie? Druzie doesn't. I think he blames me."

"I know and understand your feelings for her as a mother, but your daughter cannot run wild. That's not fair to her or to anyone."

Celie admired Aunt Agnes. Even garbed in the black she'd worn since Uncle Wash died, Aunt Agnes was radiant. Her hair graying, eyes soft and gentle, forehead wrinkling, she always listened and smiled, waiting, as if she had the most wonderful, assuring surprise to offer. There was music at White Oaks, not gloom and guilt. There was the compassion and love God asked his disciples to have. "Tell you what we'll plan. I'll invite Mary Caroline to a tea party tomorrow. We'll have lemonade and ginger cakes or tea cakes."

"Monica served me those a long time ago. Do you remember? When I was little and came over from the bluffs."

"I do. Celie, Your daughter may enjoy a tea party, as you did, but I don't think she is ready for grandmother's psaltery, do you?"

"No. She would probably break it and brag about it."

"I'm so glad you're here, my dear, and so is Druzie. You know how fond of you he truly is."

"Oh, I love him, Aunt Agnes. He is my soul-mate."

"That I am, Coz," Druzie said, as he came into the room and sat beside her on the sofa. He poured himself a glass of brandy.

"Where have you been?" his mother asked, her tone non-judgmental.

"Talking to Prince down at the grist mill. You know, he's remarkable. He wouldn't tell me his age. Says he doesn't know, but he thinks he's close to 100. Did Grandfather keep records?"

"I don't know, Son. I don't think so, all I ever heard about Dr. Bain was that he received land in Blisland County and began to build this plantation. Prince was young when he was sold to your grandfather.

"Coz, one day, Mother and I are going to free the slaves," Dru said, turning to Celie.

"Yes," his mother interrupted, "that's about the only thing your father and I ever agreed on, Celie. Even before your father met that Dr. Wemyss, we thought slavery was wrong."

Celie agreed, then asked Druzie if he had seen Mary Caroline.

He began laughing.

"Druzie, what did you do to Celie's child?" Aunt Agnes teased. "You have that tone of mischief in your voice. I can tell."

Celie marveled at the ease with which mother and son talked and hoped one day her relationship with Hugh and Burr might be that relaxed.

"Oh, Aunt Agnes, I want to learn from you. You're so calm....you never seem to worry."

"It doesn't do any good. What is to be will be, and all of the fretting in the world will not change it. I told Druzie that long ago when he was a little boy. He remembers the hymn I used to sing about giving fears to the wind."

"Yes, he's quoted the words to me more than once."

Druzie nodded as his mother continued, Celie, thinking to herself, "No, his brown eyes are not funny. They do gaze, but they are kind and gentle. They smile, like his mother's. His hair style is antiquated, and yes, dark brown, curly waves frame his rosy cheeks, but..." She put her head on his shoulder as he took her hands in his cloth-covered ones.

"What shames me, is knowing my child burned you, Druzie, and I've done absolutely nothing, absolutely nothing, to punish her because I am afraid of her. Isn't that pathetic? But I can't whip a child who is not right, who didn't ask to be born, let alone be delivered by a rapist who calls himself a doctor and an elder in the church. You probably tire of hearing my tale, but I will never forget the shame, the pain, the humiliation, the violence that afternoon. I can't forget." She shivered.

"We don't believe in whippings either, Celie. You know that, but my dear, you must not allow Mary Caroline to go untaught, undisciplined," her aunt said. "That would not be fair to her or to you. We live in a civilized world. I enjoyed some of Rousseau's views when I was in Paris, but certainly not all of them. Sometimes he seemed too free. I've been thinking, and I would like to send your daughters to Mrs. Gray's Seminary in Millsborough. It would be my gift. Would you give me permission?"

"Oh, Aunt Agnes, I will be grateful for anything you do. I cannot go on like this. I think I'd rather be dead," Celie answered. "These fears are against my psaltery."

"Well, Elizabeth Gray is a friend from Virginia. I believe she played with Edgar Allan Poe when they were both children. She's a gifted teacher whose views you and Druzie would support, based on your curriculum at Mulberry Bluffs, and your views on learning. Her husband, John Washington Gray, is an artist. You know, Celie, there are many kinds of discipline. Sometimes, I just think a punishment should equal the crime. If Mary Caroline stomped on my foot, why I might say to her, 'Do to yourself what you did to me."

Celie nodded. "Yes, I think even I could require that of my daughter."

"But not a hard stomp, just gentle one." Aunt Agnes also recommended a regular diet of exercise and herbs. "Now I'm offering Mary Caroline cookies tomorrow, but she doesn't need sweets every day, do you think?"

Druzie began laughing again. "I never finished my story. You want to hear the details?"

They nodded.

"Well, Mary Caroline came into the library where Josie was reading to me and began ripping out the pages of the book, so I caught her and pulled her to me. I untied her hair ribbons and put them in my pocket. She began kicking the furniture, so I made her kick the hearth. She kicked it so hard she hurt her foot, and then I just gave her some bourbon with sugar. As far as I know she's sound asleep in the library."

"And now I'll have to deal with her when she awakens," Celie accused. "That's not fair, and she'll be limping, too. So what do I say, Master Druzie?"

Aunt Agnes smiled, patted her son, and excused herself. "Good night, my dears. You'll have to settle this one. Things will all work out. They just take time."

"Well, Celie," Druzie continued, "If you don't do something, we'll just be allowing your younger daughter to rule us. We'll all become victims of a Deceiver."

"Druzie, stop it." Celie stood up and began walking about the room. "Mary Caroline is not a deceiver, and you know it. Oh, I feel restless, angry tonight. I want to walk down by the river."

"Then, do, my love, by all means. I won't stop you."

"No, I really want to argue…I'm tired of always yielding. But I'm really not angry with you, only frustrated with myself."

"I imagine so. Why don't you go give MC some more bourbon and sugar, and then we can walk or just listen to the crickets singing."

"I can't do that, and you know it, Druzie. Damn it, Druzie, I can't encourage a little girl to become an addict. Besides, you've never seen Mary Caroline come up and kiss me or bring me a little flower she picked in the woods."

"You're right. All I've ever seen her do is whimper, throw tantrums, and burn my hands and eyes. Maybe she's renounced the good. I don't know, but waxed eyes hurt. So do burned hands. I may be blind, but I'm not a carving yet. My sight may be gone, but my other senses are still intact. I can hear, and I can feel a touch on my hand. I'm not stupid."

"Stop it, Druzie!" Celie screamed. "You're burdening me, making me feel guilty. It's maddening."

"Come here, Coz," he laughed, extending his bandaged hands, "and let me kiss you."

"No...I'm going to bed. I'm tired and depressed, and....I'm going to have a brandy or two myself. Goodnight, Druzie." She left the room and walked into the hall adjoining the tower.

"No goodnight kiss for a poor blind beggar with burned hands?"

"No, damn you, Druzie. I'm too angry for that."

Hearing her run up the stairs, he called one last time. "Meet me at noon under our favorite white oak. I have something for you."

Upstairs in the tower, Celie flung herself across the bed and wept, confused and angry. "What would Neilly have done? Silly, if Neilly had lived, Mary Caroline would have probably had a gentle birth. Even if she hadn't, Neilly was so relaxed he would have coaxed her into behaving by playing with her. Maybe Druzie's trying to do the same thing. I don't know. I'll talk to Monica. She'll understand. I hate Barnie Dunn, and I want him to suffer," she sobbed into the pillow, her mind racing.

The next morning when she was dressing, Mary Caroline burst into the room. "Mamma, your eyes are all red. You look more like a witch than usual. Why do you always wear that silly black veil?"

Celie put her arms around her daughter, "Please, honey, witches ride broomsticks, and they are unkind. They cast spells on people. I don't believe your ma has ever done that to you, do you? Besides, Monica wants you to spend the morning with her, and Aunt Agnes has something special for you this afternoon. I want you to mind them and be sweet, will you?"

"Yes, Ma. I'll try."

"You know Monica was my grandmother Cecilia's closest friend, and she's becoming mine as well. She's very wise. Listen to her."

Mary Caroline kissed her mother good-bye and ran from the room. Celie splashed herself with rose water and looked in the mirror. "You do look like a forlorn, old woman today. Well, maybe you have a little hangover." She pushed back the black mourning veil and pinched her cheeks. "Celie, you're not even fifty years old, but you look almost 70. Stop fearing. Don't let people conjugate your name anymore. All Mary Caroline needs is a little rebuking and whatever it was Aunt Agnes called it....equal punishment or something."

"You'll feel better," a voice whispered back. "Smile. Play that psaltery. Embrace its music, its love, the psalms, our stories, too. Celie, you know, that's our psaltery here at White Oaks. Dream, and be. Become. Sing. Don't be afraid." She wondered if it was Druzie talking to her.

Deep down she knew he wasn't. He was at the white oak. Yet she still couldn't bring herself to get up and walk up the hill to meet him. Celie lay down on the bed, knowing the sun was already high over the tower, Druzie waiting, but she couldn't move.

Aunt Agnes came, then Monica. "I can't go," Celie wept to both of them. "I'm ashamed and so afraid. I drank too much brandy."

Aunt Agnes patted her shoulder and left, but Monica lingered. "Honey, your face is swollen red, and you heaving. What's wrong?"

Celie tried to talk, and Monica listened for an occasional word. "Do you love Druzie?"

"Hm...hm. With all my heart."

"Then, marry him. Give yourself to him. Don't doubt no more. Your grand mammy Cecilia couldn't say that about her heart. That was part of the problem, aside from Dr. Bain's cruelty. But you can say it, so don't ever let nothing get in the way of your heart. That's God speaking to you, dwelling in you. I guess dat's 'the holy spirit down in my heart, today.'"

Celie listened, then asked, once again. "Am I like my grandma?"

"Very much. Only difference is she felt sumpin ridin dem horses. You ain't never felt that...I think...no, I don't know right now. You seem a little more content. I just trying to tell you to give yourself to your cousin, double or no, if you really loves him...I know he loves you...I don't think your grandpa ever fully loved my best friend until she was about to die. He dun took her for granted. Don't ever take nobody for granted, honey. And don't let yo child turn yo grandma's psaltery into a tapsalteerie. You understand?"

She nodded. "Will Neilly understand?"

"Of course?"

"And George?"

"He and my son, Hebrides, waz lovers, and you know it. Massa George he ain't worried about you, so long as he can drink and not feel his body pain, and ain't nuthin you ken do...jes be kind to him when he's old...laws of Moses would abandon him cauf what he dun to you, but you goes by the faith of Jesus. You understand the difference?"

"I do, Monica. Thank you."

"Now, honey, wipe yo face, and push back that mourning veil. It's time. You ken still wear dat mourning brooch and earrings, but no more covering dem big, blue eyes. It's been nearly ten years since Massa Neilly died. Let's go down for supper, and you be kind to Massa Druzie. He won't neva hurt you."

Celie washed her face and went to the dining room where everyone was at the table enjoying fried chicken, corn pudding, apples, green beans, and biscuits.

"Mamma," Mary Caroline said, "Monica taught me how to dry herbs, and I enjoyed my tea party with Aunt Agnes. And I saw Unkie with his blind, funny eyes waiting under the white oak on the hill. He eats in a strange way. Look how he's sopping his biscuit. Why doesn't he use his fork?"

Celie looked her daughter in the eye. "I want you to go upstairs right now, Mary Caroline, and bring me my wooden sewing box, and no if's, and's, or but's about it."

Watching their baby sister obeying for a change, Hugh and Burr and Josie snickered.

"Sh...," Aunt Agnes said.

When Mary Caroline returned, Celie casually took a piece of muslin from the box, tore the cloth into two strips, and wrapped her daughter's hands. "Now, you wear these coverings for the next few days, and you'll understand why Cudn Druzie has to eat that way. His hands were burned. They hurt. Yours do not. That means, you have to eat, sleep, wash, and dress without taking them off. Do you understand? And if you disobey me, why I'll try something different. I want you to put on your nice manners all the time, and I will help you do that. Do you understand?"

Mary Caroline sulked and sat down.

"Now wipe that silly frown from your brow, and eat your pudding."

From then on, Celie began preparing the girls for Mrs. Gray's seminary, and if Mary Caroline ever misbehaved, Celie admonished her.

One afternoon, when the child splashed water on Druzie's prized hound, her mother saw her and called, "Come on, let's go to the well, Mary Caroline, and be sure to bring a bucket."

Josie followed, surprised, curious to see what her mother would do.

Celie took her daughter's bucket and told her to fill it with water. "Now, you're the hound, and I'm showering you. Dry yourself, honey. That's what Unkie's hound had to do. And he is old."

"Ma," Mary Caroline wailed.

"Don't worry. You'll be just fine. 'Do unto others as you would have them do unto you.' You'll be much happier."

Later in the week, Memnon drove Aunt Agnes and the children to Millsborough to the fair. The girls enjoyed the fortune teller and the various stunts, and they met Mrs. Gray. The boys watched students drilling on the lawn at Mount Hebron and grinned for the plum pudding.

"What did the gypsy woman tell you all?" Celie asked.

"She said Burr and I were going to fight in a war one day. That's exciting, isn't it, Ma?"

"I don't want my sons getting hurt."

"And did you like Mrs. Gray's school, Mary Caroline?" Druzie asked.

"Yes...Mrs. Gray says I can study the stars and learn to waltz."

"And I'm going to paint," Josie insisted. "When can we start, Aunt Agnes?"

"I believe the spring term begins in January. Are you excited, honey?"

"Oh yes," Celie's older daughter, always polite and courteous, answered. "And I appreciate your sending Mary Caroline and me."

On Christmas Day, Agnes and Celie passed out shoes and clothing to the few slaves who remained at White Oaks. Neither of the women realized how many servants Druzie had already freed. Christmas was different. It was a little somber, the family still in mourning for the children at the school. There were evergreens, candles, puddings, and dances in The Quarters, but nobody sang carols in the big house. The boys sneaked off and did fireworks along the river.

In mid January when her daughters left for Millsborough, Celie finally relaxed and agreed to meet Druzie under the white oak. "Don't disappoint me this time, Coz."

Celie knew the sun was rising over the house, but she hesitated, wondering why.

"Honey, he's waiting," Monica said. "He has sumpin for you. Trust yourself now, and go."

Celie wrapped Aunt Agnes' black cloak about herself and put on her black bonnet, then trudged up the hill.

Druzie was sitting there, his head against the tree, sleeping, the poke hat over his eyes when Celie finally tiptoed to his side, sat down, and kissed him. "Druzie, I'm here."

"Do you have a hangover?"

"No, darling, I don't."

"I want you to reach in my pocket and take out the little box. With my hands, I can't. Lafayette and Nathan have to help me dress, and I hate that. You know we're not like George and Hebrides."

"Silly, don't you think I know that."

Tears filled her eyes, as she looked at his wrapped hands. She opened the tiny box.

"You'll see our grandmother's emerald earrings and a Masonic ring. My father gave them to me, and I want you to wear them. This was the ring that saved Grandpa's life that night at Brookgreen. You know the story."

She nodded. "Monica says I'm like Grandmother. Do you think so?"

"From all the stories, I'd say so...you're what she dreamed of becoming. You've had the school Grandpa wouldn't allow her to open. And you have her abiding spirit of love, and I won't let anyone take it from you. Oh, even though you're wearing black, you're beautiful." He drew her down on the grass as she whispered, "Be patient with me, Druzie. You're helping me overcome that fear."

"Darling, let me take off the veil. Take it off for me, will you? This is the tenth year of Neilly's death, and I yearn for you...I want to claim you as mine. Will you come to me now and..."

"Oh, yes, Druzie, I am yours, always. Take away the veil, and...and come to me as you will."

He gently removed the veil, and with gauzed fingers, caressed her cheeks, her brows, her neck, her breasts. "Oh, you are so precious. Celie, so beautiful. Will you marry me?"

"Oh, yes, whenever you say," she answered, turning, helping him push up her long skirts, then gently moving with him as he turned her over on the grass and took her fully into himself.

"Oh, Druzie," she whispered. "Oh, I love you. I always have. I am yours...I. I feel freer than ever...I"

"Sh, love, you don't have to say anything." He unbuttoned her dress and caressed her, and came to her again and again. "Oh, Celie....my bride, my love, my psaltery."

All through the winter months, they walked along the river, talking, making up for all of times they'd missed. Druzie taught her how to operate the mill, and Celie showed him how to bow the psaltery.

In February, Celie knew her tummy was swelling. "It's our baby, Druzie. I'm carrying our child. Oh, I am so happy...I...and what will we name the baby?"

"Whatever you wish. Let's marry this afternoon..."

"I'd like that...let's ask Prince to marry us at White Oaks Chapel with your mother, Monica, and the boys there...I'll tell the girls later when they come home from school.'

"And you'll wear Grandmother's emerald silk dress, the one Ma wore."

"Yes," Celie answered.

"And the earrings."

"I've been wearing them since you gave them to me, sweetheart...and I want you to wear this ring...I don't know where it came from. Monica found it in Grandpa's chest."

"Origins don't matter, do they, when you love? That you are giving a ring to me is what matters, and I have a wedding band for you."

A bad storm forced them to postpone the marriage ceremony until March the first.

"St. David's Day," Aunt Agnes smiled…"but no leeks for good luck, only your love for each other. Oh, this is the day I've dreamed of. I am so happy for you both."

Monica beamed, "You the bride your grandmammy longed to be and feel. Oh, she's blessing you now, knowing you both are twin souls come together as one. That's what she always yearned for, dreamed of…and I can die, knowing she's at peace now. Oh, honey chile," Monica wept just before Prince opened his Bible and asked the couple to join him in pledging their troth, one to another, under the white oaks just a few feet from the tombstone of Cecilia Fears Lynch Bain, clusters of daffodils blooming among the lonely markers in the afternoon sun.

The months passed, spring yielding to summer, summer to fall, and in early September of 1851, Celie went into labor. "I want Druzie at my side."

"I'm right here with you. Hold my hand, and squeeze when it hurts. Here, drink this tea Monica made."

"Oh, you spoil me," she murmured, her face sweating. "I…I don't deserve such kindness…"

"But you do, and more…don't you ever forget it…scream, honey…just do what Monica and Nessie tell you…they know all about birthing. The only thing I know is how much I adore you…"

After a long afternoon, Monica delivered their baby, a little boy.

"Oh, he's handsome," she said, and handed the baby to his mother to suck. Celie sensed something was wrong. The child wheezed, and his tiny right hand was crooked, but he nursed easily, just like her other children.

"He's as beautiful as Massa Druzie was when he was born over forty years ago, ain't he? Why he's smiling." Celie searched for Monica's eyes, then turned to Druzie.

"Do you?"

"Yes…I feel his wheezing and his little hand, but we love him. We'll strengthen our baby, and…darling, that's all he needs…"

"Druzie, it…it's the curse…Grandma's breasts, my mother's skin, my deformity…I've passed this to our baby…it's the sins of the fathers passed on from one generation to the next…Oh, Cudn, his withered hand. A deformity is what I feared most. I've done it. Nobody else." She turned into the pillow and sobbed as Druzie took their son.

"Let her sleep," Monica sighed…"She's weary…we all are…she'll be alright, Massa Druzie…you're here for her…let the baby sleep, and you rest yourself, too."

Monica gave him a glass of brandy, and he put his arms around her. "Monica, thank you for everything…"

"You don't need to say nothing, honey. You already said it by loving Miss Celie, as her grand mammy and yours, longed to be loved long, long ago. You did it so easily simply by encouraging Celie to play that psaltery and sing."

Even Mary Caroline was excited over the baby when she visited White Oaks at Christmas. "Mamma, let's call him 'Wheezie' cause he does wheeze." Josie chimed in, "That's a nice name. It's different, but I like it. Do you, Unkie? Do you, Mamma?"

"We do," Druzie said. "And Wheezie he will be."

The baby nursed ravenously and grabbed with his good hand. Aunt Agnes ordered him a sterling rattle from Charleston, hoping that clasping might help his withered hand.

Josie and Mary Caroline returned to school for the spring term, and Celie gradually regained her strength. She cradled the baby, and sat with Aunt Agnes, often asking questions about the family, while Druzie and the boys worked in the grist mill or rode the horses.

"Aunt Agnes, I want to know more about the bluffs. Will you tell me?"

"Of course, I will. You've probably heard something. There are lots of stories about Mulberry Bluffs. Anyway, your grandfather sold the bluffs to a Dr. Boucher who wanted to build a school for orphans. He and the music teacher were both from Carcassonne. The doctor had given her a ring and promised to marry her. Well, there was a pretty young lady there, an orphan, and the doctor fell in love with her. Need I say more? The teacher became jealous and set the school and chapel on fire. Some folks believed that a Negro woman whom Dr. Boucher had once whipped set his vineyard on fire. Others said a younger child at the school experienced a vision where an angel commanded her to burn the stable. It seems that a horse had thrown the child. 'Brulez, brulez' was the command."

"They're fascinating. Which do you believe, Aunt Agnes?"

"Oh, I don't know," the older lady smiled. "It doesn't matter anymore."

"I know Mary Caroline burned the plantation the second time. That was terrible, and I wonder if she remembers any of the details, if she recalls how evil she was."

"Sh...you tend to this little baby. Mary Caroline seems content now, and Druzie is healing. I just know that sometimes on a cold October night when the moon is full, I'll hear a crackling and a chorus of wailing voices. Druzie's father heard them, too, but he wasn't ever afraid. He actually argued with them."

Celie laughed. "I can see him and hear him railing out in the night." Celie shuddered, and Wheezie stretched and opened his eyes. "Oh, Aunt Agnes, he looks like Druzie. Isn't our baby beautiful?"

"He is, and don't ever let anyone rob you of the joy you and my son share. God gave you to each other."

Celie nodded. "I won't."

"You know, time heals, and you're becoming the person God intends you to be.

Remember God wants you to embrace life and turn to him for comfort. He will never forsake you. Hold to your blessings, and share those with others. Be gentle, and trust your heart."

"Thank you. Aunt Agnes, do you think Wheezie's breathing is better?"

"I do...and his little hand, too. He has the sweetest smile, and he's looking up at you right now, honey." Celie nursed the baby, then walked down to the millpond to see Druzie, singing all the way, the berries in the dogwoods a bright red. Soon, the boys would be shooting down mistletoes and gathering greenery for the hearth. Christmas was coming.

"But it is good for me to draw near to God: I have put my trust
in the Lord God, that I may declare all thy works" (Psalm 73:28).

Book Twenty (Fall, 1853)

When Wheezie was a little over a year, Celie and Druzie decided to attend a service at their grandfather's church. "It's been a long time since I've seen his brick tower....times have changed, and maybe we will have the baby christened there," Druzie said. "What do you think?"

"Why don't we go to church tomorrow. Wheezie seems to be breathing better. In fact, we'll ask your mother and Monica and the boys. I suppose Mrs. Gray takes the girls to church in Millsborough. You know I've never even asked that question, Druzie."

"Nothing to worry about, my sweet."

"You're right. And you know, I do believe Mary Caroline has grown rather fond of you, don't you think?"

"She does seem less petulant, doesn't she? And I am proud of you for not giving in and enabling her to get away with those irritable moods."

The next morning was clear and crisp, and the leaves of the dogwood, elms, and oaks turning and whirling in the wind, the sky a rich deep blue, as Celie held the baby and waited with the boys and Aunt Agnes on the porch for Druzie. He finally came up from the stable, Lafayette following.

"Honey, Nellie's filly has a swollen eye. Prince thinks it's from the bees swarming around in that nest near the stable. We can't be sure, though. He wants to burn them out....I think I better stay near...and be with the horses. You understand, don't you?"

"Now, you know I do. We'll take the wagon."

"Let Lafayette drive you in the coach."

"No, I feel more comfortable in the old wagon. I want to drive."

"You take the Lord's Supper for me, will you. I'm sure I need it."

"Silly boy," Celie laughed.

"Hush, Druzie Bain," his mother gently admonished.

"Celie, take these tokens. You know, Grandfather left quite a collection of tokens, and we've never used them. They'll be happy to be of some use, and you'll need them."

She kissed Druzie good-bye and tucked a crocheted blanket around Wheezie, then asked Aunt Agnes to hold him. She took the horse's reins.

Hugh Fears and Burr piled in, handsome in their dress clothes, just as their mother lifted the whip. The horse took off down the lane.

"Ma, why do we have to go?" Burr grumbled.

"Well...well, I would just like for you to be with me. Besides, you may just see Miss Rosa Alison Oliphant at church. I've heard you're sweet on her. Is that right, son?"

Burr blushed, as Hugh scoffed. "Well, I'm not ever going to marry."

"And be like Uncle George and Hebrides?" Burr answered.

"I don't think so, Burr Fennell, and you know that."

When they arrived at Brick Tower Church, Wheezie was asleep. As they walked into the church, Celie found a bench and began joined the congregation in singing one of her favorite hymns, "Rock of Ages." Caught up with the melody and words, "Nothing in my hand I bring, simply to thy cross I cling; Naked, come to Thee for dress, Helpless, look to Thee for grace; Foul, I to the fountain fly; Wash me, Savior, or I die," Celie did not look up at the pulpit until she heard the preacher bellow forth the name of someone she feared.

"Elder Dunn, is there anyone here without a token or who should not be allowed to partake of the Lord's Supper, this most sacred meal, this supper of the Lamb of God 'who taketh away the sins of the whole world.' Is there a sinner amongst us this day?" The minister tugged at his grayish red beard and leered at the congregation. "Is there a sinner among us, I ask."

"Indeed, in our midst," answered Dr. Barnie Dunn who sauntered forward, "we have a woman who, unlike the woman at the well in our Biblical lesson has not repented of her sins. She sits with her wizard son to your left. Indeed, she is an abomination in the sight of all who profess to be Christians, either by faith or letter. Her sins are worse than those of China Lee who was found guilty of fornicating with Jubal at our last session meeting."

"Elder, please stop the verbosity. Does the woman have a token?"

"I do," Celie answered, standing to present hers. "All of the members of the Bain family have tokens."

Ignoring her meek voice, Barnie continued, "Regardless, I proclaim this woman a witch in the sight of Almighty God. She has never shown any sort of humility or shame or guilt and repentance for living in incest with her kinsman, Andrew Washington Bain whose mother, Agnes, herself, once a harlot in the streets of Paris, dares to sit amongst us. Yes, despite early contributions to this church of the late Dr. Colin Macaulay Bain, this woman must be removed from our midst. I have observed her body. I had the displeasure of being asked to deliver her fifth child shortly after the death of her one true husband. The woman is three-breasted, and the child who now sucks is a wizard. He has a withered hand, another sign of the malignity of one generation being passed on to the next."

"Well, then, remove her from our presence, so that we may proceed with the Word of God, of doing unto others as we would unto ourselves. Whip her at the nearest hickory, and I order you, John Ephraim Banks and Alphaeus Crowley Stephenson, to carry out this commandment."

Despite Agnes' protests, Celie was pulled from the church, stripped to the waist, tied to the nearest hickory, and whipped, Barnie counting each stroke. "I vowed I'd get even with you for humiliating me years ago, for leaving me at the creek years ago. Once again, I am punishing you, and I rejoice in the power of the Holy Spirit upon me. It is my vengeance. I call for thirteen lashes, elders in Christ."

Celie cried and twisted, tried to push herself upward, hoping to miss one stroke or another, praying to God to release her.

Dazed for just a few seconds, Hugh Fears and Burr finally ran forward and seized the whip, kicked the elders, and knocked Barnie to the ground. They untied their mother and led her to the buggy where Aunt Agnes waited with Wheezie.

With his coat and Wheezie's blanket, Burr covered his mother, and Hugh Fears drove the horse toward White Oaks.

"Nobody, not even the Dunns with all of their hypocritical religiosity get away with insulting the Bains," Burr said. "We'll defend our family's honor until the day we die."

"The Dunns have always hated the Bains, and the feuding began long ago," Aunt Agnes said, as she rocked the baby. Celie sobbed, aching from pain and humiliation.

"Even a slave hanging pales by comparison," said an old church member. "And that woman was old Dr. Dunn's own granddaughter. Did you know that, Mrs. Bailey?"

Before she could answer, another added, "At least we won't have to listen to sixty minutes of hell, fire, brimstone, and guilt."

Other members listened, wagging their heads. Some mounted their horses and followed the wagon to White Oaks. Others climbed into wagons or buggies. Lashing the ground with his whip, Barnie passed them all, "No one gets away with insulting me, and surely not a woman." Galloping with fury, he passed all of the carts, wagons, and horses, showering them with red dirt.

As soon as Hugh turned the lane for home, Burr jumped from the wagon and ran down to the stable for Druzie. "Unkie, come at once, please…Mamma…she's been whipped by that Dr. Barnie Dunn. Her back's bleeding, and that crazy man is following. Ma's hurt real bad. Please don't let anybody hurt her anymore…a crowd's gathering. Most of the church members followed us."

"What?" Druzie said, trying to understand. "Slow down a little, Son."

And Burr repeated himself. When Druzie understood, he took up his cane and pistol and walked up the hill, Prince and the others following, toward the front steps of the house, where Burr explained that, Dunn was pushing Monica down, trying to force his way into the house.

Druzie then challenged Barnie Dunn to a duel.

"What, old boy? You're blind. Remember you are without sight, and I think it would be dishonorable for me to shoot a blind man, don't you? I don't think God's going to suddenly give you vision with a wattle of red clay from your plantation, do you?"

"Not nearly as dishonorable as whipping my wife and humiliating her in front of the whole church was. Why you don't even know what honor and compassion, justice and truth mean, and yet you call yourself a man of God, a doctor. No, you have insulted my beloved wife, so now….now I am challenging you to a duel. Stephenson, I understand that you gave the lashings at the church….and you, too, Banks. Suppose one of you continue your duty to the church and count off. Do you agree? If so, which one? If not, get off my land right now!"

John Banks stepped forward. "Oh, I admire you, Mr. Bain. I am at your service, for I am ashamed of what I did."

"We all have choices, Mr. Banks…everyone of us every day of our lives must decide. You were elected to serve on Dr. Wylie Dunn's session, and I imagine you have regretted that decision ever since. But you will not regret the decision to serve us this Sabbath Day."

"No sir, I will not," the man wearing a worn tri-corn hat, answered, as he assumed the position, walked off the measurements, then gave directions to Druzie and Barnie.

"You stand here, you there. When I begin counting, you will know what to do. When I call, 'Fire,' then walk, turn, and fire. You know the rest. Do you understand?"

They nodded and waited for Banks to begin. At "Fire," Barnie fumbled to pull out his pistol while Druzie, always a superb marksman, his sense of direction clear, accurate, fired. Barnie fell and rolled down the hill immediately toward the backwoods where he died.

Cheers followed. People clapped and shouted, "Down with the Dunns, up with the Bains. Huzzah…"

Exhausted, wiping his brow, Druzie leaned on his cane and faced his audience. "Thank you. Please….there are no witches in this house or in any home nearby. There never were, nor to the knowledge of my family, have there ever been. God never wants us to be frightened by all the rigidities and laws, duties and numerous rules and commandments like those the Dunns frightened you into believing. God wants you to love and enjoy."

"Amen, Brother Bain…you should be our preacher," Alphaeus Stephenson stepped forward to say. "Thank you."

"And remember that God's blessings are upon each one of you. Serve one another. Be hospitable one to another, for you might be entertaining an angel unaware. Please, then, join us here at White Oaks for a round of punch, apples, biscuits, and cakes. We always have an abundance. There are games on the lawn—-rounders, croquet, graces, and the tilting of the ring. We have always enjoyed a variety of pastimes here, including music. I believe with all of my heart that God is present with us this afternoon. Now, I want to be with my wife and child. Thank you again for coming to our home."

"Amen," the crowd clapped. "You are a prophet." Druzie went inside.

> "He shall judge the poor of the people, he shall save the children of the needy, and shall break in pieces the oppressor… He shall come down like rain upon the mown grass: as showers that water the earth. In his days shall the righteous flourish; and the abundance of peace so long as the moon endureth" (Psalm 72: 4, 6-7).

Book Twenty-One (1853-1854)

Revived by a shot of brandy, Druzie wearily climbed the steps and went to Celie's bedside where she clutched the pillow sobbing. Monica was at her side.

"I bathed her with a damp cloth and rubbed arnica over her body, then put some muslin strips with salve on her back and made some tea, but she's in a lot of pain. Her body aches, and her spirit's sore. I know how she feels. That happened to me. I think it's best to let the air heal her. I ain't gwine tell her to dress, not for a heap of time. Oh, Massa Druzie, those mens whipped her bad."

"I know...I'm here, my darling," he said, taking Celie's hand.

"Is that mean man dead?" Monica asked, her tone a little groggy, weary.

"He's rotting in the ground by now," Druzie answered, "and I hope worms are gnawing away at his organs."

"Druzie, you don't feel the least bit of guilt in making that wish, do you?"

"No...oh, darling, not at all. I know you must ache....I am here with you now...Monica and I both are."

"But our baby? Where's Wheezie?"

"With Nessie and my mother...our little boy is fine."

"Oh, Druzie, it all happened so fast," she whispered, her voice hoarse, her head turning toward him, her eyes swollen from crying, "I didn't know what was going on." She recounted every detail. "I....I've never hurt anybody. Why are the Dunns so mean? Why are people so unkind?"

"Some people is just mean and evil, honey lamb," Monica said. "They just is, and ain't nothing going to change them."

"And you'll heal...we'll sit outside under the white oak, and by Christmas you'll feel stronger and play the psaltery. We'll sing and talk, as always, the wind stirring us, taking away all of your fears." He squeezed her hand. "But I want you to try to sleep now."

"Huh...huh," she whispered "...I'll try...you'll stay with me?"

"Yes, darling. I will."

Weeks passed, the harvest moon yielding to the colder moon of winter, the acorns falling from the white oaks. Celie slowly recovered, gained her strength, yet often felt the need to sometimes recount her nightmares with Barnie Dunn. Druzie always listened, never once silencing her. . Shortly before Christmas, Celie was able to wear clothing without her back chafing. She went downstairs, walked in the garden, and returned to singing and playing the pirate's psaltery.

Mary Caroline and Josie came home at the end of the term, and went with the boys to the woods for a tree. Wheezie jumped up and down as he watched his sisters adorn the tree with berries, popcorn, nuts, and magnolia cones.

Following New Year's when the girls returned to Millsborough, Celie's devotion to Druzie deepened in a way she could not explain to Monica.

"You don't have to tell me why. You don't have to know yourself. It just has, and Sunday coming we're going to have church here. I've aksed Massa Druzie to preach."

Celie smiled. "He is very wise, isn't he? He has given me so many lessons, as you have, best friend."

"Like a prophet, and your grandmammy would rejoice....you keep trusting yourself, too, honey, and don't neva look back...It only causes pain."

The winter passed, and in the spring when Celie and Druzie were walking and she was pointing out the flowers, dogwoods, and yellow jasmine, she stopped suddenly under their tree. "Oh, honey, feel my tummy. It's swelling. I'm carrying our second baby, and I couldn't be happier."

Druzie felt her and took her again in his arms, holding her close. "My darling, I am thrilled. That means....let's see it's Easter now...maybe a baby for our anniversary."

"Druzie, it's 1854. How old are we?"

He laughed. "Does it matter? I feel like a schoolboy all over again."

"Tell me what we should call him."

"So you're sure it's a little boy?"

"Absolutely, and I want to name him for you, sweetheart. Andrew Washington Bain."

"Or for our favorite poet, Robert Burns."

"But then I might think of the verb and be reminded of the fire, of your hands burning."

"Sweetheart, then call him 'Verb,' or give him a Scottish name you like. It doesn't matter. Just not Hebrides."

They walked to the house and shared the news with the boys and Mary Caroline and Josie who had come home from Millsborough for a few days.

Josie patted her mother's hand, then told everyone about meeting her relative, Roderick Dulligan, at one of Mrs. Gray's soirées. "Ma, I didn't know Pa had an younger brother, did you?"

"Yes, but I never met him, and your father never really talked about him, to tell you the truth, so you tell us all about young Roderick Dulligan, will you?"

"Well, he's older than I am. He's younger than Pa, though. Roderick is tall, and his eyes are brown, and his hair's black. He doesn't really look like Pa. He's rich. He owns a home near Swannkell and owns stock in the railroad. His mother lives with him. She's part Cherokee and makes pottery."

"Hmm," Druzie mused. "I'd like to meet the young man. He sounds interesting. Yes, if he owns stock in the railroad, he's well off."

"You know, I think he and Pa had different mothers, now that I remember what Roderick said," Josie said, her brown eyes pensive.

"That sounds right," Druzie interrupted. "I think Neilly once told me his mother was from Ireland. She died, and his father remarried."

"Well, we'll invite them over for a supper sometime, Josie. Would you like that? And his mother, too. Mary Caroline, what have you been doing at school?"

"Well, Josie may be thinking about marrying, but I'm not, not yet. I did meet several boys at the party. They were from Mount Hebron, but they seemed silly. All they did was talk about wanting to take their rapiers to class and hide them from the teacher."

"Like us, Sis?" Burr said, his eyes mischievous. "Is that what you think of boys?"

"Sillier," she answered, and began playing with Wheezie.

"Mamma, he's growing, isn't he?"

"I know, and before long, he's going to have a baby brother or sister. Unkie and I are expecting our second child. Are you pleased?"

"Yes."

"And when I marry, Ma, I want to wear the emerald green silk wedding dress. May I?" Josie asked, her dark eyes wide with excitement.

"Of course, and Mary Caroline, too, when she marries."

"We are going to have another wedding before long. I feel it in the air," Monica grinned.

Celie looked at her grandmother's best friend, her knees 'eaten up with arthritis,' as she herself described her tired body, her face wrinkled, and hair white. "Oh, Monica, don't ever leave us. Are those the earbobs Grandfather gave you?"

"They the ones. I don't remember when, but he'd often try to buy my attention and affection when he knew I knew he'd hurt your grandmammy."

Everyone listened as she retold some of the family stories, asking Aunt Agnes to help her with details. "My memory ain't what it was."

"Neither is mine," Aunt Agnes smiled.

The harvest at White Oaks was good that summer in late August when Wheezie was nearly two, he insisted on joining his half brothers for a fishing trip on the river, "Me wants to go to the riba, Mamma. How do you say it? Patcakee?"

"Patuxee, darling." And she pronounced the name several times.

"Can me go?"

"Not today, Wheezie. I think a storm's coming later, and I don't want your little cold to get worse if you get caught in the rain. You can go again. Can you understand what Mother is saying?" She looked at his curly brown hair and blue eyes, pale skin, and frail body, struggling to keep up with the others. In a way, he reminded her of Hugh Fears when he was a child. Unlike Hugh who was rigid and serious, Wheezie never stopped talking.

"What if I read you a story or we just go for a walk in the woods. We'll add something to the scarecrow you and Mary Caroline made with the others to keep away the crows. Why I could hide something for you to find, then give you a surprise. Would you like that?"

"No, Mammie, not today. Hughie and Burr said they were going on the Patcakee, and they promised to take me. Me can put on a blanket. I won't get cold."

She watched him wrapping a blanket around himself.

"Wheezie, not today, honey."

"But Fayette and Nafum are going, too. And so are Nafum's twins."

Still remembering all too well the time Nathan and her older boys had gone hunting with Neilly, Ceilie whispered to herself, "No...no, you can't. I won't let you." She struggled to shut out the sound of Lafayette screaming, 'Yo hubun, he ded, Missus Celie," and the image of Druzie and her brother on the Savannah River floated in her head as well. She pictured Druzie nearly drowning and shook her head...She couldn't take the chance. "Not just brain waves," she whispered again.

"Mamma," he persisted, "me want to go...can't me go? I'll be good...why?"

"Now, what's this all about?" Druzie asked, coming into the bedroom, his clothes covered with flour. He picked up his son and carried him to the window. "Now, plead your case, Master Wheezie. What do you want to do?"

"Go to the Patackee Riba with Hughie and Burr."

"Well, what does Mamma say?"

"That I've been coughing a lot."

"Tell you what...you go play for a little while, and Mamma and I will talk. Will you do that for me?"

"Hah...hah...Mammy, please."

"Darling, maybe you're just not feeling good today," Druzie said, "But it's really quite warm outside. I've been busy at the mill, and I feel the blue sky overhead and...oh the water will be calm today...maybe if I go, too. It'll be a 'gentlemen's day on the river," he continued, taking her in his arms. "Are you tired?"

"A little....I harvested a lot of herbs yesterday. Then, I had a bad dream. I know you'll tease me if I tell you, and you'll say, "Celie Fears, Celie Feared, and Celie will Fear, but I've really tried not to fear."

"I know, and I am delighted....I'm proud of you. You have such faith and strength now, and you're playing the psaltery more beautifully than ever. Do you feel it, too?"

"Yes....oh, Druzie, you have helped me so much. But I don't think you have any idea how much I adore you?"

"And you me, my darling. Don't ever forget that. Now, tell me your dream. I'll try to understand."

"Someone was flipping over under a fountain of water, and...."

"Maybe you're just remembering the time you made MC splash herself with water after she poured water on my prized hound. And it is full moon, sugar. I promise not to let anything happen. I won't. Our baby's due in two months, and I want to be right at your side when he's born. We have to name him together. Maybe we'll call him Alloway or....or how about Afton from our favorite poet's song."

"Silly!" Celie smiled and put her head on her husband's shoulder, "You're so convincing nobody could ever not believe you or disagree. It would be selfish if I said not to go, and I know that. Oh, Druzie, I don't know what I would ever do if I lost you. You are my life."

"Celie, don't ever forget that you've always been the candle that pierced my darkness. Let's lie down for a few minutes, and I'll hold you."

"Dust yourself off," she teased.

"I will."

And they lay together until Wheezie came. "Daddy, can me go?"

"We'll go....come kiss your mammy good-bye."

"Mammy, Wheezie lubs you."

"And I love you, too, little one. You have a good time, and catch a big fish for Mammy, will you?"

"Huh...huh."

"And you'll be careful, won't you, Saint Bain?" she smiled, looking up at him as he kissed her good-bye.

"I promise...Celie, did I ever quote that psalm to you about saints being joyful and singing on their beds? I remember when Ma read that psalm to me long time ago. We both laughed."

"And I suppose we're those saints."

"That's right...I'm Saint Andrew, and you're Saint Cecilia. Of course, you're musical. I'm not sure what I did to deserve my calling."

"Silly," she laughed. "I love you, whatever your calling."

"And you're with me on the river, just as I am here with you here at home, always. Good-bye, darling." He leaned down and kissed her again, feeling her arms reaching toward him.

"I'll surprise you with tipsy pudding, maybe Charlotte Russe for dessert tonight. Sometimes I wonder what the difference between Peach Charlotte and Charlotte Russe is. Maybe they're named for a queen. Doesn't that sound a little silly, Druzie? I mean I could be queen and people could name a dessert receipt after me. Charlotte Celie...or Apple Cecilia...wouldn't that be interesting? Good-bye, my darling, once again, and have a happy time."

He squeezed her hand. "I'm glad you're laughing, honey." Later Celie went into the garden where she found Monica picking marigolds. They talked for a long time. "Most too hot to eat anything....thunder clouds in the sky."

"The boys will be safe, though, for awhile, don't you think, Monica? They all were crazy to go fishing this afternoon. Maybe the storm will hold off until tonight."

Monica listened as Celie talked. They sat until the showers began. Suddenly, there were screams. Celie stiffened.

"Missus Celie, dey dun drownded," Lafayette called, "I meens Massa Druzie and de baby...De bote run onto a shole an jes flips ova...Massa Hugh, he tried to save the little boy and his pa...but dey wah tu hebbie. Massa Burr, he try too, but de bodies went limp...dat baby jes wudn't let go his pa...dey jes went plum unda. I sho iz sorry."

Lafayette was trembling, Celie shaking. "Where are my boys, Lafayette? Where's your boy?"

"Dey all bez down at de riba tryin to find dem bodees. Yessum, sho iz. Massa Druzie, why he cudn swim, and he cudn see nuthin…de babee boy…he jes kep cryin and wheezing…he got plumb blue, an…"

Celie didn't know what to say. She stood and listened in the garden in absolute shock until the sky darkened, the rain drenching her, staring straight into the scarecrow with acorn eyes that Mary Caroline had made with Nathan's twins, Linus and China Lee, to frighten the crows. "God, kill me. Take me…I don't care. I want to die." The rain finally stopped, and the night turned cold, but Celie felt nothing. She only knew that Druzie and Wheezie were not at her side. They were dead. Life without Druzie was nothing. "I'd rather die," she cried, and fell to the ground and clutched the wet earth.

Monica found her a little later and tried to get her to come inside, but Celie would not. "Maybe they're not dead yet, Monica…they'll come back. We'll find them walking ashore in the moonlight on the other side of the river…yes, and Wheezie will tell me about the fish, and Druzie….well…he'll hold me, and we'll talk about everything the way we always do…I'll hold onto that dream. Yes…that's what we'll all do…we have to dream and hope…I…I'm going to find them…you know Druzie may even be down at the grist mill just to tease me. You know how playful he is…"

"Honey, don't go," Aunt Agnes added, as she walked outside and realized Celie was delirious. "Celie, they're not coming home. Why don't you come in and try to sleep. You're with child…it's late…I'll give you something to relax, perhaps a little whiskey."

"No, Aunt Aggie, I have to find Druzie and my little boy….they may be up the hill under our white oak…he's waiting to sing 'Flow Gently Sweet Afton' to me. You knew…surely you knew I read poetry to him, and…he sang to me…sometimes ballads, sometimes hymns, maybe the songs you taught him. Then we sang together…I know he's waiting."

Aunt Agnes couldn't say anymore. Words were meaningless to souls intertwined.

And Celie wandered all through the night up and down the hills, along the river, and through the fields, calling for Druzie. At dawn, Lafayette found her under the white oak, delirious, chilled. Monica gave Celie laudanum.

Hugh Fears and Burr had gone for the girls, and Mrs. Gray offered to make all the arrangements for the burial service in the cemetery at White Oaks. Monica and Nessie prepared the bodies, and Celie sat for hours in the front parlor with them.

The priest from St. David's Church in Millsborough read Celie and Druzie's favorite psalms and poems and invited family and friends to sing a few hymns. The inscription on the tombstone read, "Here lyeth the bodies of Andrew Washington Bain, husband of Celie Fears, and their little son, Wheezie—'Til death do us part and Except ye be born again as a little child, ye shall not enter into the Kingdom of Heaven."

When the priest closed with "Dust to Dust" and sprinkled dirt before the grave diggers lowered the box into the earth, Celie wept uncontrollably. Hugh and Burr led her to the buggy for the ride home.

Aunt Agnes died a few days later from shock, and a gloomy stillness settled over the plantation like summer webs veiling over trees, whose leaves gradually crinkled yellow and fell to the ground, their acorns giving rise to yet another generation—but where? Under the oaks, behind the pines, beneath the mulberry? Only God knew.

Celie put on her veil a third time. "There will not be anyone to remove it, ever, Monica. I will remain in mourning."

"Honey, Massa Druzie wouldn't want you to grieve forever…he want you to have this baby and love it, too, same as you did Massa Wheezie…oh lamb, try."

But Celie could not keep back the tears. She walked in the garden and trudged up the hill to their white oak until she stumbled over a fallen branch and fell. Lafayette found her again. She was calling for Druzie and Wheezie. "My Wheezie was rapping his little hand on the boat, and water swished all around him, Lafayette. Did you find him?"

Lafayette carried Celie home, and around midnight, she went into labor and gave birth to a healthy baby boy.

"I want to name him…I don't know yet," and she fell asleep, exhausted. One of the wet nurses took the baby.

"You know, sometimes Ma looks like a ghost," Hugh Fears said one day to Burr and Josie. "She looks at me the way she did after Pa died when we were hunting. Sometimes I think she blames me. I was the one who wanted to go hunting and fishing. Ma's blue eyes are like crystal. If I look at her too long, I think they'll shatter. Sis, tell her I tried to save Druzie and Wheezie."

Josie comforted her brother. "Hugh Fears, Ma knows you did…she does."

But then Josie really didn't know, for she watched her mother nurse the baby, then carry him to the painting, which Mr. Gray had done of Druzie and Nellie before she foaled, and sit for hours by candlelight staring and talking. "He was your father, my little one, and there I am in the other painting." Celie looked at herself in the portrait beside Druzie's. Wearing the emerald green silk dress, she was holding the psaltery.

"Mamma," Josie gently called, "I need you."

"Sh...I'm telling the baby about Druzie and...you supervise the hog-killin later when it turns cold. You must do it, Daughter...Nessie will help you."

"Ma, that's not it...it's Aunt Monica...she's dying...she needs you to go down to the cabin...she wanted to die there, not up here...Mamma, you go. I'll hold the baby."

"Monica dying?"

Josie nodded. "Mamma, go to her side. She wants you."

Celie made her way to The Quarters where her best friend lay on a rope bed quietly singing, "Angel, Move Ova, Cause I'z Comin Home."

Sitting by her side, Celie pushed back the veil, tears trickling down her face, and kissed Monica, then soothed back her thin white hair. "Oh, I love you...I do....thank you for being my grandmother's teacher and best friend and for being mine...you and Druzie taught me how to live. Monica, how many times you were there to say something assuring. I don't know what to say...please pray that...oh, I love you, I will miss you. What will I ever do without you and Druzie? Even at White Oaks, I feel a mystery, haunting, mournful something. Surely there's nothing next. Do you think?"

Monica feebly put her arms around Celie. "Everything's gwine be alright. You remember that, honey lamb....and trust your heart. Treasure that psaltery and all it means for you and Massa Druzie. Keep it in your heart, and give it away one day. He'd want you to do that....and take this little book of Psalms. This was Misses Katie's psaltery. Read it, and listen to it when you plays the other psaltery. You'll see they's related. Both tells of God's music and his love. Missus Katie gave the little book of psalms to me long, long time ago in Georgetown. Read it to yo chillins and chaps. Talk to Massa Druzie, and remember all he told you....why he's smiling at us right now....Sho iz....name that baby soon....you'll know what to call him...but not Hebrides."

Monica's lips slightly moved, her eyes closing, and Celie smiled.

Celie sang Monica's favorite spirituals and clasped her best friend's hand. Monica squeezed Celie's hand one last time and died within the hour. She was buried a few feet, at her request, from Cecilia Fears Lynch Bain at White Oaks, the inscription, "Monica Fears Lynch Bain, wife of Elijah Bain, born on Saint James Island circa 1757, died at White Oaks Plantation, 1853, faithful friend, beloved by all who knew her."

Following Christmas, Celie asked the boys to move Elijah's grave next to Monica's. "Your mother and father should be buried together," she told Nessie and Memnon, "just as I want to lie next to my husband here."

"For a thousand years in thy sight are but as yesterday when it is past, and as a watch in the night. Thou carriest them away as with a flood; they are as a sleep: in the morning they are like grass which groweth up. In the morning it flourisheth, and groweth up; in the evening it is cut down, and withereth" (Psalm 90:4-6).

Book Twenty-Two (1854-1855)

During the winter months, Celie walked about the plantation, gathering withered collards, acorns, and early daffodils, anything to keep busy, to keep her mind from racing. She visited nursed the baby and visited The Quarters, often walked through the back orchard and across the fields to the cemetery or up the hill to that old white oak where she stood weeping, crying out, sometimes a little angry, "Druzie, where are you? I need you. Oh, I forgot to tell you Nellie died....she just missed you; the boys buried her in the field, and Mary Caroline painted a piece of granite for her marker. Oh, Druzie, what are you doing? Please come home to me, my darling. You've no idea how much I miss you."

Occasionally hearing her mother talk, Josie came and led her mother away. "Ma, maybe a little brandy will help. Druzie understands."

"Josie, do you think he really hears me?" Celie asked the next morning as she lingered at the breakfast table, unable to eat.

"Of course, he does. Mamma, and has he told you spring's in the air? I know he's heard frogs croaking in the pond and knows our garden wants hoeing. I can't do it all by myself. I need you. In addition to the garden, we have other matters. You know, we've not visited Uncle George in months. Will you ride over to the bluffs with me this afternoon?"

"And we'll take Mary Caroline with us, too. I'm very concerned about your sister. She's been acting extremely ugly again. Of course, I know she misses being with Mrs. Gray, but...but I don't have the money, not right now, not until things are settled to send her back to the school in Millsborough. Hugh Fears has helped me a lot. Burr, too. I just don't know about my money yet. Druzie paid the former slaves wages, and I don't know whether you knew it, but he also protected Nolie, the slave who escaped from a plantation down near Georgetown. He paid for her. Yes, he hid her at White Oaks and paid some money to help her escape north...maybe on the underground railroad. I don't understand those routes, but I pray she made it."

"Mamma, Druzie was a prophet, wasn't he? He did so much, despite his blindness, and he was never, ever, bitter…he inspired all of us."

"Josie, you're not only a daughter. You're my sister, my friend, my mother. Thank you."

"Ma, you don't have to thank me, but I want to tell you, Roderick and I want to marry soon. Can you understand?"

Celie looked at her daughter, at her sparkling dark eyes and dark hair, twisted in an unusual way about her head, uncertain of whom Josie resembled. "Of course, I understand. You really love Roderick don't you?"

"With all my heart, and he's kind to me…."

"Darling, I rejoice with all my heart for you, and I'll make a melody on the psaltery for your wedding. We'll go to the bluffs and visit my brother."

At Mulberry Bluffs they found George crazier than ever. He was sprawled on the bed, a bottle in hand, invoking his muses, when Celie and Josie opened the cabin door.

"Sis, you've brought me pain killer, I hope? My limbs ache, especially the ends of my fingers and the ends of my toes…did you hear those free Negroes firing pistols?"

Celie had no idea what her brother meant, but consoled herself, "Bubba talks to a ghost. So do I, I suppose, but, no, my husband's not a ghost…Druzie's absolutely not a ghost. He's real, and we love each other dearly. Get away if you don't understand."

"Sissy," George screamed, aware of her presence, "I'm writing a poem about our lake…about how Pa treated us…you were whipped, and I….I nearly drowned. But do you understand the Negroes don't like us now…they think we lashed them…and beat them. Sissy, tell them the truth."

"George, I don't understand…I don't. "No, Bubba, you're not making any sense. Tell me what you're talking about."

He continued, "The free Negroes simply heard Barnie Dunn had been shot…and…and…they wanted their money. Seems he'd cheated them too many times out of money. And for some reason, they blamed me Stupid! I never looked like the fucking Barnie Dunn."

"Uncle George, that was a long time ago. You didn't know Druzie died, did you?"

"No…no, I didn't…I…I."

Celie couldn't listen to her brother's whining. She could not relive that Sunday, not then, not ever again, especially not with her brother who was responsible for Barnie's raping her.

"No...I can't. Besides, I hear Druzie calling me. He wants me to come to the ruined chapel." She left the cabin and walked the familiar path to the chapel.

"Remember that hot summer afternoon when we made love here before the fire? My darling, always be my psaltress. Let the melodies you play lead you. Listen to them. Trust them....trust your heart." She felt him behind, taking her in his arms, whispering, "I love you. Go on living, and nobody will ever hurt you again because...because, my sweet, you won't let them...and I won't, and neither will our psaltery. You don't need to wear the veil, honey."

Josie took care of Uncle George, then found her mother in the chapel, and led her to the wagon. They all returned to White Oaks in silence.

Celie forced herself to listen to her older daughter and prepared the soil for planting.

"Ma, Unkie would want you to plant extra rosemary and...what was the other herb he enjoyed sniffing?"

"Sage...or lavender...he could recognize most every fragrance." From that day on, Josie took on the role of mother, leading Celie to heal, both aware of Mary Caroline's change in mood.

"She's so disagreeable, just the way she used to be."

"Don't let her behavior ruin our lives, Ma. There's nothing wrong with Mary Caroline. She's just jealous and strong-willed, just plain disagreeable. Sissy knows what she's doing. If you allow her, she'll ruin your psaltery. Don't allow it. She likes being petulant and disagreeable. She gets our attention that way. She likes being the dragon."

Celie smiled at her daughter's humor and wisdom and murmured aloud, "No, I can't let MC play the dragon and tempt us."

And Celie offered to pay Nathan's twin daughter, China Lee, to watch Mary Caroline.

Despite MC's varying moods and slaps, China Lee agreed, for she had her own way of dealing with Mary Caroline, nobody ever exactly knowing what they were.

On Christmas Day, Celie passed out shoes and clothes to their hired servants, Mary Caroline helping her. "Ma, who is that caramel-colored lady in the red turban? She's ugly. Look at all those wrinkles, and her ankles look like swollen tulip bulbs."

"Sh...," Celie said, but not before the woman heard Mary Caroline's words. And the old woman asked, "What you starin at me foh wid dem big blue eyez of yourn? I awin't gwine hurt you."

"Mary Caroline," Celie said, "The woman's right. She is not going to hurt you, and you must remember I've not yet met everyone at White Oaks. I didn't grow up here."

MC spit at the old woman who ignored her and called, "Christmas gif."

Celie gave her a basket of herbs.

On New Year's Eve, Burr told his family that he would be marrying Rosa Alison Oliphant, and Josie said she would be wedded to her first cousin before summer. "Ma, Roderick Dulligan will be asking for my hand in marriage."

Celie shared her children's happiness and promised to welcome Rosa Alison and Roderick into the family. But Mary Caroline resisted. She stomped her foot on the rug. "It's not fair, Ma, and you know it. After Pa died, you had Druzie, and Josie has her cousin, and Burr has his sweetheart. And Oliphant sounds like elephant."

Celie rocked the baby and shrugged her shoulders. "I don't understand what you want me to do, MC."

Before Mary Caroline responded, Hugh Fears stepped in, "Well, Sis, I'm not going to marry, at least not yet. Remember me on the porch decked out, exchanging my cigar, first one, then the other. I'll be an old bachelor, and, Josie, I'll give you away to Roderick Dulligan. You're marrying a first cousin we've never met, We'll treat all family members alike."

Celie smiled as the baby sucked at her breast. "I've never named my little boy. What shall we call him? Help me decide. Druzie suggested something Scottish."

"Ma, we don't care," Mary Caroline answered, and kicked the table, as she sucked her fingers.

Everyone waited, wondering what their mother would say, what she might do, and Celie surprised them all. She calmly led her daughter to the window. "Now, you listen to me right now. I am tired of your behavior. If I had the money, why you'd be at Mrs. Gray's in Millsborough right now, but you are with us here at home, and I expect you to behave. Further, there's nothing wrong with you, except jealousy and hostility. Why, you're just as sweet and pretty as anyone if you want to be. I am only a mother trying to teach you. I'm not a school teacher. I can only give you my love and share my dreams. I let the melody on the psaltery lead me, and if you don't understand that, I am sorry. Others seem to. Now sit down right now, and behave yourself like a lady. I have never given you a scorpion. None of us has."

"Eloquent, Ma," Burr clapped.

But her mother's words only made MC angrier. She stuck out her tongue. "It's not fair, Ma, and you know it...Josie's getting married and Burr, too."

Hugh interrupted the debate, "If you will wipe that silly frown off your face, MC, why I have a surprise for you. And for God's sake, stop sucking your fingers. You look stupid, like some sort of cow chewing its cud."

"Shall I applaud your eloquence, Bubba?" Burr asked.

"No." Within seconds Hugh returned with a basket containing two runt hounds. "We named them Littlebury and Littlemary. One's a boy, and the other's a girl," Hugh grinned, "in case you weren't sure, Mary Caroline."

MC clapped and squealed with glee, nuzzling the hounds to her face, letting them lick her fingers. "Thank you."

"Mamma, you could name the baby Davie Dumfries," Josie said.

"How'd you come up with that?" Burr asked.

"Well, because Ma and Unkie always read the poetry of Robert Burns. He died in Dumfries, and he wrote verses to someone named Davie. I just liked the combination: Davie Dumfries."

"So do I," Celie said. "Thank you. Now when will the weddings be?"

"Spring for us," Burr answered. "Why don't we get married on the same day, Josie?"

"If Roderick agrees, and I'm sure he will."

In April, there was a double wedding on the lawn of White Oaks Chapel. Burr Fennell Dulligan and Rosa Alison Oliphant were pronounced man and wife, and Martha Josephine Dulligan became the bride of Roderick Dulligan. Sure enough, Hugh Fears dressed up and accompanied his sister. "Whom God hath joined together, let no man put asunder," the priest from Millsborough pronounced." He also baptized little Davie Dumfries for Celie.

Burr built a home for his wife a few miles down the road from White Oaks, and Josie settled into a comfortable life at Forest Green where Roderick's mother taught her to make pottery and mix herbs and roots. Within a few months, both Josie and Rosa Alison were expecting babies. Celie rejoiced when she heard the news. "A baby's like a touch of heaven on earth, and they will play with little Davie Dumfries."

"You mean Dumb-Dumb," Mary Caroline said.

"MC, that's not nice, and you know it," Hugh rebuked.

Mary Caroline began complaining of how bored she was at White Oaks. "All I ever do is play with the puppies, work in the garden, or sit with China Lee. All Ma ever does is take care of Dumb-Dumb."

"You're wrong, MC, and you know it. Besides, you could marry Cudn Roderick's overseer, Bruce Murray. I understand he doesn't beat his slaves. He goes to church and has two hounds. Why you could all play together, and you might have a baby who'd give you a scorpion back. How about that?"

The more her brother teased, the angrier Mary Caroline became. She slapped her brother. "I'd rather be an old maid."

"And you'll never get laid either," Hugh laughed, pushing her down in the chair. "I don't think I'd want to marry you, Sissy. I mean, all you do is suck your fingers, kick, and scream, and there's nothing wrong with you. Why don't you act like Ma or Rosa Alison or China Lee?"

"Me? Massa Hugh?"

"Yes, you're a lady. You have a heart of kindness."

"No, she doesn't," Mary Caroline said, kicking the chair.

Hugh led her outside. "Now, you kick that post there until I count to 25. Do you understand, Sis?"

After kicking, Mary Caroline apologized.

"Be sweet, MC. You are pretty with your light hair and pale blue eyes. Just stop playing a dragon. How about that?"

In early February of the following year, Rosa Alison gave birth to a little girl whom she called Carrie for Mary Caroline. A week later, Josie had little Roderick whom she called Roddy over the next few months. Celie took Davie, MC, and China Lee to visit the babies, then added to her music club repertoire.

"I hope something's wrong with them," Mary Caroline said, as the wagon rattled along the road back to White Oaks.

"That's a very unkind wish, honey."

"I don't care what you think, Ma."

A few weeks later when Mary Caroline learned that little Carrie was deaf and Roddy club-footed, she laughed. "I caused it....I wished an evil spell upon them, and it happened. I can practice magic...maybe I'll leave this place and become a fortune-teller at the fairs, "

"Ain't you shamed, missy?" China Lee said, as she was polishing Mary Caroline's great grandmother's silver bowl out in the kitchen.

"No."

"Well, I'm ashamed of you," Hugh said. "I heard what you said, and I'm going to wash your mouth out with soap." Mary Caroline balked and screamed, but he held her down. "Now, settle down, Sis, or I'm going to tell Ma to send you to the asylum. Do you understand what that is?"

"No."

"Well, you can find out. But I hear someone coming up the lane now, and I'm going in the house to tell Ma. Celie and Hugh Fears peeked through the front door. "I think it's Barnie Dunn's widow, Ma. She's going fast. Her gray hair's tangled, and she's gotten fat, too."

"Well, I don't think she's bringing jonquils to celebrate the babies' birthings, do you?"

"No, and I wouldn't invite her in either."

Celie opened the front door. "Good afternoon, Mrs. Dunn."

"We heard over at Brick Tower, Mrs. Bain, that your grandbabies were born with maladies. I brought you one of my leftover pies as an expression of sympathy. Oh, I can't imagine having a club-footed boy and a deaf girl. Now, I know you didn't bring me anything when your blind husband shot my husband to death right here on this lawn, but Christians forgive. Tell me, do your daughters bear the same affliction you do? Are they three-breasted, like you? I've seen you, and I know there's something lurking in the Bain blood that goes way back to Scotland. Your grandmother was deformed, too. We've all heard about the curse and about the Livingston-breasted warriors. But you know the saying, 'Cast thy bread upon the waters."

Celie stood speechless, but not Hugh Fears. He took the pie from his mother, led the woman down the steps, and said, "Now, Mrs. Dunn, we surely do appreciate your concern, but you old, besom, we didn't ask you to come insult the Bain clan. Why don't you just get in your cart and take your damned, leftover pie down the road to your church and smear it on your husband's grave?"

Now, it was Mrs. Dunn who stood speechless. Hugh took off the woman's bonnet and blindfolded her, then turned her around three times and lifted her into the cart. He untied the blindfold and smeared the pie across her face, then gently tapped the mule. "Go, old boy. Take your besom home."

"Now, who was being mean?" Mary Caroline said, as she walked up to the porch and saw a grin spread across her mother's face. "Mother, you shouldn't laugh. It doesn't become you in your years of grief and mourning."

Celie ignored MC and congratulated Hugh. "Son, you're becoming like Druzie and Burr every day. It's very becoming. You don't fear anymore, do you?"

"No, Ma. I've learned to laugh and tease. Unkie taught me that."

"I'm glad, honey, so glad."

"I'll never forget that Sunday at Brick Tower Church, ever, and nobody will insult us or humiliate you again, and that means you, too, MC. No more."

Mary Caroline shook her blonde curls and screamed, "If Ma hadn't dropped me when I was born, I wouldn't be like this, and you all know it. You…"

Celie took Mary Caroline in her arms and held her tight. "You listen to me, MC. I never dropped you. It was a long, hard delivery. It was the doctor who dropped you, who delayed your birth, who wouldn't give me anything for pain, but no damage was done. I just spoiled you through the years because…because I felt guilty, but not anymore. The psaltery and Druzie and God took that all away from me. Yes, they did, and I'm not going to give in to you anymore."

Her eyes glaring, Mary Caroline scratched her mother's cheeks until they bled. "I hate you and Dumb-Dumb, and one day, I'll…"

China Lee led Mary Caroline away. Celie went inside and sobbed beneath Druzie's portrait. "Darling, look at me. Hold me, and tell me what to do."

"Listen to Hugh Fears. Follow the psaltery, my beloved."

"Mamma," Hugh said, coming in and standing beside her, "I know you won't ever give MC a scorpion, but damn it, you don't always have to give her a golden egg either. Unkie was right, and we both know that. There's nothing wrong with her. She is not brain-damaged, just willful and determined and, yes, spoiled. I want you to slap her one time, just one time."

"Oh, Son, I can't slap her, but I won't spoil her anymore."

"Well, maybe her behavior was cute when she was a child, but no longer. MC is grown, and she's strong as those oxen in the field. We never know what she might do, and I surely don't want her to set fire to White Oaks, do you?"

"Hugh Fears, you don't think?"

"Mamma, I don't know. I'm just saying we're not going to let her ruin our plantation. You've given each of us our own imaginary psaltery, and it's up to us to cherish as we will."

"Thank you, my son. Thank you for watching over us all here at White Oaks. Maybe your sister will come around. I don't know," she continued wiping her face, blood on her hands. "I need to clean myself up and nurse the baby. I hear Davie crying in the cradle."

"I will sing of the mercies of the Lord for ever: with my mouth
will I make known thy faithfulness to all generations" (Psalm 89:1).

Book Twenty-Three (1855-1860)

As Davie fussed through teething, Celie comforted him, first with one herb, then another, all the while plodding through the records Aunt Agnes had kept and passed along to Druzie who largely ignored them, except to have Lafayette or Nathan enter a deposit at the bank in Essex or Millsborough.

"Please go to the banks, Hugh Fears, and check on the accounts. I trust whatever decisions you make. I cannot go, not right now."

Hugh went and later explained to his mother that he had withdrawn the money from The Citizens' Bank of Essex and deposited it in the account at the Millsborough Farmers' Bank and Company. "It just seemed closer, Mamma, and easier if you ever have to go. And there's not a lot of money either."

She looked at him, a little wistful, remembering her first husband had left her without funds, but this time seemed different. Money didn't matter anymore. "No, you can't pay wages to everybody all the time, especially when some folks are trifling. We both know that, but it's alright. The folks here need our assistance, even if it's just food and clothing. We can always plant more potatoes. We'll survive here at White Oaks."

"No, Mamma, we won't. We can't pay all these Negroes, even in food, just because we freed them and they live at White Oaks. A lot of them don't work at all. We're just paying them to stay in their cabins, many hardscrabble now at that, I'll admit. But we must ask most of the Negroes to leave. We have to, Mamma. Otherwise, we won't make it, and really they won't in the long run either."

"Honey, I just can't do that. They were born here. This land is all they've ever known. I'll...I'll talk to Druzie. You understand, don't you, Son? He'll tell me what to do."

Hugh Fears really didn't understand his mother's imaginings, but because he loved her, perhaps still felt guilty for her husbands' deaths, he nodded.

Celie took Davie to the white oak on the hill and asked Druzie what to do.

"Let the darkies stay at White Oaks if they wish and keep a garden, and a chicken or more. Give them each a little piece of money, but ask them each to sign a little note saying they understand you will no longer be paying them wages. Sweetheart, kiss our baby for us, and don't fear. Give everybody a little gift and a note…make a copy for the records I didn't keep. If you don't understand, ask a lawyer in Millsborough…so long as people have love and something to eat or sell if they wish, why that's all they need. That's all we need. And love. You understand."

"I named our baby Davie Dumfries…I know that spells fires in another way. Oh, Druzie…I miss you so."

"I'm with you, Celie."

Even though he didn't understand it, Hugh Fears accepted his mother's decision. When he talked to the Negroes, some understood and signed the little slip of paper. Others did not. They became angry and left. Celie gave each one a bag. Even though nobody ever knew exactly what was in another's little bag, they probably wondered if the contents were all alike. But above all, they knew Miss Celie had shaken their hands and shared their sorrows.

All of Monica's descendants remained. Hugh had told them, "Ma and I can pay you wages if you want to stay." Burr didn't understand his mother's gifts any more than his brother did, but said, "Bubba, Ma's smarter than I'll ever be….and a lot stronger, so if she imagines or dreams Druzie tells her to do something, what difference does it really make?"

"It doesn't…It worked out. And right now, MC is on her good behavior. She's actually being nice. Ma's tired, though. I know it. Davie's fussy. He's different from Wheezie, and Ma says the fries of Dumfries, whatever that's called, a prefix or suffix, is a variant of fires. That's when Mamma fears, but then she's different from us. Burr, Ma's almost mystical, and I tell you this much. Even though the slaves are free, and I'm glad because I don't believe anyone should ever be chained or owned, but…but… if we go to war against the north, I will fight for the south. How about you?"

"Absolutely. It'll be about the rights of states then."

And the brothers drank to the south, each smoking a cigar, each wearing a dress suit, eyes challenging, ready for the fair in Millsborough that fall of 1855. Burr tipped his hat to Mrs. Gray who inquired about Mary Caroline and her mother. "Encourage your sister to embroider something different and to draw. Motivate Mary Caroline, and you'll see a remarkable change. Do give your mother my love…and the girls."

Hugh Fears talked to his mother, and they decided to challenge MC to design a garden for spring. "We'll plant whatever you wish, Sis," Hugh said to his sister. "But you have to draw your design of the garden first. Once that's done, we'll plant. So if you want to put something in that's different, we'll do it."

MC stuck her tongue out. "What did you ever know about flowers, Bubba?"

"Mrs. Gray sent her love and best wishes for your garden...You design it, and we'll cultivate it. Meantime, Ma and I are going to bring Uncle George home. Want to ride with us and little Davie?"

His sister nodded, and they rode to Mulberry Bluffs. Since Hebrides' death, George was scarcely aware of anyone's presence, often hallucinating that Hebrides still lived. "Somebody shot at us, Sis...maybe those free Negroes...I." And he fell on the floor. Hugh put his uncle in the wagon, and drove the buggy home where Nessie, after looking at her mother's old receipts, gave him skullcap blended with other herbs. MC immediately liked having Uncle George at White Oaks. "Then, they're not watching me," she whispered to the hounds and to Davie who was walking and did everything his half sister said.

That was until the afternoon Celie was giving directions to Nessie, asking her to write down her mother's family receipts for the family to have in the years to come.

Nessie agreed, then began talking, sensing Celie's weariness. "I ain't lik Ma, Celie. She was wise. Now....Iz older than you iz, but if yu has to drink whiskey for your nerves, take a little....and let yo brother have it, too....keep dat daughter of yours busy....busy...don't leave her with yo baby...don't leave her with Massa Davie."

Not understanding what Nessie meant, Celie did leave Davie with her brother and daughter the day Hugh Fears needed her approval on his survey of White Oaks.

George read one of his poems to Mary Caroline who was playing with Littlebury and Littlemary. Since the dogs were teething, Mary Caroline gave them dogwood twigs to gnaw on.

"And here's one for you, too, Davie. I'm tired of your crying. If it's teething, this will make you feel better."

"Ta-ta, Mawy C."

When Celie returned to the house, she found Davie had choked on the twig of dogwood. He lay on the floor near the cradle, his blue eyes gazing at the ceiling, Mary Caroline laughing, challenging her hounds to race.

"I didn't know, Ma. Maybe I did. I don't know. Davie boy... Dumb-Dumb just started fussing and crying...it tired me, so I gave him a dogwood twig. That's all. I'm sorry. So now Dumb-Dumb's gone. At least, that means one less mouth to feed. Besides that, I was trying to entertain him, help him, as you have supposedly done me...Ma, I see through you...you're the one who is crazy. You talk to a dead man. I don't do that. At least, I am who I am. Didn't God say something about I AM?"

Celie slapped Mary Caroline hard across her face. "Oh, I am ashamed of you, and you should be ashamed of yourself...killing your baby brother, mocking God, laughing at me."

Mary Caroline lingered, jeering, and Celie slapped her daughter a second time, then a third. "No more, Mary Caroline. Leave....please...and don't let me see your blue eyes again, at least not until I've buried my baby boy."

The girl fled, and Celie didn't care. She picked up Davie and talked to him, walking about the rooms, stopping at Druzie's portrait: "I've not given him the attention I gave Wheezie....I'm sorry, honey...I tried...but there was so much going on. Davie, you were precious to me, to all of us...I don't know what to say...I'll bury you at White Oaks where you were baptized and bring flowers to you and your pa 'til the day I die. I will, I promise. I should never have left you with Mary Caroline. Davie, I love you....One day you'll see your brother Wheezie in heaven...I know we'll all be there together."

"We will," she was certain Druzie answered.

"But thou art he that took me out of the womb: thou dids't make me hope when I was upon my mother's breasts. I was cast upon thee from the womb: thou art my God from my mother's belly. Be not far from me; for trouble is near; for there is none to help" (Psalm 22: 9-11).

Book Twenty-Four (late 1860)

Josie came for Davie's burial. Nathan had gone to Forest Green to tell her.

After Celie thanked the priest from St. David's in Millsborough, once again, for performing another service for her family at White Oaks Chapel, she knelt at the baby's little marker and wept. "Josie, I loved the baby, but I didn't spend the time with him I did with Wheezie...these years without Druzie have been so hard."

Celie steadied herself and stood up with her daughter's assistance. "Do you like the little angel on his marker? That's who the baby was. Josie, he fussed so much when he teethed, and....I had wanted him to play with your little ones."

"Ma, stop it...you did all you could for Davie Dumfries. You held him. You walked the floor with him. You adored him. I know what happened. I know Mary Caroline killed him. You don't have to explain anything to me."

"Do you think she did it deliberately? Don't you think your sister could have just been trying to help him?"

"Oh, Mamma, I don't know. We'll never know what goes on in that girl's mind, never, ever."

"Josie, what should I do now? I feel totally lost."

Josie's eyes brightened as she listened to her mother's question. "Ma, you ask me something. Roddy asks me something. You're far more experienced than I. You play the psaltery and read the psaltery. I don't...I just follow Roderick's advice and take care of Roddy. Besides that, the Italian villa we live in requires attention. I'll never know why my husband built such a large house."

Celie smiled as she listened to her daughter, then watched her grandson struggling to walk, his clubfoot dragging.

"When Roddy's a little older, Roderick says we'll take him to Philadelphia for an operation. I want him to be able to walk and run."

"Josie, is Roderick good to you?"

"Oh, yes, so kind, Mamma. We're expecting our second baby in a few more months. And Miss Zellie...that's what I call the elder Mrs. Dulligan....has taught Roddy to make little boats and bowls with the clay she gets down at the river. Sometimes she takes Roddy with her. My mother-in-law is a kind woman."

"Roddy reminds me a little of Wheezie, and I can't explain why. I guess it doesn't matter."

"No, Mamma...let's go home...I'll stay with you for a few days at White Oaks, then return to Forest Green."

Josie's presence comforted Celie.

Even though Roddy liked to play with MC's hounds, Josie never left her son alone with her sister. "I'll never trust her," Josie murmured to herself. "Never."

Celie talked about the former slaves at White Oaks, wondering where they had gone, asking if Roderick would free his slaves.

"Ma, I would, but my husband won't. He can't really. He depends on them for the cotton—from the planting 'til harvest-time, then the baling for market. That's Roderick's livelihood now, as I understand his investments. Of course, I don't perceive everything. Maybe his money in the railroad is related. I don't know. It doesn't really matter to me as long as he provides for Roddy and me and this second baby."

And they talked about the possibility of war.

"Roderick says he'll fight against the north. He insists the issue is not simply slavery, but states' rights as well."

"That's what your brothers say...and if the men all go, my darling Josie, we'll be together, either here at White Oaks or at Forest Green, and I'll play and read psalteries."

A few weeks later, Josie and Roddy left, and Celie felt lonelier than ever, realizing that as long as Davie lived, Druzie seemed present. With Davie's death, Druzie became more remote. Yet as the months passed, and years, she realized, once again, that the heart never changes. "It's only the spirit blending, listening, learning. Druzie's as near as you let him be," she whispered, and said aloud, "Be still, and know that I am God."

Hugh Fears and Burr left for a meeting in Abbeville late in 1860.

They returned, vowing South Carolina would secede from the Union. "That's right, Ma. At Magazine Hill, we talked about what our state will do...I know we'll soon be leaving the Union. It's a case of the rights of each state. Sure, I'm glad we freed the slaves...but I'm a Southerner born and bred, and so are you. So are MC's hounds. Ma, let's have a secession ball here at White Oaks to celebrate." His eyes brightened. "How about it? Remember how many times we've said not to conjugate our middle name?"

"Why not just a little gathering, Hugh? Winter's not even here, and I do hear the voice of the turtle dove...It's Druzie...he approves of a celebration, don't you think?"

Hugh fired a shot in the air as his mother talked of the menu for the party. "Peacock...you know your grandfather raised peacocks here at White Oaks...or we could have wild turkey and surely sweet potatoes, corn pudding, Druzie's favorite tipsy pudding, and rounds and rounds of my grandfather's special Arrack punch. I think Monica finally wrote down the recipe. What would you like, Hugh?"

"Whatever makes you happy, Mamma." Food didn't matter to her son. Neither did details. The party was simply his anticipation of secession, a celebration of the Old South, of land, of his family's way of life since 1763. That's what Hugh Fears understood. "Ma, I found one of grandpa Wash's letters from his sister in Boston. It was written a long time ago. And you know, I wouldn't want to live there. I'd hate to be in a big city, wouldn't you?"

She laughed. "I wouldn't know what to do in one either." Celie left to gather greenery for the hall and the parlor. "Maybe you'll shoot down a little mistletoe this afternoon. I do want more holly and cedar for the house," she called to Hugh.

"I will, and I'll ask Lafayette to play the fiddle. We'll dance the 'Virginia Reel' and 'The Gothic,'" Hugh answered, "And 'Soldier's Joy' is a popular dance, too."

Even MC became cheerful about the celebration, hopeful about meeting a rebel, excited over wearing the cream-colored gown Nessie had made.

While her mother was in the woods, Mary Caroline sat in the parlor where a low fire burned. She was playing with the hounds when she heard cackling and rumbling on the porch. Before she could get to the window, a big, light-skinned man and the old woman with tulip-bulb ankles forced their way through the front door.

Mary Caroline screamed, and the dogs barked fiercely, hushing when the old woman tossed crumbs to them. The man glared at Mary Caroline and shoved her to the floor, his dark eyes violent. He mounted her and thrust himself far inside and rocked back and forth.

Mary Caroline begged him to stop, and the woman laughed. "Same way yo great grand pappy used to ride me, gal. That was long time ago, but nuthin dun change...time foh yu, lik your great-grandmammy, to realize there ain't gwine be much peace on this heah earth 'til God—Gal, yo big blue eyes is starin at me again. Memba dat Christmas when you dun spat on me?"

"Who are you anyway?" Mary Caroline pleaded.

"Iz Little Numbers....name for de man wat rape yo grandma...but mos peeples run it together and calls me Lumbars...sounds Indian, don't it? But Iz really de grandson of Caleb, what was de half-brother of yo great Aunt Abbie, yo Granmammy, and her Bubba, too. Aks yo Ma sometime. Gal, yu sho feels good." Mary Caroline screamed and squirmed, kicking her legs in the air, beating Lumbars, but he slapped her back.

Riding her, Lumbars heard a door opening and withdrew. "Auntie...somebody in de house now. We betta go." He headed for the window.

"Who are you?" Celie said, rushing in from the garden. "I've never seen either one of you before." She stared at the old woman wearing a black turban and a torn calico dress and red shoes with fancy buckles.

"Of course you noz me....dat gal lauh at me wuntz and call my ankles tulep bubs. I look young dat Christmas cauf I was wearing cream on my face, but Iz an old woman. Today I be wearing de shoes wat belong to yo grandma....de red wuns she wore at some ball in Gahgtown long time ago. Yo grandpappie giv em to me. Oh, I cud make dat man happy."

"What?"

"Ma, who are they?" Hugh asked, when he came into the room. Celie shrugged her shoulders. "I don't know, Son, but that man's trying to escape through the back window. Do something..."

Hugh shot him in the leg, and Celie knelt at her daughter's side. The old woman continued to laugh.

"Yo granpappie dun kept me chained all dez yeahs down in Chinaberry Grove...it's a long story don nobody no now...all de old foks is ded and dey didn't talk no way. We all had to keep secrets. Only way we cud surviv...de white peeples didn't always want us to know. Das why dat grandpappie of yours wouldn't let yo grandmammie build a school and teach de slaves. Oh, she wanted to, but he stop her. Now yo babee gal, de wun das crazy, she gwine hab a black chile, same as yo grandmammy. Sho iz. Numbas raped huh one summer day, and she gib birth to Abbie, den gib her freedum. De gal went up north. Sho thing you had a black aunt, and you gwine hab a black grandbabee, too. Yo grandpa and me...why we had babies together...Chronicle was one of em. He wuk in de stable a little while, and I had anotha baby boy, lil Uriel. Yo grandpappy sold hem off, too. Now dis boy heah he bez my great-grandson. We jes call him Lumbars. Wez all connected, chile....de sins of one generation jes passes on to de nex...My name's Caramel. Maybe you ken read bout me in wun of yo grandmammy's diariees. Monica tole me she kep a diaree. Iz gwine hom to de grove now, den Iz leaving White Oaks, and I ain't neba cumin back."

"Oh, no you're not going free. You're not leaving White Oaks. You would just come back later on and murder us," Hugh Fears said. "We've freed every black person on the plantation, but I will not free you. You're an evil witch, and I don't trust you, no, not one bit. I've heard stories about your kind."

"Son," Celie interrupted. "Please let this old woman go...I don't want to hear those chains rattling in the night...please, release her. She's been imprisoned too long."

But Hugh Fears wouldn't. He pulled off the woman's turban. Celie saw the scar and shrieked. "Please, Hugh, please let her go...there's going to be trouble either way."

But Hugh shackled Caramel and led her down the path to her familiar home in Chinaberry Grove. Celie wept.

> "My soul hath long dwelt with him that hateth peace. I am for peace: but when I speak, they are for war" (Psalm 120:6-7).

Book Twenty-Five (late December 1860-1863)

With the help of China Lee and her brother, Celie put Mary Caroline to bed, and Nessie, following her mother's notes, rubbed her charge with arnica and offered ginger tea. Celie struggled to smile that night at the secession ball, relieved when Burr and Rosa Alison finally arrived.

"Please fill in for me, Rosa Alison. I must go to my daughter's bedside. I need you now."

"I will, Mother. I understand, and do try to rest a little."

Upstairs, Celie and MC heard Lafayette playing the fiddle and calling out the dance tunes.

Christmas Day of 1860 was somber. Celie gave members of Monica's family shoes and clothing. "Times are different, but some traditions remain the same. They always will. Today, though, I'm going to Chinaberry Grove. I wonder if Caramel ever had anyone go to see her on Christmas Day down in the grove?"

But Hugh would not allow it. "I can't allow you to be hurt. I don't trust that crazy old bitch. I'll take the gypsy-witch whatever you wish, Mamma, but I cannot let you go down to Chinaberry Grove by yourself. Promise me you won't go."

"I'm not sure I can promise you that, honey. But I won't go today." When Celie asked Nessie and the others about Caramel, they simply shrugged their shoulders, their eyes mysterious.

"Why are they like that, Hugh?" she asked that night as they sipped a little eggnog.

"Ma, some things don't change. They probably had to be that way all through the years, protection, fear, I guess. I don't know…Ma, you know Burr and me will be leaving soon, don't you? As soon as war's declared?"

She sighed. "I do, and I imagine you'll take one of the boys with you."

"Probably Nathan...maybe Linus. Josh is still here....and so are some of the others."

"They're getting old along with me, honey."

He reassured her that the war wouldn't last long. January of 1861 came too soon for Celie, but not for the boys. Not long after their own fireworks at White Oaks, there were shots at Fort Sumter, and Hugh Fears kissed his mother and Mary Caroline good-bye.

"Mamma, I'll write to you....we both will....I may surprise you and bring a wife home, and, MC, maybe I'll bring you a husband. Would you like that?"

"Oh, you're a tease," his mother answered, tucking a few biscuits and little cakes into his sack, "I'll send you and Burr boxes along the way. Just let us know where your regiment makes camp. Write to us, son. Please."

"I will, Ma..." He leaned down and kissed her and his sister once more, then kicked up a trail of dust galloping down the lane.

Celie's heart gradually gave way to loneliness, emptiness, almost desperation, especially when she heard George groaning and MC whimpering and fussing. In the late spring, Celie forced herself to work in the garden. She'd read through her grandfather's notes on flowers and herbs and planted seeds. She sang to Mary Caroline and encouraged her daughter to play the psaltery. "Darling, it will take you away from your sorrow if you let the melody lead you...It's sort of like giving your fears to the wind."

"Ma, that sounds silly. I don't understand you."

Celie ignored her daughter and began telling her stories, always trying to keep her somewhat sedated with teas, even, on occasion when she became combative, with a little whiskey and sugar, Druzie's old trick. Celie smiled, remembering their first argument so long ago. "Oh, we were closer than twins," she said aloud, hoping he would hear her.

"Misses Celie, if you wanna to get dat gal's baby killed, why we could giv huh sumpin," Nessie said. "I dun read in Ma's notes and in Prince's and yo grandpappie's about de seeds in Queen Anne's lace. You noz as well as me dat grows wild. Some folks uses blue cohosh."

Celie was glad Nessie understood. "Try whatever you will. I really don't want my daughter to have this baby....I'm not sure exactly what she remembers of that trauma in December, are you?"

The woman shook her head. "I jes hope we ain't waited too long."

Celie shrugged her shoulders. "All we can do is try. Thank you, Nessie."

Whatever Nessie did worked, for Mary Caroline lost the baby. Instead of being thankful, she became hostile, angry. Her old mood returned. "I could have had this baby. I think you and Nessie schemed together and gave me something to make me lose the child I was carrying. I didn't care if his father was colored. At least, I would be like Josie and Rosa Alison. I'd have a baby. It's because of you I don't. You killed my child, Ma."

"Honey, would you like to go visit Forest Green? Maybe have a change. I'm sure you become tired of my company and China Lee's.

MC shook her head. "I'm not going to be a nurse maid to a boy who can't walk. That's Josie's job. She's his mother. I'm not," Mary Caroline wailed as she sucked her fingers. "I hate you, Ma."

So Celie turned to her brother for comfort. Even though he primarily babbled, he occasionally recited his own poems, along with those of Edgar Allan Poe and others. All Celie had to do was mention a poet's name, and George recited their poetry. He knew the verses by heart. Listening, Celie learned a lot. "Bubba, do you know 'Flow Gently, Sweet Afton?' Druzie often sang that to me."

He nodded and said the poem, giving each word meaning and expression. Celie clapped, and she was certain her claps were echoed. "It's Druzie thanking you, too. Oh, Druzie. I've never felt so lonely."

"I miss you, too, my sweet," he answered.

Even though George wasn't living in reality, he never said anything ugly to his sister. And, of course, Celie suspected that she herself was not in reality either. "Bubba and I are alike after all. I must stay busy....I'll read to China Lee and the others if they wish. I can make sure they know the alphabet, and there's always my psaltery...yes. I wonder when we'll have a letter from the boys. I'll ask Josie when she comes....and Rosa Alison. Maybe she's received something from Burr."

A few days later, Rosa Alison and her little girl came to White Oaks. "Have you heard from Burr?"

"Yes, I have. He and Hugh Fears were separated. I'm not sure why. Burr's in Virginia, and Hugh is near Charleston. We'll stay here with you if you'd like...the house is so lonely without Burr. I try to stay busy. I've been knitting socks, and."

Celie was happy her daughter-in-law and granddaughter would stay. "White Oaks is terribly lonely, and Mary Caroline wails a lot these days. Her moods come and go. Sometimes she can be sweet and agreeable, then at other times, very petulant and irritable. She blames me for a great deal." Rosa listened as Celie reminisced and Carrie played with her dolls.

"I wouldn't leave little Carrie alone with MC," Celie added, as she looked at Burr's wife who had dark hair which was parted in the middle and grayish brown eyes. Her lips were thin, and she smiled easily. Wearing a dress with three large buttons down the front and long sleeves which slightly puffed at the shoulder seam, Rosa Alison was fashionable. Style had always been important to Burr.

"I won't...I hope MC will enjoy having her namesake here, but I won't run the risk. I know about Davie....oh, Mother, you've had such a hard time."

"Yes, but with Druzie's love and understanding, his encouragement, I was able to make changes and overcome my fears. I believe that when I play my fears into the psaltery, they leave, and I'm able to understand my heart. Druzie told me once about an old hymn his mother sang to him. It was about giving your fears to the winds. Our psaltery was more than a stringed instrument. Do you understand?"

"Oh, I do...I'd like to help you here at White Oaks. Is there something you want to do or would like for me to do?"

Celie said she wished to bury the family silver and walk for a little while. "Just your being here is a comfort. Do as you would at home. You're like my own daughter, Rosa Alison. If you'll just help us, as we move from one day to the next, why that'll be a gracious plenty."

Rosa Alison understood.

Celie walked outside and sniffed the fragrance of honeysuckle and blackberry roses and enjoyed the breeze in the white oaks. It was May. Spring had passed so quickly. She climbed the hill and buried the silver under the tree near the gold. More trees were growing near their special white oak, the one which she and Druzie always felt had magical powers. "Druzie, are you here this afternoon? And how's Wheezie? Hold me. Oh, darling....I've been playing our psaltery. I wish you could hear the melodies."

"I do, my love, and they are beautiful...always feel me there beside you while you play. I am with you wherever you are, and Wheezie's fine...Celie, you might mark our oak, lest others grow and hide it, as they will one day. I love you."

And for a few seconds, she felt Druzie's presence, his arms encircling her. And then he seemed to vanish. She tied an old copper kettle to the lowest branch.

"There, that's our sign...we played with that kettle when we were little and made mud pies. Remember?" Druzie added, before the wind shifted. The sun was almost over the garden, and Celie still had chores to do.

"Good night, darling."

She put the last two hams from the smokehouse in her grandfather's garret in the tower and wondered about the slashed portrait of the lady holding the rabbit. "Who are you?"

Then, she walked to the stable and nuzzled Dull, the old mule, and Nellie's granddaughter, whom nobody had ever named. The horse was simply called Baby Horse.

The next two years passed quickly. Sometimes Celie and Mary Caroline and Rosa Alison and Carrie would ride over to Forest Green to see Josie and Roddy. Celie enjoyed visiting with Miss Zellie who talked about getting her clay from the river and making pots. Carrie and Roddy laughed and played together. That Carrie couldn't always hear him never bothered Roddy, and his clubfoot did not disturb Carrie. The two reminded Celie in a strange way of herself so many years ago when she first met Druzie.

And there was something mysterious about the sprawling mansion with its tower, the stately rooms, and the porches. The style was different from the house at White Oaks, and Josie said she always felt like a princess in a castle.

The grown-ups talked about news they'd received from the war, who was wounded, who would be coming home. Rosa Alison occasionally heard from Burr, who sent love to his mother, and Josie received notes from Roderick, but nobody knew about Hugh Fears.

Not hearing from her son bothered Celie. She finally asked Mary Caroline again if she'd had a letter from her brother. The girl shook her head and asked if it would be alright simply to call the hounds LB and LM for short.

Shocked at her daughter's indifference, Celie said, "If you like. Why not ask Uncle George what he thinks."

"Oh, Ma, you would say that. All he does is groan when I talk to him, and I do visit him when you're out in the fields hoeing or digging in the garden. He's not interested in talking to me, so I just give him a sip from the bottle. Ma, he smells awful. Do you ever clean him? He's like a big, drooling baby now, and I'm glad he's not mine."

Of course, what Mary Caroline didn't care to know or believe was that George occasionally sat up and talked to her mother. "Yes, sometimes, MC, we have delightful conversations. We talk about the past, and I tell him what's growing in the garden, and even when he seems faraway, distant, he recites poetry. His voice is beautiful in a special way. I learn from him."

Mary Caroline only laughed at her mother. "You're crazier than I thought you were, Ma."

"Just hopeful, honey...would you like to make a scarecrow with me this afternoon, the way you did a long time ago when Wheezie was little?"

"You must be desperate, Ma. I'm 21 years old, a grown woman, and you expect me to do something as childish as that. You're really silly. Go bathe Uncle George! If you really need something to do, bathe the hounds. Can't you see China Lee and I are busy making clothes for the dogs?"

"Honey, sometimes in the late summer and early fall, I just feel lonely. That's when my husbands were killed. Wheezie died, then my grandma passed away. It's just a hard time for me."

"It doesn't matter to me, Ma. I don't care. You can't live with your dead."

Celie shook her head and busied herself with chores. There was always something to do at the grist mill. "Don't try so hard, sugar," she heard Druzie say one afternoon when she was at the mill, and she was grateful he understood.

She went to the kitchen and made cornbread and sweet potato custard, then invited Nessie and the others to join her. She resolved to make Christmas as pleasant as possible. She also made Monica's molasses tassies, using whatever was available, for many food stuffs were scarce. Then, she persuaded MC to sketch several flower pictures.

"Oh, Ma, you all sound like absolute imbeciles when you sing Christmas carols. I just want to have a baby. I don't even care if I'm married or not. At least you had babies, and you could lie down with Uncle George right now if you wanted to. Maybe you do for all we know."

"Hush up your mouth, Mary Caroline. I wish you wouldn't be so disagreeable."

"Well may I ask why you were singing and playing 'How Firm a Foundation' for Druzie when it's not even a Christmas song?"

"Because we both found comfort in the words, and...and I miss him...I've heard Charleston's in the heat of Yankee firing, and I wish I could talk to Druzie about it. Can you try to understand just a little?"

"No, Ma, not really."

China Lee rolled her eyes. "She jes dat way, Misses Celie, and I sho iz sorry, but try not to fret. It don't do no good. An I dun made you sumpin for Christmas....I made you a little bag fo your scraps when you putting togeda dem crazy quilts....das what Granny Nessie says dey iz."

"She's right. Oh, thank you China Lee. I appreciate this. Celie looked at the muslin bag which the girl had sewn together and embroidered with flowers on one side.

Celie gave China Lee a hug and an extra slice of cake. "Honey, you take the afternoon off, too. Tomorrow's Christmas, and I know you'd like to join the others tonight down in The Quarters."

"Yessum, I sho would. Iz much obliged."

Mary Caroline never looked up when China Lee left the room.

Celie prayed to God.

"Our soul is escaped as a bird out of the snare of the fowlers: the snare is broken, and we are escaped" (Psalm 124:7).

Book Twenty-Six (Winter, 1864)

A few weeks later in early February when Celie was watering Dull and Baby Horse, she looked up the hill toward that psaltered white oak. A man clothed in a tattered blue suit was untying the copper kettle.

Without hesitating, she pulled out the pistol Druzie had taught her to use and fired. The man fell immediately. Celie climbed the hill, drew her shawl closer against the wind, and dared herself to look down at the man lying in a bloody pond filled with acorns, shells caked along his lips. Had he eaten them for food? The dead Yankee wore a patch over one eye and glared at her with the other, seeming to squint against the afternoon sun.

She searched his pockets and discovered dried meat and the man's name: Private Timothy Robin O'Riley, Pennsylvania. He was Irish. Celie took the little bit of money he had and dragged his body down toward Chinaberry Grove where she buried him. After clapping the dead man's horse away, she trudged toward home and looked up at the cold moon. "Oh, I am tired tonight. Carry me with you, wherever you're going."

"Sugar, you're over fifty, so I imagine you're as tired as I am. I love you and miss you." For just a few minutes, Celie was in her cousin's arms. "I think I'll rest a few minutes, Druzie. You understand?"

Meanwhile, two other Yankees, an old, white-haired man who was short and stumpy with a stubby reddish-white beard, and a younger one with dark brown eyes, curly blonde hair, and cracked lips broke into the house. They pointed guns at Mary Caroline.

"Where's the gold, little lady?" Dan, the younger one, asked, as he jumped on the piano keys.

Mary Caroline shrugged her shoulders.

"Well, then, I'll make you know," he continued, as he smashed the picture she was painting of Mrs. Gray's school and smeared the furniture with her pastels. He threw Mary Caroline onto the floor and tore off her clothes.

Hearing screams, Uncle George stumbled down the steps, firing an old rifle, just as Baby Horse wandered through the open door. Abraham, the older soldier, seized George and strapped him to the horse, then fired a shot. The horse spooked and rode violently up and down the hall. George fell off and hit his head on the hearth.

"So these rebs live with their horses, too!" Abraham scoffed. "That's plantation life, ain't it?" He went through George's pockets. "Nothing but a verse of poetry, old fool."

Celie looked at her brother's poetry, then whispered to herself that George had fulfilled his dream, his talent. "Yes, he's helping others, the students, to realize their abilities and gifts. The younguns....they won't waste anymore time. Thank you, God," she continued, realizing she had to witness her daughter's abuse, her humiliation.

"I'm going to fuck you, little lady," Dan said, as he pushed Mary Caroline down to the floor.

"Get up, Dan. No use wasting time here."

"This little gal may be stupid, Abraham, but her pussy's better than plantation biscuits with butter and sorghum."

They heard another shot, and Abraham grabbed the horse. "Dan, I'm leaving. Somebody's fired a second shot. Maybe it's your brother. I didn't know where it came from."

"I heard a gun fire, too," Celie said, coming through the side door, hiding the pistol within the folds of her full black skirt. She took the reins from the older man, adding, her voice firm, "We don't have anything here."

"Well, that ain't what we heard in Charleston. That kin fellow of yours told us at St. Michael's Church where we shot him on Christmas Eve all about your family's gold. Lady, do you think we came all this distance out of our way just so I could fuck a stupid gal? We want that gold," Dan turned, holding MC down, riding her.

"That fellow said you had silver, too......he was kind of a scared young man, told us he was a mason, like his great-grandfather. He knew all sorts of hidden things about the church....tried to talk a lot, you know....to keep us from shootin him, but we didn't care. He was just another reb. We're deserters. Did a Yankee outside see you, Mam?" Abraham asked.

Realizing the Yankees did not suspect she had a pistol, Celie nodded. "I think he did. Somebody fired at me twice, and I ran. I didn't see anyone. I was outside picking flowers."

"Picking flowers...ain't that sweet."

"You're hurting me," Mary Caroline screamed, "We don't have any gold...Ma, make them leave me alone. Ma, I'm sorry I've been ugly."

"All we got to eat's a little spoon bread on the dining room table," Celie said, drawing closer to the horse, whispering something.

"Whoever heard of bread made out of a spoon? Do you have fork bread, too?" Dan jeered. "What kind is it? Is it silver like the kind you rebs were born with on the plantation?"

Abraham walked through the house, throwing vases and books on the floor. "So you don't have gold?"

"No...I'm a widow, and this is my daughter, and that's my brother on the floor."

Abraham began figuring things out. "Dan, I bet Tim's left us here and gone off on his horse."

"If you want some silver, there are a few pieces buried down near the chinaberry trees. Baby Horse knows. He'll lead you there."

"Lady if you're lying to me and I don't find no silver, why I'm going to set every building on this plantation on fire, and..."

Celie told the younger man to mount the horse. "And you lead....Baby Horse is accustomed to an older man leading him." The Yankees obeyed. Celie again whispered something in Baby Horse's ears and tapped his right haunch. The horse understood and took off immediately through the front door and down the steps. Dan tumbled off and died on the ground. When Abraham turned, Celie fired, then shoved him on down the steps to the brick walkway.

"Why, Mamma, you've killed three men. 'Thou shalt not kill'...you've disobeyed a commandment, and I've only been raped. But I have not sinned."

"No, Daughter, you have not have sinned," her mother answered, stunned. "I have, but right now I must bury the men. Please give me all the strength you can and help me drag them down to the chinaberry trees."

"No, I can't," Mary Caroline cried "...I can't. Mamma, it hurt more this time."

"I'm sorry...I'll try to take the hurt away." Nessie and the others ran in, scared. "We heard some shots, Misses Celie, but..." Carrie toddled in, holding her doll, "Mammy's sick upstairs. She's burning up."

Celie asked China Lee and Nessie to take care of the sick ones and watch Carrie. "Please make everyone as comfortable as you can...I..." And she dragged the men down toward Chinaberry Grove, stripped them of any valuables, and buried them. If there was moaning beyond the trees, she never heard it.

She leaned on the shovel and looked at the moon sailing across the sky, longing to jump and ride far above the white oaks.

Soaked with perspiration, her hair falling, Celie remembered the night Barnie Dunn had raped her and trembled, weary and afraid, wondering if her son was dead in Charleston, wondering what would become of all of her family.

"Pray, love. Don't forget to pray."

"I won't, Druzie. Oh, I am so tired, honey, and afraid."

> "My heart is smitten, and withered like grass; so that I forget to eat my bread. By reason of the voice of my groaning my bones cleave to my skin. I am like a pelican of the wilderness: I am like an owl of the desert…" (Psalm 102:4-6).

Book Twenty-Seven (Winter, Continued)

George sobbed and twisted in agony. Mary Caroline wailed. Rosa Alison fretted. Little Carrie cried. China Lee warned. Only Nessie, like her mother, was able to comfort Celie. "Gawd's gwine bring us through, honey. Memba dat?"

But Celie sobbed, picturing her son who too often feared being shot by Yankees as he interpreted signs in an old church, as her great grandfather once did so many years ago in Ireland.

Listening to George begging for laudanum, she thought of addictions, everyone's, her own included, whatever it was, and she knew it was guilt...GUILT. "But that was a long time ago, my love...give it to the wind in the white oaks, to the psaltery's melody," and Celie knew Druzie was talking and loving, encouraging.

"George, we'll pull through together, yet again. I promise... I know you miss Hebrides and I know it hurts, but try to sleep," Celie said, patting her brother's hand.

"He loved me," George whispered through the pain.

"Try to rest, George. Sweet dreams," she said, withdrawing from the room.

Holding the stair rail, Celie climbed the steps, one step at a time, to help her daughter.

Mary Caroline lay on the bed, turning from one side to the other, touching her legs, sucking her fingers, crying, "I want my brothers...I want Burrie and Hughie. Ma, they're coming home, aren't they?"

"I pray for them to come back to White Oaks, Mary Caroline," Celie answered, seeing an envelope on the marble-topped wash stand. She opened it and read:

July, 1863, near Charleston

Dear Sissy,

    I got your letter. Why won't Mamma write to me? I thanked her for the ginger cookies and asked for some shirts. But she hasn't written me back. Why? Sometimes, I think she still blames me for Pa's death and Wheezie's...and Cudn Druzie's. Tell her not to. My friends write more. Even Jeanette Forbes, you know that girl from Millsborough who used to laugh at my ears? She wrote. She said Lucius McFreight's leg was blown off at Gettysburg. I heard Burr was wounded at Malvern Hill in Virginia. Did you know that? I miss Burr. Member how we'd get grandpa's pipes and Burr and me and Cudn Druzie, even after he was blind, would go down behind the grist mill and puff...and then Nathan or Lafayette found us, and we all laughed?

    I'm addressing this letter to you and Mamma. Please show it to her in case you open it first. I miss all of you. How are Littlebury and Littlemary? Oh, that boy from Mount Hebron. Remember Beau Murray? He's been real sick...fever, I think. They don't think he'll pull through. I want to come for Christmas. I've been eating a lot of blackberries. Rations aren't very good. We're not far from Charleston, I don't think...maybe I'll get to see the churches there...I'm afraid, Sissy...I think the fighting will be heavy here soon. Give Ma my love...

    As ever, your brother,
    Hugh Fears

    Sitting on the side of the bed, Celie read and reread the letter and relived the last few months. If this letter was written in July of 1863, where was Hugh Fears right now? Was he really dead? Or were those Yankee deserters just tempting her?

    Celie took Mary Caroline's hand, "Honey, why didn't you show me this letter?"

    "I didn't want to...Bubba's dead, Ma...Didn't you hear what the Yankees said?"

"Yes...I heard...But...your brother dying, thinking I blamed him for the deaths of his father, Wheezie, and Druzie is horrible. I didn't blame him. Did you make him think I did just to hurt me?"

"Maybe I did, and maybe I didn't. That's none of your business, Ma," the girl answered, her voice indifferent now.

"How many other letters did you hide from me?"

"Several."

Celie sobbed into her dirty black dress as she imagined Hugh away at war, sleeping on the ground, in a tent, perhaps wounded, often hungry, wondering why his mother had not written. If only the letter had been addressed just to Mrs. Celie Fears Bain? But it wasn't. Mary Caroline's name was there, and she always took the mail first, having little else to do.

"I didn't want you to know anything about Bubba, Ma. I wanted him all to myself. You had my father and Druzie. Josie has Roderick, and Burr Fennell has Rosa Alison. It's not fair. Hughie didn't have anybody, and neither did I....so I pictured us loving each other...I let him think you blamed him...in that way, he turned to me. He didn't really need you."

Celie didn't know what to say. She only stared at Mary Caroline sliding under the quilt, sucking her fingers, and realized her daughter had manipulated both of them, brother and mother, when they were most vulnerable from war and fatigue, war and widowhood, and she hated the bitterness within her.

Mary Caroline railed on, "Yes, I wanted to make a baby with my Bubba, the way you and Unkie did, but you kept Hughie and me apart...I know you did, but you know what, Ma? Hughie and me, we played with each other out in the barn, and you never knew it. You were so busy prissing about in that stupid black dress and veil and listening to the voice of Druzie, you never heard what we needed...so...and you and Nessie took my first baby. Well, you're not going to destroy this child, even if I was raped by a Yankee. At least I will be a mother, and my breasts are normal. I don't look like a witch, and I don't think my children will ever have funny breasts, either. If they do, I'll hurt those little ones."

Celie left the bedroom and walked up and down the front lawn, then back to the garden, wondering whom she could talk to. If Druzie was trying to whisper something, she didn't hear him. She didn't hear the wind in the white oaks, nor the songs on the psaltery.

As if she sensed her mother's pain, Josie rode over one day with Roddy and little Cil, her baby girl named in honor of Celie and her own grandmother, Cecilia.

"Ma, you're so pale and thin," Josie said, removing her cape and unbuttoning her children's little coats. "What's wrong?"

Celie told her about the Yankees and about discovering the letter on Mary Caroline's wash stand. "Josie, to think my boy died, thinking I blamed him for the hunting accident and the drowning, oh, to realize Hugh Fears blamed himself and thought I'd not forgiven him grieves me to no end. My heart aches, and...and to think your sister withheld his letters deliberately is even worse...the way she manipulated all of us."

"Mamma, don't blame yourself. Mary Caroline is crazy, and you know it. Uncle George is mad. He can't really control it...but don't let MC bring you down. You're weary enough as it is..."

"I've been reading the Psalms in my Psaltery and trying to play my psaltery, but I can't do either. Josie, tell me what to do, please."

"Mamma, I know Druzie would never want you to feel this way. That I'm sure of. He would want me to shake you into living again, wouldn't he?"

Celie nodded..."Yes, he would...and you know I've been so tired lately I've not prayed or even listened to his voice, and I am ashamed, afraid."

Celie then told Josie the whole story about the Yankees in Charleston at St. Michael's Church near Christmas in 1863. "Oh, Josie, often I think you were right. I should have put MC in an asylum, but I simply cannot. Darling....she didn't ask to come into the world under the circumstances in which Barnie Dunn brought her. And if I'd been stronger, I could have slapped him and delivered MC myself, and then..."

"Ma, wipe your tears and look at me."

Celie looked up into her daughter's dark eyes. They were serious. "Ma."

"Josie, you're Aunt Aggie all over again, only much more serious today, and circumstances have brought you to that, and I am sorry."

Josie took her mother's hands in her own once again, "Ma, we will come through this horrible war, and your sons will come home again to White Oaks...I know Burr and Roderick will, too, and I'm sure one day MC will marry. Meantime, let's don't allow her to ruin our lives. We must live, too."

"Does Rosa Alison know Burr was wounded at Malvern Hill? And Roderick? Where is he now, Josie?"

"I don't know. It's been a week since we've heard anything. I can only trust, and that's what I have done, Mamma. I pray you can feel the same way...it's what you once told us a long time go...something about the wind and about giving your fears to the wind...is that the way you feel when you play the psaltery? Does that take away your fears?"

"Yes, it does...when I sing the psalms from my grandmother's psaltery, while playing my psaltery, I find comfort and healing. My fears leave, and I want you to enjoy the psaltery...and to help me with the family. Help me kick out this Satan when he tries to crawl through the house....have you met him along the way, Josie?"

"More than once...he's that evil spirit lurking in the garden to tempt you, me, any one of us, but let's not yield. Swee him out the door each morning, Ma. Please. You can do it. That's what Nolie does."

"Nolie?"

"Do you know her, Ma?"

"She's the slave whom Druzie helped escape to the north several years ago. He paid someone to take her north after she ran away from a plantation down in the low-country. I forget all of the details. Do you think she's the same Nolie?"

"I don't know, Ma. I just know my husband bought her when he was away on one of his railroad trips. She's a pretty woman. You can tell she's been whipped. She's afraid."

"If she's the one my husband helped escape, I will buy her freedom, Josie. I will." Celie looked firmly at her daughter. "And I think your husband would understand."

Josie nodded, as she sat down in a chair outside her sister's room.

"Mamma, I know you miss Druzie, don't you?"

"Oh, yes, and in my dreams, I hear his tender voice and see his loving face...one day, will you inscribe that on his tombstone? I have work to do now. I must go down to the mill, then finish making the soap...Do you hear Druzie?"

Josie smiled, a little wistful, then shook her head. "No, Mamma, but you listen. I'll go spend some time with Sissy. Maybe she will talk to me, and we want you all to come to Forest Green....will you?"

"I don't know...and leave White Oaks?"

Celie walked out the front door and waited. "It's alright, my love...you did the only thing you could do...don't look back...the Yankees are dead...move to the green...I'm with you."

And she knew Druzie was trying to tell her something.

> "I will hear what God the Lord will speak: for he will speak peace unto his people, and to his saints: but let them not turn again to folly. Surely his salvation is nigh them that fear him; that glory may dwell in our land" (Psalm 85: 8-9).

Book Twenty-Eight (1865)

Celie finally agreed to take her family to Forest Green. Some of the formerly enslaved people refused to go. Old Prince, bent over with rheumatism, was one.

"Dis been my home, Missus Celie, long as I ken memba." He scratched his white hair, taking her hands into his gnarled ones, "but I sho apprechates yo kindnesses to me all through de years."

Celie's eyes filled with tears as she remembered the old man's devotion and loyalty. She promised to send him food. Nessie and London said they couldn't leave either. "And Massa George....he too sick to go." Lafayette offered to drive Celie and Mary Caroline to Forest Green.

Hesitant to go, Celie listened to Nessie. "We be alright...if dem Yankees cum, we'll go hide in the mill. We'll watch out for yo Bubba. You go tonight."

The moon was full over the orchard, then seemed to settle above the old oak on the hill, and Celie remembered all the times she'd laughed with Druzie about the mule eating pears. "Will you come to the Green?" she whispered, leaning back.

"Where are my hounds, Ma?" Mary Caroline said, breaking into her mother's reverie.

"They ain't cumin, honey, not jes yet," China Lee said.

Of course, that disappointed Mary Caroline. That was all the young woman needed.

She railed out at her mother and slapped her skirts.

Celie took her daughter's hands. "You stop it right now, Mary Caroline. The hounds are not coming. Your sister has enough on her mind with two small children and her husband away at war, and so do I. Littlebury and Littlemary are fine at White Oaks. They can sleep with Uncle George."

"So could I, Ma, if you weren't so mean. Uncle George and I could have made a baby. He loved me, and I know it. Well, maybe I'll have a Yankee baby. What was that man's name who raped me? Oh, I hurt after that."

"And I'm sorry, honey," her mother said.

"No you're not."

"Besides, you couldn't have had your uncle. Massa George loved Hebrides, and you noz dat, Missy." China Lee interrupted.

"After Hebrides died," Mary Caroline snapped back, slapping China Lee, "Maybe he'd have welcomed me to his bed."

"Stop it right now in the name of God, Mary Caroline, and I mean it," Celie said, holding MC's hands. "Hold my daughter's feet, please, China Lee."

"Missus Celie, I dun tried and tried, but dat gal, she jus plain mean, and strong, too."

"I know, China Lee. I know." And before MC realized what her mother was doing, Celie rubbed her daughter's tongue with opium powder she'd taken from George.

Mary Caroline finally fell asleep as the coach, its interior worn and faded, jolted over the back roads to Forest Green where old Mrs. Dulligan whom everyone called Zellica or Miss Zellie, her hair white hair pulled into a low bun, her cheek bones high, welcomed her daughter-in-law's family and directed everyone to their rooms.

Celie was grateful not to have to make decisions. Her only job over the next few days seemed to be working in the garden and taking care of Mary Caroline. Celie enjoyed Roddy and Cil. The little girl was pretty and followed her grandmother around, often picking flowers for her, and counting petals. "Can me do this, Grammy?" And Celie knelt down and hugged the child. "Of course, you can." Celie read to the children and played games with them.

In midsummer Mary Caroline, who had learned to make pottery and do tatting under Miss Zellie's instruction, went into labor. She screamed and screamed and finally gave birth to a baby boy. Born prematurely, the child was frail, but gentle. "His name is Hughie for Bubba. I'm going to pretend he's our baby, Ma, and you can't change that. You know, he looks like Wheezie, but he doesn't have anything wrong with him. He doesn't pass on afflictions as you do, Mamma."

"Darling, I have no control over your fantasies. I will help you if you like."

Within a week, the baby died, and MC blamed her mother. "You plotted this, Ma. I know you gave little Hughie some poison because you resented my love for my Bubba."

"Mary Caroline, honey, I did no such thing. You're tired now...you're exhausted. I want you to drink a little tea for me, so you can sleep. It's chamomile."

But Mary Caroline sat straight up and poured the tea on her mother's face, scalding her, "You're just jealous, Ma. That's all, you three-titted witch. You can drink your damned tea."

Celie left the room and wandered over the plantation, her face burning. Later, Miss Zellie gently applied lotion to ease the pain.

Looking at her mother's burned, wrinkled face, Josie insisted MC would go to the asylum in Columbia, but Celie refused. "I can't. Josie. You'll understand as your children grow older. Losing one's child is…I can't, now."

Zellica understood her sister-in-law's dilemma and pain and suggested a compromise: sending Mary Caroline, with Nolie and China Lee to guard her, down to one of the old slave cabins. "That big one down by the corncrib, the one that wasn't burned. I know the whole story, Celie, and I am so sorry. You have suffered, my dear."

Celie reluctantly agreed to her sister-in-law's proposal, but only after she talked to Nolie. Nolie told her about being captured on her way to freedom and about being bought by Mr. Roderick Dulligan. "He was kind to me…he only took me to bed two times…said he shouldn't have done that. I think he missed Miss Josie."

"I'm going to buy your freedom. You are not going to be a slave anymore," and Celie listened, ashamed of the way white men used their servants, knowing her grandfather was as guilty as the next. "Ain't nothing you can do about dat, Miss Celie, and I much oblige to you for freeing me."

So China Lee and Nolie took Mary Caroline to the old cabin where they tried to entertain her and keep her occupied, doing what was necessary to keep her from breaking away, obeying Josie's orders. "Do what you need to do. My sister must not hurt my mother again."

> "Behold, how good and how pleasant it is for brethren to dwell together in unity…it is like precious ointment upon the head,…" (Psalm 133:1-2a).

Book Twenty-Nine (later 1865)

A week or so later, everyone heard a loud knock at the front door. It was a soldier in a ragged gray uniform. Josie opened the door and saw that the soldier was carrying a man whose right leg was missing and whose breathing was labored. The wounded man opened his eyes. "I…I'm home…Jo…Josie, I have missed you so."

Recognizing her husband at once, Josie took him and laid him on the velvet love seat in the hall. "My darling, I…"

"Your husband was wounded at Spottsylvania, Virginia, Ma'am, and he wanted to come home. I promised him. Oh, he's a fine man, Mrs. Dulligan. He wanted to see you and the little ones before….well, he insisted he had to tell you something. He's lost a lot of blood, Ma'am."

Josie thanked the man and asked Celie to give him some food, then kissed Roderick. "Oh, my sweetheart….I have missed you. The children are fine. Little Cil looks just like you. See them now?"

He squeezed Josie's hand. "Take Roddy to a doctor, my love, after the war…the house is yours. It's all in the will. Remember to take care of Mamma. Don't stay here long. Go….go to the bluffs, the Yankees are coming this way…Get the folks from the Oaks…It won't be long….Cil looks lik your Ma…I…" He died, trying to raise his head to kiss Josie one last time, as little Cil thrust one of her dolls into their faces, laughing.

Josie prepared her husband's body and buried him near the desolate chapel at the bluffs. Roderick had always liked the old place, as his older brother had, and had vowed to restore it after the war.

Josie lost no time in moving the family to the bluffs. After Christmas, the Yankees captured Millsborough and looted many plantations up and down the Patuxee. They stopped the trains from passing through Swannkell by pulling up the tracks and tying them around the trees. That was one way of cutting off supplies and ammunition for the Confederates.

Lest their own cotton be burned up in warehouses along the tracks, some Southerners stored their cotton in deserted slave cabins and turned the empty warehouses into hospitals for the wounded.

Celie thought nothing of walking the two miles from the bluffs to Swannkell to take bandages, food, and water to the soldiers. She bound up their wounds, listened to their stories, reading their letters, trying to make the dying rebels as comfortable as possible. She said prayers, held hands, lingered.

"Did you know my boys?" she sometimes asked. One young corporal talked about his sweetheart and gripped her hand as a doctor sliced off his arm before poison set in. If the wounded could walk, she took them to the bluffs where Roderick's mother spread an outdoor table with sweet potatoes and cornbread. Back down in the warehouse where others lay on the bare floor, groaning, Memnon made splints and offered water.

"Why I knew Burr Fennell Dulligan," one man said, his one green eye suddenly twinkling, when he heard Celie talking about her boys. "Yes Ma'am, I knew him at Malvern Hills. Oh, Burr could make us laugh. He was always up to some prank. He was wounded, though, and taken prisoner. Somebody said he was in the worst prison in Virginia. Then, I heard he escaped. But, Ma'am, I'm sure as I'm lying here, your son is with General Lee right now, fighting with the Army of Northern Virginia. Now, Burr had a bad cough, but...well you couldn't have had a nicer son."

Others related their experiences in prisons run by the Yankees. "That one in Washington was terrible....I know. I was there," a man with charcoal gray hair down to his shoulders said, one leg dangling over the cot, a bandage across his forehead.

"I'm sorry," Celie said. During the next few months, Forest Green was burned, and each time Celie passed the smoldering buildings on her way to Swannkell, she felt sick. "Soon it will be known as Burnt Green, a haunted plantation beneath the cold winter moon," she whispered, hoping nobody heard.

"What will become of all of us?" she asked herself, but didn't have to wrestle for an answer. Her brother was dying, and she knew they would be burying him soon. After returning from the wounded, she learned George wanted her. She hurried to his bedside. He whispered, his voice hoarse, "Sissy, I...forgive me."

"I did a long time ago, Bubba..."

"And Hebrides?"

"He's waiting for you, and we'll all be together again, Druzie, and…it's alright." George turned his head and died. Prince, at his bedside, tried to lift him, but George was more than his aged heart could handle. Prince died, and he and George were buried beside Roderick behind the chapel. "We'll move Hebrides here after the war," Celie said, as she began singing, "Nearer My God to Thee."

"Truth shall spring out of the earth; and righteousness shall look down from heaven. Yea, the Lord shall give that which is good; and our land shall yield her increase" (Psalm 85: 11-12).

Book Thirty (A Little Later 1865)

Overcome with grief and exhaustion, Celie yearned to ride Baby Horse, "Probably as much as my grandmother used to enjoy going through the woods on Dark Moon years ago," she confided in Zellie. "I think riding might relieve some of my tension. I am so tired, Zellie."

The older woman listened, but warned her, "Danger's all around us. The Yankees have camped out in the woods. Something's going to happen tonight."

"How do you know?"

"The spirits tell me."

"Missus Zellie's right," a gnarled, old woman with high cheek bones, smoking a white clay pipe, interrupted. "Iz part Indian, too, and we both feels it. Ride dat horse afta de war be over."

Celie realized she'd never talked to this person whom everybody called Aunt Sally. She had been with Zellica Dulligan for many years. Celie trusted the women.

That night Mary Caroline broke loose when Nolie and China Lee were sleeping and flaunted herself in front of the wounded soldiers who were able to go to Kell's Tavern in the village.

"I'm Mary Caroline Dulligan. We just buried my uncle and a servant back in the woods beyond that hill there. I've never seen you before. What's your name?"

The man uncrossed his legs and laughed. He was middle-aged with dark brown eyes and a graying beard. "I'm Miles Guthrie Blair from Virginia. I kind of like you, gal. You're pretty, but you seem to need something. Maybe you just want a little love. How about that?" That night, Mary Caroline gave herself to the man and got so drunk on the cheap wine he offered she could barely walk back to the cabin at midnight.

"Oh, Nolie, I liked him," Mary Caroline cried, tottering and dancing about the room by candlelight. "Did Ma know I was missing? You didn't tell them, did you?"

"No, but yo ma cum and brung yu sum custade, chile, and she figured it out!"

"Was she upset?"

"Sho was. She was worried to death. Gal, why don't you be kind to yo ma? She ain't dun nuthin to yu. She sho loves yu and she do a heap of things fo yu. Yuz blessed, and yu don't even no it."

Mary Caroline shrugged her shoulders, then took off her clothes, and pranced around the room. "Mr. Blair from Virginia said I was beautiful, and if he wants to marry me, why I'll marry him, Nolie."

"Chile, you don't eben no dat man," China Lee said, as she tried to wash the girl and put some clothes on her. "Yu otta be shamed, flauntin yoself like dat in the tavehn."

"Well, I'm not, and you might as well leave me alone. If Mr. Blair followed me home, I don't care. I'll leave with him." She slapped China Lee.

"No, yu ain't, gal," Nolie continued, coming up from behind and wrapping a rope around the girl's waist. "I gwine tie yu up right heah and dress you. Yu gwine be the lady yu iz suppose to be, not some slut."

Mary Caroline was furious. She tried to kick Nolie and bite the rope, but China Lee held her down. Mary Caroline screamed.

"Sh...yo Ma and Sissy be cumin down heah, and yu gwine get in a heap o' trouble, gal," Nolie warned.

Mary Caroline calmed down and drank the tea Nolie offered.

The next day they all stayed in the cabin, Nolie and China Lee trying to keep their charge occupied with stories and songs and fear. "That man might hurt yu. Yu don't know nuthin about hem, ceptin he frum Vaginny. Jes cauf yo teacha Missus Gray wah frum Vaginny and wah nice don't meen everybody nice frum deah."

Aware of what Nolie and China Lee were doing, Mary Caroline decided to behave. "I'll play a game with them," she said to herself. She pretended to be interested in what they said and flattered them. "I wish my skin was as smooth as yours. And why are your teeth so white?" She persuaded Nolie and China Lee to untie the rope. "If you untie the rope, I will pay you to darken my hair. What might work? My hair is so pale, and I am older, you know. I know you all know everything about herbs and roots. What should I use?"

"Why yu might use some rosemary and sage mix together in a tea. We cud do dat later on. Yu gwine pay us, yu say?"

Mary Caroline nodded. "That's what I said." At sunset, she knew the women were weary. They yawned as she asked questions about specific herbs. The fire burned low, and by dark, they had fallen asleep. So Mary Caroline took full advantage of the situation, figuring later she would get them in trouble with the ladies of the bluffs. Using the same rope they'd used on her, Mary Caroline tied China Lee and Nolie to their stools, then linked the stools together. "Even if they wake up and try to break away, it'll take awhile," she mused to herself, almost laughing aloud.

And off she went to the tavern to meet Miles Guthrie Blair. They drank wine, then walked along the railroad track, picking persimmons and throwing them at each other, laughing all the while. They finally stopped at the mulberry thicket near Swannkell and made love.

"Have you told your mother about me?" the man asked.

"No, Mr. Blair, I haven't, not yet. Ma wouldn't approve."

"But maybe I could get work at the plantation...maybe if you told her you'd met a Confederate soldier with a bad knee, she'd feel sorry for me and pay me to do a few odd chores."

"I don't know. My mother's pretty strict."

"I could persuade her," Miles Guthrie Blair continued. "I'd tell her about my days at William and Mary College and about my father who was a doctor. That would impress her, wouldn't it?"

"I suppose so since her grandpa was a doctor."

"Well, if your mother likes me, she'll give me a job. You know, I never really believed in slavery or states' rights. I only joined the Confederacy because I wanted some excitement. Actually, I've fought on both sides, but you must never tell anyone. I won't either, of course."

"What? Why?"

He pushed himself into the girl and rode back and forth upon her body as she cried out...."Do it again...oh, I feel it...let's make a baby, Mr. Blair."

"Don't ever tell anyone I'm a deserter."

"Dessert? You don't want me to tell people anyone you're pie or pudding! I don't understand. Your penis is sweet."

"And, little lady, your pussy and titties sure taste delicious, too."

He fondled her and rode back and forth, hot, sweating in the night air, a train whistling down another track.

"At least I'm not three-breasted like my ma."

"What?" he asked.

"Just what I said."

He rolled over and stared at her, shaking his head. "What have I done?"

"What do you mean by that?" she asked, rolling over on top of him this time, and pushing his penis into her vagina again. "Do it. Or are you tired? Have I worn you out?"

And he confessed he'd been with the Yankees at St. Michael's Church on Christmas Eve when they shot her brother. "Yes, your brother told us all about the gold your ma had. He thought they wouldn't shoot him if he told them about the gold. Poor rebel. Abraham and Dan didn't give a damn about him. They were just out for themselves, like me…….and if you can help me, why I'm in for the ride, especially now, that you've propositioned me. Hey, pretty little lady, you'll be in trouble if you don't lead me to the gold. Do you understand?" He twisted her arm and held it to the ground until she agreed to find out where her mother had buried the gold.

"I don't want to be afraid of you, Mr. Blair."

"Then, do as I ask, and we will be just fine. You understand what I'm trying to tell you, and you can begin by persuading your mother to hire me. Do you understand?"

She nodded, and he gave her a locket containing the picture of a beautiful woman, her dark hair coiled in a chignon. She wore a pale aqua dress which matched her eyes and a cameo at her throat. "This was my mother, Augusta Anna Blair," he said, tears filling his eyes. "She died when I was a young boy, and she would want you to have this locket, Mary Caroline."

Flattered, Mary Caroline showered him with kisses and whispered, "Come tomorrow and meet Ma. I will manipulate her as I have always done. You'll see. When you look at her cheeks, think about me. I've scratched her and burned her. I can do the same to you if you cheat on me."

"We understand each other, little lady." He kissed her good-bye.

Mary Caroline skipped across the tracks and midnight and sauntered through the fields and woods to Burnt Bluffs where her mother and Josie waited.

"Where have you been?" they cried. "Nolie finally woke up and loosened the ropes and told us the whole story. That was unkind of you to have tied her and China Lee up."

"And did they tell you they tied me up, Mother? You were cruel to have sent me to the cabin in the first place, and you know it."

Josie was furious. "Go upstairs, Sissy. My mother-in-law has a surprise for you."

The old woman did, a brew which immediately put the belligerent girl to sleep.

Nolie and China Lee avoided MC, later admitting to Celie that they were both afraid of her daughter.

Celie understood, of course, and knew she had to do something, but with Yankees surrounding them, looting and burning, she needed time. She had to put all of her energy into protecting the family.

A day or so later, Miles Guthrie Blair showed up and offered to work. He wore torn gray trousers, a plaid shirt, and the boots he'd removed from a dead soldier at the warehouse. No one ever suspected he was a deserter, for MC had never described him to her mother or sister, and Nolie and China Lee had never laid eyes on him.

Sure enough, as she had promised, MC was waiting on the rickety steps of the hovel when he came up the lane. She whistled to him, but Blair motioned her to remain silent. Before her mother ever came forward to meet him, Blair busied himself with serving cornbread to the soldiers, washing their clothes, and listening, figuring out that MC's mother would see what a good worker he was. Even as he manipulated, he hoped the Yankees wouldn't find this remote ruins in the woods. The treasure was too rich to share with anyone.

Sure enough, Celie met him and hired him to work at the bluffs, appreciative that he was already helping out with the wash and food, helping out with the needs of the Confederacy. So he repaired broken fences, took care of the chickens, and tended to whatever was growing in the field. After a few days of Mother Dulligan's frowns, Mary Caroline sauntered about the yard and flirted with the man who'd sired her baby.

"You're going to marry me, Mr. Blair, because I'm sure I'm carrying your baby."

He nodded, adding that her mother was stern. "You were right about that."

Celie, of course, never saw herself as a stern woman. There were duties. There was work to be done and finished from one day to the next: lives depended on it...feeding the wounded soldiers, binding up their wounds, clothing them, fulfilling their simple requests. Life at the bluffs was hard. "Don't ever give up, my love." She was certain that was Druzie's voice comforting her through the long nights.

"Now, I want to marry your daughter, Mrs. Bain," Miles said one day. "You've had it hard. I know that. I saw those Yankees murder your son in Charleston. You don't know, but I was with him at St. Michael's Church. Your son was my friend. Out of fear, he told the Yankees about your gold and begged them not to fire on him. They did anyway. They didn't care. He said the gold was buried under a white oak somewhere on one of your plantations. Which specific tree it was, I didn't take in. Your son said you'd tell me. Now I know one of the men planned to rape your daughter because your son told him about Mary Caroline."

Celie listened and watched this Mr. Blair as he talked, his voice buttery. He scratched his ear, avoiding her eyes. He seemed crude, vulgar. At once, Celie didn't trust him. "Trust yourself," a voice told her.

Yet, as a mother, Celie was torn, knowing MC wanted to marry the man. "Why not? Just because you don't like him doesn't mean he wouldn't take care of Mary Caroline. Just because he doesn't look at you directly doesn't mean he doesn't look at Mary Caroline. Remember you're old and wrinkled. She's not. Don't let fear block you, Celie Fears."

She wanted another sign from Druzie, but it didn't come. Clouds gathered, and the wind picked up. There was thunder in the distance, and rain came, slowly at first, then pounding in sheets on the barren, burned land.

Josie finally said that as much as she disliked Mr. Blair, he should be granted permission to marry her sister. Celie reluctantly agreed, and Zellie made a pretty dress from an old gown for Mary Caroline. The couple was married in Essex, and within a few weeks, everyone knew Mary Caroline was with child.

In the meantime, Burr Fennell came home. He'd limped much of the way from Appomattox. He was with General Lee at the surrender on April 9, 1865. Celie saw him coming through the woods one morning and wondered how he knew to come to the bluffs. Tears in her eyes as she watched her last boy, Celie cut around the back of the house to greet him. "Burr...oh, Burr, I have waited for you."

"Mamma, it's been so long. I never could allow myself to believe I'd see you again." His red hair was nearly white, his skin rough, wizened, his beard long and unkempt. "Oh, Mamma...and Rosa Alison and little Carrie. Where are they? Hugh Fears? The others? And how are you? You look so tired, Mamma."

"And old, I think," she smiled. "But it doesn't matter anymore. Tell me about yourself. Were you badly wounded?"

"In the leg," he answered, amused, his eyes filled with mischief. "That wasn't so bad. I can endure pain. The worst was being imprisoned. That's where I got this cough, but some of us...we tricked those damned Yankees and escaped. Mamma, I was with General Lee at the surrender. I would do anything for him. His wisdom, his manners, his appreciation for all of us who fought for the cause…I know some of my fellow soldiers who were wounded went to the Confederate Home in Richmond, but I had to come home…where's Rosa Alison. Is she well?"

> "All nations whom thou hast made shall come and worship before thee, O Lord; and glorify thy name. For thou art great, and doest wondrous Things: thou art God alone. Teach me thy way, O Lord: I will walk in thy Truth: unite my heart to fear thy name….O turn unto me, and have mercy Upon me; give thy strength unto thy servant, and save the son of thine Handmaid" (Psalm 86:9-12;16).

Book Thirty-One (Fall 1865-1866)

Celie took Burr to Rosa Alison who had not yet fully recovered from the fever. "I've tried to her as comfortable as possible, and little Carrie...well she plays with Roddy and Cil. They're all happy children, and they like meeting the soldiers, each only vaguely aware of what is really happening. It's all been hard, Son. Your sister—, but then I shouldn't ruin your homecoming with my problems. I'm sorry. It is wonderful to see you."

Celie left Burr with his wife and went to walk Mary Caroline around the bluffs. A few months later, she gave birth to a baby boy.

"We shall call the child Rufus Guthrie," her husband insisted, as he carried the little boy about. "Why? I'll tell you. When I was in Georgia...that's where I received my knee injury, there was a doctor from South Carolina. His name was Dr. Rufus Bratton. He took care of me, and I'll never forget him. I admired him, as Burr admired General Lee, and I will name our child for Rufus Bratton."

Burr came to see his sister and stared at his brother-in-law, immediately disliking him, then struggling to understand why. "Josie," he said later, "there's something about that man...the way he scratches his ear and avoids looking you in the eye. I know I've seen him before. I didn't like him or trust him then, and I don't now. Please tell me what you've learned about his background."

Josie shrugged her shoulders, uncertain.

And Burr didn't have to wait for friends and former servants or family to help him remember. It was at Malvern Hill...the night before the battle when soldiers had gathered around the fire, waiting, talking, the Blair man disappeared. Word got around that Blair was a spy, sometimes for the Confederacy, then for the Union, then later a deserter.

"And you traveled up and down the coast, didn't you?" Burr commented one afternoon a few weeks later when he was cutting wood with Miles Guthrie.

"I did."

"And you were with my brother in Charleston when the Yankees shot him there at St. Michael's Church on Christmas Eve of 1863? How did you feel to be fighting against him when you were both from the south?"

Blair shrugged his shoulders. "I think you're wrong, Mr. Dulligan. I wasn't there. I can usually prove my presence wherever I have been, but cannot arbitrarily account for my whereabouts every 15 minutes either. Let me know what you're trying to find out, and I'll explain."

"You knew about everything," Burr continued, piecing the story together. "I'm figuring out a crazy quilt, and I know it…I have had friends watching you. There are Blairs and Blairs, and I don't think you're really from the Blairs of Virginia. I don't trust you at all. You knew my brother. In fact, you tempted him to talk to you when he was afraid down in Charleston. You are a spy and a deserter, and I ought to hang you or whip you, but….and you fooled my sister and got her pregnant the first time, then again, haven't you, scarcely before she healed. Didn't you?"

The man nodded. "Yes."

"I've been watching you these last few weeks here at the bluffs. You're up to something, and I know it. You're trying to trick my dear mother. I have nothing but contempt for you. And now you know why, don't you?"

The man shrugged his shoulders and remained silent, busying himself at the bluffs, keeping to himself, hoping one day to fool Celie Fears Dulligan Bain and all of the others.

But his hopes didn't last long, for, after several months, when little Ruffie was barely nine months, Mary Caroline gave birth to a baby girl and stared at her. The baby's breasts were freckled, her nipples flat and firm, and a purple birthmark spread across like a creeping flame across her right nipple.

MC winced, turned her head, and shrieked. "You're ugly, just like my mother. I don't like you the way I do your brother. I hope you die, you little witch girl." The baby cried, and Mary Caroline slapped her. Miles Guthrie Blair tickled his baby daughter to quiet her.

Burr caught his sister by the arm and shamed her. "That's horrible, Mary Caroline, and you know it. This little soul is a tiny baby, unable to protect herself. She's a gift from God. Name her. Love her, and help her to grow into someone special. Blair, you are worse than I ever imagined."

"I'm going to vary her name for ma's…I'm going to call her Fears Lee…that's for ma and for General Lee. My baby girl looks like a man, and no man in his right mind would want to marry her. They would fear her. Fears Lee is what I'm calling her, and Fears Lee her name shall be."

Burr was furious with his sister and with Miles Guthrie Blair. "You are scum, an absolute low-down sleaze. Is that marriage certificate even valid, or did you write it out and forge the minister's signature?"

"No, it is valid. I owed your mother that much."

"And the locket you gave my sister. That's not your mother in the picture, is it?"

"No, it isn't, as a matter of fact. That's my sweetheart from Virginia. Her name is Anna Augusta Cary. She's waiting for me now. I said she was my mother just to make my story more credible for your ma and sister and the family."

Burr slapped the man again and again. "You are an absolute worm. You knew my sister was mentally deficient. It never takes Solomon to figure out everything. I'm sure you frightened Hugh Fears that Christmas Eve in Charleston into telling you and your damned Yankee cronies. I don't know. I wasn't there, but I aim to find, out for sure, and I'll have you hanged. My brother was afraid, and you persuaded him to tell you, saying you'd help him. Oh, you have used us all! And now, you fondle a baby! Your own daughter!"

Burr held the man tight by the collar, nearly choking him. "I have no idea where my mother hid the gold, and I certainly don't aim to find out now, not while you're on the place, if ever, because I don't care. Now go, and don't come back. If you do, I will kill you myself. To think of someone using the innocent, deceiving them, playing with their hearts is beyond anything I can ever imagine. And my sister said you claimed to have been a devout Episcopalian once upon a time. Damn you, you piece of scum," Burr railed out, as he began beating the man again.

"Yes, I was once a clergyman in Augusta County. That was before I seduced Anna Augusta"

"You're an absolute bastard," Burr said, and hit the man one last time. "If you rot in hell, I won't care. Better still, I hope the rebels capture you and take you to Andersonville….that's what you deserve."

"And do remember me to your sister, Mr. Burr Fennell. Tell her the difference between a deserter and dessert. I think she thought I was a dessert. She thought I was pie or pudding."

Burr fired his pistol again and again, hoping to injure the desserter. "Crawl in the poisonous roots, and claw the stumps, you worm, and die, damn you."

Burr was weary. Any mischief he had ever twinkled over was gone. He would tell his mother, his wife, and Josie the truth, but not MC, not now. She couldn't handle it. And his mother couldn't take much more either. "Yes," he murmured to himself, 'There is a time to hate,' and this is the time."

Of course, he knew he'd finally have to tell his baby sister about her Miles Guthrie Blair, and Burr prayed for God's strength. Then, there would be taxes. He forced himself to look at the records. Burnt Bluffs really didn't belong to the family anymore. Celie's first husband had bought the place from George, then given a part of it back to George, who was now dead, and the other part which originally belonged to Swann Creek Church, had been given back to the church. George, of course, had never paid the taxes, and neither had the church. "And, Ma, we can't afford the taxes here. Besides that, I've heard Lumbars, whoever in hell he is, is going to burn us out."

Celie knew only too well and told Burr the whole story of Lumbars and his grandma, Caramel. "I don't know where he is now, but Caramel is still chained down at Chinaberry Grove as far as I know. After Lumbars raped MC, I wanted to free his grandmother, but your brother wouldn't allow it. Hugh Fears insisted she remain chained. It's a terrible situation for one woman to have been chained all these years. Why she must be almost one hundred years old now, Burr. Even though she practices voodoo and is evil in our eyes, she's to be pitied....and we're still suffering because of the sins of my grandfather....oh, Burr, honey. It's all falling on you who laughed and played and...I am so sorry."

"Ma, I understand your compassion, but you can't have that now. The war's not yet over here. I hear Lumbars means to burn down every parcel of land, every acre, where any member of the Bain/Livingston/Dulligan family has ever lived. Further, he's inciting other former slaves to riot with him. He lives with those free Negroes who sold moonshine to Uncle George all through the years. Lumbars lives down in the bottoms, and I don't trust him."

Celie simply listened. "Do what you must, and say what you will to Mary Caroline. I trust your judgment, my son, and I will never doubt anything you do. May God's blessings rest upon you."

Burr talked to his sister. She wailed, screamed, and kicked her brother. "Why did Miles dessert me and not at least bring me some gingerbread?"

Burr tried to comfort his sister and looked down at little Rufus and the baby girl who MC claimed was a witch. "Sis, don't say that. She's just a little girl who needs love. Hold her, and claim her as your own. If you won't, at least give her to somebody who will care for her."

> "The heavens are thine, the earth also is thine; as for the world and the fullness thereof, thou hast founded them. The north and the south thou hast created them..." (Psalm 89:11-12).

Book Thirty-Two (1869-1872)

Because Mary Caroline refused to feed her baby girl, Celie took the child to Nolie who herself had just given birth to a little girl named Jupiter. Nolie nursed Fearlee as her own, and the babies grew up side by side. Certain Mary Caroline would never know the difference, Celie recorded the baby's name in the family Bible as Fairlee. The other children, both white and black, sometimes called her Fairylee which through the years was occasionally shortened to Fairy. Either one suited her, for Fairlee had a sweet disposition, a gentle smile, and crystal blue eyes.

Despite her joy and contentment, Celie was afraid. Burr's good-bye seemed too quick.

And when she heard toothless Aunt Mary say the free Negroes down in the bottoms had guns, Celie realized what Burr had meant and knew why she was afraid. So did Rosa Alison who was with child. So did Josie. So did Zellie. They all understood and were frightened. But only Celie deep down and the black people understood what Aunt Mary meant when she added that Caramel and Lumbars were present with the former slaves in the bottoms.

So his family wouldn't be murdered, Burr had rounded up friends to lynch Lumbars and the ancient cinnamon woman. And when Burr saw Caramel's earless head as he tied the rope around her neck, he almost fainted, his mouth dry. "Yo great grand pappy dun it to me, boy....it all beez recorded in the church. Read it if yo eyes ken stand de truth...all while we had to sit in the balcony. My peeples wasn't good enough to pray downstairs. And I been chained all dez yeahs down in Chinaberry Grove."

Burr stared at the wrinkled old woman, hesitating.

As Burr stood there, one of his friends from Millsborough, wearing a white robe, his eyes masked, screamed, "Hurry up! Tighten that rope, Burr. That woman's evil...they all are! We're going to set fire to all the cabins and roast them out!"

Zellie told Celie after a few days that Rosa Alison had received a message from her husband and had said, "Burr's fled to Canada for safety, Miss Zellie, and now, we must simply trust God to show us the way. He always does."

Celie listened to her sister-in-law's words: "My spirits tell me to stay busy. There's work to be done here at the bluffs," and agreed, especially whe the woman continued, "Take care of your grandchildren. We both will. They need us."

As they were talking out in the kitchen, Celie heard the door open and shivered. "Ma, it's just me. It's Burr. I've...I've come to tell you good-bye."

"Burr, darling, you're not going to leave us, are you?" She looked into his eyes and brushed back his unkempt har.

"I must go, Ma, but I couldn't leave without seeing you and Rosa Alison and the children. Rosa is expecting our second child. Please, watch out for her. I have to go. My friends and I banded together and hanged Lumbars and his grandpa's confidante, Caramel. We found the others in their party, and chased them up the river. The dogs followed and we burned their cabins. We're leaving for Canada tonight. Ma, take care. I'll be safe. I love you. Please, watch out for Rosa and for Carrie. They aren't as strong as you and Josie."

"I will," Celie promised, as she kissed his cheek and tucked an extra piece of dry cornbread into his sack. "I love you, my son. May God be with you and all the others."

Burr left during the night.

When Mary Caroline realized her brother had gone without telling her good-bye, she blamed her mother and began slapping Celie and her little girl who'd recently learned to crawl.

"I should slice off that purple birthmark and burn off those freckles, shouldn't I?" Mary Caroline screamed at the child, "And did I tell you Ruffie stutters, Mamma? Haven't you heard him? You've put the curse of my great-grandmother on both my children, on all the children here, haven't you, you three-titted witch?"

Celie didn't respond, only gathered Ruffie and Fairlee into her arms and left the room, calling to China Lee. "Please, China Lee, give my daughter some whiskey and sugar."

"Yessum."

Winter yielded to spring, and Fairlee did not walk. She only crawled, and Celie was concerned, but she didn't know where to find a doctor, not now. Zellie got hurt in her back from a fall and was little use to anyone. Celie and Josie took care of her and the others, both deep down aware that Burnt Bluffs wasn't really theirs anymore.

"The county can claim this land at any time, Josie. You know that don't you?"

Josie nodded. "Let's think about it. I can't give an answer today."

Celie nodded, but added that they could not indefinitely postpone making some sort of decision.

A few days later when they were together with the children, Josie began to talk of the necessity of leaving the bluffs. "Yes, we must, and with Forest Green burned, we can only go back to White Oaks. Let's pray that it hasn't been destroyed."

Celie smiled, "I'd like that...the bluffs is my home, but it was never like a home. My mother and father treated my so cruelly here. George, too, because he needed so much. Except for my life here during my marriage to your father, it's been an unkind place. We've made a life here these last few months, haven't we...but, you're right, we can't stay."

Josie looked at her mother, they both wore black, and said, "Don't we make a pair, Ma? The ladies in black. At least we've taken off the veil. And we don't even play cards to pass away the time...or read books."

Celie nodded, then smiled to herself, remembering that time long ago under that white oak when Druzie removed her first veil and claimed her as his own.

She walked outside and waited. Druzie cradled her in his arms and rocked her back and forth as he spoke, "It's alright, sweet. You're going home, and I'll visit you more. We'll sing under the white oak. I've missed you. I love you."

She turned to kiss him, her arms outstretched, then realized she was only embracing the darkness, and knew it was a dream, a yearning. "Oh, darling, I have missed you, too."

Standing in the doorway, Josie listened to her mother, then saw Mary Caroline slithering along the path, and called to her sister, "Don't you go near Ma. Don't you dare."

But Mary Caroline was fast. She grabbed her mother's shoulders and forced her to the ground. Celie hurt her ankle in the fall. "You stupid fool," MC railed out, "Druzie's dead. He's not talking to you, Mamma. He never has. You're the crazy one!"

Celie trembled under her until Josie grabbed MC and pulled her up and shook her. "Don't you ever do that again, Mary Caroline, ever. Do you understand me? Go to your room."

"Josie don't hurt her," Celie cautioned, "Maybe she's still in shock, you know, over her husband's departure and Burr's. And you know something's wrong with the baby. She doesn't yet walk."

"Fairlee is walking, Mamma," Josie said, turning slightly to Celie, "She took her first steps earlier today. I've not had a chance to tell you."

"But something's wrong with me, Josie. Please, help me. I can't get up on my own. I don't want to be an invalid. You would have to take care of me and Zellie. That would be too much, dear, and I don't want to be dependent. Oh, I don't."

Josie said her mother was suffering from pneumonia. "She won't last long, Mamma. Not long at all. I know we have done our best, taking care of her. I don't think she feels any pain. She doesn't say."

"You have been devoted to Roderick's mother. I know, my dear."

Josie led her mother inside. "Mamma, don't make excuses for Mary Caroline any longer. We have all suffered at her hand, but we're grown now. We have looked in the glass, into the mirror, face-to-face. We've released the past and moved on. You have surely suffered, but with Druzie's help, and your own faith, you have latched onto life. You sing, encourage, play, give love and compassion. You dream. You follow the Psaltery on your psaltery. You do, and I'm not going to let Mary Caroline, or anyone, ever rob you of that."

"No, my dear, I won't either. I promise. Maybe that's why I want to go back to White Oaks, back to where Druzie...and my grandmother...and-"

"Oh, I hate you both," Mary Caroline wailed as she watched the exchange between her mother and sister, "I'm only 27 years old, widowed with two deformed children, and it's all your fault, Mamma. It is. You carry the curse from your grandmother."

'Hush," Josie said, taking MC by the hand and leading her outside to the kitchen where she found some opium powder. Josie knew where her mother-in-law kept her medicinal secrets and gave them to Mary Caroline along with some whiskey. "Now, I'm going to give our mother something for pain, and I want you to calm down. You will meet someone and marry again. Stop fretting and pouting, and for God's sake, stop sucking your fingers. It's terribly unappealing, and you are a grown woman."

Zellie Dulligan died in the night, and Josie buried her near the chapel, close to Roderick, and mourned.

During the next few days, Josie began gathering and packing the family clothing, pots and pans, and other valuables. "We'll be leaving tomorrow," she said to her mother who was reading to the children. They were gathered around her, spellbound by her voice and her stories.

While Josie, Nolie, China Lee, and others were loading the old coach and wagon, a man driving a cart loaded down with a trunk, boxes, and a cumbersome-looking camera, came up the lane.

Ever-cautious since the episode with Miles Guthrie Blair, Celie carefully studied him. He had wavy brown hair, large brown eyes, and a moustache. Not especially tall, he wore a tattered Confederate uniform.

Aware of their stares, the man introduced himself. "I'm Jack van Eyek. Oh, no ma'am," he said, answering Celie's question, "I'm an artist, but no kin to the Dutch painter. My father lived in Maryland and married my mother, Amanda Lewis from Washington, and then they moved to the Carolinas. I am their only child, and I learned to take pictures and paint. For some reason, ma'am, you look familiar to me."

"Celie shook her head, "I don't know you. Should I?"

"Oh yes, now I remember," he continued, "I had a studio in Essex long ago, before the war. I think I took pictures of you and other members of your family once, as I did of many families of Blisland and Essex counties."

Celie vaguely remembered a trip to Essex when Mary Caroline was young. Aunt Agnes had wanted everyone to go for pictures, Druzie included.

"One of your daughters was very angry," he recalled.

Josie laughed, "That would be Mary Caroline. This is her daughter, Fairlee."

"Why, she is beautiful. She looks like an angel with her fair skin, golden curls, and blue eyes. She has a gentle smile. She's a little shy, though, isn't she? And is this her brother?"

"His name is Ruffie. We have other children here, too. I'd be glad to serve you some tea and cornbread."

Jack was appreciative, "I'd be much obliged, Ma'am."

Nathan and his son came out to finish packing. "I gwine tote dat man's valeeses," Nathan offered.

"I'd be grateful. They're heavy. And I'd be grateful, as well, if I could board here a few nights. I expect to pay, for things are hard now all across the South. I was a photographer and journalist during the war. I wrote for magazines, sketched scenes of battles and took photographs for newspapers."

They talked, and he admired Mrs. Dulligan's pottery. "These bowls will be valuable in the years to come, you know."

Josie agreed and explained that they were moving to White Oaks. "It's our old family home. Before I married and moved to Forest Green, we all lived there. The Yankees set fire to Forest Green, it was down that way. White Oaks sits so far back off the road we hope the Yankees missed it. My mother and her husband lived there. It's a long story and I suppose you are tired now."

He nodded.

"We're leaving today, though, so you must join us if you'd like to, after you rest."

Celie liked the man and continued to tell him about the house at White Oaks, in particular, about the tower her grandfather had built. "He wanted something of the Highlands here with him in South Carolina. He was something of an architect; he designed the house. Yet he loved rivers and the ocean, tidal marshes and the bay, so it's like a low-country Georgetown home, adjoined by the tower. In an odd way, the house portrays something of South Carolina and Scotland."

The artist was intrigued.

"Yes, and my daughter, Josie, paints. You should see the sketches and paintings she did years ago when she studied with Mrs. Gray's husband in Millsborough. I hope you will meet him. His name is Edward Gray. He's a portrait painter. I sing and play the psaltery. I can only hope you have a love of music."

He nodded, "Oh, yes, Ma'am. I do, indeed."

He helped the family move back into the old house. Miraculously, it stood undisturbed among the white oaks as it had for generations.

With Nathan's help, Celie climbed the hill to the old tree and lingered for hours, imagining Druzie there with her.

Jack rented the tower which he used both as an apartment and a studio. He enjoyed the family, and the children were all very fond of him. Everyone liked him, including Mary Caroline, until she learned that he intended to marry Josie.

And then MC had one of her old temper tantrums of slapping her mother and sister and children, as well as spilling Jack's paints all over the floor, then screaming uncontrollably. China Lee finally led her to bed and poured whiskey down her throat. "Ain't you shamed, girl?" she asked, shaking her head.

Josie and Celie told Jack the story of Mary Caroline. "If you don't want to marry me, I understand," Josie said, her brown eyes glistening.

"I love you, and I love your family. We will have children, and I will paint them all."

Josie wore the old green silk gown once more, declaring that it was not bad luck to do so.

"You're beautiful."

The wedding trip was only a boat ride in a rotting skiff on the Patuxee, but it was a happy occasion. The children dearly loved Uncle Jack, except MC. She came to resent him terribly and often schemed, so Nolie and China Lee figured, to poison him. But that never happened, for Jack was far too clever for MC, and she soon realized that fact.

Even when he offered to pay for Ruffie to see a surgeon for his stuttering at Johns Hopkins where Roddy would be going for surgery on his clubfoot and Carrie for surgery on her ears, MC was ungrateful. Celie insisted, and Ruffie accompanied his cousins to Baltimore where the operations, except for Carrie's, were a success. Carrie, as time passed, learned to listen through a box that she carried with her everywhere.

Rosa Alison and Carrie stayed at White Oaks with Celie and the others. Josie gave her husband several children. Celie rented out some of the former slave cabins to peddlers who came to the nearby villages to sell their wares, and Jack paid for the girls to attend Mrs. Gray's academy which reopened after the war. The boys went to Mount Hebron, and Jack painted portraits, the woods, land, churches, and houses. He was fond of painting the girls whom he called angels. He wanted to paint Fairlee, but had not yet been able to get Celie's permission. Afraid that Jack would paint her grandchild in the nude, Celie warned him not to pose the question to Mary Caroline. "Surely, you knowMary Caroline is not quite right and cares little for her daughter."

"Mother! How dare you talk about me like that!" Mary Caroline screamed, running in from the kitchen, holding a pair of scissors. She ran at her mother and slowly wrote the word W I T C H into her mother's right cheek. Blood flowed at once, staining the neckline of Celie's dress. Celie screamed and fell to the floor.

China Lee ran into the room, grabbed MC, and tossed her to the ground. "Dis girl dun gon crazy! Bring me dat whiskey bottle, Mista Jack!" And China Lee held the girl down and poured whiskey into her mouth until Mary Caroline passed out.

"Gawd a mercy, Missus Celie, your grandbaby, that Fairlee, she un angel, and I neva knowed it til now. Yu iz, too."

Jack rushed to Celie's side, "Oh, Mother Celie, I am so sorry. I feel terrible. I never should have asked. I should never have hoped to paint your granddaughter nude."

"Praise ye him, all his angels: praise ya him, all his hosts" (Psalm 148:2).

Book Thirty-Three (1879-1894)

"I never thought I'd have to commit my own child to an asylum," Celie said again and again, as she walked around White Oaks, struggling to recover and reclaim something of the past, crying out to Druzie.

And when she least expected him, Druzie came and took her in his arms, "Darling, I know it's hard, but you will survive over the next few years. I promise, and I'm waiting…Love the children, and remember our psaltery…my devotion."

Old as she grew through each decade following the war, Celie never ceased to yearn for him. "Do you see my cheeks?" she sometimes asked. "The scars Mary Caroline made? Sometimes, I ride the horse to church over at Brick Tower. Oh, Druzie, I ache for you."

She leaned against the white oak. "Take me home with you. I'm tired."

"Sugar pie, you are my A N G E L. Picture A N G E L S. You have always been my angel." Suddenly, Druzie vanished, and Celie remembered his promise.

She played the psaltery and sang those psalms from her great grandmother's psaltery, from the old worn volume Monica had given her just before she died. Celie found comfort in remembering Monica's strength and abiding love. "Druzie, she was truly our saint and our angel."

When Jack arrived at the asylum with Mary Caroline the next day, he saw naked people scratching themselves as they stood chained to the wall or floor. Some were in cages, others lying in straw, screaming, still others sitting in wheelchairs with high backs and wheels the size of those on a wagon.

"So this is how the insane really live," Jack said to the warden. "It's not a pretty way to live or die, is it? No, Mr. Cork? I cannot leave my sister-in-law here to live in such squalid conditions, crazy as she is. Do you have something else you could offer me? I have money."

"Well, what would you suggest, Mr. Van Eyck? I have little to offer. Times are hard, as you know. Besides, your sister-in-law is clearly deranged. I doubt if she would know the difference."

"I would. I will pay you to find someone to stay with her and keep her in private quarters. I cannot have her living among…"

"May I remind you that it is not easy to find help, let alone reliable help."

"Well, I will bring a former enslaved woman and pay her to watch Mrs. Blair, then pay you simply for room and board if you're so inept at finding people to work. I will not have Mrs. Blair be mistreated because she isn't well. I will not have her treated like a prisoner as these poor souls are. She hasn't been well for many years, and her presence at home is a threat to her mother and to my family. But that doesn't mean that she, or anyone here, should receive the treatment of an individual who has murdered and robbed. Do you understand the difference?"

The warden paced about the room, leaned on his desk, then gazed out the window into a garden. "I do, and I will make the necessary arrangements to accommodate you and your family. And I will find someone to attend Mrs. Blair."

So for the next several years, Mary Caroline remained at the asylum in her own quarters a part from the others, secluded from the public. She crocheted and knitted, occasionally walked, always heavily sedated, lest she become violent and escape.

As the years went by, Roddy grew up and married Elizabeth Belle Barron from Coventry, and they moved to Philadelphia. Roddy's younger sister married, and Carrie went to a special school for the deaf in Philadelphia for months at a time, happy to be near Roddy and see him on occasion.

In the spring of 1884, Celie received a letter from an official in Canada informing her that Burr Fennell Dulligan had died.

"My last son," she said, reading the note aloud. "They're all gone now, beginning with my first baby boy so long, long ago, and next…my husband, Neilly, then my beloved Druzie and our little boys, Wheezie and Davie, and Hugh Fears, and, now my mischievous Burr…and there's nothing I can do, ever again, nothing anybody can do, ever, to bring them home again. They're all gone." Celie wailed, burying her head in one of the pillows.

Josie tried to comfort her mother.

And only Druzie's spirit at the white oak, as the next few months passed into years, eased her pain. "Remember their words, my love, their laughter, their stories, our stories, our songs, for in all of them, you will find comfort and solace. We both will."

With her sons gone, Ruffie became a source of joy to his grandmother. Like Hugh Fears, Ruffie was quiet, a little withdrawn at times, but always thoughtful, and he spent time talking to his grandmother and sister.

He was sweet on a young lady named Heppie Louisa Bigham from Columbia. She was spending the summer with her cousins, and Ruffie had met her at Brick Tower Church. Celie liked her, too, and approved of her grandson's wish to marry. "You marry Heppie if you love her, Ruffie. You have a good job working for the railroad now, and you can take care of a family. I want you to be happy. We all do, honey."

When family and friends learned that their 'shy' Ruffie had given Miss Heppie a ring, they were absolutely certain wedding bells would be ringing from the belfry before Christmas.

Ruffie's happiness, however, soon turned to despair with the sudden arrival of his mother at White Oaks.

Because the new warden at the asylum in Columbia had seen only vague notes on Mary Caroline Dulligan Blair's history, he wasn't aware of who the woman was or where she lived at the asylum, and he never bothered to find out. After Mr. Cork died, the attendant left because she'd never been paid for her services. For several days, Mary Caroline had gone without food, water, medication, and sanitation.

Not until a young psychiatrist saw a woman wandering in the gardens late one afternoon, her hair wild, dress soiled, begin so strike another patient who sat in a wheelchair sketching flowers, and made a few inquiries did he learn about the woman from White Oaks.

But it was too late, for Mary Caroline had heard an attendant who knew Heppie Louisa Bigham mention her Ruffie Blair's name. "Yes, Mrs. Blair, Heppie Louisa is a family friend, and she's going to be married soon to Ruffie Blair from White Oaks. Do you know him, Ma'am?"

"That's my Ruffie, my only son," Mary Caroline shrieked, and she escaped from the grounds before anyone could catch her. She somehow made the trip home.

Days later when she saw Ruffie, MC confronted him and pulled him toward her, "You're my lover, Son, nobody else's, and I won't share you. You should have waited for me. I have loved you and nurtured you from the womb, from the time you were conceived in the mulberry thicket. This woman you're ready to marry doesn't know you at all. She doesn't understand who you are. Ruffie, don't abandon me. I need you. We'll have children together."

Ruffie froze. His body went into shock. He had no idea how to respond. Unlike Fairlee, he'd been shielded from his mother's outbursts. It didn't take long for the family and servants, of course, to hear the wailing.

Finally with the help of Josie, Linus, China Lee, Nolie, and others, Ruffie took his mother to her room. Nolie sedated her. After several weeks with the help of his grandmother and sister and Linus, Ruffie recovered and declared his intention to marry Heppie, "I love Heppie," he told Linus one afternoon when they smoking pipes down in the old cabin near the river.

"Amen, den marry her," Linus said, having seen the young lady himself at the church's strawberry festival. "She purty and seem kind. She sho got bright eyes, too." Ruffie agreed. "And her family's kind to me, too."

"Ma," Ruffie said to his mother a few days later when she seemed calm, "Please be glad I've found a sweetheart who wants to marry me. You know I've had a hard time since I was a little boy." But his mother would not be consoled. She stood up and went into a rage. She caught him by the leg and bit him, then clawed at his arms, fingernails long and sharp. "You're my sweetheart, Ruffie, and nobody else's. Your father deserted me, and I won't allow you to do the same to me now or ever. Don't you understand?"

Ruffie finally pushed his mother away and found Jupiter and Fairlee making brooms. He told them what had happened and asked them to tell Uncle Jack and Aunt Josie. "I can't right now. I'm too upset, and I have to board the train for the night ride. You know the 32 will be rumbling up the tracks from Columbia in a little while."

"But, let's try not to upset your granma right now," Josie cautioned. "She's tired, and there's absolutely no need to worry her, Fairlee. We'll talk to the servants and warn them. I'll tell Uncle Jack. But where's your mother now?"

"Ruffie left Ma in the room screaming. I know she won't stay there long."

Josie nodded and went to find Jack who talked to Nolie.

"Now that Nessie's died, I need you to tell us all what potion is best for Mrs. Blair. My wife says you're the oldest servant on the place. That's an honor, Nolie, isn't it?"

"Sho iz. I jes giv huh sum spirits and powdas. Das all."

That's what Nolie did every few hours, and Mary Caroline was quiet. She slept.

Unafraid now, family members returned to their daily activities and forgot about her presence upstairs.

Even Jack felt comfortable enough to leave the plantation for a short trip to Charleston for paints. Celie, of course, had finally heard about the episode and assured her son-in-law that they would be safe at White Oaks. "Go ahead, Jack. While you're there, you might visit the museums and receive a commission to do someone's portrait," she said, a twinkle in her tired eye. And don't forget to stop in Columbia on the way home to see your way home to see your daughters at Chicora and give them my love."

He left.

A few days later, knowing it was almost time for him to board the train again, Ruffie felt a fear he couldn't explain. He had to hear his grandmother's voice. He didn't know why. After all, he'd gone on so many trains without ever whispering anything but goodnight, for often she was asleep. Only tonight was different. Maybe it was the sheets of heavy rain beating on the roof, whipping off branches of the white oaks, lightening flashing in the distance, but Ruffie needed Gramma's assurance. She clasped his hand as he kissed her. "Be careful, honey, and God be with you," she whispered, her voice hoarse.

Rain lashing against him, Ruffie struggled down the lane toward the tracks and boarded the train. A reliable brakeman, he always leaned out from the baggage car to retrieve the mail pouch on the crane at the little village old-timers called Lochund as the train whizzed by. He did that every night.

But on the cold, rainy night in late April in 1894, however, his great coat became tangled in the wheels, and Ruffie's body was pulled down under the train and severed. The train rolled on up the tracks toward Essex, it's whistle blowing, thunder clashing, a violent orchestration that night, not far from Celie's open window.

The next day, peddlers discovered his headless body, and Ruffie was buried within the week at Brick Tower Church. His mother learned of her son's death and, heavily sedated, attended the funeral.

After the funeral, she began roaming the fields and woods in search of her son's head. She saw nothing until the grandson of Littlebury, her very first hound, found his head and brought it to her.

Looking at the teeth marks, Mary Caroline really went crazy. She beat the hound for biting Ruffie's head and began crying out for her son and his father. After all, thirty years earlier Ruffie had been conceived, and his mother sorely missed him.

Everyone missed Ruffie. Celie was devoted, of course, to Josie and Jack's children, but somehow they were a little different though she herself could not explain why.

Celie and Fairlee grew extremely close during the years following Ruffie's death.

As she'd done since Fairlee was a child, Celie continued to create imaginary characters for the two to enjoy, characters who helped to alleviate their loneliness.

Jim John, their friend who lived in the woods and knew all about flowers and trees, continued to be a part of their conversations. Celie said he went to Columbia and became a gardener at Chicora College. He met a young lady who studied music at the college and married her.

"Gamma, do you think I'll marry somebody like Jim John?" Fairlee asked one afternoon.

"Yes, one day, my dear, but something tells me he'll be a man from Scotland. He will come from the Highlands, and he'll appear one day in Lochund or Swannkell and be a merchant and a farmer. He'll meet you at church and want you to be his bride. He'll drive his buggy up the wide lane to White Oaks. You'll know he loves you. He'll have big eyes, a moustache, and large hands. He'll hold you one night and tell you that he loves you. You will wear your great-great-grandmother's green silk wedding dress, and be the most beautiful bride to ever live here at White Oaks."

"Will he love me as much as you and Druzie loved each other and as much as Aunt Josie and Uncle Jack love each other? Will he, Gramma?"

Celie's eyes filled with tears, "Oh, I'm sure, darling, for you're as imaginative and faithful as Druzie was, just as he taught me to be...but...honey, I'm a little sleepy now. Nolie gave me some tea. I think I'll say my prayers, and maybe in the morning, we'll go for a walk around White Oaks and gather mulberries. It's early May, and."

"Gamma, are you afraid of my mamma anymore?"

"Not anymore. Of course, I know your Aunt Josie's kept your ma away from me...I'm sorry it has to be like that, but your mother blamed me and...well you see the scars on my face...you know. We're alone tonight. Josie and Uncle Jack are not home yet from Columbia. I had a letter today. They will stay a few more days. She says that Jack was commissioned to paint a portrait of the governor's wife. I'm excited for him. And, of course, I know Josie's happy to visit her daughters at Chicora."

Fairlee smiled. "Isn't it wonderful that Uncle Jack came up the road to the bluffs that morning. He changed Aunt Josie's life. Why she could have easily become a lonely widow, couldn't she?"

Celie nodded. "I suppose so. Fairlee, you might like to go to Columbia with your aunt and uncle sometime and visit your cousins."

Her granddaughter shook her head. "Grown up as I am, I don't want to leave you, and I won't ever let anybody hurt you, Grandma." She walked to the window. "The rain has stopped, and the sky is clearing. Good night. I love you."

"Sweet dreams, sweet repose. Half the bed, and all the clothes, my child."

Way in the night, Celie stirred, aware of someone's presence, as the full moon dappled patterns of light through the heavy draperies. She sat up quickly, lighted a candle, and saw Mary Caroline leaning over the high back walnut bed, her long, white hair cascading over the quilt. Celie screamed, and her cry frightened MC so much she stumbled and fell, something in her arms. Celie drew the quilt closer and drifted back to sleep.

China Lee, still paid to watch MC, rushed in and took led her away, but not without a fight. Mary Caroline kicked China Lee to the floor, then ran upstairs to her room, and later wandered down to the old cabin on the river.

Not until the following afternoon did Fairlee realize what had happened. She was troubled, yet somehow began to believe that with love, her mother might just change and heal. "Yes, I'll find Ma," Fairlee kept saying to herself, as something led her down to the river. "Things will be better. Mamma will begin to love me. I want her to care about me." Fairlee listened to birds singing in the trees. But their notes were suddenly interrupted by moaning. Fairlee listened. The sound was coming from the cabin window.

Fairlee tiptoed through the vines to look. She saw her mother rocking back and forth holding Ruffie's head. "Mamma," Fairlee dared to call. "You want a little company? I'm here. I love you."

"Get away...don't you dare come near me...I want your brother all to myself. He's mine, not yours, not my mother's, and never, ever, his lost sweetheart's."

As Fairlee turned to leave, she saw her grandmother. "Sh…"

They watched together, spellbound, as MC continued to rock back and forth, occasionally holding the head to her face, then putting it back in the reed basket on the broken table, and painting the cheeks red with one of Jack's brushes. She sang spirituals. "Ruffie, my love, Ma has her Druzie. She talks to him. Now I can talk to you. At least I have your head, and I can paint your eyes as blue as the sky, your brows dark as your father's."

Celie stared in silence.

"That's the basket I keep my psaltery in, the one the pirate gave to my great grandmother," she finally said. "I noticed it was missing when I finally got up this morning. My psaltery was cracked, too. Was your mother in my room last night? I thought I saw her standing over me, but I may have been dreaming. I don't know, Fairlee."

They saw MC put the head in the basket, stand up, and leave, holding the basket under her arm.

"Let's follow her, at least for a little while, Granma."

"Slowly, though. You know I'm old now, honey. I'm on the crutch now on account of my leg. It's late in the afternoon, too."

"Where's Mamma going, do you think?" Fairlee whispered, as she explained her sudden hope of trying to bring her mother around through love. "I've always been so afraid of her, Granma, but when I awakened this morning, I decided I didn't like that fear. Maybe I had a dream, too. I don't know."

"We've all been afraid, darling, and we've all tried to show love to your mother. We'll talk about that tonight...we're both tired now, and we have something else to do."

They followed MC through the woods, then north along the railroad tracks, listening as she wailed and howled, then sang spirituals, all the while swinging the basket back and forth from side to side, then up and down, as if the head were a ball.

Celie looked up at the sun. "It's getting late. The 28 southbound will be clattering down the tracks soon, Fairlee."

Suddenly, Mary Caroline stopped at the mulberry thicket where Ruffie had been conceived years before. She threw the basket toward the thicket, and Ruffie's head bounced out and rolled toward the ditch. Fairlee screamed and picked up her brother's head.

Mary Caroline shrieked, "Ruffie's mine." She grabbed the head from her daughter and pulled Fairlee by the hair toward the tracks, then turned to beat her mother. But Celie saw her daughter and pointed her crutch at Mary Caroline. "Daughter, Ruffie doesn't belong to you or anyone, except God. Now give me his head to bury now." With the tip, she butted Mary Caroline in the stomach. Her daughter fell backward onto the tracks, her eyes glaring. Celie stared as the train rolled on down the tracks.

"Granma. Mamma's dead."

"I know. Maybe she's at peace now. 'The strife is over, the battle done' after fifty years, child. Fairlee take me home. I am so tired, so weary. I....I'm ready to go home. It's almost twilight now, and there's a going in the tops of the mulberries." Do you hear the sound?"

"What does it mean, Granma?"

"Sh...God's telling us something. We'll know in time, child."

Celie took off her petticoat and covered her grandson's head and gave the basket to Fairlee, then took the crutch in one hand and held her granddaughter's arm with the other.

Somehow, the two made it to White Oaks, one supporting the other, As they walked up the lane, Celie saw the moon rising over the old house and imagined Druzie calling her to come home. Celie paused and listened. Before long, they were at the front steps. Celie climbed them slowly, holding onto the rail, lingering for a few minutes to enjoy the fragrance of the honeysuckle…"Oh, I'm so tired." She went to bed immediately. Nolie gave her a little whiskey and said, "You got another letter from Miss Josie today."

"Please read it to me, will you, Nolie?"

"It jes say, 'Ma, the girls are happy at the college. I went to their Maypole dance on the lawn today, and Priscilla was crowned Queen of the May. She looked so pretty. Jack says he'll finish the portrait tomorrow. We'll spend another night in Columbia, then come home. I miss you all.Devotedly, as ever, Your Josie Columbia, May the 5, 1894"

"I'm glad they're having a good time. Fairlee, please hand me the psaltery, will you, and remember it's yours, my darling. When you play it, sing the psalms from the little book of psalms. That's a psaltery, too, you know. And remember Druzie and me, and follow your dreams. Trust yourself and God. Share your faith, your music, your stories, and your love, as Druzie and I did. That was our Psaltery at White Oaks, and it's all yours now."

"Granma, I don't understand…"

"It's alright, honey. You will, and you remember that gentleman from the Highlands…yes. He'll be coming. Please hand me my glasses now. I want to read a little before prayers. I'm most too tired to sing tonight. You understand. And maybe we'll find mulberries tomorrow, maybe."

"I know we will, Granma…I love you."

Celie opened her book and read to her granddaughter.

"Time like an ever rolling stream, Bears all its sons away; They fly forgotten, as a Dream, Dies at the opening day."

She closed the worn volume and took her last breath just as the fairy clock began to strike the twelfth hour. Cecilia Fears Dulligan Bain died at White Oaks Plantation on May 5, 1894, the ancient psaltery at her side.

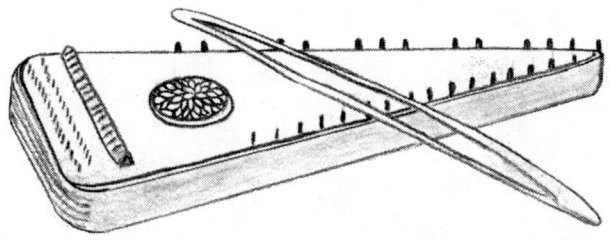

THE END

"Receipts" in *Psaltery at White Oaks*

Southerners are known for their oral culture. They treasure telling stories, sharing memories, and simply passing along the news or "gossip." In fact, there's nothing as interesting and rewarding as listening to a grandmother or great grandmother talk about the happenings of days gone by. In addition, Southerners are certainly remembered for a variety of pastimes, including holiday celebrations, feasting, and merriment. My story about making eggnog, peanut soup, and turkey gravy every year at "Lombardy Hill" in Virginia, and accidentally serving "the nog" in the gravy boat to accompany the roasted turkey one Christmas dinner remains a favorite, especially when I share the "receipts" for these old-time culinary delights.

Indeed, the characters in *PSALTERY AT WHITE OAKS* ate many of the dishes which Southerners have enjoyed since the seventeenth century. A few are included for your sampling. As the saying goes, ENJOY. And while you're enjoying one of the cookies with a cup of tea, why not play a word game with the Scottish TAPSALTERRIE? How many words can you make from it? Do some rhyme? Does one word sound a little like the name of one of the early families in Georgetown?

Let's get started.

Here are some words: tap, salt, tear, pie, rear, lap, rap, pear, are, Lear (one of Shakespeare's characters). Remember? And the list goes on and on. A game like this is a wonderful ice-breaker not only in a classroom setting, but also at a party.

Then, let's try rhyming.

Tap
Rap
Sap

Lap
Tear
Pear
Rare
Tip
Lip
Rip

You might also try writing a nonsensical verse using some of the words. For instance, you could say,
John put his head on his sister's lap
And listened to a song of rap.
He ate a pear
That was too rare.

Have you ever eaten pear pie? Even Dr. Bain might have enjoyed pear pie with a shaving of chocolate.
In any case, the possibilities go on and on. Just use your imagination, and have fun creating games from this wonderful Scottish word which Robert Burns often used: TAPSALTEERIE. It Means 'topsy-turvy.'

Peach Charlotte

Line the bottom and sides of a dish with fresh sponge cake. Pare some ripe peaches; cut them in halves and sprinkle sugar over them. Now, whisk a pint of sweetened cream. As the froth rises, take it off. Pile the cream on top of the sugared peaches, and serve.

Beaten Biscuits

Knead together 2 pounds of flour, ¾ pound of sugar, ¼ pound of butter, 1 teaspoon soda dissolved in a little warm water, a little salt, and milk enough to form a dough. Knead well until dough becomes smooth and light. Roll in sheets about 1/8 inch thick. Cut with a biscuit or cookie cutter. Prick each with tines of a fork, and bake in a moderate oven.

Corn Pudding

A little butter, ¾ cup sugar, 4-5 eggs, separated, ½ teaspoon salt, pepper to taste, a touch of mace, 2-3 tablespoons of flour, 2 cans cream-styled corn, and a generous teacup of milk. Mix, stirring in beaten egg whites last. Bake in lightly greased casserole for about an hour or until set.

Tea Cakes

1 cup sugar, 1 stick butter, ½ cup buttermilk or sour milk, pinch of soda, 1 egg, about 2 ½ cups flour, maybe more to make a smooth dough, and flavoring to taste, e.g., vanilla or lemon.

Mix, and roll out on floured board. Cut in circles, and bake on ungreased tin at about 300 degrees til golden brown. You may prick cakes with a fork before baking.

Blackberry Roll

Make a pastry of ½ tsp. Salt, 2 tsps. Baking powder, 2 ½ cups flour, 1-2 eggs, 1 heaping tablespoon shortening, and a bout 1 cup, more or less, of water. Roll out on a floured board, and spread with 2 cups sugared blackberries (about 2 cups and your favorite spice or flavoring). Roll dough over berries and tuck ends. Gently lift roll into oblong greased pan. Fill with 1-1 ½ cups of water. Bake at 325 degrees until golden brown. Serve with ice cream or sauce. MULBERRIES and/or other fruits may be used as well.

Charlotte Russe

1 quart whipping cream, 3 tablespoons gelatin, whites of 4 eggs, and sherry to taste.

Beat cream 'til stiff; add some top milk. Beat egg whites 'til stiff, and add cream to egg whites, one spoon at a time. Add sugar and flavoring to bottom of cream before blending with egg whites. Meantime, soak gelatin in cold water for 10 minutes (set up in hot water for dissolving). Cool. Carefully add soaked gelatin to cream, beating generously. All of this, by the way, is done before adding cream to egg whites.

Tipsy Pudding

For many years, Southerners have truly enjoyed English trifle and tipsy cake or pudding, both of which traditionally include ladyfingers (some folks substitute angel food cake or pound cake for the ladyfingers), custard and sherry or wine, fruit or jelly, and whipping cream and almonds.

(Generally, layers of sherried ladyfingers, custard, almonds, and whipped cream with fruit jello; some prefer to add jelly).

Layer a pretty glass bowl with lady fingers soaked in sherry. Add custard, almonds, and some whipped cream, and add jello or jelly if you like. End with cream, which may be adorned with candied fruits or mint leaves, depending on your taste.

My mother always used the following "receipt" for custard. Be sure to use a double boiler. Scald 4 cups of milk. Let it cool. In a separate bowl, beat 5 eggs with about 1 cup sugar and a pinch of salt. Pour a little milk into the egg mixture; then pour all of this back into the double boiler. Do this slowly, gradually, stirring until mixture coats the back of a silver tablespoon. Do not overcook or it will curdle. Put in a bottle, jar, or pitcher to cool. Stir in a little vanilla or brandy, and sprinkle with nutmeg. When this is cool, begin the layering procedure.

Don't forget, of course, that many folks, especially the young and the frail, enjoy boiled custard by itself.

Eggnog

Wonderful on all festive occasions.

12 eggs, separated, 1 and ¼ cups sugar, 6 cups heavy cream (may use 2 cups of ½ and ½, if desired), 2 ½ cups whiskey and spirits, pinch of salt, and a lacing of nutmeg or mace.

Beat egg yellows first, and gradually stir in sugar. Beat 'til thick. Slowly pour in cream which has been whipped. Some people gradually pour in the spirits, adding rum last. Now, beat egg whites still stiff with a pinch of sugar. Fold into the mixture and chill thoroughly. Serve cold with a sprinkling of nutmeg.

Spirits, your choice, of course, include Bourbon and Cognac, or Bourbon, Rye whiskey, Brandy, Rum, even sherry. Of course, some folks just like vanilla flavoring.

Arrack Punch

Put 3 cups white sugar in a pot with the juice of 3 oranges. Cover with 2 cups mellow red wine, a quart of boiling water, and 2 cups of Arrack. Add a couple of cinnamon sticks or a few cardomom seeds. Stirring constantly, heat over a low fire. Serve hot in winter or cold in the summer. You may add sweetened tea to this beverage for a large crowd, especially if you don't want such a potent punch!

Candied Sweet Potatoes

5-6 large potatoes (boiled, peeled, and cut in pieces), one teacup of warm water, ½ stick butter, teaspoon of vanilla or your favorite flavoring, a little cinnamon and nutmeg, 1 and ½ cups brown sugar (or a combination), and a little salt. Put potatoes in greased casserole, and make a syrup of the remaining ingredients. Pour syrup over potatoes, and heat in a warm oven, about 30 minutes. You may use orange juice and water to make one teacup if you like an orange flavor.

Molasses Tassies

Cream ¾ cup butter, and blend in one egg, one teacup brown sugar, and 4 tablespoons molasses. Mix well. Gradually stir in 2 ¼ cups flour (more or less), 2 teaspoons baking soda, ½ teaspoon salt, and a blending of your favorite ground spices: cloves, cinnamon, ginger, nutmeg to equal about 2 ½ teaspoons. You may wish to use mace as well. Mix well, adding more flour, if needed. Thoroughly chill the dough. Form into small cakes or balls, and flatten. Sprinkle gently with sugar. Brush with a little warm water. Bake in a moderately hot oven, 350-400 degrees for about 13 minutes. Watch carefully, so tassies do not burn. Delicious with tea, lemonade, coffee, or cocoa.

Spoon Bread

Boil 2 ½ cups water. Remove from heat, and stir in a little more than one cup white cornmeal. Mix well. Blend in a teaspoon salt, a little white sugar, and 2 heaping Tablespoons butter. Mix well. Cool. Add 2 cups milk, 2-3 small beaten eggs, and one teaspoon baking powder. Pour into a greased casserole dish. Bake at 350 degrees for about an hour until firm. Delicious with butter.

Other old-time favorites are, of course, grits, pecan pie, chess pie, apples, bread pudding, fruit cake, damson pie, gingerbread, water melon pickle, peach preserves, rice custard, or floating island. The families in this novel would surely have enjoyed these at one time or another. You should, too!

CPSIA information can be obtained at www.ICGtesting.com
Printed in the USA
LVOW101957160212

268925LV00002B/79/P